THE TANAISTE

Finola clawed helplessly at the meaty hand tightening on her throat. The hulking Norseman had dragged her to the ground and pinned her there, dropping his knee to her chest with such force that the air had fled from her lungs, stifling her screams and leaving her gasping for breath. Unable to move, she stared up in wide-eyed horror at the black–bearded face of her attacker as his lips parted to form a malevolent smile that revealed black and rotting teeth. The stench of him filled her nostrils and her stomach churned with nausea. Slowly, as if to savour her terror to its fullest, the Viking raised the short handled axe in his free hand high above her head. With macabre fascination, Finola's eyes followed its ascent, seeing nothing but the gleaming edge of the blade. It stopped suddenly and hung motionless for a moment.

And then he struck.

THE TANAISTE

by

Donald T. Phelan

ERIN BOOKS

An Erin Books Paperback
THE TANAISTE

This edition published 1994
by Erin Books
9860(A) - 33 Avenue,
Edmonton, AB, CANADA T6N 1C6
All rights reserved
Copyright © 1994 Donald T. Phelan

ISBN: 1-896-320-33-3

Printed in Canada
by Ronalds Printing, Edmonton, AB

Cover Illustration by
Richard Conor

For LORRAINE, *the love of my life*,
SEAN, DANNY, ALANNA, ERIN,
and especially
RYAN, *my Tanaiste*

ACKNOWLEDGEMENTS

My thanks to the following individuals without whose assistance this book would not have been possible:

Ms. Morgan Llywelyn, best-selling author of LION OF IRELAND, for her friendship and guidance.

Dr. Katherine Simms, Department of Medieval History, Trinity College, Dublin, for her gracious assistance with the research.

Mr. Eoghan Ragallach, Department of Gaelic Studies, Trinity College, Dublin, for some much needed help with Gaelic pronunciations.

My father, **Thomas Phelan,** the eternal seanachie who led me back into Irish history.

My mother, **Betty Phelan**, who taught me the discipline the arts demand.

ERIN
(Ireland)
circa 840 a.d.

L. Swilly
AILECH
Swilly R.
Foyle R.
DERRY
Magh Bete
Bann R.
Magh Itha
Spertin Mts.
ULSTER
L. Erne
DUNGANNON
L. Neagh
ARMAGH
Sligo Bay
Garavague R.
ENNISKILLEN
L. Gill
Brickelive Mts.
SLIGO
Bann R.
Carlingford Bay
CONNAUGHT
L. Owel
TARA
CLONARD
L. Ree
MEATH
L. Gabhar
CLONMACNOISE
Magochtair
DUBHLINN
CLONFERT
CLONCURRY
BRAY
NAAS
Liffey R.
L. Derg
TERRIGLAS
MULLAGHMAST
Nora R.
LEINSTER
Ardagh Mts.
LIMERICK
KILKENNY
Shannon R.
Barrow R.
CASHEL
WEXFORD
MUNSTER
WATERFORD
CORK

0   MILES   50

PART ONE

CHAPTER ONE

Bran stood on the crest of the mossy hill that overlooked the battlefield, his sword hand clutched over the throbbing wound on his left shoulder, staring vacantly at the scene of carnage in the valley below. The excitement he had reveled in on the eve of his first battle was gone now, leaving him with a profound sense of shame. So many dead – fine warriors on both sides whose lives had been cut short by blind loyalty to their respective clans.

There should have been some other way, Bran thought bitterly to himself. *For as long as I can remember, Ragallach Ui Muiredaig has refused to acknowledge my father as king of Leinster, swearing that he would someday destroy the clanna Ui Faelain and claim the title of Ri–Ruirech for himself. Over the years our two clans have chafed at one another, alternately initiating the petty skirmishes and cattle raids that have perpetuated the long–standing feud between us. What was once mere rivalry between two chieftains has fermented into a hatred that we have all been too eager to embrace. Even as a child I listened to the exploits of our own warriors, thriving on their stories of bravery and heroic deeds and anxiously awaiting the day that I myself would become a blooded warrior. But I never expected or wanted… this.*

The brisk north wind whipped his matted red hair about his face and carried to Bran the haunting cry of the Bocanach. The legendary demon of battle had not one voice but many, the moans of the wounded and the dying mixing with the wailing laments of the women who prostrated themselves over the corpses of their husbands and sons. Bran's blue eyes filled with tears of remorse. He had grappled with death and proven himself as worthy a warrior as any other. A warrior who had killed.

Bran doubled over and vomited. When the spasms subsided, he suddenly sensed that he was not alone and spun around, his hand going from his wound to the hilt of his sword.

Etach took a half step back and gestured reassuringly. "Easy lad," the older man said gruffly. A leather patch covered the empty socket where his right eye had once been, and the livid purple scar that ran down his forehead and across his cheekbone was gruesome testimony to the fact that the slash of a sword was responsible for the loss. "This is no place for the king's son to wander about – alone and unguarded," he said, tilting his head skyward. "It will be dark soon and the Ui Muiredaig may still have some men about."

Bran released the grip on his sword and wiped his mouth with the back of his hand. He was certain that Etach had been there long enough to see him retching uncontrollably and he silently cursed himself for his weakness. But he knew that the champion of the Ui Faelain clan would offer neither the embarrassment of comfort nor the sting of criticism. Without a word he turned and looked back down into the valley, drawing his cloak about his shoulders against the chill of the rising wind.

"Come, my lord," Etach persisted. "Let us return to the warmth of our fires. We will fill our goblets and drink to our victory." They began to move down the hill, Bran clutching the cloak and Etach striding robustly beside him.

"Victory?" Bran challenged, thrusting his hand toward the battlefield. "There's your victory, Etach. Those we have slain number in the hundreds."

"Aye, and in the morning we will kill hundreds more," Etach stated flatly. "Do not forget that many of our comrades lie among the dead and they must be avenged."

"But nothing changes!" Bran pleaded. "And Leinster is no different than the other provinces. The clans war among themselves for the kingship of their own territories then turn on each other. Connaught and Meath squabble and Munster still feuds with Ulster, while we of Leinster are content to slaughter one another. At least for the moment. The men of Erin will butcher each other until not a single one is left standing. Where's the glory in that?"

"You're alive, aren't you?" Etach reasoned, reaching across to jab a long bony finger into Bran's chest. "There's your victory! You have slain those that would have killed you and taken your father's kingdom – a kingdom that will someday be yours. Mother of God!" The old soldier shook his head then glanced sideways at Bran. "In our camp tonight, the warriors who have survived this day's battle are laughing and drinking each other's health. They celebrate because they are still alive and they know that tomorrow they may not be. But tonight the victory is theirs."

"Theirs – not mine," Bran said bitterly.

"And who are you to reject that which has been paid for in blood? What is it you want?"

Bran sighed as he lowered his head and watched the swirling mist part before his leather-clad feet. The sounds of battle still rang in his ears – screams of pain, the clanging of metal on metal. "I want peace," he whispered.

"Sometimes it is the sword that is the key to peace," the old warrior retorted evenly.

Bran slowly shook his head. "How can I expect a man like you to understand?" he asked quietly. "You are the champion of the Ui Faelain, the *Airechta* who is honoured and revered because of the number of men he has killed. Throughout the passing of the seventeen summers that I have seen, you have always been our champion, a warrior whose prowess is second only to that of my father. It was you who taught me the skills of the warrior – how to wield a sword, to hurl a spear, how to guide the stone from my sling to its mark. It was you who taught me how to kill."

Etach's eye narrowed. "If that is truly all that you have learned, then my time was wasted," he said solemnly. "I taught you how to survive. Someday you will rule Leinster and all that you have learned of the Brehon laws, the philosophy and the poetry will be of no use to you if you do not have the strength to hold what is yours." The old warrior looked past Bran to the distant horizon. "If my lord feels that I have done him some injustice by teaching him these things, he may have his father dismiss me as his personal retainer," he added with stiff formality.

"That will not be necessary," Bran replied softly, realizing that his words had cut into the old man's heart as deeply as any dagger's blade. For as far as his memory could reach back, there had never been a time without Etach. In many ways, Etach had been more of a father to him than the king. Although they had never openly displayed their affection for one another, Bran loved the man who strode beside him and knew that Etach's devotion to him was beyond question. "There is none more capable than yourself, Etach, and you have taught me well. It is myself that I doubt. I fear the day I shall have to order men to their deaths in defense of my throne and my authority. Can the kingdom of Leinster be worth the price of so many men's lives?"

"That is a question for men of education," Etach said thoughtfully, scratching his shaggy grey beard. "I am a soldier. I take orders and do what must be done. One day, when Leinster's future rests in your hands, so will you."

Etach had set a brisk pace and Bran was tiring, slowed by his wound. He stumbled, winced at the shooting pain in his shoulder, and gasped. Etach stopped and gently lifted the edge of Bran's cloak. "You're hurt!" he exclaimed. Catching the blood–soaked tunic between his gnarled fingers, he carefully widened the tear in the already gaping fabric, then squinted in the fading light as he surveyed and probed the wound. Resigned to the inspection, Bran bit down on his lower lip. "It is a decent enough gash alright," Etach observed, raising an eyebrow and clucking his tongue. "You see what comes of carrying your shield too low."

Bran laughed and rolled his shoulder back out of reach. "Forgive me, my friend. It would appear that there are lessons you have yet to teach me."

Etach smiled as he nodded and pointed at the wound. "And some for you to relearn, eh? Come," he snorted, the familiar gruffness returning to his voice. "The camp is not much further."

The two men continued slowly down the steep embankment to the base of the hill. They avoided the roads and open country, seeking instead the security of the oak trees and hawthorn bushes that twisted between the rolling hills. The night sounds of the forest assaulted Bran's ears and brought to mind the strange tales he had once listened to spellbound and wide–eyed. From the past came evenings spent in the firelight of his father's great hall where the *seanachies* told their stories of hellish creatures and demons, ghosts and *banshees*, of the fate of those foolish enough to venture out into the jaws of darkness. As the mist from the bogs rolled between the trees, dark shapes seemed to lurk around them, as if the shadows themselves were coming to life. Bran silently reproached himself for the sudden apprehension he felt. Superstitions and tales spun by old men were of no concern to a warrior who had proven himself in battle. Even so, he unconsciously tightened his grip on the hilt of his sword.

After a time, the drone of besotted revelry and the squeals of women laughing came to them, and they emerged from the forest into a clearing surrounded by hills and illuminated by the soft glow of the open fires. Scores of tents and pavilions were spread across the valley, the largest of which dominated the centre. Shadowy figures moved about the tents and fires.

At the perimeter of the camp, the two warriors were challenged by a drowsy sentry who quickly moved aside when he recognized the king's son. They made their way through the throng of people that enveloped them, exchanging greetings with comrades whose coherence seemed to vary in direct proportion to the quantity of ale and mead they had consumed. A pretty red–haired girl giggled impishly as she ran to Bran and threw one arm around his neck. He kissed her quickly on the cheek, then sent her back to her amused companions with a playful slap on her well–rounded rump.

When they reached Bran's tent, the two guards that

slouched at either side of the entrance snapped to attention. "That wound should be cleaned and dressed," Etach suggested. "Let me bring you the physician."

Bran shook his head wearily. "I will attend to it myself. There are many whose need is greater than my own."

"As you wish, my lord," Etach replied, bowing and disappearing into the darkness. Bran turned to one of the stone-faced sentries. "Bring me fresh water and linen," he commanded. "Then see that I am not disturbed." Without waiting for the man to obey, he turned and stepped between the flaps of his small tent.

The interior was dimly lit by two tallow lamps that hung from the centre post. In the corner, a bed of moss and freshly cut rushes had been carefully laid out by his bodyservant. As a new wave of fatigue washed over him, Bran unbuckled his sword and tossed it onto the bed. He bent over and opened the heavy wooden chest that constituted the only piece of furniture in the tent and after rummaging with the contents, withdrew a flagon of wine and a bronze goblet. Kneeing the lid shut, he sat down on it heavily. He poured the rich red wine into the goblet, then raised it to his lips.

"I see you have no need of water, my lord."

Bran's head jerked around at the sound of the rich velvet voice. He held his goblet frozen in mid-air. "Taillte," he whispered hoarsely.

The woman who stood motionless just inside the tent smiled back at him with full inviting lips. Her face was flawlessly structured, her high cheekbones and delicately curved jawline the elegant features of a noblewoman. Her complexion was milk white and magnificently contrasted by the raven black hair that cascaded down below her shoulders. Her shining emerald eyes held him transfixed as she glided toward him. "Your man told me that you had been wounded," she commented. Only now did Bran notice the basin and squares of linen she carried. His gaze shifted to her swaying hips.

The pale orange light danced along the curves of her body as she moved toward him and the ankle length *lena* she wore did little to conceal her figure. The garment was of thin, red samite with the neckline cut low enough to reveal the ivory swell of her ample breasts. A thin girdle of black kidskin was tied around her delicate waist.

Bran regained his composure enough to remember the goblet in his hand. He took a long draught of wine before looking back at her. "How did you get past the guards?" he asked casually.

She came to him and stood looking down. "I told them that the king's son should have a woman's gentle touch to bind his wounds. Besides," she added coyly, "they know who I am and that I am no stranger to your royal chambers in Naas."

The light from the far side of the tent revealed the silhouette of her shapely legs beneath the translucent fabric. Bran smiled at the memory of the pleasures he had found between her thighs. He was suddenly aware that Taillte was watching him, reading the expression on his face. Looking up, he discovered the peculiar gleam of satisfaction in her green eyes that he had so often resented. His smile faded. "An armed camp is no place for a woman," he said flatly.

Taillte placed the basin and the linen on the chest beside him where he sat and stepped between his outspread thighs. "My only wish is to be near you in your hour of triumph over the Ui Muiredaig," she cooed softly. She unfastened the silver brooch at his shoulder and tossed his cloak on the bed. "Would you have me leave you?"

The scent of her perfume filled Bran's nostrils. She shifted her weight slightly so that her thigh touched his own, separated only by the silky smoothness of her lena. "As you wish," he replied with feigned indifference.

Her creamy fingers slowly unfastened the rawhide thongs that bound his tunic at his throat, gently eased the garment over his broad shoulders, and she grimaced at the sight of the ugly gash on his shoulder. But as she stripped him to the waist her expression changed and he watched her study the play of muscles in his arms and chest, the lean hardness of his belly. Taillte leaned forward slightly and soaked a piece of linen in the basin.

"You are indeed a fine warrior, my lord," she said quietly as she gently sponged the blood-caked wound. Tiny rivulets of water slowly trickled down his arm and chest. "But you must become a better swordsman if you are to survive and succeed your father."

Bran caught her wrist and drew her closer to him. "The sword that found my shoulder no longer has a hand to grasp it," he said fiercely. "I will survive. But I am not eager to take my father's place on the throne. Kenan is my father's firstborn son and by right of birth it is he who should be tanaiste."

"But the council of elders judged him unworthy and selected you in his place," Taillte reminded him, laying the linen aside and cradling his face in her hands. "It was a wise decision and much favoured by your father."

Bran slowly nodded. "And scorned by my brother, perhaps with just cause. I have taken away everything that ever mattered to him – his father's love, his birthright and even the woman he loved."

Taillte wrapped her arms around his neck and bent down to face him. Her voice was soothing and sympathetic. "You took nothing from Kenan – including me. It was I who chose to come to you."

Bran studied her face closely, his eyes searching hers. *You only allow me to see part of you,* he thought. *Behind the shields of your eyes there lies some secret, some part of you that you will not reveal.* "And was it me or what I will become that brought you to me, my love?"

Taillte gazed back at him steadily. "I am yours now, and I will be yours when you are king." She pressed her lips against his, gently probing with her tongue. Bran's will surrendered to the rising heat in his loins, his lips wandering down her face, her throat, the white flesh of her breasts. In her embrace his tormented conscience found a kind of peace where thoughts of battle, thrones and kingdoms gave way to the solitary desire to possess this woman – to thrust himself deep between her satin thighs, to be engulfed by her passion. Her hand moved beneath the coarse fabric of his tunic, her slender fingers inching up his thigh with deliberate slowness. Bran moaned as his eyelids drooped shut, his heart pounding in his ears.

Then, as if heard in a dream, there was noise. Shouts. It took several moments before Bran realized that the voices were directly outside his tent. People arguing. Bran frowned as he gently pushed Taillte away, then leaped hastily to his feet, adjusting his tunic about his shoulders as he strode to the entrance of the tent. He tore the flaps open, eager to vent his anger on the source of the commotion.

A young red-headed woman stood before the burly guard who had blocked her entry, pounding her dainty fists against his chest and spitting a barrage of curses into his face. Her efforts were having no effect whatsoever.

"Muireen!" Bran bellowed. At the sound of his voice the woman fell silent and took a step back, her still clenched fists on her hips. The relieved guard quickly stepped aside.

"Would you kindly tell these numskulls that I will not be denied entry to my brother's pavilion!" Muireen shouted.

In spite of himself, Bran was amused at the thought of his sister bullying two of his personal guards. "They are acting under my orders," he said with some difficulty, scarcely able to contain himself. "And I'll thank you to refrain in future from pummeling my men about." He looked from one guard to the other. "Are either of you seriously wounded?" The two warriors grinned back at him for a moment, then all three men burst into laughter.

"I see nothing funny about being manhandled by some hulking brute of a man," Muireen said indignantly. "Especially by the likes of them." She took a step forward and looked up at Bran, her face suddenly serious. "I have a message from your father." The urgent tone in her voice silenced their guffaws and Bran lifted the tent flap higher, gesturing her inside. As she brushed past him, he dropped the flap behind her and turned, his arms folded across his chest. It seemed unusual that the king should send Muireen instead of one of the servants on such an errand and his mind was already busily considering the reasons behind his father's actions. "Well... what is it?" he asked tentatively.

Muireen's eyes moved from Taillte to Bran, her lips tightly pressed together in disapproval. "What is she doing here?"

"Your brother was wounded in battle today, my lady," Taillte answered before Bran could reply. Her lips curled into a saucy smile. "I was merely attending to him."

Muireen grinned back at her wryly. "Seeing that he is half–naked, you seem to have been doing just that. But there are plenty of other men in the camp that you can... attend to. I'll take care of my brother."

Taillte took a step toward Muireen, but Bran caught her by the arm. "I will send for you later," he said flatly, the tone in his voice matching his firm grip. He detected a flicker of defiance in her eyes before she nodded her head.

"As you wish, my lord." She strode briskly toward the entrance but paused in front of Muireen, bowing formally, her fiery gaze fixed on the younger woman's eyes. "My lady," she said between clenched teeth. Muireen glared back at her and nodded curtly, as if dismissing a servant. As Taillte stormed out of the pavilion, Bran noted that his sister's face shone with satisfaction.

"I'll never understand why you two are always at each other's throats," Bran muttered as he struggled to adjust his tunic.

"Leave that off and sit down," his sister ordered, walking toward him. Bran perched again on the edge of the wooden chest. "She is a predator," Muireen said as she took over the task of cleaning and binding his wound. "She preys on men like you to get what she wants."

Bran chuckled. "Am I to live in fear of such a woman?" He winced as Muireen tied the bandage a little more tightly than was necessary.

"Perhaps you should. You are tanaiste to the king and that should mean more to you than the favours of a common whore."

Bran roughly pushed her away. "I do not need you to remind me of my duties. And as for Taillte..."

"No man can compete with her lust for power," Muireen interrupted. "She is making a fool out of you, and I will not allow anyone to hurt you or bring shame to us all simply because you refuse to see the truth."

Bran's fury began to subside as he saw the determination in her steady grey eyes. He knew how much she loved her father and her brothers and how much she had sacrificed since the death of their mother. At thirteen years of age she had become the lady of the household, an obligation which she had taken to heart. Now, five years later, she remained without a man of her own while others much younger than her had already married and begun to raise a family. Although much sought after by courtiers, she had devoted herself exclusively to the care of those she called "her men." Bran reached out and gently held her freckled cheeks in his huge hands. "You worry too much little sister – about all of us. The sons of Crimthann were not raised to bring dishonour to Leinster."

Muireen touched her fingers to her lips. "I had almost forgotten why I came," she said quickly. "Father wishes to see you. He bids you to meet him in his pavilion when the moon rises and brings sleep to the others."

"Please tell him that you have delivered the message and I will do as he asks," Bran replied, puzzled by the apparent need for secrecy. He stooped down and lightly kissed her on the cheek. "Have one of my men wake me when the camp is quiet."

"I will." As Muireen tightly wrapped her shawl around her and hurried off into the cool night air, Bran reflected on how like her mother she looked. He stretched out on his simple bed and fell into a fitful sleep.

CHAPTER TWO

With the deepening of night the din of activity in the camp gradually gave way to subtler sounds — the crackling embers of the dying fires, a drunken snore and the occasional bark of a startled dog. With the exception of those warriors who had been posted as pickets, the camp seemed to breath collectively in deep rhythmic sighs, gathering its strength for the light of day and the new battle that would have to be fought.

As was his habit when on campaign, Crimthann Ui Faelain had decided to check the sentries once more before allowing himself the luxury of sleep, and he was absent when a solitary figure emerged from the shadows and staggered drunkenly toward the guards at the entrance to his pavilion in the centre of the camp.

"Out of my way," the unsteady figure slurred, gesturing the guards aside with an expansive wave of his arm. Recognizing him, the warriors obeyed instantly. The man belched loudly as he stumbled past them and through the entrance.

Once inside the pavilion, Kenan Ui Faelain looked past the tapestries and couches to the platform that had been erected opposite the entrance and upon which sat the richly ornamented bench that served as the king's place when he traveled. Kenan walked unsteadily past the other furnishings and stepped up onto the platform. He glanced quickly about to ensure that he was alone, then collapsed into his father's chair, languidly swinging one leg over an armrest. He took a mouthful of wine from the flagon in his hand, then leaned back and laughed.

"So this is how it feels to be a king," he mused aloud.

"This is where I belong. On the throne of Leinster." He felt the familiar anger coursing through him and he scowled into the dimness. *But it is Bran who shall become king and not I,* he thought bitterly. *My little brother, who would rather spend time with his harp and his poetry than on the practice field learning the skills of a warrior. And yet, it was always him that our father favoured and praised and even boasted about in the great hall for all to hear. Always bragging about what Bran had done or accomplished, no matter how trivial the deed. But what of me? I have always been the strong one – the one that Bran could never beat in wrestling or racing. Yet my own father chose to shame me in front of the entire clan by picking that pup over me. And for the wrong you have done me I will never forgive you. Neither of you. The time will come when I will make you both pay for what you have done.*

Kenan tilted his head back and drank deeply from the flagon. The strong wine fueled his fury instead of providing the escape he sought. His hatred gave him a sense of purpose; to hurt them the way they had hurt him.

A few minutes later he heard voices outside, and Bran walked into the pavilion followed by his younger brother Conor. It had always disgusted Kenan how much the two looked alike with their pale complexions and coppery coloured hair. Two beardless youths whose looks favoured their mother while his own dark hair and beard and skin were those of his father. He smiled sardonically and beckoned them closer.

"Come in, come in, my dear brothers," he invited with an air of authority, although he had some difficulty enunciating the words clearly. "Don't be shy now, there is no one here but myself. The almighty and all powerful king of Leinster has yet to show his face."

With Conor at his heels, Bran strode across the pavilion. He smiled at Kenan but his voice was chill. "I judged as much from the boldness of your words. Crimthann will be displeased to find you full of the drink again and yourself perched in his rightful place."

Kenan's dark eyes burned with contempt. "And is it my father or you that is more offended by my sitting here – in my rightful place?" he hissed. "This seat is meant to be occupied by a warrior – not a poet who has no stomach for battle."

Bran averted his eyes and Kenan knew that his words had found their mark. He leaned forward, anxious to probe deeper. "A ruler governs by the strength of his will and his arm. And you know I have always been your better in – "

"That is not what I have heard," Conor blurted, starting forward.

"What are you talking about?" Kenan growled. Conor's affection for Bran was something he had never quite been able to understand, but over the years he had grown to despise it.

"I listened to the soldiers around the fires tonight," Conor said. "They say that you sent your men forward to be slaughtered like sheep when you should have held your position in the line."

"What do you know of battle?" Kenan countered. "I thought it best to advance."

Bran looked up at him incredulously. "Advance? Father gave you orders to protect our left flank and your foolishness nearly cost us the battle. It certainly cost us many good men. Perhaps you would have been a little less anxious to order

your warriors forward if you had been leading them into battle yourself instead of sitting in safety behind the lines like a
coward and ordering them to their deaths."

The insult was more than Kenan could bear and he sprang
to his feet, his legs unsteady as he groped for the dagger at his
belt.

"Kenan!" Crimthann's voice boomed. Kenan's hand froze
on the hilt of his dagger and he squinted through red–rimmed
eyes at the man that stood opposite him, filling the entrance
to the pavilion. The king of Leinster was an imposing figure,
taller than most men, lean and well muscled for his years. His
thick black hair fell to his shoulders and was flecked with
grey, as was the beard that covered his square jaw. The only
visible evidence of his royal authority was the plain gold circlet that rested on his forehead. He was otherwise dressed in
the modest garb of a soldier. Over his plain woolen tunic he
wore a heavy bearskin cloak, pinned at the shoulder by an
iron stake and his *cland*, the sword of a champion, was suspended from his shoulder by a belt of stamped deerhide. He
gave the other two boys a cursory glance, then glared at Kenan.
"How dare you draw a weapon in my pavilion. Get down from
there!"

Kenan quickly sheathed his dagger and grunted slightly
as he obeyed. "I meant no insult," he retorted, slumping into
a nearby couch.

The king strode slowly toward him, jolting Kenan into
some measure of sobriety and he sat up, bracing himself for
the blow he was certain would come. It would not be the first
time that his father had struck him and he knew that it would
be useless, perhaps even dangerous to make any effort to de-

fend himself.

"This is the second time today that you have crossed me," Crimthann bellowed at him. "Do not let there be a third." He stood for a moment glaring down at his son, then turned and ascended the platform, seating himself in his place of honour. Kenan breathed a sigh of relief as the king fixed his gaze on Bran. "You fought well today, my son," he said, making no effort to disguise the pride in his voice. "They told me you were wounded."

"The hurt is only slight," Bran replied.

Conor's face beamed with excitement. "The warriors say that Bran stood against a score of the Ui Muiredaig wielding his sword like a scythe." He gently laid his hand on his older brother's injured shoulder. "I'll wager that the man that gave him this is not nursing his wound tonight – not in this world anyway."

The young lad's idolatry filled Kenan with envy. He laughed scornfully. "You are indeed fortunate to have a god as a brother," he scoffed.

"Enough!" Crimthann commanded. "I did not call you here in secret to listen to you squabble among yourselves. I have received an urgent message from Niall Caille – a message that will affect all Leinstermen." The name of the high king of Erin was enough in itself to catch the attention of the young men and they listened intently as their father spoke. "Feidlimid of Munster has broken the treaty of Cloncurry and declared himself *Ard–Ri* in Tara. He has plundered Meath at his leisure and plans to march south into Leinster. If that happens, we will be facing enemies on two fronts – the Ui Muiredaig to the West and the Munstermen to the North."

"Why doesn't Niall stop them in Meath?" Kenan suggested indolently. "It is, after all, his authority as high king that Feidlimid has challenged."

Crimthann shook his head. "The Munstermen will be across our borders before Niall's army can reach them. The high king has asked us to march north and hold them until his forces arrive."

"Then that is what we should do," Conor said excitedly. "We will sweep the Ui Muiredaig aside and march north. Our warriors —"

"Do not presume to advise me, boy," Crimthann growled, grabbing a handful of his son's hair and worrying the lad's head back and forth. "The wisest chieftain is one who plans how to avoid a battle rather than how to win it. What will happen to us if Niall does not arrive in time? Eh? The clanna Ui Faelain cannot stand alone against the entire army of Munster!"

"In one respect Conor is right, my lord," Bran said slowly, choosing his words carefully. "The Ui Muiredaig were badly shaken today. They may be ready to negotiate."

"Aye," Crimthann replied thoughtfully. He rose to his feet and began to pace back and forth, stroking his beard. "Ragallach Ui Muiredaig and I have been enemies for many years, using Leinster as our own personal arena. And while we brawled, outlaws like this Feidlimid of Munster have raided us freely, unopposed, looting and murdering as they pleased. To the north, the Norsemen have fortified themselves on the banks of Lough Neagh, terrorizing Ulster despite Niall's efforts to stop them. In time, we may have to face them, too. But first, Leinster must be unified if we are to survive." He paused for a moment, eyeing their anxious faces. "This night I have arranged a truce with the Ui Muiredaig. We will meet with them in the morning to negotiate an alliance between our clans."

Crimthann's announcement was like a physical blow that left the three young men dumbfounded for several moments. Then Kenan sprang to his feet, his face contorted with anger and disbelief. "An alliance?" he exploded. "Why should we sue for peace with an enemy we have already defeated? Are these the words of a king – or an old woman? Has our father grown too weak to – "

"Get out before I have you thrown out," Crimthann snarled. Their eyes were fixed on one another, locked in silent combat, carefully gauging each other's strengths and weaknesses. The primeval contest of youth challenging experience raged without words.

"Damn you and your treaty!" Kenan shouted, glaring back at him defiantly. "I'll have no part of it! You already decided what you were going to do before you called us here tonight and it is clear that our opinions are worthless to you." His voice crackled with emotion as he pointed an accusing finger as his father. "The Ui Muiredaig are not to be trusted and if you do this thing, you will have turned your back on the clanna Ui Faelain and on those warriors who died to protect your throne." He held his father's gaze for a moment, then stormed out of the tent.

"Follow him," Crimthann instructed his youngest son. "Make certain that he reaches his quarters without incident. Kenan needs little provocation when the fire is in his blood."

As Conor hastened to do his bidding, Crimthann turned

to Bran. "Like so many other warriors, your older brother has yet to learn that he cannot stand alone. God grant that I have more success convincing Ragallach that the clans must stand together against the Munstermen."

"You intend to negotiate with him personally?" Bran asked, frowning. "I must ask you to reconsider, my lord. Send another in your place. With an invader approaching our borders, Leinster cannot afford to risk the life of her king."

Crimthann raised his eyebrows. "Then you share Kenan's mistrust of the Ui Muiredaig?"

"I do," Bran replied evenly. He paused, then went on. "You once told me that only a fool turns his back on a wounded boar. With the sour taste of defeat still in their mouths, the Ui Muiredaigs' desire for revenge may well outweigh their obligation to honour the truce."

Courage and foresight, Crimthann thought with satisfaction. *I have indeed chosen well, my son.* "No matter the risk, I cannot afford to have Ragallach think me a coward," he said aloud. A grin touched the corners of his mouth. "Nor will we wait for the boar to charge before we act, eh? Summon the officers and chieftains to my pavilion. If the Ui Muiredaig mean to betray the peace tomorrow, they shall not find us unprepared."

The sweet songs of larks and wrens floated above the valley which only the day before had been filled with the screams of men in pain. The sun was already beginning to burn off the early morning mist and countless beads of dew sparkled across the grassy plain. Only the dark red blotches remained as a gruesome reminder of the recent battle.

Mounted on horseback, Bran and his father waited beside the small pavilion that had been erected in the middle of the valley. Ragallach Ui Muiredaig had stipulated that Crimthann bring only one man as escort, as he himself would. When Bran learned of the condition, he had insisted on accompanying his father. Crimthann had reluctantly agreed but taken the precaution of positioning his warriors in the hills behind them, ready to sweep into the valley on a pre–arranged signal in the event of treachery.

From somewhere beyond the hills he faced, an almost imperceptible sound reached Crimthann's ears. The noise crescendoed until he recognized it as something he knew only too well – an army on the march, moving toward them. Bran looked at him anxiously, but the king's features gave no indication of surprise or fear. As the Ui Muiredaig army flowed from between the distant hills and positioned itself on the far side of the valley, Crimthann fought the impulse to raise his hand and summon his warriors forward. But even as he considered this, two riders separated from the main body of the Ui Muiredaig army and galloped toward them.

The king shielded his eyes against the sun and squinted at the two men as they approached. He saw that the stouter of the two was dressed in the tunic of a nobleman, the elaborate multicoloured cloak of a chieftain flowing out behind him. The other man wore only a sleeveless leather vest and a pair of tight fitting *truibas* which were tucked neatly into the fur leggings covering his calves. Crimthann might have taken him for a huntsman were it not for the heavy sword that was slung across his back. Unlike his companion, the huntsman did not bear a shield. They reined in their horses a short distance from the pavilion and dismounted. The nobleman handed his reins to the huntsman and sauntered toward them.

Ragallach Ui Muiredaig was a far cry from the way Crimthann remembered him. Although he had obviously once been quite muscular, his short thick legs now supported a corpulent body, the result of many years of savouring life's pleasures. The bulbous red nose and mottled cheeks were evidence of his long–standing passion for heady wines and ales. His thinning hair was a non–descript shade of brown and matched the colour of his beard which had been carefully groomed. Crimthann noticed that his old enemy still walked with a slight limp, favouring his left leg, and he remembered that it was he who had wounded Ragallach in personal combat years earlier.

Crimthann swung out of his saddle and handed his reins to Bran. "Wait here," he ordered without looking up. As he walked briskly forward to meet the chieftain, he sensed the huntsman's eyes following him, wary of his every move.

"Greetings, old friend," Ragallach hailed. The two warriors embraced as if they were comrades rather than enemies. "The seasons have changed many times since last I looked upon the great wolf of Leinster."

Crimthann smiled back at him, amused by the pun which implied that the name Ui Faelain meant more than "Clan of the wolf". "Much time has passed," he agreed. It had been years since he looked into the other man's face – a time when they had both been young warriors, each seeking to slay the other. But that was long ago, he thought to himself, and we are becoming old men. Perhaps the long standing grievances we have held against one another no longer matter. Everything – and eve-

ryone – changes.

"I have brought my son Rowan to witness our treaty of peace," Ragallach stated, beckoning the huntsman to join them with a wave of his hand.

"Bran!" Crimthann called loudly in his turn. Leading their horses behind them the two young warriors joined their respective fathers. After the formal introductions had been completed, Crimthann firmly grasped Ragallach's shoulder. "They are fine looking boys, the pair of them. There is our future, my friend."

"Aye," Ragallach said thoughtfully. "And perhaps Leinster's."

"Come, we have much to discuss," Crimthann said, directing him to the pavilion. Together they walked to the entrance and Crimthann lifted the flap, motioning the chieftain to enter. "I have saved our finest ale for this occasion. I would be honoured if you shared a cask with me."

"Gladly," Ragallach replied, smacking his lips loudly. "It would indeed be bad manners to refuse such fine hospitality." Crimthann followed him inside, dropping the flap behind and leaving the two young men to attend to the horses.

Once inside the pavilion, the two chieftains took their seats on opposite sides of the table upon which sat several small oaken casks and two finely crafted gold tankards. Crimthann pulled one of the casks toward him, withdrew the small wooden stopper and filled their goblets with rich brown ale. As he moved to replace the stopper, Ragallach caught his wrist and winked. "There's no need to do that," he suggested, grinning. "We'll only have to take it out again."

"Crimthann laughed as he discarded the lug and raised

his tankard in salute. "To the warriors of Leinster," he said heartily.

"And the chieftains they serve," Ragallach added, raising his drink to his lips. He quaffed the ale in a single draught, then held his tankard out to be refilled. "I'm thinking there would be less battles fought if men spent more time at diversions such as this."

"Feel free to drink your fill," the king replied benevolently, refusing to allow himself to be reduced to the status of a servant. "Matters of state often prevent men such as you and I from pursuing more... pleasurable pastimes."

"That's the truth of it," Ragallach agreed somewhat sadly as he refilled his goblet. "Even so, such concerns can lead enemies like us to share a dram or two."

"Aye," Crimthann replied, nodding his head. "But I am afraid it is more than our petty differences which brings us together." He related the details of the message he had received from the high king, watching the other man's face closely for any change of expression. When he mentioned the impending invasion, Crimthann detected a glimmer of pleasure in Ragallach's eyes and he realized that the chieftain's obsession with the crown of Leinster blinded him to the destruction that was marching toward them both.

"I see now why you so anxiously petition us for peace," Ragallach stated after the king had finished. "But I don't understand why you are telling me all this. What's to prevent me from ordering a withdrawal and allowing the Munstermen to annihilate the Ui Faelain?"

"Because it is not just us that will be overrun," Crimthann explained. "When Feidlimid is finished with us he will certainly march on the only other clan capable of offering any resistance to him at all – the Ui Muiredaig." He paused for a moment while Ragallach considered the import of what he had said.

"There is merit in what you say," Ragallach agreed. "If either of our two clans stands alone against them, we shall surely be defeated."

"Then we shall not face them alone," Crimthann said emphatically. "The clans of the Ui Muiredaig and the Ui Faelain will band together to face the invader. Together, we have a chance."

Shock suddenly spread across Ragallach's face. "I cannot ask my men to fight alongside the warriors of the Ui Faelain in defense of a throne to which I have laid claim," he retorted.

The king slammed his fist onto the table. "Don't you understand?" he argued hotly. "If we fail to stop the Munstermen there will be no throne – no Leinster to fight over." Abruptly, he rose from the table and strode to the far side of the tent, running his hand over his face in frustration. *I must not lose my temper,* he thought to himself. *Far too much depends on securing this man's cooperation if we are to survive.* He turned and looked at the chieftain apologetically. "It has been many years since we first vied for the crown of Leinster," he smiled, "but you have continued to fight a battle that has long since been decided. I am king and will remain so. All the minor tribes and clans have sworn allegiance to me and pay their tribute to the Ui Faelain."

"And the Ui Muiredaig has suffered for it," Ragallach said between gritted teeth. "When you were crowned king, you exacted the *boruma* from those tribes who had once paid tribute to us and left us to fend for ourselves. You reduced us to raiders and scavengers and forced us to fight for our very survival." Ragallach leaned forward in his chair. "Now your time has come and you dare to ask us for our help!"

"If all we have ever fought about is the tribute, then let the wealth of Leinster be divided equally between our two clans," Crimthann replied quickly while his mind raced to find some means of appeasing Ragallach. "If your warriors fight alongside the Ui Faelain I will – "

"The Ui Muiredaig are not *amhuis!*" Ragallach roared indignantly, tipping his chair backward as he sprang to his feet. "We will not serve you as paid mercenaries!" He stood there glaring down at Crimthann, his chest heaving with fury. He paused for several moments before drawing himself up to his full height. "I did not come here to discuss a division of Leinster's cattle and gold and whatever other trinkets you may think I can be bought off with." He repeatedly jabbed his index finger onto the wooden table. "What we are nego-tiating is a sharing of power between our two clans. If you want to divide something, then let it be the crown of Leinster."

"The people cannot divide their allegiance between our two clans," Crimthann said shaking his head. "The ancient ties are too strong and old wounds too hard to forget."

"Then Leinster's destiny will be decided on the battle-field," Ragallach replied, hoisting his swordbelt on his round belly.

Now is the time, Crimthann thought as he leaned for-ward in his chair. "There may be another way," he said slowly. "A way in which both of us may rule as one." He casually refilled the Ui Muiredaig chieftain's tankard and waited.

Ragallach hesitated, then took his seat and reached for the tankard. As he raised it to his lips, Crimthann began to unfold the plan which he had conceived months earlier.

For nearly an hour Bran and Rowan ignored each other and waited in an uneasy silence while the fate of Leinster was being decided, their ears straining to decipher the murmurings within the tent. Frustrated by the unintelligible conversation, Bran watched Rowan as he busied himself with adjusting the bridle of one of the horses. "Your men fought well yesterday, son of Ragallach," he said at last. "They fought and died bravely. Erin will mourn the loss of your kith and kin."

Rowan swung around abruptly, his eyes full of fire.

"And yours. My sword tasted the blood of many an Ui Faelain yesterday."

His reaction and the bitter tone in his voice surprised Bran. "Peace, warrior. I do not mock your dead. My blade has no thirst for the blood of Irishmen, whoever they may be. I would rather have it quenched on the blood of the Norsemen."

Rowan studied him for a moment and then relaxed visibly. "That ambition is shared by many. We ourselves have long suffered at the hands of the *Finn Gail* – the white strangers. But their numbers are great and there is little any one clan can do against them."

"That is true," Bran agreed. "But if we were united under one standard, they would not be confronting just one clan. They would have to deal with all of Leinster."

For several moments Rowan looked into Bran's guileless

blue eyes. Abruptly he turned and looked back at the ranks of the Ui Muiredaig's army. "One standard," he muttered under his breath. But Bran did not hear him and the two fell back into their uncomfortable silence.

Near midday, hoots of laughter suddenly erupted from the pavilion and a short time later the two chieftains emerged, their arms around each other's shoulders. Ragallach, who had obviously enjoyed his ale, clapped Bran solidly on the back. "You have a wise father, lad." he declared loudly. "From this day forward our two clans will live in Leinster in peace, and the bards will sing your father's praises for what he has done here today."

"For what *we* have done," Crimthann corrected, grinning broadly.

Ragallach took the reins from Rowan and with some difficulty mounted his horse. "Aye, Crimthann. For what we have done." He turned to his son. "Come Rowan. Let us return to our warriors and tell them of the new Leinster." The bewildered youth hurriedly swung himself up into the saddle and followed his father who was already trotting back toward his waiting army, waving and shouting his farewells to the king.

Bran turned to his father, full of a dozen questions. "How much territory did he want? Will he accept the tribute? Will he recognize your authority as king?" he blurted.

Crimthann smiled and held out his hands to ward off any further interrogation. "You will know everything in good time," he laughed. "For now it is enough for you to know that there will be one Leinster." Bran started to ask another question, but Crimthann snatched the reins from him and quickly mounted his horse. "Come. We must announce the news of the alliance. For this day at least, there will be feasting instead of battle. Follow me!"

Bran's heart pounded wildly as they galloped across the open plain and between the gently rolling hills, behind which the bulk of the Ui Faelain army had been positioned. When the king appeared before them, the warriors sensed the bloodless victory and cheered wildly, banging their swords against their shields. The deafening roar subsided as the king raised his hands. His deep voice thundered along the valley.

"From this day forward we are at peace with the Ui Muiredaig!" He paused for a moment while the cheering crescendoed again and waited until it began to fade before continuing.

"We have formed an honourable alliance with our brothers in Mullaghmast. Together we shall march to meet Feidlimid and his Munstermen and they will see soon enough that it is not just the Ui Faelain they face, but all of Leinster. When the invader is defeated, the alliance with the Ui Muiredaig shall be forged together by the union of our two clans. To celebrate our victory, Ragallach Ui Muiredaig shall bring his clansmen to our royal city in Naas where his daughter shall be wed to Bran, my son and tanaiste to the throne of Leinster."

While the voices of thousands of elated warriors filled his ears, Bran stared slackjawed at his smiling father.

CHAPTER THREE

For three days the warriors of the Ui Faelain and the Ui Muiredaig marched north, the columns stretching out behind Crimthann and Ragallach as the two chieftains rode side by side. Rumours about the enemy they were soon to face rippled through the ranks, distorted with each fresh retelling until the exaggerated version that reached the men in the rear bore little resemblance to the original comment. Men who only days earlier had been sworn enemies, spoke freely to one another as the miles passed beneath their sandals. They discussed the upcoming battle, some openly confiding their apprehension, while others boasted of their own prowess with sword or javelin. Many of them talked of the women who waited for them and although the occasional lewd anecdote produced an explosion of guffaws, wives and lovers were generally spoken of with great respect and a tender affection born out of the awareness that many of them would soon be widows. Nevertheless, the spirit of the warriors was high, the old rivalries and grudges melting into a new found confidence in their joint ability to deal with the task before them. The treaty had fused the two opposing clans into a single body of warriors who would fight, and die alongside their countrymen if necessary, in order to defend their homes and their loved ones.

The army of Leinster.

On the afternoon of the third day, the advance scouts that Crimthann had sent out returned with news that Feidlimid had crossed the border into Leinster and was marching south, leaving a chain of charred villages and farmsteads in his wake.

"What of the survivors?" Crimthann asked of one sandy-haired scout.

"There were none, my lord," the man replied through clenched teeth. "It would appear that the Munster king is taking no prisoners."

"And what of his strength?" Ragallach asked anxiously. "Did you actually see the Munstermen?"

"Aye, my lord," the warrior replied, shifting uneasily in his saddle. "He has three, possibly four warriors to every one of ours."

"In what direction were they moving?" Crimthann asked.

"Toward Magochtair."

"Then that is where we will stop them."

"And what if Niall does not arrive in time?" Ragallach asked.

Crimthann smiled back at him confidently. "Then we shall have to stop Feidlimid ourselves," he replied. He turned to the scout. "Tell the officers that we will have to double our pace if we are to reach the plains of Magochtair by nightfall." The king spurred his horse forward, and as he left the Ui Muiredaig chieftain behind, the smile faded from his lips. *We cannot win this battle on our own*, he told himself. *Everything depends on Niall. Without him, there won't be enough of us left to bury our dead*. Such thoughts were dangerous, promoting weakness and mistakes, and he set his mind to work on the strategic details of the upcoming battle.

By nightfall, the army of Leinster had reached the dense woods that fringed the plain of Magochtair, the warriors' stamina exhausted by the rigors of the forced march. They camped behind the concealment of the trees and as soon as the pickets were posted, Crimthann called his chieftains and senior officers together in his pavilion. As the last of them filed into his tent, Crimthann stood alongside Ragallach, a large parchment map spread out on the table before them. He surveyed the anxious faces of the men who crowded around him, knowing that each commander secretly hoped that the battle plan would delegate his men to a position of advantage against the Munstermen. With some annoyance, he noted that Bran had failed to attend the assembly. Crimthann cleared his throat and leaned forward, resting his hands on the edge of the table.

"The emissaries that I sent to the King of Cashel have returned," he announced in a loud voice. "When they presented him with my proposal for peace, that... whore–son had their tongues cut out."

Protests and oaths of vengeance filled the pavilion and Crimthann raised his hands for silence. "Our scouts have informed me that Feidlimid's army is encamped on the far side of the open steppe that stretches beyond the trees. We must assume that he likewise knows our position and has no doubt been informed that our warriors are vastly outnumbered by his own." He paused momentarily, watching for the slightest flicker of apprehension in their eyes. Success would depend on men who did not fear the odds they faced.

"Any one of my men is worth a score of spineless Munstermen," one black bearded chieftain declared loudly. Several others grunted their agreement.

Crimthann grinned back at the chieftain. "Even with such noble warriors in our ranks, Feidlimid still knows that he will have superiority on the battlefield. Perhaps we can turn that knowledge against him. While we may not be able to deceive him into believing that we have a larger force, it may be to our advantage to face him with somewhat fewer warriors than he actually expects." Puzzled murmurs filled the room as Crimthann pointed at the map. "If we present Feidlimid with a force which he believes can be easily defeated, he may well hold a greater number of his warriors in reserve."

"Aye," Ragallach sighed, grinning broadly. "There is more of the fox in you than the wolf. This pompous king of Cashel cannot know of our alliance. The emissaries you sent will lead him to believe that only the Ui Faelain will face him on the battlefield."

Crimthann smiled smugly back at him. "And his high opinion of himself is well–known throughout all Erin. Such a man will not be content with merely defeating us, he will seek to humiliate our efforts to stop him. I am certain that he will commit only enough of his men to sweep us out of his way."

"He will indeed be surprised to see the Ui Muiredaig fighting alongside the Ui Faelain," Ragallach added.

"Let us not be too anxious to advise him of your presence," Crimthann said thoughtfully. "Gather your standard bearers together with one hundred of your finest warriors. In the morning, have them circle around to the hills behind the Munstermen's camp and tell them to conceal themselves there. Make certain they are not seen or they will have lost their usefulness to us. Tomorrow, when the standards of the Ui Faelain drop, I want them to make all the noise they can and march to the top of the hill in two ranks so that the second rank is barely visible from below. If fate smiles upon us, Feidlimid will think that the whole of the Ui Muiredaig army is behind him."

"And what of the remainder of my warriors?" Ragallach interrupted. "They will not be content to leave all of the glory to your men."

Crimthann laughed. "On the morrow they will have their fill of battle. At sunrise you and your son Rowan will divide your men equally between you and lead them through the trees and thickets that flank Magochtair. You must advance in stealth and no more than three hundred paces, remaining hidden from the enemy's eyes until the signal is given and the Ui Faelain have begun to fall back. When the Munstermen advance to pursue us, the Ui Muiredaig will attack their flanks. With the sudden appearance of what he assumes to be the Ui Muiredaig army at his back, Feidlimid may hesitate to commit the remainder of his reserves to the battlefield."

"But what if he does?" Kenan asked, his dark eyes flashing in the light of the tallow lamps. "What if he commits all his warriors from the outset?"

"Then we will fall back to the trees behind us," Crimthann replied. "It will be easier for us to deal with them there than on open ground."

Ragallach shook his head. "My men will not care for this creeping about like frightened children," he complained. "They would rather face the Munstermen foot to foot than to dishonour themselves."

"There is no honour in defeat," Crimthann stated.

After the senior officers and chieftains had been given

their battle orders, Crimthann took Etach aside as the grim—faced men shuffled out of the tent.

"I fear that many of them will not see home again," the old warrior commented gruffly.

The undercurrent of apprehension in his voice surprised Crimthann. "Do you not approve of the plan?"

"I do not trust the Ui Muiredaig," Etach stated frankly.

"We must rely on each other," Crimthann objected.

"With all due respect, my lord, it is at best a rearguard action. Whatever innovations we may employ tomorrow, there is little more we can do other than fall back before Feidlimid's advance. We may be able to slow him down for a few days if we continually strike and fall back. But without the support of the Ard—Ri we are doomed to defeat."

"Do not assume that the battle is lost before it has even been fought," Crimthann said shortly, turning his back on the warrior and striding toward the handler who was leading his horse to him. Without a word, he snatched the reins from the startled groom's hands and flung himself up on the back of the uneasy stallion.

"See to it that such thoughts are laid aside," Crimthann commanded Etach. "They have been known to weaken even the strongest man's swordarm."

Etach bowed deeply. "I will fight for you as I always have," he replied evenly.

Crimthann jerked the reins to one side and drove his heels into the horse's ribs, galloping off into the night in an effort to leave the old warrior's misgivings behind. But the truth of Etach's words clung to him like a shadow, preventing his escape.

The chill of the night air gradually cooled his temper and he slowed his horse to a walk as he approached the edge of the forest. Not once in his life had Crimthann been compelled to face the possibility of defeat, the strength of his own will precluding such a consideration. Now a host of doubts gnawed at his confidence. He knew Etach was right. Without the army of the Ard–Ri, it would be only a matter of time before they were overrun by the Munstermen. *God*, he prayed silently, *give us the strength to hold until Niall arrives.*

The gnarled branches of the aged oak and elm trees created eerie silhouettes against the pale moonlight as the king of Leinster urged his horse into the forest. The nervous animal shied away from the dark shapes that loomed above his head, forcing his rider to dismount and lead him through the forbidding maze.

Uncertain of his footing in the darkness, Crimthann tested each step before committing his full weight to the moss blanketed ground. His progress was further hampered by dense thickets that surrounded the base of the trees, and he cursed under his breath as he brushed against a hawthorn bush, the needle–like thorns piercing the fabric of his tunic and lacerating his skin.

These woods will be like a wall at our backs, he thought as he pulled his garments free. *If we disengage and withdraw beyond this barrier, it could work to our advantage. But if we allow the Munstermen to drive us back into it...*

Defeat.

Leinster conquered and her people subjugated.

Crimthann shuddered. The land he loved had become his sole mistress and he had willingly committed his life to protecting and guiding her toward his vision of the future. But now, she had been savagely violated at the hands of a dispassionate stranger who sought to destroy the dream he had so carefully nurtured. For a man who had never lost in battle or game, the mere suggestion that his beloved Leinster could ever be forced into submission was incomprehensible. He would fight, and die if necessary, to defend her.

Death had been his constant companion in the seemingly endless series of campaigns Crimthann had been obliged to undertake against those who sought to expand their own kingdoms at Leinster's expense. The prospect of dying in battle had long since ceased to hold any fear for him, secure as he was in the knowledge that the dynasty which he had established would continue to flourish and grow under his tanaiste.

Bran.

My son is my future, Crimthann thought to himself. *Why did he not attend the war council?*

Suddenly, his mind was filled with the mental image of Bran lying upon the battlefield, a pool of blood welling about his head like a grotesque halo. Instinctively, Crimthann thought of ordering him to remain behind, safe from the flashing steel of the enemy's front line. But he quickly dismissed the idea. The alternative would compel his son into a even crueler fate. *If we are defeated and I fall in battle,* he thought, *the only legacy I shall have left my son is a kingdom under siege and the people of Leinster will need a leader who has the strength to hold them together. He must be prepared to stand before his people, leading them toward their collective destiny even at the risk of his own life.* No, he reasoned, *we will face the Munstermen together tomorrow and trust our lives to God.*

The ground rose abruptly, forming a narrow ridge that bordered the southern edge of the plain that lay beyond. Crimthann tied his horse's reins around the trunk of a sturdy oak, then climbed the steep embankment to the top, pausing to survey the spectacle beneath him.

The scouts' reports had been right. Hundreds of amber lights glowed and flickered in the distance, arranged across the far side of the plain in the disciplined symmetry of a military camp – the fires of the Munstermen.

A horse softly whinnied nearby and Crimthann cautiously moved toward the sound, unsheathing his sword as he wound his way through the thick brush. A short time later, he came upon a small clearing where a solitary figure stood looking across to the ominous campfires.

The king smiled to himself as he recognized the familiar profile and stepped out into the open, easing his sword back into its scabbard.

"You may count on at least a dozen for each of those fires."

"Father?" came Bran's started response.

"It would be an almost beautiful sight were it not for the evil it represents," Crimthann added as he came to stand alongside his son. "I expected you to attend the war council tonight. Your assessment of the battle plan would have been appreciated."

"I'm afraid that my contribution would have been of little use to you," Bran replied.

"What troubles you my son?" Crimthann asked, puzzled by Bran's tone. Guilt swept through him as he realized that the question was one he had never asked before. Over the years, the affairs of state had occupied the bulk of his time, forcing him to entrust the raising of his sons to Etach. It occurred to him that the young warrior who now stood before him was little more than a stranger – a stranger whose eyes were filled with the same look that Crimthann had seen countless times before on the faces of other men. Their glassy–eyed stares looked through the present and into the future, each warrior praying that he did not find death waiting for him there. "If it is the swords of the Munstermen you fear, remember that the ranks of Feidlimid's army are swollen with mercenaries and conscripts, all of them scavengers who fight for personal gain. It has been my experience that such men soon lose sight of profit when they are confronted with honourable warriors who are willing to die in defense of their homes and families."

"I am no coward," Bran said indignantly. "But I do not share your enthusiasm for war, father."

"So you think me barbaric, do you?" Crimthann snapped back, angered by the remark. "Perhaps you think we should stand back and allow Feidlimid's troops to rape Leinster, as they did Meath."

"No, my lord," Bran replied, shaking his head. "But the sword is not the only answer. I am certain that the king of Cashel would be prepared to negotiate if we – "

"I sent emissaries to Feidlimid this very day," Crimthann interrupted. "He – sent them back."

"Then we must try again!" Bran countered emphatically. "I cannot believe that we who call ourselves civilized men must resort to bloodshed to resolve our differences. Have you become so accustomed to killing that you have forgotten the value of human life? Surely Feidlimid is no more anxious than we to see his own men slaughtered on the battlefield. Why not increase our mutual strength by forming an alliance as we did with the Ui Muiredaig?"

"You can compare neither the situations nor the men involved," Crimthann explained. "Despite the fact that Ragallach and I have been enemies for many years, this is our home and we came to terms because we did not want to see it destroyed. But for Feidlimid, Leinster is little more than a glittering prize – another kingdom to be conquered rather than protected."

"Can the throne of Leinster be worth the price of so many men's lives?" Bran persisted.

The expression on his son's face was one of sensitivity and concern, a look that flooded Crimthann's mind with memories which he thought had been long since forgotten. His deceased wife had spoken often of her own hatred of war and the grief it brought to innocent women and children. It occurred to Crimthann that Bran had inherited far more than his mother's blue eyes and red hair.

"The throne is nothing more than an over–ornate piece of furniture," he said softly. "But what it represents is worth dying for." He laid his hand on the younger man's shoulder. "Your mother, God rest her soul, was devoted to me beyond words and never once failed to stand beside me, even when the paths I chose cost many of our people their lives in battle. But she had a dream. And since she passed away I have given myself to that dream – a united Leinster. A land of peace that you will one day rule over as king, with the daughter of the

Ui Muiredaig at your side."

Bran studied his father in silence for a moment, then smiled. "Until now I have seen you as nothing but a warrior whose life had no other purpose than to wield a sword in combat. I see now that we are much alike and that our visions of the future are one and the same. But I must confess," he added, "the prospect of marrying the Ui Muiredaig woman fills me with more fear than the sight of Feidlimid's camp."

Crimthann grinned back at him. "One adversary at a time, eh? If we are to have any future at all we must first deal with the Munstermen." He placed his arm around his son's shoulder and gazed down at the open plain. "Now let me explain the order of battle to you. Our success tomorrow depends upon it."

CHAPTER FOUR

In the early morning light, while the mist still clung to the lower regions of the plain, the warriors of the Ui Faelain arranged themselves according to Crimthann's battle plan and waited. An unusual quiet hung over the ranks while sweated palms tightly grasped weapons in anticipation of the order that would send them forward to meet the enemy.

Bran stood in front of his men, sword in hand, and glanced along the line to where his father had positioned his mount at the head of the army. To the rear of the main body, Kenan's warriors stretched across the unprotected flank – a contingent to be held in reserve which would provide support to the rest of the army should a retreat become necessary. Despite the relative security of such a position, Bran noted that his older brother had taken the precaution of surrounding himself with his personal bodyguard, many of whom were not warriors but criminals and brigands, reputedly well paid by their employer.

Bran turned his head and looked across to the distant columns of Munstermen that filled the far side of the plain – row upon row of stone–faced men arranged in several large phalanxes, their mounted officers frantically riding between the ranks shouting last minute commands and encouragement to their individual companies. Above them, their respective banners fluttered in the gentle breeze.

The intimidating spectacle of Feidlimid's army was further augmented by the insults and jeers that his men hurled across to their silent foe. Crimthann had given strict orders that there would be no verbal response to such provocation and more than one man found himself biting his lip in frustration. As time dragged on, the warriors of the Ui Faelain became increasingly uneasy, shifting their weapons from one hand to another, adjusting their shields and whispering anxious complaints about the delay to their comrades – their patience diminishing with each passing moment.

We cannot ask these men to bide their time much longer, Bran thought to himself. He caught his father's eye and as if in response to his concern, Crimthann drew his sword and held it high above his head, sunlight glinting along the polished blade.

"Advance!" he roared, and kicked his mount forward.

All along the line, the Leinstermen began to move, banging the flat of their blades against their shields, a thundering cadence that synchronized the rate of their advance.

As he strode forth, Bran could see that the front line of the Munstermen had also begun to move, the blades of their weapons flashing in the early morning sun. A new sensation twisted his belly into knots as the gap between the two armies gradually narrowed. Fear gripped him, tightening its hold until his entire body was covered with a thin film of sticky sweat and his garments clung uncomfortably to his skin. Perspiration beaded his forehead and rolled down his face in tiny rills, stinging his eyes.

All thoughts pertaining to the morality of war and the sanctity of life were gone now, replaced by the more immediate and urgent consideration – survival.

The Munstermen were closer now, their shields held tightly against their bodies, weapons at the ready.

Behind him, Bran's men moved as one, their individual

wills dissolved into the singularity of loyalty and purpose that propelled them forward. He filled his lungs with the cool morning air and raised his sword above his head.

"Leinster!" he cried in a voice that resonated with power.

First one man, then another and another, took up the battle cry, the chanting building to a pulsating roar.

"Leinster! Leinster!"

The pace of the warriors quickened as they neared the enemy. They trotted, then ran at the line that bristled with blades and iron tipped spears, their chant crescendoing.

In the final moments before the two armies came together, the front ranks of the Leistermen suddenly halted and dropped to one knee. The spearcasters behind them launched their missiles with a speed and accuracy that caught the foremost Munstermen unprepared. The decimation of Feidlimid's advance formations created the desired effect and in the ensuing panic that immediately followed, Crimthann's warriors launched themselves against the surprised Munstermen who stumbled and tripped over the bodies of their fallen comrades.

Bran advanced alongside his men, shoulder to shoulder, pressing the advantage of the momentum which the initial attack had given them. He deflected a savage blow with his shield, burying his sword in the skull of the red bearded Munstermen whose poor aim had left him off balance and exposed. The man groaned as he crumpled into a heap and Bran stepped over him, slashing at an unprotected throat. His sword sliced through the soft flesh and the wounded warrior fell to his knees, staring up at him wide–eyed while he clutched frantically at the spurting wound on his neck. A second blow severed the man's head from his body.

Bran felt nothing.

He moved with precision and agility, reacting instinctively to his opponents, his movements dictated by pure reflex. The continuous clanging of metal on metal rang in his ears.

Etach was suddenly beside him, shouting wildly as he eliminated yet another of Feidlimid's warriors. "These bastards'll rue the day they ever laid eyes on the hills of Leinster!"

But already the impetus of the initial attack was beginning to fade. A few of the warriors turned and fled, pushing their way toward the ranks in the rear.

"Hold your ground!" Bran shouted hoarsely as the onslaught drove him back.

The Munstermen kept coming, a sea of spears and swords to which there seemed no end. As one man fell another took his place and they pressed forward, sensing that victory was only a few paces away.

Suddenly, over the din of battle, Bran heard his father cry out in a voice that resounded across the plain to the distant hills.

"Ui Muiredaig!"

The standard bearers who had been left with Kenan in the rear heard the signal and lowered their banners.

Trumpets blared beyond the hills at the rear of Feidlimid's army and a few moments later the brightly coloured banners of Crimthann's phantom army became visible in the distance. As the Munstermen on the battlefield nervously glanced over their shoulders, Ragallach and Rowan's men exploded from their concealed positions in the trees and charged toward the startled Munstermen, screaming wildly. The warriors of the Ui Faelain moved up, completing the formation that virtually contained the enemy on three sides. But as effective as the maneuver was, it could not match the strength of the Munstermen whose ranks continued to swell with wave upon wave of reinforcements from the reserves on the far side of the plain. Within an hour, the lines of the Ui Muiredaig had begun to erode and once again the men of Leinster were forced to fall back.

And then they heard it, faintly at first, but growing steadily louder with each passing moment, the blaring of scores of clarions and trumpets. The standards of the Ard–Ri suddenly appeared alongside those of the Ui Muiredaig in the distant hills.

"It's the high king!" Bran shouted, pointing excitedly at Niall's warriors as they swarmed down the sides of the grassy slopes. "It's Niall!"

The Munstermen were now surrounded on four sides and no longer possessed the advantage of superior numbers. Lines and formations dissolved into melees where warriors fought individually or in small groups, often finding themselves cut off from their comrades.

Through the mass of men fighting for their lives, Bran glimpsed Crimthann. The king had lost his mount and was down, standing alone against three Munstermen who had managed to encircle him.

Bran screamed his father's name, trying to make himself heard over the noise of the battlefield as he started to move toward him. He glanced over his shoulder at the reserves on the far side of the field and saw that Kenan had not yet committed his men to the battle. Bran turned and pushed his way through the horde of warriors, roughly shoving comrade and enemy aside. One Munsterman stepped forward to challenge him and Bran hacked him down, stepping over his body without breaking stride.

"Father!"

The warriors around Crimthann had begun to close in. The king stepped forward to meet one of his attackers, then spun around abruptly, his sword flashing through the air. The man behind him screamed in pain as his swordarm was severed at the elbow. But in the same instant that Crimthann had turned, one of the other warriors dashed in and thrust his sword deep into the King's unprotected back.

"No!" Bran cried out.

Crimthann somehow managed to pivot quickly, swinging his bloodstained sword at his assailant's neck and decapitating him. But the effort of the stroke expended what strength he had left and he collapsed to his knees, leaning forward on the sword to support himself.

A cruel smile crossed the thin lips of the remaining Munsterman as he casually stepped behind the king and raised his broad sword high. The blade sliced through the air. But instead of connecting with flesh and bone, it rang out like the toll of a churchbell as it met the steel of Bran's weapon. The blow deflected, Bran twisted his sword upward and into the man's throat. As the warrior fell, Bran turned and knelt beside his father.

"I'll get you back to camp," he said with quiet urgency, gently placing a hand under his father's head. "The physician will —"

"There is no time," Crimthann said faintly. He drew his breath in sharply, fighting for the strength to speak. "I always knew you were the one."

"Don't talk," Bran pleaded, tears welling as he caught the expression in Crimthann's eyes. Weakness and defeat were unknown to his father – an invincible warrior who had spent a lifetime cheating death.

But Crimthann had begun to cough up thick clots of blood, an indication that the lungs had been pierced and his time was short. When he finally managed to catch his breath he looked about anxiously. "Where is my *cland?*"

The long–bladed sword lay alongside the fallen king and Bran picked it up slowly, holding it for Crimthann to see. The hilt of the weapon had been crafted in gold and worked into the shape of a wolf's head with two glittering rubies that made the eyes seem to Bran as if they were on fire.

"To be king is to be as the wolf," Crimthann whispered. "The leader... always protects... his pack and his territory – even if..."

The blood red eyes of the wolf seemed to flicker for an instant, then fade. When he looked down again, Bran Ui Faelain was alone.

CHAPTER FIVE

By midafternoon, most of Feidlimid's warriors had laid down their weapons. Under the watchful eyes of their captors, they were pressed into the grisly task of collecting the dead and carrying the wounded to an area where the physicians of both armies could attend to them. The few scattered pockets of resistance that remained were easily overpowered, and Niall ordered that those Munstermen who had deserted and fled the battlefield were to be hunted down and executed as common criminals. Only the warriors who had surrendered honourably were entitled to the protection of the law which governed the rights and treatment of prisoners.

As the fighting subsided, Etach and the warrior who accompanied him found Bran sitting alongside Crimthann's body and staring at the bloodstained sword that rested in his lap. He raised his head slowly, eyes reddened with weeping, and fixed his gaze on the captain of the king's personal bodyguard.

"Where were you, Flann?" he asked unsteadily.

"I... we couldn't reach him in time. When he saw Niall's banner, he charged ahead of us and — " Flann could not continue.

Etach rested a calloused hand on Bran's shoulder. "You cannot fault him lad," he said in a low voice. "Your father always exposed himself to the same danger his men faced. He has died as he lived — a warrior." He bent down and knelt beside his fallen king, his gnarled fingers fumbling with the iron brooch at Crimthann's shoulder. He removed the king's bearskin cloak and wrapped it around Bran, pinning it at the shoulder in the same manner Crimthann had worn it.

"We must go my lord," he said softly, helping Bran to his feet. "The Ard–Ri has summoned you to his pavilion. Flann and his men will take your father back to camp."

Bran started to follow then paused, glancing over his shoulder at the pale, lifeless form that had once been his father. The chieftain of the clanna Ui Faelain and king of all Leinster had united the clans but died without having realized his dream – his kingdom at peace. *Only through death have you found the peace you sought*, Bran reflected sadly as he turned away.

He walked beside Etach in silence as they made their way toward the camp that Niall had established on the far side of the plain. Bran was becoming aware of the organized confusion that followed the battle's aftermath. Prisoners loaded the dead into scores of small wooden carts while the soldiers of Niall's army roamed the battlefield collecting the weapons of fallen warriors. Others bustled from one wounded man to the next, carrying their burdens to the area where the physicians labored to mend the casualties from both sides. Wounds were cauterized and limbs severed. The screams of comrade and foe alike mingled in bone chilling harmony while from the camps came the sounds of a dozen different choruses, the victors voices heavy with wine as they celebrated their triumph.

When the two men reached the perimeter of Niall's camp, they were challenged by several guards who were dressed in the royal blue tunics of the Ard–Ri's personal guard. The soldiers escorted them to what had previously been Feidlimid's headquarters, an expansive pavilion surrounded by dozens of the king's finest warriors. Bran and Etach followed their escort inside.

The luxurious interior of the quarters was lavishly adorned with the spoils of Feidlimid's raid into Meath. Intricately stitched tapestries covered the ground. Opposite the entrance a mound of booty piled to the height of a tall man's shoulders glittered in stark testament to the avarice of the king of Cashel. Drinking vessels, platters and finely crafted jewellry in gold and silver, all inlaid with precious stones, had been tossed in the heap with total disregard for the beauty or delicacy of any one piece. Anger filled Bran as he noticed that Feidlimid had included several chalices and crucifixes in his collection. It was apparent that the Munstermen had little respect for the sanctity of the monasteries and churches which had had the misfortune to lie in their path of destruction.

Niall's senior officers were resting comfortably on large, well-padded cushions. The loud conversations Bran had heard with such clarity from the outside, died to faint murmurs the instant he and Etach entered. All eyes were upon him as he stood with his father's bloodied sword still clutched in his hand. Bran glanced around at the bearded weather beaten faces.

Then his eyes met Kenan's.

His brother had positioned himself next to one of the older warriors whose hand still poised in mid-air as if to silence him. *What is he doing here?* Bran wondered. *By whose authority does he dare to intrude on a council of war called by the Ard-Ri himself?*

The warrior beside Kenan abruptly rose to his feet and moved toward Bran. Although his hair and beard had begun to show traces of grey, his muscular body was that of a young man. His coarse woolen tunic and his forearms were splattered with dry blood. The modest sandals of a soldier covered his feet. As he drew nearer, Bran realized that a golden circlet of kingship rested on the man's wrinkled brow.

"I am Niall Caille," he said quietly, gripping Bran's forearm in the traditional gesture of greeting. "I am sorry we had to meet under conditions such as these." His brown eyes softened suddenly. "I have been told what happened to your father and I am sorry. All Erin grieves the loss of a man such as he. I cannot help but feel responsible. If only we had arrived sooner, he might well have been with us here today."

"The fault was not yours, my lord," Bran assured him, his gaze shifting to Kenan. "Had our reserves advanced when they were supposed to, my father would still be alive."

"You were closer to him than I!" Kenan protested loudly, leaping to his feet. "But why should you want to save the king's life? He was all that stood between you and your ambition to seize the throne."

Before Bran could respond to the accusation, Etach stopped forward, raising his hands to quell the speculative whispers that had erupted. "Any man who was there knows that Bran Ui Faelain speaks the truth," he said loudly. "Kenan's men were positioned to cover our retreat but they never came." He glared at Kenan. "I see that you wasted no time in positioning yourself here."

Kenan reseated himself, then shifted uneasily under the speculative stares of the warriors.

Niall studied him for a moment, then turned back to Bran, the creases in the corners of his eyes deepening. "It would seem that your brother now contests your right to succeed Crimthann. He feels that your election as tanaiste was contrary to the traditions of the Brehon laws. However, he has suggested that rather than see you relinquish your title, it might be in Leinster's best interests to be ruled by both of you – jointly."

"My brother would appear to be somewhat misinformed," Bran retorted carefully. "My appointment as tanaiste was quite legitimate as the councilmen and any of the chieftains who were present can confirm. My father spent a lifetime uniting the clans of Leinster and I assure you it was not his intention to have it divided again, even between his two sons."

"But I am the first–born!" Kenan argued hotly. "By tradition, it is I who should have been delegated his successor and I will not be cheated out of my inheritance." He turned to Niall, his face contorted with rage. "Under the law you are obliged to –"

"In Erin, I am the law," Niall stated firmly. "And I can see nothing in what you have said to support your claim. Bran was duly elected by council and approved by Crimthann himself. I see no reason why he should not succeed your father as chieftain of the Ui Faelain and king of Leinster."

Kenan's dark eyes narrowed. "It is not just I who questions his ascendancy. There are those whose allegiances lie... elsewhere, and I fear that if Bran is crowned king, Leinster will erupt into civil war."

Niall, who was taller than Kenan by a head, looked down at him and grinned. "Although I think you have exaggerated somewhat, it is obvious that your brother does face some opposition. But let me say in front of both of you right now, if he is confronted with any dissension whatsoever, Bran Ui Faelain will have my complete support in suppressing it." His smile faded. "Is that clear?"

After a moment Kenan muttered resentfully. "Aye, my lord."

"Good," the high king gestured his dismissal as he turned to face Bran. "Leave us now – all of you. There are affairs of state that I must discuss with the king of Leinster."

Kenan's face flushed red as he marched out of the pavilion. Etach followed Niall's officers.

When they were alone, Niall raised a bushy eyebrow. "I am afraid that it will not be long before a move is made against you," he cautioned. "Despite what I told your brother, I cannot guarantee that I will be able to respond should you be confronted with such a problem. Since they first sailed up the Bann River five years ago, the Norsemen have gradually tightened their stranglehold on Ulster and despite our initial victory at Derry, we have been powerless to stop them. Their leader, Thorgest, has erected a fortress on the banks of Lough Neagh which has so far proven to be impregnable. He has kept us off balance by sending raiding parties to attack our villages and monasteries throughout the northern province, then withdrawing to their stronghold before we can intercept them. More often than not, we arrive only to find the smoldering ruins and rotting corpses that they have left behind."

"But I have heard the bards sing of your victories," Bran blurted incredulously. "Surely a few barbarians are no match for the army of Erin!"

Niall laughed sardonically. "What you have heard is more

the product of a poet's imagination than anything else. Aye, we have had some success in ambushing a few of the smaller raiding parties. But I would not call those victories. The Norsemen are highly organized and fight as if they are of one mind. Ships full of reinforcements continue to arrive while our ranks are plagued with desertions and low morale that worsens with each defeat. It is only a question of time before they dominate all of Ulster. I am told that Thorgest already refers to it as his Kingdom of the North."

The fatalistic tone of Niall's words shocked Bran. "Their numbers cannot be so great that they would not be overwhelmed by the armies of Erin's five kingdoms!" he uttered.

"But it is not five kingdoms they face," Niall explained. "The army of Erin consists mainly of Ulstermen and most of them are from my own clan, the Ui Neill. Connaught and Meath are no different than Leinster, the tribes and clans warring among themselves over the provincial kingship, unaffected by that which lies beyond the realms of their respective territories. Meanwhile, under Feidlimid's guidance, Munster has prospered by openly trading with the very enemy who invaded our island. But even wealth could not sate his lust for power, driving him to the point where he could accept nothing less than being recognized as Ard-ri. I'll wager he is now wishing that he had sought a lesser ambition.

"Feidlimid is alive?" Bran had not seen the king of Cashel on the battlefield and merely assumed that he had escaped in the confusion.

"For the moment," Niall replied. "He was found in this very pavilion, cowering beside the same plunder he took out of Meath."

"What do you intend to do with him?"

"I thought I would leave that up to you. He is, after all, responsible for your father's death. But I tell you this – he would not be long for this world if the decision were mine. Feidlimid is a dangerous man, a threat to both of us, and as such should be eliminated."

The compulsion for vengeance flared inside Bran and he considered how simple it would be to inflict the ultimate punishment on Feidlimid. A few words, an uttered command would send the king of Cashel to his death. *Even so*, he thought to himself, *the scales will remain unbalanced*. "The life of a Munsterman cannot compare with my father's honour price," he said aloud. "We will send him back to Cashel in the dignity befitting his station, providing he agrees to pay an *eraic* for the slaying of Crimthann Ui Faelain."

"Your offer is more than generous," Niall said slowly, a puzzled expression on his face. "Feidlimid would be a fool to refuse. But it surprises me that you would accept blood money as compensation for your father's life."

Bran's face remained expressionless. "As Crimthann Ui Faelain devoted his life to Leinster, it seems only fitting that an entire kingdom be held accountable for his death. If Feidlimid wishes to be spared, he will render full half of Munster's profits to Leinster each year."

Niall threw back his head and laughed until the tears streamed down his cheeks. "You have done far worse than kill him," he finally managed. "The king of Cashel will scramble for the executioner rather than have you tamper with his coffers."

Bran allowed himself a faint smile. "I do not think that

Feidimid will object. I suspect he puts far greater value on his life than I do."

Niall's expression grew suddenly serious. "You realize of course that you will have made a powerful enemy for yourself – one who will likely move against you at the first opportunity. When that day comes, Leinster may have to face him alone."

"We will be ready," Bran said with conviction. "Leinster already owes you a great debt and we can offer you little but our gratitude and loyalty. I wish we could do more."

"Be my eyes in the south," Niall beseeched him. "I must return immediately to Ulster and the Viking may be dealt with more effectively if we are not concerned about the Munstermen at our backs."

"I would consider it an honour, my lord," Bran replied, bowing deeply. As he rose and turned to leave Niall caught his arm.

"The most powerful enemy is the one that strikes from within," he cautioned. "There is hunger in your brother's eyes and I have seen that look before. It is born of evil and treacherous thoughts."

"Kenan is many things," Bran replied. "But he is not a traitor. In time, his ambition and our differences will both be forgotten." Bran bowed, then turned and disappeared between the flaps. Niall stood for a moment in the empty pavilion, staring after him.

"For both our sakes, I pray you are right," he said softly.

CHAPTER SIX

The following morning the sky had taken on a sickly grey pallor and a light drizzle was falling as the army of Leinster began its journey back to Naas, marching solemnly behind Bran as he rode alongside the two–wheeled cart that carried his father's body. The jubilation of victory had faded quickly at the news of Crimthann's death and the sullen mood of the warriors matched the gloom of the rain–laden clouds.

Behind Bran, Etach and Ragallach rode together, an unspoken camaraderie developing out of their mutual respect for Crimthann. The Ui Muiredaig chieftain had petitioned Bran to allow his soldiers the honour of escorting the fallen king back to Naas. The sincerity of the old warrior's request had touched Bran deeply and he had readily given his consent. Now, as he glanced over his shoulder, he could see no discernible divisions between the two factions. Warriors from both clans were trudging beside one another as comrades. It occurred to him that no greater tribute could be afforded the memory of Crimthann Ui Faelain.

Bran rode back along the column several times, scanning the sea of stoic faces that gazed up at him, but Kenan was not among them. After he had left Niall's pavilion, Bran had returned to his own camp to find his older brother, anxious to ease the tension that had exploded between them. Although the incident could not be overlooked, he concluded that fear had been the source of Kenan's anger and jealousy. He obviously felt that he had been passed over and now that his father was gone, he would somehow be excluded from the inner circle of Bran's royal court. Such degradation and loss of status would be an insult which Kenan simply could not bear and Bran was eager to reassure him that he would retain the same rank and privileges he had possessed under Crimthann's rule.

That day, the search had proven fruitless and after nearly an hour of casting about and inquiry, it became evident that Kenan and his personal guard had broken off from the main body of the army. Bran had speculated that he would rejoin the column once they were enroute to Naas, but dismissed the notion as they drew nearer to their destination.

As sunset pried through the darkening clouds on the second day of their journey, Bran sighted the familiar hills that surrounded Naas, ancient stronghold of the Ui Faelain. In the valley beyond, hundreds of lime-washed cottages, the simple homes of the *bothachs* who worked the land, surrounded the grey stone ramparts of the massive fortress that towered beyond them. The farmland stretched north and west for several miles to the banks of the River Liffey which snaked through the Leinster countryside and into Meath, emptying into the sea when it reached the distant eastern coast. To the south of the community, several thousand head of cattle grazed on the pastoral meadows that gradually gave way to dense forests of oak and ash.

Thunder began to rumble as Bran led his men down into the valley and in the distance he could see people beginning to congregate around the main gate as they approached. The rain suddenly deluged in deafening sheets before him. Lightning flashed across the sky like a jagged blade of fire and illuminated the faces of those who had gathered to pay their respects to their dead king. Women, young and old, their heads covered with rain drenched shawls, wailed and lamented. Nobleman and peasant alike stood in the chilling wind, their soaking hair and clothes slicked against their flesh, staring grim-faced at Bran. Their eyes followed the small cart as it slowly passed them and was pulled into the main compound.

Then Bran saw her – arms flailing wildly as she frantically ran across the cobblestone courtyard. Wet tendrils of hair straggled down her face and her shawl had slipped from one shoulder, billowing out behind her as she dashed through the puddles to the cart.

Muireen threw her arms around her father's neck and cradled his head against her breast, rocking his lifeless body to and fro.

"Father!" she sobbed. "You can't be dead! You can't!"

Bran swung out of his saddle and hastened to his sister's side. "Muireen, don't," he said awkwardly. "He's gone."

"No!" she shrieked, twisting away from him.

"Muireen!" Bran shouted, grasping her arms and turning her toward him. She struggled for a moment then grew suddenly quiet, raising her blue–grey eyes to meet his, her tears mixing with the rain that rolled down her face.

Bran held her tightly against him, willing her sorrow into his own body. "I know," he said softly, his throat constricted with the grief. Looking over her head, he caught Etach's eye and subtly gestured, easing Muireen's arms from around his neck and guiding her toward him.

"Take care of her," Bran instructed. Etach protectively wrapped his brawny arm around her shoulders and led her away to her quarters.

Bran watched them for a moment then turned, nearly

colliding with Conor who had been standing quietly behind him. His younger brother's lip quivered as he fought to stave off his tears.

"He told me to stay," the wretched lad whimpered, "but I should have gone with you."

"He thought it best for you," Bran told him, laying his hand on his brother's head. "There was nothing that any of us could have done." He turned and leaned heavily against the side of the cart, staring down at his father's face. "Go and tell his manservants to prepare him for... the ceremony," he said without looking up. "Tonight he will rest among his ancestors."

As Conor hurried off, Bran raised his head wearily and summoned his senior officers, ordering them to dismiss the warriors who had steadfastly remained in formation while the rain pelted them mercilessly. "Tell them to go home to their fires and their families," he ordered in a subdued voice. "They have fought well and Leinster is grateful for the victory they have given her."

While the other officers moved to carry out his instructions, Bran signaled Flann to remain behind. "I want you to see to the needs of the Uí Muiredaig warriors," he went on, wiping the rain from his face. "Food, blankets, physicians – anything. And send Ragallach to me. I will wait for him in my father's great hall."

Slogging across the saturated courtyard, exhaustion weighed down Bran's every step. Sleep had eluded him for two nights and his eyes and muscles ached for a respite. The world he knew had changed so quickly, presenting him with a myriad of situations and problems he was not certain he could cope with.

Pushing open the heavy oaken doors at the entrance to the great hall, he stood while the warmth from the open hearths in the centre of the room washed over his face. His nostrils filled with the acrid scent of soot and smoke and with it came memories of feasts filled with laughter and song, often lasting until the early light of dawn.

He moved slowly toward the king's place of honour atop the dais on the far side of the hall. The heavy high-backed throne of carved yew consisted of intricate spirals and patterns inlaid with silver and gold. As he ran his hand along its polished surface, he pictured Crimthann presiding over the festivities as he had so often done, his favourite wine goblet in hand and his face flushed with laughter.

Father.

He stood motionless, unable to ascend the dais, transfixed by the power it represented. He was not his father – had never aspired to be – and the thought of ruling in his stead filled Bran with a profound sense of inadequacy.

The doors behind him creaked open and he turned to find the Ui Muiredaig chieftain standing in the entry.

"You summoned me, my lord?" Ragallach asked, crossing the space between them. The formal acknowledgment of Bran's authority sounded strange and uncomfortable on the lips of the older man. *I must not let him see the insecurity I feel*, Bran told himself as he stepped forward and grasped the chieftain's arm in greeting.

"I have been contemplating the treaty between our two clans and it has occurred to me that our alliance is based on an agreement between yourself and my father," he said quietly. "Now that he is gone, there are those who will say that the pact is nullified."

Ragallach slowly shook his head. "I swore an oath of allegiance to the king of Leinster, not to your father. Providing that all conditions of the treaty are met, the Ui Muiredaig will continue to honour it."

"As will the Ui Faelain," Bran quickly assured him. "But regarding my marriage to your daughter, I – "

Ragallach held up his hand. "Say no more," he interrupted. "Under the circumstances, I cannot fault you for wishing to postpone. There will be plenty of time for wedding celebrations after a decent period of mourning for your father has passed."

"I am grateful for your patience and cooperation," Bran said quietly. "And I give you my word that I shall honour my father's bond. When the time for grieving has passed, I will summon the clans to Naas so they may witness my marriage to your daughter. Leinster's future will begin with our sacred union, and from that day forward, the Ui Faelain and the Ui Muiredaig shall be as one people."

Ragallach's features gradually relaxed and he smiled warmly. "Your father chose you well," he said thoughtfully. "Tonight the Ui Muiredaig will grieve the loss of a great king. But tomorrow, we shall return to Mullaghmast with the news that Bran Ui Faelain now sits upon the throne of Leinster."

As the Ui Muiredaig chieftain left the great hall, Bran turned and faced the throne of Leinster. The intimidation and uncertainty were gone. Slowly, he stepped up onto the dais then eased himself onto the throne, leaning back and raising his eyes to the rafters.

One people – one Leinster, he thought to himself. *And I am their king. Father, your dream is still alive.*

That evening, Crimthann's body was laid out in state upon the heavy oak table that had been placed on the dais next to the throne. The deceased king had been clad in his finest tunic and sandals, and the circlet of gold which signified his authority rested upon his head. His weapons and personal ornaments lay by his side, to be buried with him, so that he might journey into the afterlife with the honour and dignity of a warrior king.

Charged with the care of the candles around the edge of the table, Muireen stood near her father's head, her face shrouded by a black veil of mourning. The two professional *keeners* stood opposite one another on either side of the king. Bran and Conor sat nearest the dais surrounded by their relations and friends, and behind them were the nobility and tribal chieftains of Leinster. As they waited in silence for the ritual to begin, Bran's eyes scanned the congregation, but Kenan was still nowhere to be seen.

Muireen began the recitation of the dirge, her voice a lamenting cry. Her song was an ancient *Cepog* that recounted the passage and adventures of the dead in the world beyond. She followed with a part of equal length, her gentle crooning weaving through the haunting melody to produce an intricate tapestry. The long part was then chanted by the two keeners, with the congregation joining in the common chorus at the end of each stanza until the room was filled with the sound of heartfelt woe.

When the mourning part of the ritual was completed,

a handful of warriors bore Crimthann's body upon their shoulders out of the ringed fortress to a clearing in a nearby thicket of trees where the remains of bygone generations of Ui Faelains rested undisturbed in their *duma*, the ancient burial mound of the clan. Crimthann was interred standing upright alongside the warriors and champions who had preceded him, facing Naas and the surrounding countryside he had loved.

Bran had kept his eyes on Muireen throughout the ceremony, noting that she had somehow managed to maintain an uncharacteristic poise. It was not her way to reveal her innermost feelings to others at such a time, but when the huge boulder which sealed the entrance to the duma was rolled back into place, she abruptly dropped to her knees and embraced it, her shoulders convulsing with sobs. Bran started to reach for her.

And then he heard it. High up in the air, from somewhere beyond the surrounding hills, the sound drifted down to him on the wings of the wind. The haunting howl of the beast paralyzed him and brought back the words he would never forget. "Be as the wolf... as the wolf."

He blinked his eyes rapidly several times then bent and helped his sister to her feet.

"He's gone... gone," she wept, burying her face in her hands as Bran wrapped his arms around her. He shifted his gaze to the distant hills. "Our father's blood flows in our veins and he will forever be a part of us. So long as any one of us lives, he will never die."

CHAPTER SEVEN

The *dun* at Mullaghmast contained several hundred buildings ranging from the stone and mortar residences of the Ui Muiredaig nobility and freemen, to the simpler mud and wattle huts of the retainers. The ringed fortress was surrounded by concentric earthen mounds between which were deep trenches filled with water. The stone ramparts of the innermost wall were terraced on the interior with flights of stairs leading up to the battlements and galleries.

Finola sat in the *grianan* of her father's house, her delicate fingers occupied with the task of embroidering the hemline of a satin lena with fine threads of silver and gold. The lofty windows in the room were positioned to admit as much sunlight as possible, and the white bronze of Finola's hair sparkled as the light from above danced along the curling locks that fell about her shoulders and down to her waist. Her skin was as white and immaculate as the first snowfall of winter, the natural blush that kissed her cheeks augmented by the gentle caress of the warm afternoon sun. Her maidservant, Morallta, sat across from her at the square oak table that dominated the room, preoccupied with her own sewing. Finola was only a year older than the girl and over the years the relationship that had blossomed between them had come to be based more on friendship than on the duties of rank.

For nearly an hour the two young women worked in a comfortable and contented silence that was only periodically interrupted by the curious wrens that perched on the ledges of the open casements, their melodic warbling accompanied by the shouts and laughter of children playing in the courtyard beyond. Gradually, the golden rays that bathed the girls slipped away to pool on the heavy carpet that covered the centre of the stone floor, its colourful designs radiant in the patch of sunlight.

Morallta laid her work on her lap and fidgeted with an unruly braid of auburn hair, her eyes twinkling mischievously.

"It is rumoured that Donnchad, son of the Owenachta chieftain sat beside my lady in the banquet hall last night and could not take his eyes from her," she remarked nonchalantly. "They say that he will surely not leave Mullaghmast without first offering you a proposal of marriage."

Finola raised her violet eyes. "It was not Donnchad, but Dermot, prince of Connaught." It amused her that so innocent a gesture was enough to stimulate speculation and rumours throughout the court.

"Forgive me," Morallta said, turning her attention back to her sewing. "My lady has had so many suitors since she came of age, I have difficulty remembering them all. But I am told that this one is by far the most handsome." She paused for a moment, as if a comment or reply was expected. When there was none she sighed heavily. "And if he petitions for my lady's hand, will she reject this young prince as she has all others before him?"

"I don't know," Finola replied pensively, her hands momentarily stilled. She lifted her head and stared across the room, looking beyond the tapestried walls. "He is a fine man and of noble birth – as they all have been. But he should be... I should feel..."

She shook her head, exasperated. Despite his charm, Dermot had been no different than his predecessors, all of them lacking that elusive quality Finola could not quite define. Though many had been fair of countenance, with wealth and prestige enough to flatter even the most particular woman, she had politely declined all proposals. *He will be different, the one for whom I wait*, she thought to herself, *and I will know him when he comes*.

Finola frowned back at Morallta. "Oh... Dermot's feet are too big," she complained and the two girls broke into a fit of giggling.

At that moment Finola heard her name being called, and recognizing the booming voice she leapt to her feet excitedly. The door to the grianan swung open and Ragallach strode into the room, his arms outstretched to embrace his daughter. "Finola," he shouted happily.

"Father!" She ran and hugged him tightly. "When did you return?"

"Only just this moment," he answered, unpinning his mantle and tossing it onto one of the benches positioned along the wall. "It has been far too long since last I looked upon my daughter's face."

"Mother and I have been so worried about you," she said softly, smiling back at him. "She will be glad to see that you have come back to us safely." Finola started to move toward the door but her father caught her arm and drew her back to him.

"Wait," he instructed, suddenly grave. "I have already spoken to your mother and there is something that I must tell you." He paused, his gaze shifting to Morallta. "Leave us." The startled maidservant glanced quickly at Finola, then bowed and hurried from the room.

The abrupt change in her father's mood puzzled Finola. "What's wrong?" she questioned, realizing that he had not yet spoken of the battle, and for the first time she noticed that his face and clothes were still soiled with dust and sweat.

"Are we defeated by the Ui Faelain?" she asked slowly. Before he could reply her eyes suddenly widened in horror. "My brother – Rowan," she demanded, clutching the sleeves of her father's tunic. "Is he wounded or..."

Ragallach shook his head slowly and caught Finola's hands, holding them tightly in his own. "No, my little bird, God has kept your brother safe. And we do not come back to Mullaghmast in defeat, but with news of peace." He told her of the alliance with the Ui Faelain and how the Munstermen had been defeated by the united clans of Leinster. She noted the remorse in his voice as he spoke of the untimely death of Crimthann. "From this day forward the clans of the Ui Muiredaig and the Ui Faelain shall never face each other again as enemies." But his deep brown eyes, eyes the colour of the rich soil of Erin, were strangely lacking the reassurance she had expected to find there. What she found in its place was the remoteness she had often seen on his face when he mediated disputes within the clan.

"What troubles you?" she probed nervously. Ragallach averted his gaze and began to pace across the room. When he turned to face her again, his jaw was set.

"The treaty that I have made with the king has united not only our clans, but our two families," he began. "In the great hall this very afternoon we will announce your betrothal to the son of Crimthann Ui Faelain."

Finola gaped at her father in astonishment, the blood

draining from her face. "You – you cannot have promised me to the son of your greatest enemy," she stuttered.

Ragallach's face was granite. "My enemy is dead and Ui Faelain are no longer our foe. We shall share equally in the tributes of all Leinster and our clan will be prosperous again."

"But you will remain as servant to them," Finola protested, fighting to regain her composure. "As will we all. Even to the point where you have consented to give me up as a hostage!" She suddenly became aware of the chill breeze that teased the curtains as it whiffled through the open windows and she felt the icy press of the stone floor beneath her kidskin slippers. She shuddered and rubbed at the gooseflesh on her forearms.

"You will not be a hostage, but a member of the royal family," Ragallach explained. "Bran Ui Faelain shall be crowned king and as his wife you will be afforded all of the respect and privileges due to your rank." He strode across the room and grasped her shoulders. "You must trust my judgment in this, daughter."

"But I have never even met the king's son," she protested. "What if he is not pleased with me? Or I with him?"

Ragallach sighed heavily. "Try to look beyond your own desires, Finola. We have battled the Ui Faelain for years in an effort to gain control of Leinster. And with each passing year the Ui Muiredaig has grown weaker. Now Bran will be king and you will rule as queen by his side, ensuring that the interests of your clan are protected. Would you deny those of your own bloodline such an advantage?"

With the welfare of the clan to consider, Finola felt

her options rapidly dwindling. *The plight of our people becomes more desperate with the passing of each summer,* she thought. *Without the tribute of the lesser tribes who have since sworn allegiance to the Ui Faelain, the territories held by our clan are scarcely enough to sustain those who have remained loyal. And for the second year in a row, the harvest has been blighted. Even my father's army has been plagued with desertions and those who remain often fight on empty bellies, foraging for food and supplies in the villages and farms through which they march. Something must be done if we are all to survive, and if that means selling my heart into captivity, I have little choice. If one life will ensure the survival of so many others, there is no choice.*

"It is not my wish to displease you father," Finola said resignedly. "When is the courtship to begin?"

"There will be no courtship," her father replied flatly. "You are to be wed to Bran Ui Faelain at Naas in a fortnight's time. I have given him my word on it."

Finola drew back, her face flushing crimson. "Not only do you take away my right to choose a husband for myself, you deny me the decency of a proper betrothal!" she cried out, clutching the apricot folds of her heavy skirt in agitation and thrusting her face close to Ragallach. "Although a year would be preferable, I was prepared to settle for six months. But fourteen days! Have you any idea how many old tongues will wag, all of them speculating on the need for such haste. I will not be made a fool of," she told him defiantly, folding her arms across her breast. "And I will not be traded like a sack of grain just so you can pacify your new master!"

"Forgive me, daughter," Ragallach entreated. Finola felt his hand tremble as he touched her cheek and she saw his pain and frustration. "You are more precious to me than my own life's blood," he continued, "and I would rather have my soul damned to hell than ever see harm come to you. But there is much more at stake here than you realize. If I break my oath to the Ui Faelain, the killing will begin again and this time there will be no end to it until our clan is destroyed."

Finola stared at her father in disbelief as he trudged past her to the oak table in the middle of the room and leaned heavily on its polished surface. He seemed suddenly old, worn out, and the abrupt transformation frightened her. She desperately sought after the words that would bring him back to her.

"You have defeated them before, father," she declared with counterfeit poise. "You will – "

She started as Ragallach slammed his fist onto the table and whirled to face her.

"Damn it, Finola, don't you understand?" he cried out. "We cannot win against the Ui Faelain! They have the support of the Ard–Ri and if we do not abide by the conditions of the treaty we could well have the whole of Erin at our throats!"

He gazed at her in silence for several moments, his chest heaving. When he spoke again his voice was subdued but determined. "The Ui Faelain have offered us an honourable alternative to war and we have no option but to accept. We have no choice – and neither do you."

Finola stepped forward. "But father, I – "

Ragallach raised his hand, his face implacable. "There is nothing more to be said," he declared firmly, then turned away. "I have given my word and I cannot – will not break it."

Finola stood paralyzed for an instant, her thoughts a labyrinth of uncertainties and newly acquired fears. The world she had known and the future she had always dreamed of had been irreparably shattered, her destiny forever altered by a cruel circumstance over which she had not been able to exert any influence or control. Never more so than at that moment had she felt so completely alone – so powerless.

Then, through the depths of her despair, a flicker of light appeared – a glimmer of hope in her otherwise hopeless dilemma.

Mother!

Finola fled the grianan, the tattoo of her own heartbeat muting Ragallach's voice as he called after her. She ran blindly through the corridors, hot tears streaming down her face, until she reached her mother's chambers.

Lady Agnes had been studying and adjusting her carefully coiffed hair in a mirror of polished silver, when Finola burst into the room and threw herself at her mother's feet.

"Oh Mother," she pleaded. "You've got to help me!"

"Dear lord!" Agnes gasped as she reached down to embrace her. "What in God's name happened?"

Between sobs, Finola told her. When she had finished, Agnes drew her close, cradling her head against her breast.

"I cannot help you my child," she said sympathetically. "Your father will not break his oath to the Ui Faelain. The wedding preparations are already underway in Naas. If you refuse this young chieftain it will be too great an affront for them to ignore and we shall be plunged into war again."

Finola clutched the folds of her mother's lena. "Then

what am I to do, Mother?" she wept. "Must I marry him?"

"By all accounts he is a fine warrior and nobleman," Agnes replied in a strained voice. "Your father will be given half of the tributes of Leinster as your brideprice and you will rule alongside Bran Ui Faelain as his queen."

"Then you want me to..."

"You will marry this man because it is your father's wish. Would you disobey him and see him dishonoured? Are you prepared to see more blood spilled because of your girlish notions of love and romance?"

Finola remained silent.

"You are not a herdswoman who may take up with any man she fancies," Agnes went on crisply. "You are of noble blood and along with all the privileges you have received comes a responsibility to your family and your people. To deny that responsibility is to deny them."

To deny them. The words echoed in Finola's mind. *How many of you have died in the name of the clanna Ui Muiredaig?* she wondered. *How many of our women have lost their sons, their husbands, their fathers to this mindless slaughter? Perhaps we are too ashamed to count our dead. Their sacrifice has been for nought, for the outcome of every battle has always created an imbalance between victor and vanquished, defeat and revenge feeding on one another. No, the sword will not bring us peace. I am the only one who can put an end to the bloodshed. Only I have the power.*

She wiped the tears from her face. "You may assure my father that I will do what is expected of me. But tell him this – when I marry Bran Ui Faelain my first loyalty shall be to him, not to the Ui Muiredaig. And I will work in my husband's best interests, even if they are contrary to those of my father."

She rose and started to leave, then paused and looked over her shoulder. "And you may tell the chieftain of the Ui Muiredaig that he has my word of honour on that," she added coldly. "And like him, I will not break my oath."

CHAPTER EIGHT

Without final confirmation from the council of elders, Bran's ascendancy to the throne was subject to dispute, leaving the kingship of Leinster prey to any *tuath* chieftain powerful enough to lay claim to it. A kingdom without a leader invited dissension, perhaps even invasion. The near fatal clash with the Munstermen was still fresh in their minds and rumours had begun to circulate throughout Naas of Norse raids along the coast of Meath. It was not surprising therefore that a certain air of urgency hung over the assembly that would elect the new king. But as there had been virtually no doubt as to the outcome of their meeting, a message had already been sent to Forannan, Archbishop of Armagh, requesting that he preside at the upcoming coronation. There were no objections or other challengers, so the elders did little more than verify the tanaiste's right to be named *Ri–Ruirech* of the province. Their deliberation was short and their vote unanimous. Three days after he had laid his father to rest, Bran Ui Faelain was named King of Leinster.

The announcement breathed new life into the royal city and the gloom that had shrouded Naas following Crimthann's death gradually began to fade. A new king meant new life and the people talked excitedly of a future filled with peace and prosperity. Crimthann had been well loved by his subjects and his passing had left them lost and uncertain. But Bran was of the same blood and they saw in him a youthful vitality and strength that filled them with hope.

The Archbishop of Armagh and his entourage arrived at last and Bran received them in the great hall, surrounded by noblemen and chieftains who had come to pay their respects to the holy man. As Primate of Erin, Forannan's authority and power extended far beyond the religious who served under him. He was noted for his wisdom and kindness, but he had proven on numerous occasions that he would not compromise his principles or beliefs. More than one tuath king had been humbled by the quiet spoken archbishop who intervened whenever he felt the edicts and policies of men contradicted the laws of God and jeopardized the immortal souls of the faithful. So great was his power over their hearts and minds, that even the Ard–Ri himself did not dare to oppose him.

Like Bran, Forannan was a tall man, but the lack of muscle on his frame made him look thinner. His skin was pale, the result of the countless hours he had spent in scriptoriums studying the word of God. There was an unearthly quality in his large blue eyes and his finely sculpted features gave him the ethereal appearance of a saint. He was beardless and his tonsure, unlike the Roman custom of shaving the crown of the head, took the customary Irish form of shaving the hair to the front of the head, allowing his thick, white–gold hair to grow long at the back. A shimmering robe of scarlet, indigo and viridian shot through with gold thread was draped over his lean body and he carried a crosier of polished hazelwood carved into the crook that symbolized his status in the church. Even so, he wore the modest sandals of a simple monk, the scuffed and worn leather testimony to the leagues that had passed beneath his feet.

Forannan smiled warmly at Bran. "I knew your father," he remarked, extending his hand. "He was a just king and dearly loved the people of Leinster." Bran dropped to one knee and kissed the ring that sparkled on the thin hand. "His devotion to them was well known," he replied respectfully. "I pray that I will be worthy of the honour that they have bestowed on me."

"Have no fear, my son," Forannan smiled, resting his hand on Bran's head. "You will guide them toward their destiny even as the King of kings guides your footsteps."

Bran met his eyes. *I hope your faith has not been misplaced,* he thought to himself as he rose. *God give me the strength to be the man – the king I must be.*

That night, Forannan occupied the place of honour during the evening meal. Seated next to him, Bran was surprised to find that the aging ecclesiastic had a refined sense of humour.

"Your coronation and your wedding present me with a unique opportunity indeed," he stated casually to Bran as he delicately picked at his food. "It is a rare occasion where I am called upon to officiate at two such paradoxical ceremonies."

"Paradoxical?" Bran was bewildered.

"Aye," Forannan replied, his eyes twinkling. "Tomorrow you will be made king, with power over thousands. But in a few days you will be fettered to a wife whose needs and desires will no doubt govern much of your life. A strange contradiction don't you think? You are a man who will soon become both master and vassal."

Bran pressed his lips into a thin smile. It suddenly occurred to him that he had given little thought to his upcoming marriage. Until now, he had regarded the arrangement as a matter of diplomacy – a political necessity if the alliance with the Ui Muiredaig was to be maintained. But Forannan's innocent jest had aroused his curiosity and he found himself wondering what his bride would be like. Apart from her name, he knew little about her and his lack of information generated a parade of alarming and tantalizing images that danced across his mind. But he knew that his fantasies were of no consequence. The union of the two clans overshadowed any consideration of his own feelings. Still, her name fired his imagination.

Finola. The white–shouldered one.

Abruptly, Bran made his apologies to the archbishop and excused himself from the great hall immediately after the evening meal, blaming his fatigue on the long days he had spent preparing to assume the reins of power. Much of his time had been filled by tedious conferences with his council of advisors and intensive sessions with the *Brehons* who tutored him on the subtle distinctions between the Urradus laws of Leinster and the Cain laws which were upheld by the high king according to the statutes contained within the copious volumes of the *Senchus Mor*. But in truth, the dark circles that had begun to appear under his eyes were born of the nagging sense of expectation which robbed him of sleep, as night after night he paced in nervous anticipation of the day his father's dream would become a reality.

When he reached his chambers, Bran threw himself on the freshly prepared bed without bothering to remove his tunic, desperate for a few hours sleep. He dozed uneasily until he was awakened by a persistent knock at his door.

"Enter," he muttered drowsily, propping himself on one elbow. The door creaked open and a woman slipped through, the light from the hallway momentarily revealing the sensuous curves of her body beneath the thin shift she wore. Bran eyed the familiar figure hungrily and grinned to himself in the dim light of the oil lamp that flickered on the far side of the room. "You seem to have lost your way home, my lady – again."

Taillte quietly pushed the door closed and leaned against it, a wanton smile revealing her pearl white teeth. "I am where I wish to be," she whispered softly. "I have no interest in those who waste their time drinking their fill and listening to the old seanachies' tales of ancient heroes." She crossed the short gap between them and gracefully seated herself on the edge of the bed, her movements executed with a leisurely precision that made them all the more provocative. "Some men do more than just listen to stories of great deeds," she added as she leaned forward, her emerald eyes beckoning him closer. "They create them."

"And you think me such a man?" Bran asked uncomfortably as he sat up, leaning away from her slightly. The fresh fragrance of lilac oil mixed with the lusty scent of her body enveloped him, drawing him toward her. He felt the heat rising in his loins and shifted self–consciously. "What great deeds do you foresee in my future?"

"More than merely the kingship of Leinster," she replied, laying her hand on his knee. "The eraic that you have exacted from the king of Cashel is but the first step. But why settle for only a portion of the prize? The whole of Feidlimid's treasury would easily make Leinster more powerful than any other province."

Bran drew back and blinked in astonishment. "To what

end?" he asked incredulously. "The Munstermen are defeated and we no longer need fear invasion."

"Power," she uttered in a throaty whisper. "Leinster will only be safe so long as you have the power to protect your kingdom. And power can only be accomplished through conquest. Once you have dominated Munster, Connaught and Meath will fall easily. Then all that remains in your path is Ulster, and Niall is already sorely pressed by the Norsemen. With his defeat, all Erin would be united under the banner of Leinster – with you as Ard–Ri. You will have accomplished what Niall could not and the foreigners will be driven back into the sea."

Bran looked at her pensively for several moments. Her scheme involved not only treason to the high king, but wars that would result in the death of countless thousands. And all the while she had given no indication of guilt or even compassion for those who would suffer, her eyes glistening with lust for power. Although he disapproved of her strategy, Bran realized that it contained elements of truth. Power was the key to Leinster's security, and as Niall himself had said, the Norse and Danish invaders would be quickly routed if the clans of Erin gathered under one banner. Unity was the answer – but at what cost?

He rose slowly and walked across the room to a small table on which rested several flagons of wine and drinking vessels. After filling two bronze goblets with the heavy, rich red wine he preferred, he turned to find Taillte stretched out comfortably across his bed. "I have no desire to subject the people of Leinster to further misery," he stated flatly as he handed her one of the goblets. "Until now, their lives have been filled with nothing but senseless feuds and battles. And death. They have suffered enough."

Taillte sipped her wine delicately, her eyes locked on his. "And how long do you think it will be before Leinster is invaded again? A year? Six months – maybe less? Peace is only an illusion unless you have the power to enforce it. Look to Niall for the truth of what I say. The clans and provinces feud among themselves because he no longer has the strength to enforce his will upon them. But you – you could bring peace to Erin by proclaiming yourself Ard–Ri."

Bran sat down heavily on the edge of the bed and stared at the goblet in his hands. "I cannot accept that war is the only road to peace," he said slowly. "Can't you see the pain it would bring to –"

"A true king must be prepared to sacrifice anything or anyone to protect his kingdom," Taillte interrupted. She sipped her wine slowly, then ran the tip of her tongue along her full lips. Bran's eyes involuntarily followed its erotic path. "Could you be such a king?" she queried softly.

"Not without the warriors of the Ui Muiredaig," Bran admitted. "And I doubt they would be anxious to fight battles which do not advance their own interests."

"Surely they would respect your authority as king of Leinster," Taillte said coyly. "And have they not already agreed to an alliance with the Ui Faelain which is soon to be... consummated by a royal wedding?"

Bran's face reddened. He was annoyed and embarrassed at the smug confidence in her voice and manner. "The marriage is not of my choosing," he protested. "I –"

Taillte put her fingertips against his lips. "You misunderstand me, my love. Did you expect me to be jealous of your Ui Muiredaig bride? We both know that the only reason she will warm your bed is to secure the treaty with her father. But understand this, Bran Ui Faelain — no milksop of a girl will ever come between us. Once you are married we will continue to meet, in secret if we must, until you have become Ard–Ri."

Her assumption that he would mindlessly submit to the dictates of her scheme infuriated Bran. "You take much for granted," he snapped angrily. "I am not some infatuated fool who will scramble to do your bidding. Tomorrow I will be crowned king, and the decisions I make regarding my future, and Leinster's, will be made without any thought of consulting you. As for Ragallach's daughter, she will be treated with the honour and respect due to her as my queen and I will not risk offending her by indulging myself in... other pleasures." He reached up and caught her wrists, freeing himself of her embrace. "After tonight we will not meet again in private," he added decisively.

Rage flickered in Taillte's eyes for an instant. "Spoken like the dutiful husband," she mocked him. "I suppose a king is not prone to human weaknesses – or desires."

The velvety richness of her voice was like a soothing caress, blunting the impetus of Bran's ire. "I will not jeopardize all my father worked for by betraying my vows to Finola," he stated with quiet conviction.

Taillte raised her eyebrows and tilted her head to one side. "Finola, is it?" she muttered thoughtfully. "She must indeed possess great beauty to inspire such... loyalty."

"I have never laid eyes on the lady," Bran protested,

suddenly feeling the need to defend himself. "We will meet for the first time when we stand before the altar to take our vows."

Taillte nodded slowly as she drew her legs beneath her. "But tonight, there are no vows to be broken," she reminded him as she leaned forward and took his face in her hands. "Let me show you the future that awaits you."

Poor Taillte, Bran mused to himself. *You have always been mistaken about which of us was using the other.* He gently eased her onto her back, sliding his hand beneath her flimsy shift and along the satin softness of her thigh until he found the moist warmth he sought.

Taillte moaned.

CHAPTER NINE

Bran woke alone the next morning. He was mildly surprised that Taillte had left his chambers so early for she had often taken great delight in setting the court tongues wagging by leaving his quarters late enough to ensure she was seen. Her unpredictability had always been part of her fascination, but Bran put any thought of her aside, his mind focusing on the details of his coronation. *Today my destiny is fulfilled,* he told himself as he hastened to prepare for the forthcoming ceremony. *Today, my father shall have his victory. Leinster will be a kingdom of peace, a land in which our people are free to build a future for themselves and their children.* Excitedly throwing open the doors to his chamber, he called for his body servant.

Near midmorning, the warriors of his personal guard arrived to escort Bran to the destiny that awaited him in the great hall of the Ui Faelain. Etach, dressed in his finest tunic and cloak, walked by his side, beaming with fatherly pride beneath his carefully trimmed beard. As they made their way across the courtyard, the cobblestones beneath their feet still glistened from the light rain that had fallen overnight and Bran filled his nostrils with the sweet scent of the wet grass and moss. The sun highlighted his thick copper hair and danced along the intricate patterns of the heavy gold torque that hung about his neck. He wore the multicoloured cloak of kingship pinned at his left shoulder by a large brooch inlaid with precious gems. His tunic was of royal blue, girded at the waist by a belt of embossed leather from which his father's sword hung along his left side. His sandals were of the finest quality and the long straps which criss—crossed his legs were fastened securely just below each knee with small brass buckles.

The cheering throng of spectators filled the courtyard and the guards were hard pressed to force a path through the teeming mass of humanity. When at last they reached the great hall, the warriors pushed open the huge oaken doors and stood at attention on either side of the entrance. Bran suddenly hesitated. He glanced nervously at Etach, but the old soldier smiled back at him reassuringly.

"I wish your father could see you now," he remarked. "This is the day that he lived – and died for."

"I know," Bran replied softly. The two men regarded each other in silence for several moments, the understanding that passed between them transcending the need for words. Bran smiled warmly at his mentor, then turned and stepped through the entry.

The walls of the king's great hall, previously smudged with the smoke and soot of countless feasts, had been white washed with lime and bedecked with the brilliant standards of the tribes and clans of Leinster. The room was filled with chieftains and nobility of only the highest rank, richly attired in a vast array of finery that rivaled the hues of the rainbow. They stood on either side of the uniformed guards that formed a pathway to the dais where the chief Brehon and the Archbishop of Armagh waited patiently on either side of the throne. The young page who nervously stood beside Forannan held a bronze tray upon which rested the plain gold circlet Bran had ordered fashioned to match the one his father had worn.

A single deep toned drum marked each footstep as he

slowly marched toward the dais, the throbbing beats resounding in the confines of the hall.

He glimpsed Muireen and Conor standing behind the guards to his left, their faces radiant with pride as he passed in front of them. But even as he smiled back, Bran was disappointed that his older brother had not seen fit to attend his coronation. There had been no word of him since the battle with the Munstermen and it was now apparent to Bran that Kenan's jealousy and bitterness far outweighed his sense of loyalty to his family. There would be no reconciliation between them.

When he reached the dais, he genuflected before the archbishop who stood above him. Forannan bowed deeply in acknowledgment, then stepped to one side. The chief Brehon came forward and stood between Bran and the throne of Leinster. For nearly an hour, he quoted the laws to which Bran would be bound as king, his failure to comply with any one of them during the course of his reign resulting in his immediate deposition by the council of elders. As each ordinance was uttered, Bran responded with a solemn oath pledging his intent to follow its dictates. The Brehon concluded by enlisting Bran's vow to uphold the laws of Leinster and Erin according to the provisions of the Senchus Mor. His part in the ceremony concluded, the Brehon moved back to his position beside the throne and glanced at Forannan.

The Archbishop came forward and traced the sign of the cross in the air. Laying his venerable hands on Bran's head, Forannan raised his eyes to heaven, his voice resounding with strength and clarity.

"May God Almighty bless and preserve our chosen

king, Bran Ui Faelain, and fill him with the grace of the Holy Trinity to guide his thoughts and deeds, even as we your humblest servants are directed by the word of God. Grant him the wisdom to lead his people in peace and the strength to defend them in times of war, his decisions tempered by the faith in you, Lord, with justice and mercy to all men."

Forannan turned to the page at his side and delicately picked up the golden circlet with his fingertips, raising it above him as he turned to face the assembly.

"Dear Lord, we humbly beseech you to bless and sanctify this ancient symbol of our king's sovereign authority and may it serve as a constant reminder to him of his sacred duty to govern his kingdom and his people according to your commandments and the laws of Leinster and Erin."

He gradually lowered the circlet until it came to rest on Bran's head. "May your rule be long and blessed with peace and prosperity for the people of Leinster. In the name of the Father, the Son, and the Holy Ghost." Forannan smiled at Bran as he signed the cross over him, then held out his arms, palms turned upwards. "God go with you, Bran Ui Faelain, King of Leinster."

A chorus of cheers erupted in the great hall as Bran ascended the dais and took his place upon the throne.

"Wait!" a voice suddenly thundered from the entrance to the great hall. "That man cannot rule as king!"

The acclamation trailed away into terse whispers as all eyes turned to discover the source of the outrage. Bran stared in shock at the solitary figure standing in the doorway. "Kenan," he whispered.

Uncertain what to do, the guards looked hesitantly at

one another and the crowd buzzed with speculation as Kenan swaggered across the room, coming to stand before Bran.

"You seem surprised to see me, brother," he said loudly. "Did you expect I would not attend this travesty which has placed you upon the throne?"

Bran slowly rose to his feet, setting his jaw in an effort to control the fury building inside him. "Little you do surprises me," he replied stiffly. "But now that you are here, you are welcome."

Kenan snorted his contempt as he turned to address the nobles. "He offers me hospitality," he cried mockingly, gesturing at Bran. "This... this loving brother of mine denies me my rightful inheritance then graciously invites me to enjoy the circumstance." He turned his head abruptly and glared at Bran. "Have you no conscience?"

"I did not ask to be made tanaiste," Bran replied evenly. "It was our father's wish that I accept the title and I will not dishonour his memory by rejecting it. Your bitterness is ill placed, Kenan. You were always treated fairly in this family."

"Fairly?" Kenan roared. "Perhaps your attitude would be different if it had been you left with nothing."

"You have been given your equal share of our father's property," Bran said coldly.

"Don't speak to me of land and a few head of cattle," Kenan replied with a perfunctory wave of his hand. You know full well that it is I who should be sitting in your place."

Bran's eyes narrowed. "You know the law of tanaistry as well as I do. There was never any question which one of us would succeed our father. If you had objections you should have presented them before the council when you had the opportunity. But now the matter is settled and whether you acknowledge me or not, I am king and will remain so."

The great hall was hushed but for the occasional cough and shuffling of feet from the stiff crowd as they watched and waited. A heavy silence hung between the two men as they glowered at one another. Then Kenan hissed, "And am I to prostrate myself before you?"

"I have not asked for that," Bran replied, shaking his head. "I ask only that there be peace between us. If it is status and land you desire I will – "

"Damn the bloody land!" Kenan shouted. "What you offer me is nothing more than your table scraps." He shook a clenched fist. "Mark me, Bran. You cannot buy me off with your petty bribes and empty titles. I will have what is mine!" He whirled abruptly to face the murmuring crowd. "Listen to me – all of you. Since the defeat of the Munstermen, I have traveled the length and breadth to Leinster and I tell you this – not all of the clans have been deceived. Look around you – see how many have chosen to abstain from witnessing this conspiracy. They know that the council manipulated the law at Crimthann's urging in order to place the crown upon my brother's head. But there are men of honour who do not condone such a blatant disregard of our traditions. And neither they, nor I, will ever bow before this usurper."

"And what promises did you make to secure the loyalty of these honourable men?" Bran challenged, his face flushed with rage. "Was it land? Wealth? It is you who have deceived them because you have promised that which is not yours to give. Only men as treacherous as yourself would put any credence in such promises."

"They will stand with me against you," Kenan declared vehemently. "As will any of those present who do not wish to see Leinstermen needlessly shed each other's blood." He looked out on the assembly, surveying the faces that stared back at him. "Who among you will follow me to keep the peace in Leinster?"

"Enough!" Bran roared. "There will be no further talk of treason and civil war in my hall. If the people do not want me for their king it is they, not you, who will depose me." He stood before the royal families of Leinster, his feet planted wide apart and his arms crossed over his chest. "Are there any among you who acknowledge my brother's claim? If so, you may speak with impunity for I have no wish to see Leinster torn asunder by rebellion."

The silence roared in Bran's ears as he counted his heartbeats. After several moments, he gazed down at his older brother. "There is your answer."

Kenan glanced quickly about the hall. "Is there no one? None of you?"

"What manner of man seeks to betray his own brother?" a husky voice spoke up from the back of the crowd. "Such a man would surely not hesitate to turn his back on his own people."

"It's only himself he's thinking about," another pointed out.

The great hall was suddenly filled with scores of voices muttering curses and condemnations.

"Banish the traitor! Let him rot in exile!"

The sudden shift in the mood of the crowd startled Bran and he leaned toward his brother. "I think you had better leave," he advised, straining to make himself heard above the uproar. "You have made many more enemies than friends here today."

"This is not over yet," Kenan snapped, his features etched with scorn. "Remember it when the valleys of Leinster run red with blood." Before Bran could reply, he turned and marched haughtily toward the entrance, oblivious to the jeers that followed him.

Bran started after him thoughtfully, then turned as he felt a hand on his shoulder. Forannan stood by his side "You must find it in your heart to forgive him, my son," he said quietly. "His soul is tormented with envy and visions of what might have been. You must look beyond his anger if you are to understand the man within."

"But I do understand him, your grace," Bran retorted. "I understand him all too well."

That evening, Kenan staggered through the deserted cobblestone streets, his belly full and his head light from the wine he had consumed in an effort to blot out the memory of his humiliation in the great hall. With each goblet he had raised to his lips, Kenan's resentment of Bran had intensified and he had found no consolation in the company of his bodyguards who had inadvertently mocked him by toasting the health of the new king. At the first opportunity he had slipped away from them and fled alone into the darkness.

When at last he found the small mortar hut he had been seeking, Kenan slumped against the wall and pounded heavily on the door. It opened a moment later and he stepped back quickly to avoid losing his balance.

"Are you mad?" Taillte demanded angrily. "I told you not to come here anymore."

Kenan brushed past her, scanning the dimly lit interior of the room. "Are you alone?"

Taillte closed the door and stood eyeing him suspiciously, her lips pressed tightly together and her arms folded across her ample bosom. "I am expecting no more visitors this night," she replied coolly.

Kenan grunted and helped himself to the flask of wine he found on the small ornate console. He wiped his mouth with the back of his hairy forearm and surveyed the furnishings. The open hearth was surrounded by richly embroidered couches and several large silk cushions. The table and chairs were of the finest wood, intricately carved, and the tapestries that draped the walls were no less resplendent than those that hung in the king's great hall. Kenan's gaze drifted back to the solid gold goblet in his hand. "I have always been amazed how a mere dancer in the king's court has been able to procure such treasures for her services," he said thoughtfully.

"I choose my own way and am answerable to no one," Taillte replied evenly as she strolled across the room. She reclined on one of the couches, her legs drawn up beneath her, and grinned back at him. "But you, on the other hand, are accountable to your brother, who is now the king. Tell me, Kenan, how does it feel to be Bran's vassal?"

Kenan's eyes narrowed. "My brother may not always be king," he said slowly.

"Of course not," she agreed mockingly. "One day he will die of old age and the throne will be vacant again. But until then you will remain a vassal – to him and his child queen."

He knew that her words were calculated to hurt him. "I take it you have heard about the wedding then," he snapped.

Taillte tossed back her hair. "How could I avoid it? The whole of Naas is abuzz."

Kenan walked to the couch and sat beside her. "This is the first time I have heard jealousy in your voice, my love. It doesn't suit you."

"Don't confuse disgust with disappointment," she stated flatly. "Bran has his faults and this – this Ui Muiredaig girl will only serve to weaken him further. But even that may have its advantages." She stared thoughtfully at the flickering flames of the hearth and Kenan wondered what plots and schemes prompted her eyes to glisten in the pale amber light. His eyes wandered down the white flesh of her throat to the ivory swell of her breasts, and he saw that her nipples were erect and firm beneath the sheer fabric of her lena. When he looked up, Taillte's lips were drawn back in the alluring smile that still haunted him in his dreams. She had been his once – and would be again.

"Bran is not without enemies," Kenan said quietly, making no attempt to disguise the loathing in his voice and eyes. "If something were to happen to him it would be my right to claim the throne. And as king, I would naturally need a queen who is my equal." He laid his hand on her thigh and started to lean forward, but Taillte braced her hand against his chest.

"You flatter yourself Kenan," she asserted coolly. "You will never be king and Bran is not yet lost to me. Many a married man has been lured away from his connubial bed by women far less persuasive that I and I would rather be mistress to a king than the mere consort of a disgruntled servant."

Kenan checked the impulse to strike her and rose slowly to his feet. "Bran is lost to you now," he sneered. "In a few days he'll be wed and I can assure you that my self–righteous brother will never compromise himself or his position for the favours of a common whore."

"Get out, you bastard!" Taillte snarled.

Kenan ambled across the room and opened the door, pausing nonchalantly at the entrance. "We are cut from the same cloth, you and I. Someday you will see that. And when you do, my love – I'll be waiting." As he stepped out into the cool night air and closed the door, Kenan smirked at the sound of smashing crockery.

CHAPTER TEN

On the day that he was to be wed to the girl he had never seen before, Bran awoke in the early afternoon from a fitful and uneasy sleep, his mouth feeling fur-coated from too much ale the night before. The bridal party had arrived from Mullaghmast the previous day and erected their pavilions in the meadow just beyond the somber, grey stone walls of Naas which had been hastily adorned with flowers and garlands and banners of every shape and colour. As was the custom, the bride had been sequestered in her own tent and Muireen, being the groom's closest female relative, had gladly accepted the honour of assisting Finola to prepare for the upcoming ceremony.

After he had bathed, Bran dressed himself in a tunic of white silk and strapped a pair of gilded sandals to his feet. The sash that he wrapped around his waist was of a deep forest green and matched the cloak pinned to his shoulder, its edges embroidered with spirals and swirls of gold thread. He felt uncomfortable as he struggled to adjust his sash, preferring the familiar weight of a swordbelt.

He had watched the preparations for his marriage to Finola with a certain degree of detachment, feeling strangely isolated. It seemed as if everyone had been caught up in the spirit of the impending event, attending to the few remaining preparations for the feast and arranging accommodations for the numerous guests who had been invited. For the most part Bran had kept to himself, ignoring the celebrations given in his honour and the invitations of friends wishing to drink to his health and his future. But his curiosity would not be denied and he became preoccupied with speculation about his bride.

The sun had already begun its descent when Etach and Conor came for him, walking by his side across the courtyard to the small beehive shaped chapel that stood alongside the great hall. Bran forced a grin and tried to ignore the smirks and ribald whisperings of his friends and comrades–in–arms as they fell in behind the trio and followed them inside, nudging and winking at one another in perverse pleasure. Dusty beams of light filtered through the stained glass windows, filling the room with an eerie illumination that seemed unnatural. An icy shiver ran through Bran's body and he fought the impulse to break and run as he walked to the front of the altar where Forannan waited for him. The archbishop's sympathetic countenance did little to allay Bran's fears and his mind was filled with a variety of hideous possibilities regarding his wife to be. He swallowed with difficulty and smiled weakly.

Crowds thronged behind the bridegroom and filled the chapel to overflowing so that many jostled each other back outside. Bran's coronation had been a rare occasion indeed, but the romantic appeal of a royal wedding had captured all imaginations and excitement rippled through the crowd.

Suddenly there was silence, followed by a low, collective sigh that prompted Bran to turn around.

Finola stood in the aura of her own beauty. She was dressed in a sleeveless gown of pale lavender silk, revealing the milky whiteness of her shoulders. A belt of gold, studded with precious gems, girded her slender hips and was knotted in front so that the free ends dangled down to the hemline of her gown. A delicately patterned silver diadem encircled her forehead and her hair fell like sunlight about her face and shoulders. The crimson bracelets on her wrists matched the colour of her finely shaped lips and the slippers on her dainty feet were of white kidskin, stitched with silver thread.

Bran did not even notice Ragallach as the Ui Muiredaig chieftain escorted his daughter toward the altar. Finola glided down the aisle like the whisper of a prayer, her graceful steps seeming to barely touch the ground. Bran took her hand, delicate and soft as down. She raised her large violet eyes to meet his and Bran felt himself drawn into their shimmering warmth, lost in the lilac depths of her unblinking gaze. When the wedding ceremony proceeded, the traditional responses which he had been obliged to commit to memory took on new meaning as Bran pledged himself to her with reverence and tenderness. He listened spellbound as Finola pronounced her vows, her voice a sweet melody of innocence and virtue. When at last the archbishop pronounced them married, Bran smiled at his new wife, his soul elated beyond any emotion he had ever known before.

"I will spare no effort to see to your happiness, my lady," he declared fervently. She looked back at him with the moist eyes of a saint – trusting and content. But the expression lasted only an instant, replaced by an abrupt remoteness that surprised Bran.

"I am honoured that you have found me worthy, my lord," she said softly, lowering her eyes.

Bran leaned forward and kissed her. Her lips were soft and pliant, but she did not respond to his embrace. An inexplicable barrier had suddenly been placed between them and he felt her tremble slightly in his arms.

A deafening cheer exploded from the onlookers and the newlyweds found themselves surrounded by family and well wishers. Amidst a shower of rose petals they were propelled out of the chapel and into the courtyard. As sunset transformed the white mortar of the surrounding buildings into burnished bronze, they entered the great hall for the marriage feast which had been prepared in their honour.

Once they were seated, Bran watched with amusement as the servants scurried back and forth between the main chamber and the kitchens, carrying an endless quantity and variety of food. He knew that Muireen had taken it upon herself to supervise its preparation and it was obvious that she had spared no effort in organizing the lavish feast. His mouth watered as platters of veal, mutton, and roast suckling pigs seasoned with leeks, onions and watercress were marched beneath his nose and served with wheat and barley meal cakes, along with curds and cheese. He waited with thirsty anticipation as large kegs of *cuirm*, the dark ale favoured by the men, were rolled into the banqueting hall only to be immediately surrounded by a parched congregation, their empty tankards in hand. The ladies, on the other hand, seemed content to remain at their tables, sipping discreetly from goblets which the servers were hard pressed to keep filled with honeyed mead or *nenadmin*, the sweet tasting crabapple cider potent enough to fell a husky man.

Throughout the course of the banquet, Bran's repeated attempts to speak to Finola were continually frustrated by a seemingly endless series of congratulations and toasts in their honour. He glanced at the elegant young woman who was now his wife and found himself longing to be alone with her, the memory of her lips against his still fresh in his mind. But each time he spoke to her, he was reminded of the wall that had sprung up between them and try as he might, Bran could not breach it. She responded to his questions and comments with formal politeness, maintaining the distance between them for reasons which evaded him.

When the meal was concluded, they were entertained by the individual skills of the best harpists, bards and poets in Leinster. One of the older poets, Fiontainn, an *Ollamh* from Bray who had spent twelve years of his life becoming a master at his craft, was particularly well received and after much coaxing from his audience, humbly consented to supply them with another recitation.

"I put down this verse a short time ago to commemorate the crowning of our king," he announced in a resonant voice that compelled the hall to silence. He turned and bowed deeply to Bran. "With your permission, my lord." Bran nodded his assent and Fiontainn faced the assembled guests, raising his head dramatically.

"Remember the wolf that howled in his den
For he came to be a leader of men.

Remember who brought two together as one
For the wolf gave us hope when there had been none.

Remember invaders we marched out to meet
For the wolf brought us glory from certain defeat.

Remember the blade that slashed through the air
For the wolf lost his life at Dun Magochtair.

Remember his sacrifice made out of love
For the wolf now runs free in fields above.

Remember the dream death couldn't erase
For the wolf left behind one to rule in his place.

Forget about war and sheath bloodied sword
For the son of the wolf is our overlord."

The old poet bowed as deeply as his frail frame would allow and the great hall was instantly filled with thunderous clapping and whistles of approval.

"It is a great honour that you have bestowed upon my father and I, Ollamh," Bran told him sincerely. "For now we, like your words, shall become immortal." The poet smiled back at him gratefully before returning to his table and Bran turned toward Finola only to find that her brother's grinning face had suddenly appeared between them. As they shifted in their seats to face him, the ale slopped over the sides of the tankard in Rowan's hand, splashing onto the floor.

"Forgive me for not congratulating you both earlier," Rowan said drunkenly, turning from one to the other. "But I have been distracted by the finest cuirm I have ever tasted."

Bran grinned back at him as Finola touched his hand. "You are forgiven, brother. How can I fault you for celebrating my happiness?"

"You are fortunate to have found such an understanding wife," Rowan said to Bran. "Although as her brother I can tell you she is not without a temper."

Bran nodded slowly and looked at Finola. "I thank you for the warning, my friend, but I think that there are many things I have yet to learn about your sister."

The high–pitched voice of a young page rose above the din in the hall. "What did he say?" Rowan queried as he raised the tankard to his lips again.

The smile faded from Bran's face. "We are to be entertained by one of the court dancers."

A lone harpist struck a single chord and repeated it at equally spaced intervals, its slow rhythmic pulse bewitching the guests into silence. All eyes were on Taillte as she entered the hall, her long strides matching the musician's meter. The sleeveless *caimsi* she wore was blood red and girt at the waist with a *cris* of black leather, the tight fitting garment revealing the sensuous curves of her body. The hem was cut high on her thigh, leaving her long, shapely legs exposed, muscles rippling with each step. She was barefooted and her hands hung loosely at her sides. Her shoulders were back and her breasts thrust forward as she strutted toward them, her demeanor that of an animal stalking its prey. When she reached the bridal party's table, a second harpist joined the first, the intricate passages of the melody skillfully woven around the lilting chords.

Taillte's head fell back, her glossy black hair spilling down her back as she extended her arms and swayed hypnotically from side to side. The tempo quickened and her hips undulated seductively. The dance was one of passion and lust, and her thighs shone with a fine sheen of perspiration as her suggestive movements intensified to frenzied desire. Abruptly, she threw herself across the table in front of Rowan, her outstretched hands reaching for him. But her intense gaze was fixed on Bran. Taillte paused there for but an instant, then retreated, drawing herself up to her full height, her back arched. She moaned as she ran her hands along the curves of her breasts and down her belly to the inside of her thighs. The music suddenly climaxed and she screamed, falling to her knees in front of him, her chin dropping to her heaving breast.

There was silence for a moment, then the great hall broke into applause. Taillte rose slowly to her feet and bowed to Bran, her blazing green eyes locked on his. He acknowledged her with a slight nod of his head but his face was stone. Then he felt Finola's hand on his and he turned in time to catch a glimpse of the warning that her large violet eyes had flashed to the woman who stood before them. He glanced back at Taillte and was surprised to see her blink uncomfortably beneath Finola's unwavering glare, the confidence which had shone in her eyes moments earlier replaced by defeat. She turned impulsively and bowed to the still applauding audience, then trotted lithely out of the hall.

"It would seem she has danced for you before, my lord," Finola remarked, her grip on Bran's hand tightening slightly. "Who is she?"

"Her name is Taillte," Bran said evenly, avoiding her eyes. "She has been at Naas these past three years."

"Then I regret not coming to Naas sooner," Rowan interjected. He quaffed the remaining ale in his tankard and set it down on the table with a thud. "With your permission my lord, perhaps I can convince the lady to visit us in Mullaghmast... to entertain us with her dancing."

Bran shrugged. "Taillte is free to do as she pleases." Rowan bowed and repeated his congratulations before taking his leave.

"I am sorry," Bran muttered when he had gone.

"A woman such as that embarrasses only herself," Finola reassured him. "I am not so naive as to think that you have not known other women. But they are a part of your past and are of no concern to me now."

Bran reveled in the warmth of her smile and leaned toward her, encouraged by the unexpected tone of intimacy in her voice. But as he opened his mouth to speak, a covey of giggling young women descended upon Finola, her mother and Muireen among them. Lady Agnes smiled gracefully at Bran, then rested her hands on her daughter's shoulders as she stooped forward between them, her lips close to Finola's ear. "Come child," she murmured softly. "It is time to prepare for your wedding night."

Shock flooded Finola's face, her fearful gaze darting from her mother to Bran. Her eyes were those of a frightened fawn, but Bran could only stare at her with disbelief, unable to understand the source of her sudden panic. Without a word she rose from the table and followed her entourage across the great hall, the small procession winding its way between the tightly packed guests who heartily shouted their encouragement and advice to the newly wedded bride. As he watched them disappear through the huge main doors on the far side of the room, a startling revelation flashed across Bran's mind, filling him with a mixture of remorse and anger.

It's me! he thought to himself miserably. *Mother of God, she is afraid of me!*

The design and furnishings of the chamber which had been prepared for Finola were far more elaborate than her own in Mullaghmast. The walls were fully wainscoted with polished planks of oak and ornamented with several brilliantly coloured tapestries which stretched from ceiling to floor. Cabinets and chests for clothing lined the wall to her left and on the far side of the room a huge mirror of polished silver as tall as Finola rested in a heavy rack of carved yew beside which stood a delicately crafted table and bench of darkly stained hazel. The mirror had been positioned in such a way so as to derive the most benefit from the twin windows beside it, into each of which had been set thick panes of glass. A spinning wheel and loom had been placed in the opposite corner, complete with reels for winding warp and weft.

With some trepidation, Finola focused on the large canopied bed which dominated most of the area to her right.

"Is something the matter, my lady?" Muireen inquired uncertainly. "If the chamber is not to your liking, you have but to tell Bran and – "

"The room is fine," Finola replied quickly. "Forgive me, gentle lady," she added calmly, managing a half smile. "But the day has been long and I find myself growing fatigued."

"Don't you worry yourself, dearie," a plump, ruddy-faced maidservant crooned, winking to her companions. "Your husband will soon see you tucked snugly into bed." As the other women snickered, the corners of Lady Agnes' mouth twitched into an uneasy smile.

"Come Finola," she said, taking her daughter by the arm and guiding her toward one of the cabinets. "There is little time left if we are to make you presentable."

"Presentable?" Finola asked curiously. "What do you mean 'presentable'?"

Her mother opened one of the cabinet doors and reached inside. "You surely don't want to meet Bran in your wedding gown," Agnes replied as she withdrew a pale pink shift and held it out, smiling at her daughter through the gossamer–like fabric. "I had it made especially for your wedding night. You will look lovely in it, my dear, and it is certain to meet with the king's approval."

"I will not dress as a harlot!" Finola fumed, snatching the flimsy garment from her mother's grasp and flinging it aside. "Not to please you or the king of Leinster!" She angrily stamped across the room to the windows and gazed out into the darkness, her back turned on the awe–struck women.

"You misunderstand your mother's intention," Muireen offered, her voice tinged with concern. "She – "

"There is no need to apologize on my behalf," Lady Agnes interrupted. "But perhaps it would be best if all of you allowed us a few moments alone."

Finola closed her eyes and tried to ignore the gently clucking tongues of the maidservants as they filed out of the chamber. When she heard the door close after them, she moved to the table in the far corner and collapsed onto the bench in front of it, burying her face in her hands. "Forgive me mother," she sobbed softly. "I did not mean to shame you so."

"I have never been ashamed of you Finola," Lady Agnes

replied as she moved to her daughter's side. "Your father and I were truly blessed with our children. You and your brother Rowan have filled our lives with pride and joy and we are pleased with you both." She picked up a brush from the table and gently pulled it through her daughter's shining hair. "I cannot help but recall doing this when you were a little girl," she went on. "Now, here you are, grown into a beautiful young woman with a fine husband. Where did the time go?"

"I sometimes wish I was that little girl again," Finola said, lowering her hands to her lap and staring past the wall in front of her to her memories of her childhood. "My life was so simple then – so free of worry and responsibility."

Lady Agnes bent down and kissed her head. "You must count your blessings and look to your future, child. You are married to the King of all Leinster and will never want for anything so long as you live. At least some of the dreams I have always held for you are coming true."

"But I am frightened, mother," Finola confessed, pivoting in her seat and lowering her gaze. "Other girls much younger than I have already had many lovers, but I – I have never been with a man before. What if I do not... please Bran?"

"You need not concern yourself, my dear," her mother answered earnestly. "Men please themselves. Giving yourself to your husband is a duty you will soon learn to perform with a certain degree of... detachment."

Finola looked up at her, aghast. "But you make it sound so cold. You yourself said that in time Bran and I would come to love one another."

"Love is an elusive fantasy that torments maidens and confounds young men. You can waste a lifetime in pursuit of it."

"Do you and father love each other?"

Lady Agnes gazed back at her thoughtfully. "Over the years we have been through much together and a certain bond of mutual respect and fondness has developed between us. We live our lives separately and together, with neither one of us demanding or expecting anything of the other. In time, perhaps you and Bran will come to the same understanding." She laid the brush back on the table. "Now I must be gone before your husband arrives. I do not want Bran to think me a meddlesome mother – not yet anyway." She kissed her daughter lightly on the cheek. "May your marriage bring you happiness and the blessing of children."

Finola shuddered as Lady Agnes turned to leave, wanting to call her mother back but knowing she would not. There was nothing left to say or do – no hope of a last minute reprieve that would alter the course of the inevitable. The door closed with a thud of finality, imprisoning her.

Alone.

She stood up and paced slowly around the room, her thoughts drifting to Bran. She wondered with what sort of man she had solemnly vowed to spend the rest of her life. Throughout the wedding feast he had treated her with quiet courtesy and respect, his manners and skillful conversation reflecting his noble ancestry and breeding. She knew that he had made every effort to make her comfortable in what was no doubt an awkward situation for them both, and Finola regretted the chilled fashion in which she had responded to his attempts to ease the tension between them.

The sudden recollection of the pronounced difference

in their physical statures amused Finola and she smiled to herself. Bran was at least a head taller than she, a giant by comparison, and he had towered above her like one of the ancient heroes in the stories the seanachies told. She suspected that such a man had rarely wanted for female companionship – nor would he ever, regardless of his marital status. Like the dancer in the great hall, few women would consider the existence, or even the presence, of a wife a serious deterrent to their amorous advances. Even the most faithful husband would eventually succumb to such temptation – if his desire was not appeased at home.

The prospect of her husband taking his pleasure in another woman's arms disturbed Finola, not for any possible consequences it would have to her or her marriage, but because of the humiliation and disgrace she would suffer at the royal court. She imagined the rumours and gossip that would quickly circulate throughout Naas, describing how Bran had been driven from his bed by a cold–blooded wife.

I will not be made a fool, she promised herself as she walked to the foot of the canopied bed. The coverlet had been dyed in the deep indigo extracted from leaves of woad and painstakingly embroidered with threads of gold and silver. She bent down and ran her hand along its glossy surface, relishing the sensual texture of the fabric against her fingertips. As wary of Bran as she had been, the smooth play of the muscles in his arms and thighs had not escaped her attention and she pictured herself beside him on the elegant bed, her fingers wandering down his chest to explore the knotted ridges of his belly. The erotic pleasure of her fantasy consumed Finola and she closed her eyes, a warm, tingling sensation beginning between her thighs.

"I trust that everything is to your liking, my lady."

Finola started at the sound of the voice behind her. Bran was standing just inside the doorway, a flagon in one hand and a goblet in the other. His face was flushed and he stood unsteadily, his lips drawn back in a fatuous grin. Finola blushed with embarrassment as she realized that he had been watching her.

"I did not hear you enter, my lord," she stammered helplessly.

"I am not in the habit of announcing my entry into my own chambers," he stated bluntly as he kicked the door closed behind him. "Or should I say – our chambers?" Bran poured the remaining wine into the goblet, then recklessly cast the empty flagon aside and strode across the room to stand beside her. He stared at her with bloodshot eyes as he leaned sideways and grasped the coverlet, massaging it between his fingers. "It is gratifying to the touch, isn't it?"

Finola smiled at him nervously, anxious to change the direction of his thinking. "Your flagon is empty, my lord. Shall I have the servants fetch you another?"

"I have already drunk my fill," he replied. "But you certainly look to be in need of a drink. Here," he added, thrusting his goblet forward. "Take mine."

Finola took the bronze drinking vessel in her delicate hands and raised it to her lips, drinking deeply. *This is not the same man I married this afternoon*, she thought in panic as the fiery liquid slid down her throat. *Is this what I have to look forward to for the rest of my life or has he just taken too much of the drink?*

Bran stretched luxuriantly. "That terrible press of people today wearied me to the bone," he yawned. His arms dropped limply to his sides and he smiled at her. "It's glad I am to be alone with you now."

"It has indeed been a trying day," Finola replied uneasily. "But now we will have a chance to get properly acquainted with one another. A marriage between strangers, they say, is a poor proposition."

"There will be plenty of time for that kind of jabber later," Bran said decisively as he stepped toward her. "You and I have other things to resolve before this night is through." He reached out and touched her naked shoulder, his fingers tracing a path along her collarbone to her neck. "Finola," he said softly as if testing the feel of her name upon his lips. "Of the white shoulders. You are, in truth, well–named."

The blood drained from Finola's face. "Please my lord... I ..."

"There is no need to explain," Bran interrupted, shaking his head. "I know that you were forced into this marriage even as I myself was. But we are man and wife now and if there is to be harmony between us, certain... adjustments must be made."

Blessed Mary, Mother of God, she silently prayed as she stared at him in horror. *Don't let me be taken – not like this!*

Bran abruptly released his grip and paced across the room, his hands clasped tightly behind his back. When he reached the far wall he pivoted and looked back with the same remoteness she had often seen in her father's eyes. "I have decided it would be best if we did not share the same quarters," he said evenly. "I will stay with Etach until such time as I can make other arrangements for myself."

Finola's jaw dropped in amazement. "I... I'm afraid I don't understand, my lord," she stuttered breathlessly.

"I am not blind, my lady," he explained, moving toward her. "Any fool could see that you do not wish to be here – and I have no intention of forcing myself upon you. So where does that leave us?" He shrugged and smiled at her sympathetically. "We must both face the reality of our situation. Our marriage is nothing more than a political necessity to insure peace between our two clans. So be it then, but there is no need for you to suffer because of this agreement. I will make life in Naas as pleasant as possible for you and you will, of course, be entitled to all the rights and privileges of your status as my wife. But, for now at least, ours will be a marriage in name only. Perhaps in days to come you may regard me with less apprehension."

"Am I to have no say in your decision?" Finola objected. "I don't understand why you are doing this."

"I am doing this for your sake, my lady," Bran sighed wearily. "And because I already have more problems than I can handle. If Thorgest and his Norsemen defeat Niall, it will only be a question of time before they look to Leinster. And though the Munstermen do not pose an immediate threat to us, Feidlimid is notoriously treacherous and must be watched. Even my own brother, Kenan, could become a problem that I will eventually have to deal with." He grinned at her wryly. "I do not need another foe at my back."

"I had no idea you regarded me as such," Finola replied coolly, then turned and walked briskly to the window so he would not see the tears brimming in her eyes. Torches danced in the courtyard below as well wishers congregated around the royal residence, their voices resounding in choruses praising the king and his bride–queen. Finola bit down on her lower lip in an effort to suppress the hurt and anger that welled inside her. "I am not your foe, my lord," she told him after several moments, then touched the gold band that now graced her ring finger. "The discords that once made us enemies no longer exist. Our two clans are united, even as we ourselves are bound to one another."

"Forgive me, lady," Bran said awkwardly. "It was not my intention to offend – "

"Then you are a fool," Finola interrupted as she turned to face him. "Either that or you are the most callous individual I have ever had the misfortune to encounter. How could I not be insulted? I have abandoned my own dreams and done everything that was expected of me – only to be spurned by the very man who is responsible for my being here." She jabbed his chest with one long, delicate finger. "Hear me, Bran Ui Faelain. If my father and my clansmen knew of the dishonour you have heaped on me, I assure you their reaction would not be a favourable one!"

Bran threw up his hands in exasperation. "What in the name of God do you find so objectionable? The arrangement I suggested was for your sake – not mine. Yet, you oppose me in this. What do you want of me, woman?"

"Don't you understand?" Finola demanded, her voice rising. "I want our marriage to be more than just a political necessity! I want a husband that I can love and who loves me. And I want to give him children, many children so that someday I can see him choose one of our sons as his rightful tanaiste. That is my dream – and our common destiny. And if you deny my right to that future, the feud between the Ui Faelain and the Ui Muiredaig will begin again – starting right now with you and I!"

Bran studied her for a moment. "If I live to see a thousand summers, I will never understand the workings of a woman's mind. I will waste no more time on you this night." He turned to leave but Finola flung herself at him.

"You motherless bastard! You slime coated slug!" Tears streamed down her face as she lashed out at him. Bran warded off the blows easily and caught her wrists, but a well–aimed kick found his ankle and he lost his balance, falling forward. Before she knew what was happening, they had crashed to the floor, his weight upon her robbing the breath from her lungs. Pinned beneath him gasping for air, Finola tried to move, but Bran had somehow managed to keep his grip on her wrists.

"By all the saints in heaven!" he exclaimed breathlessly. "Your brother was right. You do indeed have a fine temper."

Finola's chest heaved convulsively. "Get – off – me!"

Bran released her and rolled to one side, propping his head on one elbow. He reached out and gently brushed her disheveled hair off her forehead. "Are you hurt?" he asked softly.

Her breathing was becoming easier and she shook her head. The touch of his hand on her face was cool and reassuring. She lay motionless, gazing into the deep blue eyes of the man beside her. Bran smiled at her.

"Forannan told me that I would be both king and vassal." he lightly chuckled. "And here I am – already a slave to your commands." His hand quivered slightly as it moved down her neck to the milky whiteness of her shoulders. She lay patiently, her eyes encouraging him as he caressed her satin soft skin. Then he bent down to kiss her and her lips parted slightly, yielding beneath his. He ran his hand between her shoulder blades and along the small of her back to her firm buttocks, drawing her toward him.

"Finola," he whispered, helping her to her feet and guiding her toward the bed.

They undressed awkwardly, their fingers fumbling with each other's clothes, then sank naked onto the soft feather mattress. His lips explored her face, her throat, her breasts. At the touch of his tongue, the small virginal nipples stood erect in their delicate pink aureoles, and Finola moaned. Her legs shook uncontrollably as he moved his hand between her thighs. He gently coaxed them apart, then moved over her. He entered her gently and she moved with him, surrendering to her desire. Consumed with passion, the intensity of his thrusts increased until the pliant wall of the hymen gave way and Finola cried out in the voice of a small child – a child in pain. Bran started to pull away from her, but she held him close, her hips undulating rhythmically beneath him.

"Don't leave me," she moaned, the sound coming from deep within her throat. "Please don't leave me."

They made love to each other with passion and tenderness, not feeling or wanting any other world than the oneness of their own.

PART TWO

CHAPTER ELEVEN

The River Bann snaked across Ulster from the quiet waters of Lough Neagh, flowing north to the rocky coastline of Magh Bele and south to Carlingford Bay. With the inland *lough* as his base, Thorgest had ordered a string of forts built along the banks of the great river, enabling his longships to slip out unmolested to ravish the helpless coastal villages then return to the security of the fortified harbour, their holds laden with plunder and slaves. Free from fear of attack, the Norse cargo ships glided up and down the Bann at will, frequently stopping to trade at the river outposts which guarded the approaches to the Viking base.

Since its establishment five years earlier the settlement of Lough Neagh had become a thriving commercial centre, its crowded waterfront bustling with activity as merchant ships from as far away as Iberia, Carth and Stygia filled the harbour, their owners eager to barter for the Irish goods which the Norse could now provide at considerably reduced costs.

Behind the waterfront was a tight cluster of buildings crowding in on dirty wood–paved streets jammed with goods, people, and domestic animals. The large wooden houses of the wealthier inhabitants were set in isolation on the outskirts and arranged in a series of neat rows. The entire town was surrounded by a palisade of felled timber above which rose sentry towers at various points.

The firehall, where the men gathered in the evenings, was the hub of the settlement. Its two longer walls curved inwards toward the gabled ends and several thick roof posts were arranged in two rows down the middle of the building.

Down each side of the room ran a broad, low, flattened bank of earth, its edge held up by boards and slabs of stone to form a smooth raised floor. The central strip was left as a rough lower floor in which was set a huge stone–lined hearth. The interior walls were covered with wood paneling and were decoratively carved as were the roof and door posts. Throughout the summer months, the raiding season, drunken laughter and singing from the firehall had filled the warm night air as the Viking celebrated their mounting victories over the Irish.

On the same evening as Naas celebrated Bran's marriage to Finola, Thorgest presided over the firehall from his customary place of honour, smoke from the open hearth stinging his ice–blue eyes while the stench of sour wine assailed his nostrils. The *jarls* and sea chieftains before him sat at long oaken tables surrounding the central firepit and from one side of the hall came the drone of voices extolling the Danish leader who had returned from a successful raid earlier that afternoon. With mounting concern, Thorgest eyed the sullen–faced Norse who sat segregated on the other side of the firepit, murmuring among themselves and casting envious glances at the Danes opposite them. *We will not escape a brawl this night*, he thought uneasily. *Thor's blood! I should have taken command of the raiding party myself. By taking only the Danes with him, Ragnar insulted every Norseman in Lough Neagh. If he now denies them an equal share of the booty he will drive a wedge into the gap that already exists between our two peoples. What was he thinking? I do not understand his reasoning – his motive. Beneath the ripples on the surface flows a current I cannot see. But I can feel it. Ragnar himself knows that when I chose him to sit at my right hand, I did so to ease the tension between our war-*

riors. Many of my own jarls have long regarded the Danes as un-trustworthy mercenaries whose loyalty varies in proportion to the gold in their purses. They in turn fear that there will be no place for them on this island once the Irish are conquered and we have no further use for their swordarms. But despite their suspicions both sides have always tolerated one another, if only for the sake of their mutual greed. Until now. If Ragnar refuses to divide the spoils equally, the earth will drink the blood of Norseman and Dane alike. And such a feud I will not abide, for I need them both if the final prize, this kingdom called Erin, is to be mine.

Thorgest snatched up the drinking horn before him and drained its fiery contents in a single draught. Slamming the empty vessel back down on the table he belched loudly, then glanced up at the young whey–faced girl who stood at his side.

"More," he grunted, pushing the vessel toward her.

The girl averted her eyes and fumbled with the stopper on the wine sack she held, then leaned forward to refill his drinking horn, her rust coloured hair spilling over the freckled ivory of her naked shoulders. Thorgest smiled to himself as his eyes roamed along the enticing curves that shifted beneath the shear fabric of her knee–length caimsi. He had taken her during a raid on a small Ulster village nearly two years earlier and although she had not yet seen the passing of fifteen summers, her lithe body had already yielded pleasures that both sated and whetted his sexual appetite – an appetite which his wife had long since refused to appease.

Reaching beneath the hemline of the caimsi, Thorgest slid his hand up along the inside of the girl's thigh. She stiffened momentarily, then glanced down at him over her shoulder, her grey–blue eyes defiant.

    I will never truly possess you, little one, Thorgest surmised as he held her gaze. *Beneath the veneer of your quiet servility lurks rebellion and contempt. I have seen the look before, in the faces of your countrymen who labour in our fields as thralls. Like you, they bear the yoke of slavery in order to survive, but their hatred and desire to avenge themselves upon us remains unbridled. If so small and insignificant a girl as you is capable of nurturing such resolve, we can expect no less of the Irish as a people. Such a race may well be conquered, but their spirit will never be subjugated.*

    Thorgest slowly withdrew his hand, then jerked his head to one side, dismissing the girl. As she hurried off, he rose from his seat and drew himself up to his full height. The voices of those seated nearest to him died suddenly and silence gradually spread across the firehall as others followed the example of their comrades. Thorgest was taller than most men and his well–muscled frame was testimony of his prowess as a warrior. His hair and braided beard were the sun–bleached gold of his people and his complexion was that of a man who had grown accustomed to a constant exposure to the elements, his face tanned and weathered by a lifetime of seafaring. His woolen breeches were neatly tucked into the bearskin leggings which were secured about his calves with criss–crossed thongs and the shoes upon his feet were of hardened rawhide. The sleeveless leather jerkin he wore was pocked with metal studs that caught the firelight as he moved, and the muscles in his bare arms rippled as he raised his drinking horn.

    "Hail Ragnar Evilbrooder!" he shouted heartily, grinning down at his second in command. The others likewise raised their drinks in salute.

"Hail Ragnar! Hail the fist of Oden!" As wine and strong black ale were greedily swilled back, soaking neatly pointed beards and curled mustaches, Thorgest watched Ragnar smugly revel in the praise of his comrades. There was a sinister quality in the man's raven black eyes that glistened beneath his bushy brows and a lifetime of cruelty was etched in his harsh features. His physical appearance was made all the more grotesque by the loss of his right ear, sliced off in combat. As if in retribution for the injury, Ragnar personally saw to it that those who could not be taken captive in each raid were left behind disfigured and horribly mutilated. Although Thorgest himself had condoned such atrocities as a necessary means of demoralizing the Irish, he viewed the practice with distaste, for there was no honour in brutalizing helpless women and children. But Ragnar was different – he enjoyed it. Still, his abilities as a warrior and sea captain had made him chieftain of the Danish jarls and as such, a valuable asset whose aberrations would have to be... indulged.

Thorgest quaffed his wine, then wiped his mouth with a rough calloused hand. "You must take care, old friend," he cautioned in a loud voice as he took his seat again. "Or someday the weight of your greed will capsize your ship."

While the firehall echoed with laughter Ragnar flashed a yellow-toothed grin. "If a heavy cargo pulls the River Witch to the bottom of the sea, and my crew is sent to Valhalla, it will be because these Irish are so generous with their treasures," he shot back. "We took enough gold and jewels for a dragon's hoard, and many captives, some of whom will serve us better in our beds than working as thralls in the fields."

"But what of their men?" Thorgest asked, leaning forward. "Were there no warriors to resist you?"

Ragnar snorted and shook his head. "It was as you predicted, lord," he replied. "We were without opposition. The brown robes of their holy places will not take up the sword against us – this strange god they worship forbids it. So I am told." Abruptly, he drew his dagger, skewered a piece of meat from the platter in front of him and stuffed it into his mouth. "What use is a god who does not strengthen a man's arm?" Several of the others around his table nodded and grunted their approval. "As for the villages we raided, the only fighting men we encountered were a few hot–headed farmers who charged at us like madmen, wielding their scythes and hoes as if they were broadswords. But those were easily dealt with. Apart from our wounded, we lost only six men in battle." His dark eyes glinted as he smirked at Thorgest. "In return, we slew every man in each settlement and left boys who were coming of age without hands to grasp weapons."

"You have done well," Thorgest remarked thoughtfully, his fingers unconsciously tugging at his blond beard. "But it is unfortunate that none of my Norsemen were among those chosen to accompany you, for they are always eager for combat and the opportunity to share in the glory of another victory."

Ragnar glanced warily across the firepit to the glowering Norsemen, then slowly shifted his gaze back to Thorgest. "I meant no insult to you or your countrymen, lord. But our crews have always been under the command of Norse sea chieftains and, as my brother suggested to me, here was a chance to demonstrate that we have the ability to execute your orders without direct supervision. I saw no harm in Saxulf's proposal for I was certain that our success would convince you of our fealty."

So you are behind this, Thorgest thought to himself as he peered at the man seated at Ragnar's left. A pair of pitch black eyes, cold and lifeless as a shark's, glared back at him in silent response. In contrast to his older brother, Saxulf was tall and well-muscled, and his jaw was clean shaven to reveal a roguishly handsome profile. Famed for his love of women, few nights passed when his bed wanted for the press of warm flesh. But it was his reputation as a stormy petrel that had first drawn him to Thorgest's attention and he knew that much of the dissension between the Norse and the Danes had found its roots on Saxulf's tongue.

Thorgest rested his arms on the table and smiled at Ragnar. "Our Danish brothers need not prove themselves to us," he assured him. "They have already done so in battle many times. Are we now to abandon the tactics that have brought us our victories?"

Mumbled accord rippled across the firehall.

"Do not allow him to deceive you, brother," Saxulf cautioned Ragnar in a voice loud enough for all to hear. "It is gold, not glory that he seeks us to partition."

"And so we shall," Ragnar answered without hesitation. "Have we not always equally divided the spoils among all of us, including those that were left behind?"

"But it was we who took all the risks," Saxulf protested.

Ragnar shook his head. "Were you so intimidated by the old men and farmboys we encountered?" he asked grinning. Several of the warriors around him chuckled at the criticism. "No, we shall do what we have always done," he added as he glanced across the firepit to the Norsemen. "We will all have a share in the booty."

Saxulf lowered his eyes.

As cheering filled the firehall, Thorgest rose from his seat and raised his drinking horn. "Well spoken, Ragnar. Together we will crush the Irish. All that stands between us and the kingdom of the north is Niall Caille."

Ragnar threw back his head and laughed. "The one they call high king is no obstacle to us. He and his army still cower within their fortress at Ailech, as they have since their return from Leinster. As you ordered, we put the torch to all the villages and monasteries we could find along the banks of Lough Swilly so that this feeble king who had sworn to protect them could watch the fires burn from the safety of his battlements. And still he would not venture out to challenge us." He squared his shoulders haughtily. "We are free to strike where we will, for the king of Erin has forsaken his land and his people."

Thorgest frowned. "A man such as Niall does not easily relinquish his kingdom."

"What kingdom?" Ragnar scoffed. "His chieftains quarrel amongst themselves and he is powerless to stop them. A king such as Niall is little more than a symbol to his people."

"Which is exactly why he is all the more dangerous to us now," Thorgest countered. "This island is divided into scores of petty kingdoms which are constantly at war with one another and it had been our good fortune that their interests rarely extend beyond the borders of their own territories. But if ever they unite, few of us would see the shores of home again. As long as Niall lives, he is like a standard – a banner around which the Irish could well rally. If we are to conquer this island, we must first defeat its high king."

"Then let us finish him now and be done with it!" Ragnar bellowed, slamming his fist down on the table.

"He is right!" one ruddy-faced warrior roared, springing to his feet. "Let us take what we want as we have always done!" Several of his comrades murmured their agreement.

"And face two swords instead of one?" Thorgest set down his wine and leaned forward against the table, his eyes fixed on the warrior before him. "Or have you forgotten what happened to the Munstermen?" From the startled expression on his face it was evident that the question had caught the burly Norse jarl off guard. He glanced anxiously at his companions who had fallen suddenly mute, then lowered his eyes sheepishly and sank back into his seat without uttering a word.

Thorgest scratched his beard thoughtfully as he rose and slowly moved around the table to stand behind the embarrassed warrior. "You are a brave man, Bothvar," he said reassuringly as he laid a hand on the man's shoulder. "As are you all. But the bear cannot rely on his strength alone if he is to defeat the fox. He is a shrewd one, this Irish king. He has deliberately gathered his forces in Ailech to provoke us into laying siege to the fortress, drawing us out into the open, away from our own stronghold. With our backs to Leinster, we could well find ourselves caught between two armies, with a retreat to Lough Neagh completely cut off."

"But perhaps caution is our greatest enemy," Ragnar interposed. "If we do not move against Niall now, winter will be upon us and he will have all the time he needs to consolidate his forces."

"My brother is right," Saxulf added quickly, leaning back in his chair and grinning confidently. "You look for foes where none exist, lord. The Leinstermen will not risk turning their backs on their homes – not even for their high king. I say we attack now!"

The challenge to his authority was unmistakable and Thorgest sensed the others watching him. *Hatred and jealousy swirl in your eyes,* Thorgest thought as he met Saxulf's gaze. *When the thoughts of a man such as yourself tend to ambition, he becomes unreliable ... and dangerous. I had reason enough before to kill you, for I have not been deaf to the whispers that speak of you and my wife in the same breath. Even so, I have stayed my hand because I know that slaying you would cost me your brother's allegiance and perhaps that of all the Danes. But your defiance tasks me Saxulf, and by the gods, I will be rid of you.*

"The threat that Leinster poses to us cannot be ignored," he told Saxulf in a carefully controlled voice. "If we are to defeat Niall, we must be prepared to face the Leinstermen as well." He allowed himself the flicker of a grin as he peered deep into the young Dane's eyes. "It would be foolhardy to think otherwise. When we attack, it must be at a time and place that gives us the advantage. Until then, we wait." He turned suddenly and strode to one of the large wooden bins that rested against the wall.

"But the winter, lord," Ragnar objected. "If we wait..."

"The winter will serve our purposes even better than it will those of the Irish." Thorgest extracted a thick scroll from the bin and moved to Ragnar's side. The parchment crackled dryly as he unrolled it across the table, revealing a finely detailed map of Erin. Thorgest himself had taken it from the scriptorium of a monastery he had raided months earlier. Shadows crept along the carved panels of the firehall as the jarls crowded around him, their faces distorted by the ocherous glow of the hearthfire.

"While Niall tries to build his forces and his confidence, we too shall build," Thorgest explained. He picked up a meatknife from the table and lightly tapped the parchment. "Here – on the banks of the Lough Ree. The great river the Irish call Shannon flows from there to the sea. From such a base we will be well positioned to strike out at Niall once we have lured him into the open." He glanced up at Ragnar. "You and I will sail with a vanguard within a fortnight. While we are gone, Bothvar will be in command of our warriors at Lough Neagh."

"A Norseman," Saxulf sniffed. "Does my lord not consider any of the Danish jarls... suitable?"

Thorgest stood erect. "In truth, I did take account of you, Saxulf. But there is another task, one of far greater importance that I thought more appropriate for one such as you." He grinned warmly at the open–mouthed Dane. "Before the snow comes, you must journey back to our homeland. When the ice floes melt you will return with the remainder of our fleet – one hundred and twenty ships and eighteen thousand fresh warriors, eager for battle. And their bloodlust shall not go unsatisfied for it is you, Saxulf, who will bring Niall to us."

"But you said that the Irish king dare not leave the safety of Ailech!" Ragnar argued.

"A man will fight for many reasons," Thorgest replied.

"As these Irish put so much faith in their god, that is where we shall strike. Armagh is the seat of their church and lies between Lough Neagh and Lough Ree. When Saxulf returns in the spring he will land here," he explained, indicating the position on the chart. "At Dubhlinn, the black pool. We will then see to it that Niall receives word that a fleet of raiders is poised to attack his holy city. "When he moves to prevent its destruction, we will spring the trap from both north and south."

"And if he does not respond to the threat?" Ragnar asked.

"Then I will convince him to act by destroying the monastery at Clomacnoise," Thorgest replied coldly.

Saxulf grinned knowingly. "Otta will be pleased. As high priestess to Oden she has long despised this nameless god the Irish worship."

Thorgest clenched his jaw and pushed back the vision of his hands wrapped around Saxulf's throat. The man before him was obviously well–acquainted with his wife's desire to eliminate all who did not pay proper tribute to Oden and Thor. Her sacrifices to the gods were many and she was obsessed with seeing the body of the Archbishop of Armagh hung from the sacred oak alongside the others.

"I do not share my wife's convictions," Thorgest said flatly. "Which god a man worships is of no concern to me. The fear of his warlord is the only faith a thrall needs. With Niall defeated, we will strip this land of its riches and the Irish will be a conquered people, with us as their masters – rulers of a new empire even as our kinsmen rule the Britons."

"But what of Niall's ally?" Ragnar protested. "With our

forces divided we will be easy prey for the Leinstermen."

"They will be too preoccupied to be of any use to him" Thorgest answered. "When Saxulf has drawn Niall into Armagh, he will send half his ships to raid the eastern coasts of Leinster. Then they will sail south, around the island and up the River Shannon to reinforce Lough Ree."

"And the rest of the fleet?" Ragnar queried.

Thorgest smiled. "Your brother will have the honour of leading the remainder of our vessels down the River Liffey to cut out the heart of Niall's ally." He suddenly stabbed the chart, pinning it to the wooden table.

"Here – at Naas!"

Near midnight, while the drunken snores of the jarls who lay sprawled beneath their tables rattled throughout the firehall, Saxulf stepped out into the deluge of the thunderstorm which had descended without warning on the dormant community. His anxious footsteps slopped through the murky puddles that had already gathered as he hurried along the wood–paved street, keeping to the shadows and glancing furtively over his shoulder every few paces. The message he had received earlier had been blatantly insistent and he pondered its urgency.

When he reached the main gate, Saxulf gave the bleary–eyed sentry who huddled there a perfunctory nod, then jogged across the rain–soaked cornfield to the clump of trees which shielded the Viking base from the chill of the north wind. Finding the well–trampled path that cut into the dense woodland, he followed it by the scant light of the half moon until at last he came to the edge of the clearing he sought.

Saxulf crouched beside a cluster of thickets and wiped the rain from his face, listening to the unbroken sigh of the downpour through the canopy of leaves overhead, waiting.

A jagged shard of lightening abruptly slashed across the obsidian sky, illuminating the sacred oak which stood isolated in the centre of the glade before him. In that brief instant, Saxulf saw the disemboweled carcasses that hung from its gnarled branches and an icy shudder coursed through him as he realized that two of the twisted shapes among them were those of men. Beneath the hideously adorned branches a stone altar had been erected at the base of the ancient oak.

With the crackling boom of the thunder clap that followed, the awestruck Dane raised his eyes to the heavens. "*Mjolnir*," he whispered under his breath, invoking the name of Thor's hammer, the weapon which generated the lightening bolts as it sped to destroy its target with a mighty crash before returning to the hand of its master. He knew that a great battle raged above him.

Glancing back at the sinister oak, Saxulf tensed suddenly and stared at the tall, shadowy figure that had somehow materialized out of the darkness and now stood poised before the altar, back arched and arms stretched out in supplication. The rain–drenched robes of Thor's high priestess clung to her body, revealing the sensuous contours of Otta's breasts and long legs as she tilted her face skyward and began to chant.

"Hail the day, hail the sons of day," she droned as the lightning flashed again, revealing the golden tangle of her hair, unbraided and spilling down past her waist. "Hail the night and your children of the night. Glance you with gentle eyes upon us and grant us who serve you victory. Hail Thor, hail the feeding earth. Grant power and wisdom to us, your faithful ones, for as long as we may live."

From within the folds of her cloak, Otta suddenly produced a dagger and raised it high above her head, clutching the hilt with both hands. Only then did Saxulf notice the tiny bundle on the altar. Squinting in the darkness, he thought he saw it move. At first he guessed the sacrifice to be a small pig or perhaps a lamb. Then he heard the frail cry as the knife flashed downwards, and knew. After several moments, Otta laid the dagger aside and raised her arms again. Steam rose from something she held in cupped hands.

. "THOR!" she howled, the eerie pitch of her voice raising the hackles on Saxulf's neck. When finally she lowered her hands, Otta collected the bundle and carried it around the altar, to place the offering at the base of the massive oak. She gazed down at it for a moment, then pivoted abruptly and looked directly at Saxulf.

"Come to me," she called. "I have been waiting for you."

Saxulf drew himself up to his full height and strode angrily to her, the condescending tone of the command grating on him. When he reached her she threw her arms around his neck, but he rudely broke her embrace and held the high priestess at arms length, frowning.

"Why did you summon me here?" he demanded irately. "We risk much by meeting like this, especially now. I could not avoid the sentinel at the gate and even if he is dim witted he will eventually reason that it is not mere devotion to Thor that brings me to this place on such a night. Besides," he added uneasily, "a few hours ago in the firehall I caught your husband watching me. There was something strange in his eyes, Otta, something he was trying very hard to conceal. Suspicion or jealousy, I could not tell which, but the look was there, as if he knew it is I who have taken you from his bed."

"Don't be a fool," Otta chided, droplets of rain clinging to her face. "Of course he knows. Thorgest has many shortcomings but stupidity is not among them. Why else do you think he had chosen you to return to our homeland for the remainder of the fleet?"

Saxulf gaped at her in astonishment. "How can you know that? I only learned of it myself a short time ago."

"Many are faithful to the god I serve," Otta replied. "And to his priestess. Matters of the slightest consequences to me are always brought to my attention – quietly. The loyalty of those who supply such information, and they are many, provides me with a certain measure of... security."

"But many more are loyal to lord Thorgest," Saxulf pointed out. "And if, as you say, he has already discovered that we have dishonoured him, there will be little either of us can do to safeguard ourselves. Perhaps he has arranged that this voyage I undertake be my last."

Otta took his face in her hands. "You worry at nothing, my love. Nothing. You are brother to the Danish chieftain. Thorgest will not dare harm you for fear of provoking Ragnar and starting a blood feud. He cannot afford to lose the support of the Danes in his war against Gael. As for me," she went on, slipping a hand to the nape of his neck while the other moved to caress his chest, "not even my husband dare raise his hand against the high priestess to Thor. No, my love, both of us are safe – so long as Thorgest does not uncover our intent."

The lightning flashed again, and in its brief radiance Saxulf searched the sapphire blue of her eyes. "And what if he already has?"

"We would be dead by now if Thorgest even suspected we have plotted to kill him," Otta replied, now drawing away from him. She shrugged. "But obviously he has not and soon we will be able to carry out his elimination as planned."

"How can we?" Saxulf objected. "If I do Thorgest's bidding I will not return until spring, and then only after a long campaign has been waged against the Gael." He paused, looking for the slightest hint of treachery in her expression. "But perhaps you have already decided to proceed on your own, without me."

"And risk having your brother or some other sea chieftain replace Thorgest?" she raised her eyebrows. "There would be no guarantee that any of them would take me as their queen – a position I have grown much accustomed to. Do not concern yourself, I will wait for you. The attack you will lead against the Irish is well suited to our purpose, and your victory over them will bring the fame and patronage that will support your claim to Thorgest's place of honour – once he is dead."

Saxulf sniffed dubiously. "How can you be so certain of the outcome? I could well be defeated."

"You will prevail," Otta assured him as she stepped forward once more and curled her arms about his neck, her body pressing firmly against him. "I have consulted the gods and they have assured the success of your enterprise, and mine.

On the day you return to me, Thorgest will die. The potion I shall put in his drinking horn will cause his heart to cease beating and speed him on his way to Valhalla. Then, I will be free and you shall rule in his place as emperor of the Irish."

Saxulf looked past her at the *Hlaut*, the blood of sacrifice that stained the altar, his eyes coming to rest on the crimsoned dagger. "I wonder what my fate might be," he speculated aloud, "if ever I incur your displeasure."

Otta grinned wantonly, then gradually lowered herself to recline in the oozing mud, pulling him down between her outspread thighs, her voice thick with desire.

"You will not displease me."

From the shadows of the woods that fringed the sacred glade, Thorgest stood in the driving rain, watching them. Slowly, he relaxed his grip on the hilt of his broadsword, then turned and walked away.

CHAPTER TWELVE

The passing of summer was the time of year that had always filled Finola with a strange melancholy – a sadness born out of the realization that the life and vitality of mother earth would soon flicker and fade and the warmth of the sun would be devoured by the icy greyness of winter. Soon would come the cold, an invisible foe against which men barred their doors and huddled together around the comfort of their fires. Everything that brightened the world would be temporarily extinguished and survival would become the primary concern of all living things.

But as the patchwork cloak of autumn enveloped the countryside surrounding Naas, the sadness that Finola had experienced in previous years was replaced by the newfound contentment which flourished in her breast. The prospect of change in any form had always disturbed her deeply, for she had come to believe that it spawned only an uncertain future, often at the expense of the familiar and the reliable. Now, as she watched the transformation of the world around her, she came to realize that the changes in her own life had been as dramatic and inevitable as the passage of seasons and in the process she had discovered the love for which she had secretly yearned.

In the weeks that had followed her marriage to Bran, Finola had discovered that the man with whom she shared her bed possessed qualities which her initial fear and anger had blinded her to – qualities which aroused her curiosity and drew her closer to him. He was a carefully guarded mystery. Each day she learned a little more about her husband

treasure the time she spent with him – the
one together at dusk, the shared laughter, the
gs by the hearthfire. She listened as Bran spoke
on of his dreams for the future, for Leinster and its
people, and she saw in him the man who had been the essence of her fantasies; a warrior king whose eyes betrayed his secret dreams and fears. The man she loved. Never before had Finola experienced such intense emotion and each night as he took her in his arms her heart soared. She believed that her happiness could not be more complete.

But on the day of the first snowfall she felt Bran's child move inside her, a sensation that filled her with shock and elation. At first her body seemed to rebel and waves of nausea plagued her daily. But these soon subsided, as the older women told her they would, and in the months that followed her belly began to swell with new life. The winter that others feared took on new meaning for Finola, for it now seemed a time of peace, a time to nurture and safeguard the life within her.

The following spring she gave birth to a son, a sturdy little boy endowed with his father's red hair and his mother's fair complexion. As she gazed down at the infant that suckled at her breast, the pains of labour were quickly forgotten. She tenderly caressed his smooth, pink skin and marvelled at the miracle in her arms. *A part of me… a part of us*, she thought, smiling to herself. *And yet, a separate person – an individual in his own right, who will someday grow into a man. There is so much I have to teach him about this world, this life he has entered. And yet, there is much that I myself do not know or understand. I can but guide him toward his future and from his father he will learn the strength that he will need to make his own decisions and choices. Bran will teach him how to stand alone when he must.*

Three days later Finola and Bran presented their son to the court at the feast given especially in his honour. Finola could not help but be amused by her husband's fatherly pride as he walked beside her through the great hall, his shoulders back and his head held high while the nobles and chieftains applauded the newborn. They had no sooner taken their places when Bran rose to his feet and gestured for silence.

"Etach Mac Cennedig," he called. "Come forward."

The champion left his place at the table and walked across the room until he stood opposite the king and queen. Bran stooped down and took his son from Finola's arms, then held the infant out before him. "Even as my father entrusted me to your tutelage, I place the life of my son, Devlin Ui Faelain, in your hands," he smiled.

Finola watched Etach's face as he took the child in his huge, rough hands and knew at that moment that her husband had made the right choice. Etach held the infant with an awkwardness that made him seem clumsy, but his face shone with a radiance that made the old man beautiful. For several moments he looked down at the infant which squirmed in his arms, then slowly raised his head, his one good eye glistening with emotion.

"I... I thank you my lord... and my lady, for the great honour which you have bestowed upon me, and by the holy name of St. Padraic I pledge my sword and my life to the child you have placed in my care. So long as I may live, he will never want for an ally or companion."

As the great hall filled with the sound of cheering and

squinted down at the tiny bundle he held, hand the child back to Bran. "Devlin, eh? he is it?" His grey eye twinkled with mischief. ot daggers bigger than him." As if insulted by the remark, the baby suddenly reached up and grasped a tiny handful of the old warrior's tangled beard. "Ah!" he exclaimed, wincing in mock pain. "I meant no offence, little lord!"

Bran had less trouble freeing the infant's hand than he had controlling his own amusement. He handed the child to Finola then turned back to Etach, wiping tears of laughter from his eyes. "Perhaps we should begin his warrior training without delay," he suggested.

"Aye," Etach agreed, stroking his mangled beard. "It would appear that young Devlin is indeed well named. That will stand him in good stead. Sometimes all a man has is the strength of his name."

Finola's eyes followed the champion as he returned to his place. *Here is a man much like my own Bran*, she thought to herself. *Beneath his harsh exterior beats a gentle heart. My son will be fortunate indeed to have such a warrior as his mentor.*

In the weeks that followed, Finola spent her days attending to her newborn child together with Morallta and Muireen. From the time of their first meeting the three women had taken a liking to one another and throughout the course of Finola's pregnancy they had become as sisters, dividing the chores among themselves and sharing those delectable bits of gossip to which no male member of the household would ever be made privy. Both Muireen and Morallta loved the baby as if it were their own and Finola was never at a loss to find an extra pair of arms to cradle the child.

The days grew warmer until, on the feast of *Bal*
when the sweet scent of spring proved too powerful to resist,
the three women took the infant out to the lush meadows
that surrounded the ringed fortress. Finola laid him on the
thick, sweet smelling moss and he dozed serenely in the
warmth of the sun while the women busied themselves with
their sewing and embroidery. Around them, the fields and
forests were painted in countless hues of green and speckled
with the assorted colours of spring's flowers. The swallows
and larks that soared overhead filled the air with a medley of
sweet lilting melodies that announced the coming of summer.

The sun gradually climbed across the sky until, near
noon, Finola put her work aside and raised her head, reaching back to massage the aching muscles in her neck. As she
looked past her companions she noticed two figures in the
distance, moving along the main road that led to Naas. "Who
might they be I wonder?" she mused aloud, squinting and
shielding her eyes against the brilliance of the sun.

Muireen and Morallta lifted their heads and followed
her gaze. "Whoever they are they are no doubt weary,"
Morallta observed. "See how one leans on the other. Without horses it's a fair stretch of the legs to the nearest village.
A good day's walk."

"Then they have been walking all night," Finola said,
rising to her feet. "Whatever would possess them to do such a
thing?"

Muireen stood up beside her. "A strange time indeed
to make such a journey."

As the travellers drew nearer Finola instructed Morallta

...ng infant, then turned back to study the ...gers who had left the main road and were ...ctly toward them. One of the men appeared to ... an the other, white haired, and he stooped slightly as ... walked with the aid of a long staff. His free arm was wrapped around the shoulders of a younger man whose head drooped to his chest as he limped alongside his companion.

"Is that not a bishop's crozier the older one carries?" Finola suggested uncertainly. The tattered and begrimed tunic that the man wore seemed contrary to any such idea.

"If that's a bishop, he is in a terrible state," Muireen replied. "And I think the other is hurt."

"We will find out soon enough." Finola adjusted the blanket around her son's tranquil face. "Take Devlin away from here and find my husband," she ordered Morallta. "Tell him what you have seen and ask him to come at once." As Morallta hurried back toward the main gate, the two other women walked slowly to meet the strangers. The older man saw them coming and raised his staff, calling out to them in a hoarse voice.

"Have mercy! For the love of God help us!"

The two women gathered up their skirts and ran. As they reached the hapless pair, both women gasped at the sight of the scalp wound on the younger man's head. Although the bleeding had stopped his skin was a ghastly white, his forehead and face streaked with blood. They eased the old man's burden from him and gently lowered the wounded stranger onto the ground.

"God bless you both my children," the aged traveler

gasped weakly, leaning on his staff with both hands. Muireen stooped over the prone figure, doing her best to cleanse the wound, but Finola stared in horror as she suddenly recognized the white–haired man. His beardless hollow cheeks were stained with soot and the red–rimmed eyes that looked back at her were underlined with dark circles of fatigue.

"Archbishop Forannan!" she gasped, sinking to her knees. She grasped his hand and kissed the ornate ring on his finger, the seal of his sacred authority.

Forannan forced his cracked lips into a half smile. "God's blessings on you both, my children. It's glad I am to be among friends again."

"Have you been robbed then?" Finola queried as she rose to her feet. "What outlaw would dare to raise a hand against a holy man such as yourself?"

"No, no daughter," Forannan replied, closing his eyes wearily. "The worst of Irish cutthroats are not capable of the savagery that these old eyes have witnessed. It was those god-less heathens the Norse. They have destroyed our monastery at Clomacnoise and there are rumours that they will next raid Armagh. Imagine! The very seat of the church in Erin!"

Bran and a score of warriors from his personal body-guard suddenly exploded from the main gate and raced to-ward them, the naked blades of their swords glinting in the sun. He gazed at Forannan in surprise as he halted before them, then shot a puzzled look at his wife. "What in the name of God has happened?"

Forannan grasped his tunic, his bloodshot eyes wide with remembered horror. "They came at night, screaming like demons from hell itself as they appeared out of the darkness.

Axes, longswords cleaving any who stood in their path. Scores of our unarmed brothers and priests were slaughtered and brutally mutilated, and anything that would burn was put to the torch. A few of our brethren, those who had time, ran to the great round tower and locked themselves inside. But the barbarians built great fires at its base, as if it were a giant's hearth, and the poor souls were burned alive. They screamed hideously and clawed at the iron bars on the windows – trying to escape but..." His voice cracked and he put his hand to his head, swaying unsteadily.

Bran caught him as he fell forward, then hoisted the unconscious archbishop into his arms as easily as he would a child. He stared for a moment at the limp form then shifted his puzzled gaze to Finola.

She knew the question even before he had uttered it and the answer was one that filled her with terror. She reached out and touched her husband's arm, her throat suddenly dry, and her voice was reduced to a ragged whisper.

"Vikings!"

News of the raid on Clomacnoise spread so quickly through Naas that by the following day rumours of impending invasion had already begun to circulate. The foreigners' reputation for brutality was legendary and fear swept through the stronghold and the huts surrounding it like an icy wind that chilled the blood of those it touched, carrying on it the whispers of half–remembered tales which told of the campaign of terror the Vikings had waged in the north. There had always been a certain unrealistic quality to the stories, due in part to their remoteness and to the suspicion that each account had been embellished in the retelling. But now that death lurked just beyond Leinster's borders, imagination became a plausible reality.

Bran sensed his people's panic and knew that their mood was tempered with outrage over the destruction of the monastery. Although Clomacnoise was located along the western border of Meath, its accomplishments had been a source of pride for all Irishmen. The school which was located there had been founded over two hundred years earlier by Ciaran who, under the tutelage of St. Finnian of Clonard, came to be revered as one of the twelve apostles of Ireland. The high scholastic standards of the school attracted students not only from the ranks of Irish nobility, but also included princes from distant lands. The monastery was also renowned for the missionaries it had produced and sent throughout Britain and the continent of Europe.

The wanton destruction of the institution filled Bran with a rage he knew was shared by the people of Leinster. There would be cries for vengeance, retribution, and they would look to him, the king, for satisfaction. But although he shared their fury, he had no desire to see Leinster plunged into war again. *Clomacnoise is – was the responsibility of Meath, he told himself, and I will not see the blood of Leinstermen shed on their behalf, not even for such a grave tragedy. There were nearly one hundred monks at Clomacnoise, with at least ten times as many students. The Viking force must have been indeed large – perhaps an invasion vanguard. But the heathen have so far seen fit to leave Leinster untouched and we will not provoke them to act otherwise. We will not make war on the Viking until they become a threat to Leinster herself.*

In the late afternoon the court physician sent word that Forannan had regained consciousness and was asking for the king. Bran immediately made his way to the guest chambers where he found the archbishop sitting up in his cot, his back propped against the wall, the food and drink on the table beside him untouched. As he entered the room, Forannan looked up at him anxiously.

"What news of Brother Dallan?"

"The physicians say that he lost much blood," Bran replied, closing the door behind himself. "But he will recover. What of yourself?"

"Your healer told me I have slept an entire day away," Forannan answered quietly, then lowered his eyes. "It would appear that I will not yet be called to our heavenly Father, as have so many of my brothers in Christ."

"That is our good fortune, your Grace," Bran said solemnly. He looked down at his hands for a moment, choosing the right words. "Although we are honoured that you have come to us for refuge, I am puzzled why you and your companion did not flee to Meath. Such a journey would have surely been logical."

Forannan raised his eyes. "We had little choice. I am convinced those heathens would have followed us to Tara itself."

"Then you believe it is their intention to invade Meath?" Bran asked, frowning.

Forannan nodded. "I'm afraid I do. There were so many ships, some of them huge. And hundreds – maybe thousands of armed men. In the moonlight they appeared as a massive black wave washing onto the shore. No, it was more than a simple raid and we knew that Meath would not be safe to us."

"But you and your followers could have escaped south to Clonfert or Terriglas in Munster. Either one would have been less wear on your sandals."

"It is because of the Munster king that I journeyed south from Armagh. Feidlimid has declared himself not only king but archbishop of Cashel and has petitioned me for acknowledgment of his status. We only planned to rest a few days at Clomacnoise before continuing our journey." The old man's eyes narrowed. "It would now appear that it is all the more urgent that I meet with him."

"Why is that?" Bran asked quickly, startled by the exigent tone in his voice.

Forannan looked at him in silence for a moment, then spoke in a voice laced with contempt. "The Viking were not alone – there were Munstermen among them."

"What?" Bran jerked back in shock. The Irish had always feuded among themselves but until now they had never sided with an invader and taken up the sword against their own. "Can you be certain of what you saw? After all, it was dark and – "

"I heard them," Forannan said slowly. "And in the light of the flames of our monastery I saw the banners of the king of Cashel flying alongside the black raven of the heathen."

Bran rose and paced slowly across the room, his fists clenched behind his back. Feidlimid's plan was clear and he would soon exact his vengeance on Leinster. The time for war had come again, a war which Bran knew would not be prevented.

"The foreigners will no doubt use Meath as a stepping stone for their campaign in the south," Forannan said as if reading Bran's thoughts. "But perhaps Leinster need not face them alone."

Bran turned and squinted at him. "The high king is the only one who would stand beside us in the event of invasion and he is hardly in a position to come to our aid. Even if he were able to break through the chain of Viking fortresses that isolate Ulster, his army would be cut to pieces moving through the territories held by the heathen."

"I was not referring to Niall," Forannan said quietly. "After I have rested for a few days, I shall resume my journey to Cashel. Perhaps Feidlimid can be reasoned or negotiated with."

"To what end?"

"Whatever evil he has done, Feidlimid is still a son of Erin. Granted, his allegiance is to his own greed and ambition, but that may be used against him. Even as he believes he is manipulating the Viking to his own advantage, he himself has become their tool. When they have subjugated the rest of the provinces, they will turn on him. He is not a stupid man, merely short–sighted. If he can be made to realize that his dream of someday becoming Ard–Ri will only be fulfilled if Erin is free of the invader he may reconsider his alliance with the foreigners. Failing that, I will subtly suggest to him that his association with pagans will be an impediment to his appointment as archbishop. If nothing else, the king of Cashel is a merchant and I will tactfully remind him that every commodity, no matter how intangible, has its price."

So this is how you have gained the respect of chieftains and kings, Bran thought as he studied Forannan's face. *You may well have been able to meet with others on their own terms, but you will not get the better of the devil when the bargain is struck in hell.* "Forgive me, your grace, but Munster will never ally itself with us and you would be a fool to put yourself in Feidlimid's hands. Without you to oppose him, his claim to the bishopric of Cashel would be unchallenged and he would be able to use his position to exact the servitude of his own people and those of any other region he claims as his jurisdiction."

Forannan smiled. "You are forgetting Rome, my son. In the event that I... cease to represent our Holy Mother The Church in Erin, another would be appointed in my place and Feidlimid would be compelled to bow to the authority of my successor." He raised his eyes to the ceiling. "Besides, there is a higher authority to whom he will someday have to answer to."

There was silence in the room for several moments as Bran searched for the slightest flicker of apprehension in Forannan's clear grey eyes. But he saw only determination. "Is there no way I can dissuade you from your decision?"

The archbishop looked at him thoughtfully. "As king of Leinster your duty is to your people, to protect and guide them to the best of your ability, and I know that you would not dishonour yourself by doing otherwise. Although I am not a king, I too have a responsibility and it cannot be ignored."

Here was the same fervour that Bran had seen in his own father, a love for the people that transcended all other concerns, even at the expense of the man himself. "At least let me provide you with an armed escort to ensure your safe passage."

Forannan shook his head. "I cannot enter Cashel surrounded by warriors. I will go to Feidlimid alone and greet him in the spirit of peace. God's holy angels shall be my guardians. I would, however, ask you to oblige me with a horse to speed me on my mission, for the sooner that Munster and Leinster stand together, the sooner the Viking shall be defeated."

Bran nodded. "I do applaud your intentions," he said skeptically. "But the eraic that Feidlimid still renders to Leinster is a bitter reminder of his..." The door suddenly swung open and Etach stood in the entrance, red–faced and out of breath. "Forgive me, my lord, but your brothers quarrel in the great hall. You must come at once or I fear blood will be shed."

Bran glanced quickly at Forannan in apology and stepped out into the darkness. Nightfall had already spread its velvet mantle across the sky, the stars glittering in its folds like precious stones, and he realized that the evening meal was long since past. Many a warrior's thinking would already be clouded with drink. It was a time when innocent jest was often mistaken for innuendo and tempers flared unreasonably at the slightest provocation. From the far side of the compound the muted din of shouts and angry voices drifted across to them from the great hall.

"What started this fray?" he queried Etach as they began to jog across the courtyard.

"I do not know... my lord," the already winded retainer panted as he strained to keep pace with the younger man. "But neither would heed our pleas to desist and we dared not lay hands on a member of the royal family. But they are both armed and I thought..."

"Aye," Bran exhaled loudly, quickening his pace. His older brother had gained a reputation as a swordsman, brawling at every opportunity, more for the perverse sport of each encounter than in response to any inducement. Given his brothers' intense dislike of one another, Bran knew that Etach had not overstated the potential for disaster. If Conor was fool or drunk enough to draw his sword against his older brother, Kenan would not hesitate to kill him.

Within a few strides of the huge oak doors, Bran halted abruptly and reached for the weapon that hung at his side, his eyes fixed on the dark shapes that lurked in the shadows between the great hall and the mortar buildings on either side.

"Your *amhuis*," Etach explained. "Flann would not hear of you going in there unescorted."

Bran grunted his approval as the captain of his bodyguard stepped forward. "I hope we shall have no need of your men."

"They will do what they must," Flann replied, unsheathing his sword. The anonymous mass of men behind him followed his example, their blades gleaming in the moonlight.

The clamouring in the great hall suddenly swelled to a frenzied pitch and Bran sensed the nervous anticipation of Flann's warriors as they shifted their weapons. "Follow me," he ordered Flann, "but do nothing unless I give the word." He glanced quickly at Etach, then turned and threw his weight against the huge double doors that barred his path. Above the creaking of the ancient iron hinges, the uproar from inside washed over him, carrying with it the fury in Conor's voice.

"... for traitors such as yourself in Leinster!"

Bran strode into the great hall.

The smell of roasted meat and ale permeated the air and the thick smoke from the hearth and cooking fires still clung to the timber rafters that spanned the ceiling. In the flickering torchlight Bran saw that the chieftains and noblemen had left their tables and positioned themselves around his two brothers who glared at each other directly in front of the dais. Kenan stood sword in hand, a crooked grin curving his thin lips as Conor grasped the hilt of his own weapon.

"Conor! Kenan!" Bran barked as he marched into the hall, the warriors of his bodyguard fanning out beside him. "Put up your weapons!"

The silence was instant as every head in the room turned toward him.

For a moment Conor stood motionless, staring defiantly at Bran, his teeth clenched, his chest still heaving with hatred and fear. But resignedly he gradually released his grip, dropping his swordhand to his side and turning to glower at Kenan who had made no move to sheath his own weapon.

Bran shouldered his way through the chieftains and stood so close to Kenan that he could smell the sour ale on his brother's breath. "I have tolerated the insolent remarks of this pup long enough," Kenan fumed.

Bran looked down at the white-knuckled hand clutching the sword, then slowly raised his head and gazed levelly into his brother's bloodshot eyes. "Put up your weapon or I will take it from you myself," he said.

Kenan glared defiantly at him, then glanced around at the others in the room as if expecting their support. When no one moved, he grudgingly sheathed his sword.

Bran shifted his gaze to Conor. "Now, what is it that set you two at each other's throats?"

Conor scowled as he pointed at Kenan. "That slug would have us ally ourselves with the same defilers who ravaged Clomocnoise. I say the blood of our countrymen calls out for vengeance!"

"Aye!" a red-bearded warrior behind him cried. "Let us see if those spawn of hell bleed like ordinary men!"

Those around him shouted their approval.

"Silence!" Bran demanded. "Are you all so hungry for war that you would journey halfway across Erin to find it? So far we have had no quarrel with the foreigners, nor they with us. Only a fool would start one now."

"That is exactly what I told Conor," Kenan said brashly. "We do not want to jeopardize the peace we have all struggled for – and some of us died for. The only way to avoid war with the Viking is to make a treaty with their leader, the one they call Thorgest."

"Have you taken it upon yourself to dictate policy on my behalf?" Bran snapped. "No man here desires peace more than I – but the price you place on it is too high."

Kenan raised his eyebrows. "Then you would have us fight the Norsemen? The same Norsemen who so easily annihilated the high king's army?" He laughed sardonically. "Don't you see, the time is coming when there will only be two types of Irish – those who rule alongside the Viking and those who work as their slaves in the fields."

"Your outlook for the future is dim," Bran replied, his eyes narrowing. "So long as I live and Niall Caille is high king, he will be the only one to whom Leinster gives her allegiance."

"Then we are destined to battle the Viking for they will not continue to ignore us much longer. There are many who would oppose any decision that leads to such disaster."

"That would indeed be a grave mistake on their part," Bran stated coldly. "And you, my brother, where will your loyalties lie if we are compelled to march against the heathen?"

Kenan flashed a malicious grin. "Why, where they always have, brother – with the crown of Leinster."

CHAPTER THIRTEEN

Finola clawed helplessly at the meaty hand tightening on her throat. The hulking Norseman had dragged her to the ground and pinned her there, dropping his knee to her chest with such force that the air had fled from her lungs, stifling her screams and leaving her gasping for breath. Unable to move, she stared up in wide–eyed horror at the black–bearded face of her attacker as his lips parted to form a malevolent smile that revealed black and rotting teeth. The stench of him filled her nostrils and her stomach churned with nausea. Slowly, as if to savour her terror to its fullest, the Viking raised the short handled axe in his free hand high above her head. With macabre fascination, Finola's eyes followed its ascent, seeing nothing but the gleaming edge of the blade. It stopped suddenly and hung motionless for a moment.

And then he struck.

With a start Finola opened her eyes and sat up, her heart beating frantically and her bedclothes damp with sweat. She blinked rapidly several times, then anxiously peered into the darkness that surrounded her. But there was no Norseman – no axe. Only the familiar shadows of her own bedchamber. She rubbed her eyes and caught her breath, grateful that her assailant had been left behind in the world of dreams. Only then did she realize that she was not alone.

Bran sat on the far side of the room, his bench turned toward the hearth as he stared into the dying embers of the fire. Finola rose and quietly padded toward him, the stone floor beneath her bare feet as smooth and cold as the surface of a frozen lake. The cool breath of night sent a draft throughout the chamber and she rubbed at the gooseflesh on her bare arms. Bran did not move as she approached him but sat slumped forward, his forearms resting on his knees as if he bore the weight of some unseen burden. She stepped behind him and reached out to touch his shoulder, then paused and withdrew her hand. She wanted to comfort and console him but did not wish to intrude on the privacy of his thoughts.

All at once Bran twisted around and looked up at her with eyes that yearned for the sleep which would not come. "Forgive me, love," he said wearily, wrapping his arm around her waist and drawing her to his side. "I did not mean to awaken you."

"It would seem that sleep eludes us both this night," she replied, studying the lines and creases in his face which she did not remember seeing there a year earlier. She frowned at the dark circles under his eyes. "What troubles you, my husband?"

He lowered his head, sighing deeply and running his hands over his face. "The Viking have accomplished far more than merely invading Meath – their presence has split the clans of Leinster in twain. Most of the chieftains think we should go to the aid of our countrymen, but those whose territories are farther south do not regard the danger as imminent, and favour sending emissaries to the foreigners to sue for peace."

"Perhaps the men of Meath will defeat the Viking."

Bran shook his head. "The clans feud among themselves, even as we once did. The heathen will defeat them one clan at a time until all of Meath has fallen. Then they will look to us. We must be prepared to fight them." He grasped her hand. "But we must stand united. In two days, Forannan leaves for Cashel. He will petition Feidlimid to ally himself with us, but I have little hope for the success of his plan. Even so, I have decided to accompany him as far as the Munster border. From there, I will make a circuit of the southern clans, meeting with those chieftains who hesitate to take up the sword against the Viking. They must be made to realize that unless we act together, Leinster will surely fall."

Finola ran a hand up the nape of his neck. "How can they refuse you, my husband? A personal visit from the king and queen is a great honour and the chieftains will be anxious to win your favour. The change will be pleasant for us all. How long shall we be gone?"

"Our journeys will not lead us to the same destination, my love. I want you to take Devlin to a place where I know you will both be safe. I have already spoken to Conor and he has agreed to escort you to the coast – to Bray."

"I will not leave you," Finola protested. "Not now or ever. My place is by your side and that is where I intend to stay."

Bran stood and caught her face in his hands. "Try to understand. I will be better able to deal with the situation here if I am not worried about you both."

"Then I will send Devlin with Muireen and Morallta." Finola twisted away. "Whatever perils you face, we will face them together. I will remain here, with sword in hand if I must, to protect my home and my family."

"No. You will all go to Bray," Bran insisted with quiet finality. "Even if I have to tie you to your horse myself. I would never forgive myself if anything happened to you or Devlin."

Finola suddenly capitulated under his determination. *What if the Norse do come?* she asked herself. *Bran is right, the only way to protect our son is to take him away from here.*

"For the sake of our child, I will do as you ask," she agreed, wrapping her arms around him and nestling her head against his chest. "But every hour away from you will seem a lifetime."

"We have no choice," he whispered. "When Leinster is at peace again I will come for you both and we will never be separated again." He smiled down at her reassuringly and gently touched her cheek. "I promise."

Two days later, on the morning that Finola and Forannan were to begin their respective journeys, Etach and Bran watched Conor as he supervised the loading of the women's baggage, then rode back and forth along the length of the small caravan, barking last minute orders to the drivers who were irritably repositioning their carts for the third time. All was confusion.

"I've seen entire armies maneuvered with less difficulty," Etach commented gruffly.

Bran nodded. "He is inexperienced, but he will learn. Besides, giving him command of the caravan's escort was the only way I could be certain that he would leave Naas with the others."

"Aye," Etach sighed resignedly. "But I would still feel better were I going with them."

"I need you here," Bran replied. "With Kenan at my back I dare not leave Naas unattended while I am in the south. You are the only one I can trust to see that my authority is not... challenged in my absence."

"As you command," Etach replied formally. "When do you expect to return, my lord?"

"Without any carts to slow us down, we should be able to complete our circuit within a fortnight – providing we aren't detained by one of the more obstinate chieftains."

"You could well be detained by more than that," Etach stated with concern. "I have already spoken to Flann and he agrees. It is foolhardy for you to undertake such a journey escorted only by the warriors of your bodyguard. Forgive me, my lord, but it is a mistake that creates great opportunity for your enemies."

"And what would you have me do?" Bran protested. "Drag the army halfway across Leinster, leaving Naas unprotected and showing my enemies that the king fears touring his own kingdom unescorted? No, old friend. I am taking a lesson from Forannan. If we want to strengthen our ties with the southern clans we dare not intimidate them with a show of arms. A king who governs his people by force inspires only rebellion."

Etach started to rebut him, but Bran waved his objection aside. "Whist now!" he whispered as he glanced over the warrior's shoulder. "Here come the women. Let's have no more talk of this."

With Devlin in her arms, Finola emerged from the royal residence and walked to them across the courtyard, Muireen and Morallta at her side.

"We have a fine day for travelling," Bran called out as he stepped forward to meet them. He gestured overhead. "There is not a cloud in the sky and only the hint of a breeze to keep the heat from the horses. Ah, it will be lovely for you all in Bray." He wrapped his arm around Finola and she managed a faint smile, but her eyes glistened with tears. "I have never been to the sea before," she said quietly. "They say that it is like a great lough without end."

Bran gently caressed her cheek. "There is no distance so vast it cannot be crossed."

They walked in silence along the length of the column until they reached the empty jaunting cart which awaited them. As Etach helped Muireen and Morallta up, Bran bent over the tiny bundle in Finola's arms and kissed his infant son. When Finola passed the child up to Muireen, Bran removed the gold Celtic cross which hung at his throat and, reaching out, gently fastened the delicate chain about her slender neck.

Finola bowed her head as she fingered the intricately crafted cross, then slowly raised her eyes to Bran. "I cannot take this," she told him. "It was your mother's."

"She would approve of your having it," Bran replied, embracing her. "God grant you all a safe journey. I will come for you when the danger has passed."

"God keep you, my husband," Finola whispered into his ear, her voice quivering with emotion as she clung tightly to him.

Conor drew up beside them, his buckskin mare prancing with nervous anticipation. "All is ready, my lord."

Bran nodded, then lifted Finola into the cart. He looked at Muireen. "Take care of them for me. They are all I have."

His sister leaned down and hugged his neck. "You need not have asked."

Conor reined his horse around and galloped to the head of the column. With a shout, he ordered the caravan forward. As the carts and mounted warriors began to move toward the main gate, Bran's eyes remained locked on Finola's, a strange sensation sweeping over him as he gazed after her, wanting to call her back, and knowing he would not. Even when they had turned out of sight, he stood looking after them, unable to move.

"Etach," he muttered slowly. "See to it that the archbishop has been made ready for his journey. Tell Flann and his men that we leave within the hour."

Later that night, in the small hours when all was quiet and weary guards dozed comfortably at their posts, Kenan led his horse through the shadows of Naas undetected and out the fortress gate. An hour later, he turned off the main road, riding cross country toward the great forest that stretched out before him like a wall obscuring the landscape which lay beyond. When at last he reached the edge of the trees he dismounted and wrapped the reins around the trunk of one towering giant, then walked into the dense wildwood.

Veils of dark clouds drifted past the moon and he moved slowly in the darkness, his progress slackened by the tangled thickets and underbrush. Overhead, a gentle breeze rustled through the leaves of the aged oak trees and their gnarled branches were like skeletal fingers that swayed and clutched at him. Feral eyes glared at him out of the darkness and from somewhere off in the distance, the bone chilling howl of a wolf pierced the stillness of the night. The sound seemed to emanate from all directions at once and he hesitated, his muscles tense. The superstitious yarns of the simple folk who still followed the old ways spoke of how the spirit of Crimthan Ui Faelain still roamed the hills surrounding Naas in the shape of a great black wolf. Kenan listened for a moment longer then moved on, nervously deriding himself for his own fearful imagination.

A short time later he came upon a circular clearing and shuddered involuntarily as he peered between the trees. Shadowy figures, some in long hooded cloaks, milled about a huge open fire in the centre of the space, its flames licking at the stars, crackling and popping as ruby embers exploded up into the blackness overhead like a sprinkling of blood. The ancient site that lay before him had once been the heart of the sacred oak grove where *druids* and their acolytes had gathered to perform their pagan rituals before the pillar of *Crom Cruach*, the heathen deity they worshipped.

A massive stone idol of the god presided over the area on the far side of the clearing, the archaic *ogham* symbols that the old ones had laboriously carved into its smooth surface still clearly visible, mysteriously impervious to the assault of the elements over countless generations. Smaller granite slabs, tilting at drunken angles, radiated out from either side of the pillar to form a circle that bordered the entire area.

Kenan suddenly remembered the tale he had heard the seanachies tell of how, centuries before the birth of Christ, the legendary warrior Tigernach and his soldiers had been turned to stone when they attempted to pillage the forbidden sanctuary. His eyes moved to the fire that now blazed in what had once been the sacrificial pit in which it was said animals, and even men, had been slaughtered as offerings to Crom.

Kenan clenched his teeth and stepped out into the open.

"Which one of you fools lit this fire?" he snapped angrily, glowering into the startled faces of his bodyguards.

One of the men, shorter than the rest, stepped forward and drew back the hood that concealed his face, revealing a tangle of russet hair and the smooth–cheeked features of a warrior who was little more than a lad. He gestured apologetically.

"Forgive me, my lord," Eoghan stammered helplessly. "But the night is chill and I thought... "

Kenan clutched the young warrior's coarse woolen tunic. "Don't you realize that the fire may be seen from the battlements?" he fumed, pointing back at Naas.

"I meant no harm, lord," Eoghan stammered. "Domhnall said it would be all right."

Kenan eyed the captain of his bodyguards, a burly warrior whose dark mane and beard were threaded with silver.

"'Tis midsummer's night and there is no lack of those who still practice the old religion," Domhnall commented. "Many's a farmer will be burning a circle around their crops to ensure their fertility. Even if the guards back at Naas do see our fire, they will take little notice. But let's get on with it," he added, glancing about furtively. "This place makes my flesh crawl."

"Aye," the ferret–faced warrior next to him agreed. "What is it that is so important that you would call us away from the warmth of our fires and our women?"

Kenan scowled at the warrior. "Your comfort matters little, Aengus, when the fate of Leinster rests in our hands."

Aengus smirked. "In the king's hands, you mean."

"It is as you say," Kenan replied sardonically. "Even though there are many who oppose his decision to move against the Viking, he is determined to drag us all into a war that is wanted by none, branding those who question his wisdom as traitors. And yet, is there a man among you who loves Leinster less than he – who would not lay down his life for his home and his family?" He paced back and forth as he shook his head. "No, oh no, the path that my brother has chosen will surely lead us all to destruction – unless we have the courage to act."

Several of the warriors muttered their agreement and Kenan smiled inwardly as he sensed their bitterness.

"What is it you propose we do?" Domhnall asked.

Kenan felt the attention of the others upon him, waiting for his response. "We must ally ourselves with the foreigners if we are to ensure peace in Leinster."

Aengus laughed. "Your brother will never agree to that. We all heard him in the great hall. So long as he is king, his allegiance is to Niall."

"Then another must rule in his place," Kenan stated flatly.

Eoghan stared at him in wide–eyed disbelief. "What you speak of is treason," he whispered hoarsely.

"Is it treason to protect our people from the death and misery that war will bring?" Kenan demanded hotly. "Leinster has seen enough of war."

"There is much truth in what you say," Domhnall replied slowly. "Even so, we are but few while many more are loyal to your brother."

"We have no other option," Kenan answered, his gaze moving from warrior to warrior as the smoke from the fire curled around him like the coils of a serpent. "Bran must die."

The crackling of the fire was the only sound in the clearing as the warriors stood motionless, their complete attention focused on Kenan. *Now we shall see*, he thought to himself, *where loyalty ends and fear begins*.

"Leinster will never follow the murderer of their king," young Eoghan muttered apprehensively. "The deed will blot out the intention."

"Only a fool would contest you," Kenan replied, smiling as he moved closer to the youth, but his eyes shifted to Aengus. "However, my brother is accompanying Forannan to the Ardagh mountains, an area well known to be infested by outlaws. With only three score bodyguards escorting him, his party might well be set upon by brigands and thieves."

"Such men have but one loyalty," Aengus growled. "A thief's efforts should be rewarded in gold."

"As they will be," Kenan replied. "With my brother dead, the council of elders will be compelled to recognize me as king, and I shall be very generous to those who helped me gain my rightful inheritance."

Eoghan suddenly stepped forward, then knelt at Kenan's feet. "My loyalty to you is beyond reproach, my lord, and from the first day I entered your service I have followed your orders without question. But I am no assassin."

Kenan rumpled the lad's hair, then helped him to rise. "Think carefully, my lad," he said benevolently, as he moved behind the young warrior. "Can your loyalty to your king be worth the price of your future?" His hand moved to the dagger at his belt.

"I will not raise my sword against the king," Eoghan declared adamantly. "Even if that means – "

Kenan caught him from behind, wrapping his arm around Eoghan's throat while his free hand wrenched out the dagger at his belt. Before the boy could utter a cry, he thrust the blade into the exposed back then twisted the knife savagely. Eoghan quivered for a moment, then went limp. Kenan released him and he fell face forward to the ground.

"Such will be the fate of any man who seeks to betray me," Kenan snarled, blood dripping from the weapon in his hand as he surveyed the faces of the dumbfounded warriors. "Are there now any others among you who will not fight for Leinster?" When there was no response, he knelt and wiped the blade of his dagger on the dead man's cloak. "Then it is agreed," he said flatly, sheathing his weapon. "We leave tomorrow. To spare ourselves further... complications, we will camp here tonight." His eyes moved to Domhnall. "If we are to avoid arousing suspicion, we must split up in the morning and travel by three separate routes. At sunset, we will assemble at Kilkenny."

The dark–haired warrior acknowledged the command with a nod, then gestured the others to move. "You heard him – see to your horses and your beds. We ride before daylight."

He paused, then turned to Kenan. "Perhaps the boy was right. If you are absent from Naas when Bran is slain, there will surely be much whispering among the nobles at court."

"Rumours," Kenan snorted. "Few will risk their reputations on accusations that they will not be able to prove. I must see Bran fall with my own eyes – and preferably by my hand."

Domhnall joined the others and Kenan watched his men file past him, feeling their mixture of awe and respect. More than one warrior glanced uneasily at the heap by his feet. *Now I truly understand the Viking*, Kenan thought to himself. *The only genuine key to power is fear. When I am king, a new era shall begin in Leinster.*

CHAPTER FOURTEEN

Three days after they left Naas, Bran and his men made their way through the narrow pass in the Slieve Ardagh, the mountain range which separated the kingdoms of Leinster and Munster. He had planned to reach the border in two days, but had not taken into account the welcome they received when they arrived at one of the *bruideans* which, according to law, he was required to maintain.

Honoured that the king had chosen to visit his public house of hospitality, the *brughaid* who oversaw its operation had begged Bran and his company to spend one more night as his guests. So eloquent were the man's pleas that Bran was finally compelled to acquiesce.

Now, as his stomach churned with the movement of the horse beneath him and the sound of hooves against granite thundered in his ears, Bran reflected on the wisdom of his decision. The time spent at the bruidean had been full of revelry and laughter, the ale flowing as freely as a mountain stream. He smiled to himself at the memory and tried to ignore the persistent throbbing in his skull. His only consolation was that, judging by the red eyes of his companions, he did not suffer alone.

Forannan abruptly reined his horse in and turned in his saddle to face Bran. "This is where I must take my leave of you," he said quietly, motioning to the vast plain that stretched out beneath them. "Beyond lies the territory of the Munster king."

Bran frowned. "I wish you would reconsider and allow us to accompany you to Cashel. I do not like the idea of you going there alone."

"He who walks in the shadow of the Almighty is never truly alone," Forannan replied, smiling. "Besides, if Feidlimid does not agree to my terms, your mission to the southern clans will be even more vital to Leinster's security."

"You are a stubborn man, your Grace," Bran replied, grinning wryly as he grasped the archbishop's forearm in farewell. "And a brave one. May God keep you in the palm of His hand."

Forannan made the sign of the cross. "And grant safe passage to you." He held Bran's gaze for a moment, then turned and urged his horse forward.

As the archbishop slowly moved away from them, Flann maneuvered his horse alongside Bran's mount. "Will he be returning to Naas after he has met with Feidlimid?" the warrior asked.

Bran's eyes remained fixed on the solitary figure ahead of them. "I do not know," he answered thoughtfully.

Flann shielded his eyes with his hand and glanced up at the sky. "It is near midday, my lord. Even if we hasten our journey back, we shall not reach the Ui Drona before morning, and there are no bruideans so near the border."

"Just as well," Bran snorted, clapping him on the back. "I do not think any of us would survive another such encounter. Come," he added heartily, swinging his horse around, "we will make our way back through the Slieve Ardagh and camp tonight on the banks of the River Nore. Tomorrow we will seek out the chieftain of the Ui Drona."

As they retraced their route through the mountain pass, Bran marvelled at the beauty of the landscape around him.

Sheltered from the westerly winds, clusters of bracken and oak appeared on the eastern side of the granite ridges with mountain born streams cutting down dramatically into spectacular waterfalls. Below them, several small farms dotted the valley floor with fields of oats and potatoes interspersed across the lush pastureland. Patches of heather flourished in the hollows and glens that fringed the steep ridges, the slopes gradually giving way to the treeless hillsides of drumlins which were blanketed with the vivid splash of bluebells and violets and the dainty pale gold of primroses quivering in the noon breeze.

How can a land such as this be plagued by such disunity, Bran wondered. *We are all children of the Gael, descendants of the same ancestors, and yet we feud among ourselves as if we were strangers. We have butchered this island of ours into hundreds of petty kingdoms, each clan claiming this territory or that as their own, making it a simple task for the Viking to conquer us a little at a time. If we but stood together as one people, one nation, the invader would be driven back into the sea from whence he came.*

They forded the River Nore by late afternoon and made camp in a glade within the dense, brooding forest that stretched along the eastern bank of the sparkling water. They spent the remainder of the afternoon hunting and fishing, returning to the site at sunset with the carcass of a large stag and several fresh trout. Once they had eaten their fill the warriors wearily prepared their beds, laying brushwood next to the ground, then covering it with moss and fresh rushes.

Bran ensured that the horses had been properly attended to and the pickets posted, then stretched out on the ground beside the fire, its warmth easing the tension in his muscles as he drowsily stared up at the tiny pinpoints of light that glittered overhead in the ebony heavens.

Sleep brought Finola to him – a dream in which she stood in the midst of a great void, her arms outstretched, reaching for him. He began to walk toward her, and then ran, but the gap between them remained constant, though she did not move. She desperately cried out to him, her voice laced with panic and fear. Sweat stung his eyes as he struggled to reach her. Her image began to fade and Bran screamed out her name. An answering wail floated to him, then she was gone.

Abruptly he opened his eyes, lying motionless as he listened to the snores and deep breathing of his comrades. The sound that had penetrated the veil of his consciousness had been unnatural – out of place, and his ears strained to hear it again.

The horses whinnied nervously and a low moan drifted across to him from the perimeter of the camp.

He felt for the broadsword that lay at his side and turned his head cautiously, slowly surveying the woods on the far side of the clearing. His breathing quickened – the guards that he had stationed there earlier were nowhere to be seen. Instead, dark shapes glided ominously through the shadows between the trees, and from their midst, came the almost inaudible rasp of a hoarse voice, muted to a menacing whisper.

Bran scrambled to his feet.

"To arms!" he cried as he drew his sword and cast the empty scabbard aside. "We are ambushed!"

Hands fumbled desperately for weapons amid a torrent of confused curses as the alarmed warriors struggled to their feet, bracing themselves against the onslaught of shadows that charged them from the cover of the trees. The element of surprise lost, the faceless entities screamed wildly as they hurled themselves into the clearing. The eerie illumination of the fire transfigured the specters into a horde of heavily armed men who surged forward, flames reflecting along the polished steel of their naked blades.

The two factions collided with the horrendous clanging of steel against steel, dissolving into a mass of battle–hardened bodies that glistened with sweat as spear and sword sought soft flesh. Shrieks of pain soared above the grunts and shouts of the combatants, and the air hung heavy with the oppressive scent of perspiration and blood.

Although surprised and outnumbered, Bran's soldiers fought with precision and discipline, responding instinctively to their captain's barked commands. Each warrior gradually maneuvered around his adversary, then drove him back. Their assailants soon found themselves crowded shoulder to shoulder in a tight circle with the searing heat of the fire at their backs. With every avenue of escape or retreat cut off by the warriors who surrounded them, they frantically fought back with the blind panic of doomed men. But the king's soldiers continued to press them.

"Yield now!" Bran roared at last as he saw their resistance crumble into panic and confusion. "Or die where you stand!"

But sporadic fighting continued until those who had refused to lay down their weapons were slain. The defeated warriors eventually stood in silence. Bran suddenly stepped forward and pointed at one of them.

"I know you," he said in astonishment. "You are

Aengus, one of my brother's – "

A lone rider suddenly exploded from the woods and charged across the small clearing, his sword held high. He swung wildly as he passed but Bran easily dodged the blow that was intended for his head.

"Flann!" he bellowed over his shoulder as his attacker galloped toward the main road. "I want that whore–son brought back here alive!" The captain and two burly body-guards ran to the horses. As they thundered away into the darkness, Bran turned and peered at Aengus.

"Was it Kenan who sent you?" he asked.

Aengus remained silent, eyes lowered.

Bran pressed the point of his blade against Aengus's throat. "Answer me by Jesus, or the devil will have company in hell this night."

The tip of the weapon broke the skin and a tiny rivu-let of blood trickled down Aengus' throat. "Aye... aye," he mumbled, passing his tongue over dry lips. "He seeks the crown that should have been his."

Bran's hand trembled slightly, but he resisted the urge to kill the man. Lowering his sword he turned and walked to where the wounded were being attended to, stepping over the bodies that lay strewn on the damp moss. *I have underes-timated Kenan*, he thought bitterly as he surveyed the casual-ties. *We have always been rivals, but I never realized the full ex-tent of his obsession until now. What was once boyhood envy has matured into an intense hatred. He has become an enemy who will stop at nothing to see me destroyed.*

Nearly a quarter of an hour passed before the sound of hoof beats announced the return of Bran's warriors. The captive they had taken rode between the two bodyguards, his hands bound behind his back, while Flann led his horse into the clearing. As they rode into the amber flow of the fire, the flickering light washed over Kenan's face, revealing a bloody gash on his forehead.

"Help him," Bran said flatly, moving toward them. Flann and his men dismounted, then hauled Kenan from his saddle. As they led him to stand before his brother, his expression was as stone, his cold eyes void of fear or contrition.

"I could have you executed for this," Bran said coldly.

The corner of Kenan's mouth lifted into a contemptuous sneer. "All my life I have stood in your shadow and been forced to watch while you took my birthright, my woman – everything that ever mattered to me. Now you covet all I have left. My life. Forgive me if the prospect does not surprise me."

"I took nothing from you," Bran snarled, clenching his fists in an effort to control himself. "Taillte had already ceased being your woman long before she came to me. And as for the crown, it was the council of elders, not I, who placed it upon my brow."

"What are you going to do with me?"

Bran regarded him in silence for several moments. "I do not yet know."

"The fate of those who would slay their kin requires little thought, my lord," Flann interjected. "The penalty for *fingall* is death."

Bran's gaze shifted to his captain. "And by so punishing him, am I not committing that very crime myself?"

Flann opened his mouth to reply but Bran gestured

him to remain silent.

"You have proven yourself an enemy to Leinster and to me," he said to Kenan. "And according to Brehon law, I would be more than justified in killing you now. But as you are my brother, I will spare your life and those of your men. From this day forward you will all be banished from the kingdom of Leinster. On pain of death do not let yourselves be found within our borders again."

"You cannot simply let them go, lord," Flann objected vehemently. "You only give them the chance to strike at you again."

Kenan grinned triumphantly at him. "My brother dare not slay me, captain. My murder would weigh heavy on his conscience."

"What do you know of conscience?" Bran said contemptuously. "Your weapons and horses will remain with us," he ordered. "Perhaps the journey on foot will allow you an opportunity to reflect on the path you have chosen." He nodded to Flann. "Release him."

When Flann untied the leather bindings Kenan rubbed his reddened wrists and scowled. "I had envisioned the circumstances of our parting somewhat differently," he said, unrepentant. "But I am certain that we shall meet again."

Bran's eyes narrowed. "For your sake, brother, I hope that you are wrong."

They glared at each other in silence, then Kenan flung around and marched off, signaling his remaining warriors to follow. Bran watched as they disappeared into the darkness. "Have them followed," he instructed Flann. "Then tell the others to make ready. We leave for the Clanna Ui Drona at once."

CHAPTER FIFTEEN

Kenan and his men crossed the border into Munster under cover of darkness, travelling cross country to avoid the main roads. By day they sought the protection of the woods, making their camps in small clearings to avoid detection by any of the local clans. Few would be without bitter memories of their defeat at the hands of Leinstermen, and Kenan had no doubt that they would welcome any opportunity for reprisals. The plan he had conceived was not without risk, but he had no intention of falling into the hands of some minor chieftain before he reached his destination. For fear of attracting attention he ordered that no fires be lit and posted guards each night.

On the third night of their journey, just before sunrise, they reached Cashel. The bleak stone fortress sat atop a rocky outcrop which, according to legend, had been cast upon the open plain by magic centuries before. As they made their way toward the ancient citadel of the Munster kings, the early light of daybreak transformed it into a sanctuary of shimmering golden radiance.

"It is truly worthy of a great king," Kenan commented to Aengus, awed by the beauty of the scene before him. "Any man capable of attaining and holding such power will no doubt prove a valuable ally."

"Aye," Aengus answered dubiously. "But of what use are we to such a man?"

Kenan smiled knowingly. "We shall soon see."

When they reached the main gate a bleary—eyed sentry leaned over the wall, and cupping his hands around his mouth, shouted down.

"What men are you?"

Kenan stepped forward and pulled back the hood of his cloak. "Tell your king that it is Kenan Ui Faelain, Prince of Leinster, who seeks an audience with him!"

The startled sentry hesitated for a moment, then disappeared from sight. Within the fortress came a torrent of a muffled commands, followed by the dull patter of scampering feet and the rattle of weapons being assembled. A few moments later the massive timber gates slowly swung open, revealing several hundred heavily armed warriors whose unblinking eyes followed Kenan as he led his own men into the compound. He marveled at how the arrival of a few Leinstermen appeared to evoke such apprehension among the Munstermen. But he also noted, with some surprise, the speed with which the sizable force had been mustered.

They were taken to the great hall of Feidlimid Ui Eoganachta, *Ri–Ruirech* of all Munster and self–proclaimed archbishop of Cashel. The interior was divided into scores of compartments which surrounded the centre hearth, each constructed of beautifully carved red yew, the front of which was trimmed with bronze. Exquisitely enameled shields lined the walls, each hung above the compartment of its respective owner, the nobles of Munster occupying one side of the hall while the captains of the army sat along the other. The silver and gold goblets at their tables were inlaid with precious gems and it was obvious to Kenan that despite the heavy eriac which Bran had imposed on Feidlimid for the death of their father, the coffers of the Munster king had somehow secretly continued to swell.

On the far side of the hall a meticulously woven tapestry depicting Erin in minute detail covered the wall behind
the gilded throne in which Feidlimid slouched languidly.
Pouches sagged beneath the small, watchful dark eyes that
appraised Kenan. The man's head was clean shaven. He wore
a long black mustache that drooped past the corners of his
wide mouth to a jawline that was well concealed within the
folds of his fleshy jowls. An ankle–length robe of embroidered red satin covered his corpulent body and he wore a pair
of ruby–studded slippers which, though delicately crafted, appeared ludicrous on a man of such bulk.

A young girl reclined idly at Feidlimid's feet, her arms
resting on his thick thighs, and Kenan stared at her with una-
bashed fascination. She was naked but for a scanty loincloth
of apricot–coloured silk. Her skin was black as pitch; a bluish
sheen slithering across her taut body as she leisurely shifted.
Her glossy raven hair was fashioned in tight curls that spilled
over her shoulders to her small, firm breasts. Alluring, almond
eyes, flared nostrils, and pouting lips gave her face an erotic
quality that held Kenan transfixed.

Feilimid rose abruptly, brushing off the girl, and hooked
the thumbs of his pudgy, manicured hands in his wide belt.

"No enemy of Munster has ever willingly stood before
me in this hall," he announced in a high–pitched nasal voice.
"What is it you seek, Leinsterman?"

Several of Feidlimid's men rose from their tables as he
spoke, positioning themselves around him. Kenan guessed
them to be mercenaries, warriors without allegiance to any
tribe or clan. He sensed his own bodyguards shifting uncomfortably behind him.

"We have come before you unarmed," he replied calmly. "Not as a foe but as ally. He that rules in Leinster is an enemy to us both."

Feidlimid tugged thoughtfully at the small gold ring that pierced his right earlobe. "Your disaffection for your brother amuses me," he remarked. "Judging by your wounds, I suspect he regards you and your comrades with equal contempt." As the warriors around him snickered, Feidlimid glanced down and nudged the black girl with his toe. "Some wine for our guest, my precious. Rarely are we entertained by so noble a prince."

The girl rose and glided to a nearby table, filled a goblet, then presented it to Kenan. He guessed her to be much younger than his own sister, but the eyes that met his were those of a woman. Raising the wine to his lips, he watched her swaying buttocks over the rim of the goblet as she returned to Feidlimid's side.

"The whore is Nubian – the wine from Stygia," the Munster king informed him, grunting as he lowered himself back onto the throne. "Luxuries that we have grown accustomed to, thanks to the Viking traders."

Kenan raised his eyebrows. "I had heard rumours that you have established such an agreement with the foreigners. But I must confess that I am surprised that they have continued to honour it. Raiding your territory would have been simpler."

"It would be less profitable for them to do so," Feidlimid explained, laughing. "Such a venture would cost them many more lives and ships than they are prepared to sacrifice. Instead, we both get rich by... cooperating with one another. It has been my experience that anything may be bargained for – if the price is right." He leaned forward and looked directly into Kenan's eyes. "And everything has its price, does it not?"

"And what price would you place on Leinster's loyalty?" Kenan asked without hesitation.

Fiedlimid sighed heavily as he leaned back. "It is my understanding that Leinster is not yours to bargain with," he said flatly.

Kenan grinned. "You are indeed well–informed, your grace. But my brother is not a man of vision. He still renders tribute to Niall Caille who calls himself Ard–Ri of all Erin." He paused, then quaffed the remainder of his wine. "Were I able to assert my rightful claim to the throne, Leinster could prove a valuable ally to you. Cashel, after all, is closer than Ailech."

"There is much merit in what you say," Feidlimid agreed slowly. "But to wage war on Leinster would be to drive her into Niall's arms and Munster would again be faced with two enemies."

Kenan stepped forward. "Not if your Viking allies could be convinced to take up the sword against Leinster. Have they not already cooperated with you against Niall? With their support, your victory would be assured – particularly if resistance to such an invasion were to prove considerably less than anticipated."

"What are you talking about?"

"My opposition to Bran is not unique. Even though the Ui Muiredaig are his wife's kinsmen and his most powerful ally, there is one among them who would embrace any opportunity to strike at him. If, through the influence of my contact in Mullaghmast, the clanna Ui Muiredaig could be persuaded to remain neutral, many of the southern clans will be inclined to do likewise rather than stand against us."

Feidlimid raised his eyebrows. "Us?"

A thin–lipped smile spread across Kenan's face. "Leinster conquered is not Leinster held. My countrymen would never submit to a king who is not one of their own and your reign would be plagued with incessant rebellion. I, on the other hand, could rule in your stead as a sort of intermediary, and my claim to the throne could not be disputed. Especially if Bran were dead."

The hint of a grin twitched at the corners of Feidlimid's mouth and he nodded appreciatively. "You are a shrewd and dangerous man. How am I to trust one who would so readily betray his own brother?"

"Trust has nothing to do with it," Kenan replied evenly. "And as you yourself said, everything has its price. I would be a fool indeed to estrange so generous a benefactor."

"Wisely spoken," Feidlimid snorted. "Many a man has regretted making an enemy of me." He gazed coldly at Kenan for a moment, then threw back his head and roared with laughter. "Come," he chuckled as he collected himself and struggled awkwardly to his feet. "Let me show you something that may be of interest to you."

He led Kenan out of the great hall and through the compound to a small stone oratory, a windowless structure that had once been used by monks for private worship. Feidlimid grunted as he threw back the heavy iron bolt and opened the door, stooping as he stepped across the threshold. Kenan winced at the stench that assailed his nostrils as he followed him inside.

The prisoner who had been lying on the straw pallet in the far corner sat up as they entered, the iron shackles rattling as he moved. He was an older man, his long white hair and beard tangled into thick mats and his threadbare tunic soiled with his own filth. His grubby hands shielded his eyes from the sudden brightness.

"Good day, your holiness," Feidlimid mocked, leaning over him. "And a lovely day it is to be at peace with God and the world."

"Don't speak to me of God, you motherless heathen," the old man hissed, lowering his hands to reveal the drawn features of archbishop Forannan. He squinted at Kenan for a moment, then his eyes widened in horror. "Merciful father! By what misfortune have you fallen into this butcher's hands, my son?"

"Your compassion is overwhelming," Feidlimid drawled. "Unlike yourself, the Leinsterman is here of his own accord."

Forannan's eyes flashed back to his tormentor. "When Bran Ui Faelain hears of this outrage he will bring all the might of Leinster down on you and your legions of darkness."

Feidlimid threw up his hands in feigned surprise. "Can this be the same man who so eloquently entreated me to make peace with the Leinster king?" He turned to Kenan. "Archbishop Forannan has been somewhat intolerant of my suggestion that Erin would benefit greatly were it ruled by Munster, with Cashel the capital of the rightful Ard–Ri."

"For whose benefit?" Forannan questioned accusingly. "You are a murdering pig, Feidlimid, and the Brehons will never recognize what you call your legal right to the high kingship, no more than I recognize your claim to the bishopric of Cashel."

"Was it not from the rock of Cashel that holy St. Padraic first used the shamrock to explain the Holy Trinity?" Feidlimid demanded. "I am king of Cashel and all of Munster, and therefore his successor!"

"Not in the eyes of Rome," Forannan replied calmly. "And Rome will never acknowledge you. You have bestowed the title of archbishop upon yourself for no other reason than to better control the poor people under your rule, to use their devotion to Christ as a weapon against them."

"Have not my subjects benefited from my benevolence?" Feidlimid argued hotly. "The land is prosperous and the people happy."

Forannan nodded slowly. "Aye, in Munster they are. But you trade with the very demons that ravage this land and you yourself have pillaged and burned as many churches as they. Munster thrives at the expense of all Erin."

"Only those within Niall's domain have endured such misery," Feidlimid said hotly. "Without my protection, they must suffer the consequences of their misplaced loyalties."

Forannan's hand trembled with anger as he thrust a bony finger at the Munster king. "And you dare to call yourself a man of God! You are a tyrant and a blasphemer! I warn you Feidlimid, not even you are above the law. Someday you will be called to account for your crimes."

"Don't be a fool," Feidlimid laughed. "It is I that make the laws."

"It is the laws of Almighty God I speak of!"

Feidlimid's hand flew to the dagger at his side, but Forannan stared back at him unflinchingly. "Kill me then!" he shouted defiantly. "It won't be the first time that Gaelic blood has stained your hands!" The king of Cashel stared down at him for a moment, then sheathed his weapon. "I'll not give you the satisfaction of a martyr's death," he muttered. "At least not yet." He gestured Kenan to leave, then followed him out into the daylight.

"Why do you let him taunt you?" Kenan asked as Feidlimid bolted the door behind them. "Why not just kill him and be done with it?"

"The archbishop of Armagh may yet prove useful," the other man replied thoughtfully. "I think you will find that in our dealings with the Viking, Forannan will be of considerable value. But that is my concern. In the meantime, see to it that your friend in Mullaghmast is as cooperative as you claim."

Kenan smiled beneficently. "I assure you, my lord — she will be."

CHAPTER SIXTEEN

One week later, as the midday sun warmed the stone walls of Mullaghmast and radiated through the windows of her private chambers, Taillte luxuriated in the steaming water of her afternoon bath. As was her habit, she had not awakened until late morning, exhausted by another night's revels in the great hall of the Ui Muiredaig. The nightly ritual of feasting, drinking and dancing frequently lasted until dawn and life at court had become central to Taillte's existence; her afternoons consumed by tedious hours of beautifying herself in preparation for each evening's festivities.

When she had first arrived in Mullaghmast a year earlier, Rowan had taken great pride in escorting her to the great hall each night, anxious to display the prize he had returned with from Naas following the marriage of his sister to Bran Ui Faelain. He had been the envy of every warrior who saw her and many vied for the attention of the sultry dancer whose every movement seemed an exercise in seduction. Taillte had basked in their attention, flirting openly with them and lowering her eyes with counterfeit modesty at their bawdy jests. On such occasions, she had been almost oblivious to Rowan who had sat by her side in stoic silence.

As the months had slipped by, and each morning found the autumn landscape frosted with the first icy breaths of winter, Rowan had begun to accompany her to the great hall less frequently, leaving her to her own devices for days on end while he accompanied the hunting parties on their expeditions into the surrounding hills. Her irritation at his prolonged absences had been further compounded by her own fading popularity at court, the novelty of her presence being gradually overshadowed by the daily routine of the clan and by the numerous guests who frequented Mullaghmast.

It was then that Taillte had taken a lover. He had not been a particularly attractive or witty man, but he had fawned upon her shamelessly, stumbling over himself in an effort to fulfill her every whim. His blatant idolatry had rescued Taillte's dwindling self–esteem, providing her with some semblance of the affection she so desperately craved, and she had taken him to her bed more out of gratitude than desire. But her contentment had been only temporary, for within a matter of weeks her lover had begun to avoid her, feebly excusing himself from their discreet meetings. A short time later the liaison had ended bitterly, leaving only a sense of betrayal and emptiness that gnawed at Taillte's soul.

Throughout the harsh months of winter and the early days of spring, she drifted through a labyrinth of lovers, seeking refuge from her loneliness in the obliging arms of selfish men who themselves mattered even less to her. Each encounter left her more unsatisfied than the last – a futile quest for an elusive fantasy she had not been able to define.

But now, as she rested her head on the edge of the bronze bathing vessel and watched the water lap at the almost imperceptible bulge of her belly, Taillte smiled serenely to herself.

A child, she thought wistfully. *My child. Mine to hold and to love. To be loved in return without qualification. A part of me that can never be taken away.*

I do not know who the father is, but it matters little. Rowan will believe the child to be his own. And why should he not? I have

*been discreet with the others and we have lain together often enough
that he may well be the father. None will dare challenge such a
claim, for Rowan would be honour bound to respond to the insult
and his prowess as a swordsman is well known. No. He, like everyone else, will accept that he is the sire.*

*Perhaps the prospect of a child will prompt him to recon-
sider marriage, particularly if I present him with a son – an heir
who would bear his name. Until now, the so–called proper ladies
at court have looked down on me as his mistress, his concubine –
an immoral woman who does not warrant their respect. But with
a bride–price of my own, it will be I who regards them with a
critical eye. The marriage portion paid by a chieftain's son to his
bride will surely exceed that of even the highest ranking noblewoman.*

*God grant me a son who will one day be chieftain of the Ui
Muiredaig. Then we shall see who...*

The fantasy that had begun to take shape in her mind
disappeared suddenly as her maidservant hurried into the
chamber.

"My lady! My lady!" the girl babbled excitedly as she
scuttled across the room. "A holy man from the monastery at
Armagh awaits you in the great hall!"

Taillte sat up and peered at her inquisitively. "A monk?"

"Aye, my lady," the girl replied enthusiastically. "He
comes bearing an urgent message for you!"

"Armagh," Taillte repeated slowly, searching her
memory in vain as she stepped out of her bath and accepted a
fresh linen towel from her maidservant. "See to it that he is
given food and drink," she ordered as she hurriedly dried herself. "I shall attend him presently."

The girl hesitated. "Pardon, my lady, but he would speak to you in private."

Taillte paused to consider the unusual request. "Very well," she replied cautiously. "Allow me time to dress, then bring him to my chamber."

As the servant bowed and hurried off to do her bidding, Taillte quickly slipped into the pale blue lena which had been laid out on her bed, then sat down at her dressing table and stared at her reflection in the mirror of polished silver. *It has taken so long to find the home and the life I have always dreamed of*, she fretted to herself. *Am I now to be plagued by some forgotten ghost from my past, to have my future destroyed before it has even begun?* She pushed the spasm of despair aside and hastily set about the task of coiffing her hair.

A few minutes later she was startled by an abrupt rapping at her door.

"Enter," she called apprehensively.

Slowly the door creaked open. A monk was stepping into the room. He was a huge man, heavy boned and thickly muscled, and the hood of the simple woolen robe he wore concealed most of his face, giving him a dark and sinister appearance. He stopped, then suddenly reached out and slammed the door on the anxious maidservant who hovered in the passage.

"Forgive this intrusion, lady," he murmured apologetically. "But I have urgent business with you." Reaching up, he drew back his hood, revealing a mass of burnished bronze hair that fell to his shoulders.

"You're not a monk!" Taillte protested indignantly. "Who are you?"

"That is of no consequence," he answered, making no effort to disguise his frank appraisal of her. "I merely bear a message from my lord – Kenan Ui Faelain."

Taillte shifted uncomfortably beneath his gaze. "I left Naas over a year ago. What reason has he to contact me now?"

The stranger grinned. "My lord now resides at Feidlimid's court in Cashel where he is considered... a much greater asset than he was in Naas."

"What is it he wants?" she insisted irritably.

The monk casually strolled across the room until he stood over her. He picked up a gold brooch from her dressing table and examined it closely.

"Kenan Ui Faelain has long disputed his brother's claim to the throne of Leinster," he replied. "It is a dispute that he now intends to resolve."

Taillte shrugged. "I fail to see how that concerns me."

"You have, shall we say, the ear of Ragallach's son. Were you to use your influence to ensure the neutrality of the Ui Muiredaig, my lord would be eager to express his... gratitude."

"My past is a legacy of unfulfilled promises," she retorted. "I have built a life for myself here in Mullaghmast. Why should I jeopardize what I have for the sake of a man who is no better than a stranger to me?"

"Kenan Ui Faelain can be a very generous man," the messenger replied slowly. "To those who are his allies. He has instructed me to tell you that when he ascends the throne, you will rule at his side as queen. Should you, however, refuse to cooperate with him now, he will regard you somewhat less favourably when he is king."

Taillte's first instinct was to lash out at so blatant a

threat; to turn the man who stood before her over to Rowan's warriors. But a lifetime of weighing options and possibilities had taught her to control such spontaneity. She smiled graciously. "I will need time to consider so handsome a proposal."

"I leave for Cashel in the morning," he stated flatly. "I will expect to hear from you before then." Without waiting for her to reply he bowed curtly and strode from the room. "Is everything all right, my lady?" Taillte's maidservant queried excitedly a moment later as she peered round the door.

Taillte nodded slowly. "Where is Rowan?"

"I know not, my lady. I have not seen him since early morning."

"Find him and tell him I must speak with him immediately," Taillte ordered. "We have much to discuss."

The white–tailed stag raised its head from the water and pricked its ears forward, the muscles in its powerful legs tensed for flight. Although the surrounding woodland was silent but for the rustle of a gentle breeze through the trees and the light murmur of the sparkling brook, the animal had instinctively sensed imminent danger and its wide nostrils flared as it tested the air.

Rowan had positioned himself downwind from his quarry, concealed within the undergrowth that fringed the small clearing. He had stalked the deer for nearly an hour, moving silently over the fallen leaves and spongy moss that carpeted the forest floor. Once within range, he crouched slightly and drew back his throwing arm, holding his iron tipped casting spear at eye level. Unconsciously shifting his weight and gathering his energy, he paused for an instant, adjusted his aim, then hurled the spear toward the point he had selected at the base of the deer's neck. Almost simultaneously he detected the dull pounding of horses' hooves. The noise startled the stag and it bolted sideways, charging toward Rowan's position. The sharp iron tip of the missile sliced across the right flank of the fleeing animal, embedding itself in the soft turf, its shaft still quivering as the pain panicked stag veered sharply and plunged into the brush.

"Rowan!" a husky feminine voice called out, shattering the stillness of the forest. A flock of frightened quail exploded from a nearby hawthorn bush with a staccato fluttering of wings. "Rowan!"

Livid with fury, Rowan marched across the clearing and retrieved his spear. Recognizing the voice that had become a growing source of irritation to him, he cursed its owner aloud. He cut the string of obscenities short as Taillte rode into the clearing on the black mare that he now regretted having once given her a token of his affection.

"By all the saints in heaven, woman!" he bellowed at her. "You are enough to make Christ want to get back up on his comfortable cross!" Angrily, he grasped the horse's bit with his free hand and jerked it. The skittish horse reared, tearing the reins from his hand. Taillte was thrown backwards and landed heavily in the shallow brook, the water spraying into countless glistening drops above her As her mount galloped back toward the security of its stable, Rowan dissolved into laughter. Taillte lay helplessly gasping for breath. When she had recovered her wind she raised herself onto her elbows. The raven hair which had been so carefully coiffed hung limply about her face in dripping tendrils. Her best lena was thoroughly soaked and clung wetly to her. "You whore–son bastard!" she screamed indignantly. "I spent my entire afternoon dressing to please you! And look what you have done to me!"

"And it's all afternoon that I have been tracking that stag!" Rowan gestured angrily toward the spot where his quarry had stood.

Taillte hauled herself to her feet and stepped onto the turf, then stopped to wring the water from her hair. "When my girl told me that you had made other plans for the afternoon, other than to speak to me as I had requested, I could not believe what I was hearing. How dare you ignore me! Am I your harlot to be kept waiting for your favours?"

"Certainly not *my* harlot," he snapped gruffly. "To me you are little more than a spoiled child – a squalling brat whose demands I will no longer cater to!"

Taillte stared at him incredulously for a moment, then threw herself forward, arms flailing wildly. Rowan instinctively lashed out, cuffing her along the jaw and sending her reeling. She sobbed as she rubbed her reddened cheek and slowly looked up at him, but Rowan saw that there were no tears in the large blue eyes. "Hell roast you," he muttered under his breath as he turned to leave.

"Please, my love," she implored pitifully. "I think I am hurt. I..." The helpless quality in her voice was almost genuine and Rowan hesitated. It was more of a conditioned reflex than a conscious reaction. She had long since discovered the compassion in him and he often resented her for using it. Still, he found himself turning to face her. He stood stiffly as she embraced him, nestling her head on his chest.

"Forgive me," she whimpered. "It is frustration that drove me to anger. Each day that passes seems to find us further apart than the day before. That is why I want to speak to you... why I came looking for you. Let us go back to Mullaghmast and we will spend the evening together, as we used to."

Rowan's face remained impassive. "You have no need of me," he replied coldly. "And I have grown weary of feigning ignorance while you amuse yourself in the beds of half the noblemen in Mullaghmast."

Taillte stiffened at the rebuke. "But now we have a life together – a future. We are going to have – "

"We have nothing," he interrupted, shaking his head. "The ambition in your heart has left no room for love of anyone but yourself. Our dreams are not the same, Taillte. I am content with life and gratefully accept whatever it has to offer. But you – you will never be satisfied."

The soft eyes that gazed back at him suddenly filled with fire. "Don't be a fool, Rowan," she urged him. "There is a storm coming that will soon sweep through all of Erin and the opportunities for you and I will be almost limitless."

"What are you talking about?" he asked, eyes narrowed.

Taillte stepped closer. "They say that Kenan Ui Faelain has allied himself with Feidlimid and that he will soon replace his brother as king of Leinster. If we join them now in their enterprise, our future will surely be lined in gold."

Rowan frowned. "I have heard no such rumours."

"What you hear depends on where you listen." Taillte was watching him closely.

"You are indeed a remarkable woman," he breathed,

retreating from her reach. "If not a devious one. The only true love in your life is power, and what you think it will do for you." He took in the glistening sheen of her black hair and the exquisite curves of her face. There seemed such a striking contrast between what he saw before him and what he knew lay beneath the surface. "I am sorry for you, Taillte," he went on. "And for what your lust has already done to you." It took more effort than he had imagined, but he turned and strode away from her, his feelings a mixture of sorrowful regret and relief.

"Be off with you then, you mealy–mouthed bastard!" Taillte screeched after him. "And I will go my own way – just as I have always done. Do you hear me? I am leaving you, Rowan! You and Mullaghmast and your whole damn clan! Do you hear?"

Rowan kept walking.

CHAPTER SEVENTEEN

The following morning, as Taillte set out on her journey to Cashel, the Viking sacked Armagh. Forty leagues north of Mullaghmast a billowing canopy of thick black smoke hung over the smoldering ruins of the once magnificent holy city, filling the air with the acrid scent of charred timber and seared flesh. The individual wooden cells of the monks had blazed like tinder leaving only a few skeletal frames rising above the landscape where hundreds of the simple dwellings had stood just hours before. The stone and mortar of the three churches, the refectory and the scriptorium had proven impervious to the torch, but their lime–washed walls were now stained ashen–grey with the grimy particles of soot that drifted on the gentle morning breeze.

Although nearly seven thousand inhabitants, mostly students and cenobites, had resided at Armagh, few had escaped the steel of the Norse and Danish raiders. The twisted and mutilated bodies lay where they had fallen, some piled one atop another, their faces hideously contorted by their final death throes while puddles of blood, urine and excrement pooled beneath them.

Parties of scavenging warriors moved among the corpses, laughing as they stripped the dead of their ornaments and clothes. The wounded who were unfortunate enough to be discovered alive were set upon with knives – their ears, noses and fingers hacked off until they mercifully lost consciousness. Only then were they quickly dispatched.

One poor man, an elderly monastic who had suffered a head wound, was caught as he attempted to crawl to safety through the graveyard. He screamed himself hoarse while his hands were summarily hacked off, then stared in wide-eyed horror as his tormentors indulged in a macabre game of catch – tossing his still twitching extremities back and forth while blood spurted from the severed stumps at his wrists. He did not live long.

Thorgest squinted as he made his way through the carnage, his eyes and throat burning from the dense smoke that snaked throughout the monastery. He wiped the back of his bare arm over his sweat and soot-streaked face, then cleared his throat and spat. The globule of spittle sizzled as it landed among the glowing embers. In anticipation of meeting Niall's army at Armagh he had worked his men into a blood frenzy. But there had been no enemy to slay and the battle hungry warriors had appeased their lust by massacring the defenseless inhabitants. To have interfered with his warriors, Thorgest reasoned, would have been a grave mistake.

When he reached the scriptorium, the door was already open and from inside came a strange breezy sound, like the air leaving a dying man's lungs. Thorgest tightened the grip on his sword and stepped through the doorway.

Ragnar stood at the far side of the room, his back to Thorgest, swinging his long handled battle axe at the scores of manuscripts suspended in satchels by leather straps from the walls. With each stroke countless pages exploded into the air, then gracefully fluttered to the ground, falling among the pieces of parchment, waxed tablets and stylos that lay scattered among the overturned benches and tables.

Destruction for its own sake had always appalled Thorgest. "Ragnar!" he snapped. The dark-haired Dane pivoted quickly, his weapon poised in mid air. "I told you to send out scouts to watch for Niall's warriors."

"And I have done so," Ragnar acknowledged, lowering his axe. "But still there is no sign of him. It is as I said before, the coward intends to remain in Ailech."

"Do not mistake caution for cowardice," Thorgest replied. "I am beginning to understand this Gaelic king and he is a man of few errors." A splash of colour among the debris at his feet caught his attention and he bent to pick up a page of manuscript that had somehow survived Ragnar's onslaught. As he stared at the patterns of spirals, braids and interlaces, the design seemed to slowly come to life, the light tonality of the coloured animals and ribbons set against the dark background making them appear to move in and out slightly, then back and forth, creating the illusion of movement on several different planes. The animals themselves were brilliantly abstract, true evocations rather than representations. But unlike the fat, biting serpents and quadrupeds of Norse ornamentation, there was a peculiar fluidity to this variation of the same motifs. Here was the essence of Celtic imagination, flowing freely within the clear bounds of intellectual control.

Abruptly, he crumpled the page and cast it aside. "What of Forannan?" he asked.

"He has not yet been found, lord. And all the buildings still standing have been thoroughly searched."

"Then they must be searched again," Thorgest said, annoyed, as he turned to leave. "The holy man must be taken alive."

Once outside, the two men made their way to the nearest of the few remaining structures which still stood intact.

The largest of the three churches at Armagh was located several hundred paces north of the scriptorium and as they drew nearer to it, Thorgest's eyes roamed along the intricacies of the Romanesque architecture. *Perhaps Otta is right*, he thought, recalling his wife's insistence that the archbishop of Armagh be brought before her. *Forannan and his one god are all that links this country together and they may yet prove a greater threat to us than any Irish chieftain or king. If ever this island is to be ours we must see to it that they are both destroyed.*

A few minutes later they arrived at the front entry of the church. The main doors had already been battered down and the two vikings warily stepped into the dimly lit interior. Smoky shafts of tinted light beamed through the stained glass like rainbows, casting an iridescent mosaic on the smooth oaken floorboards. Ragnar moved ahead of Thorgest, holding his battle-axe against his chest as he stepped over the upended benches, winding his way to the ornate altar on the opposite end of the sanctuary. On the wall behind it hung a massive sculpture of carved yew, depicting a man crucified to a narrow beamed cross. Thorgest looked up into the figure's face; into eyes that were the quintessence of sorrow and peace.

That is no way for a warrior – for anyone to die, he told himself. *And yet this god the Irish call Christ is much like the all-father Oden who was nailed to the Ash Yggdrassil, his side pierced with his own lance, himself a sacrifice to himself to win the knowledge of the runes. Perhaps we are not that different from...*

"There is something here!" Ragnar exclaimed suddenly, squatting down behind the altar. Thorgest moved to his side and watched as he pried at the loose flooring with his axe. He tipped the long plank aside and reached into a shallow hidden compartment, extracting a narrow bundle of satin. Rising to his feet, he unfastened the silk cord which bound it at the centre and slowly unwrapped the smooth material, revealing a simple wooden crozier.

"A walking stick," he snorted with disgust, angrily flinging the satin aside.

"It is more than that," Thorgest speculated. "Why else would the brown robes have taken such trouble to conceal it?"

"It is the staff of Christ!" a youthful voice behind them shouted wrathfully.

The startled warriors twisted around to face a wild–eyed lad who glared back at them from the entryway, his face streaked with blood. The soiled woolen tunic he wore had been torn in several places and hung in tatters from one shoulder. Thorgest guessed him to be a kitchen servant or perhaps a stable boy, but he raised his sword as he eyed the short handled scythe in the young Irishman's hand.

"It was given to St. Padraic by an angel of God," the boy snarled, raising his weapon as they moved around the altar and inched toward him. "It does not belong in the hands of murdering barbarians!"

"You are right, little one," Ragnar growled balefully. He grasped the crozier with both hands and poised it above an upraised knee. "We have no need of this."

"No!" the youth screamed in horror, brandishing his scythe as he charged. Caught off guard by the unexpected attack, Ragnar lost his balance and stumbled back against the altar. Thorgest stepped in front of his fallen comrade and thrust his sword into the boy's belly, the blade passing through his lean body and out his back. The impaled youth drew his breath sharply, his eyes bulging with shock. He stared down at the shaft of steel that protruded from his belly then raised his eyes to Thorgest, a puzzled expression on his face. His eyelashes fluttered, then the scythe fell from his hand and he toppled heavily to the floor.

As Thorgest withdrew his sword from the limp body, Ragnar scrambled on hands and knees to the dead boy's side, dagger in hand. He grabbed a handful of the corpse's hair and poised the dagger beside one of the ears.

"Leave him," Thorgest grunted, lightly tapping the jarl's shoulder with the bloodied blade of his sword. "Put the staff back where you found it and lay the boy over the place. He has earned the right to safeguard it."

Ragnar stared at him in amazement for several moments, then grudgingly dragged the body behind the altar. When he had returned the staff to its hidden crypt and replaced the planking, he rolled the slain youth over it.

"I do not understand your concern for a dead servant," he grumbled.

"That servant journeys to Valhalla as a warrior," Thorgest said solemnly. "Of all those slain here today, he is the only one who has died with honour. The brown robes of this land are not like their brothers across the sea. From Fiesole to Jumieges, the holy men have met our ships with sword in hand and fought with skill and courage. But here – here on this island of bitter winds and strange mists, they drop to their knees to invoke their God and willingly bow their heads beneath our blades."

"I too grow weary of slaughtering cowards," Ragnar

agreed as he stooped to retrieve his battle–axe. "Let us march north to Ailech that we may once again honourably battle the warriors of the high king and defeat them as we should have long ago."

"No," Thorgest replied decisively. "We must return to Lough Ree before Saxulf arrives. By now he will be moving his fleets down the River Liffey and along the coast of Leinster." He dropped his eyes to the dead boy who lay at his feet. "Soon we will discover if Leinstermen know how to die."

That afternoon, as the longships of the Viking fleet moved down the coast from Dubhlinn, Finola strolled along the secluded beach which stretched below the precipitous moss–crowned cliffs surrounding Bray. The ivory sand felt cool beneath her bare feet and she clutched her cloak about her shoulders against the chill of the sea breeze that tugged at her clothing and fanned her bronze hair out behind her. She smiled at the antics of the long–billed curlews that erratically scurried in and out of the foam fringed waves which gently lapped at the shoreline. Their musical cries mixed with the high–pitched screams of the cormorants and gulls that hungrily circled above the distant curraghs bobbing on the surface of the sapphire blue water.

There is such peace here, Finola reflected, filling her lungs with the crisp sea air. From the first moment of her arrival at the small community she had been constantly surrounded by people, mostly a bevy of petty officials and the higher ranking members of the tuath who continually vied to monopolize her attention. No effort had been spared in welcoming the queen of Leinster and her entourage to Bray and Finbar,

the local chieftain, had ordered a month long festival to celebrate the royal visit. In the evenings she had attended the
feasts given in her honour, smiling graciously and
complimenting her host on his hospitality. In the days that
followed she was called upon to inspect the fishing vessels,
tour the surrounding farmsteads and conduct a seemingly endless series of private audiences. Finbar even pressed her into
taking an active part in the affairs of the tuatha by attending
meetings and personally adjudicating cases brought before the
elders by the Brehons.

Within a short time, Finola had begun to feel smoth-
ered, her need to escape prompting her to cancel her appoint-
ments on this day. She had left Devlin with Muireen and
Morallta and slipped away to the beach without her bodyguards – a liberty that she suspected Conor would reprimand
her for later.

Never before have I felt the weight of such responsibility,
she thought, idly kicking at the sand. *Only now am I beginning
to understand the pressures that my husband has faced and endured alone. In all the time that we have been together he has
never allowed me to see how the task of kingship gnawed at him.
Instead, he has shielded me from the liability of my own position,
shouldering the burden himself while I have been little more than
an ornament upon his arm. I have been permitted to share his
dreams and victories, but never the anxieties that I know must
torment him. Though he has often told me I have been a good
wife, I fear that I have failed him as his queen.*

Bran. The image of him waving farewell filled her mind.

"How much longer, love?" she whispered aloud, fin-
gering the gold Celtic cross at her throat. "When will you

hold me in your arms again? At night I lay alone in the darkness and long for the gentle press of your flesh, to lose myself in the love that has become my lifeblood. In my dreams I reach out to draw you near but I awake instead to the embrace of this chill loneliness that has been my steadfast companion since we left Naas. I know that it was your concern for our safety that prompted this separation, but you have deceived yourself, my husband. It is foolish to pretend that any one of us can alter the future course of events or otherwise escape our destiny. That remains in God's hands. Even so, you need not bear the burden of life's ordeals alone. Draw on the strength of your family, for our lives are intertwined and whatever fate befalls one is shared by all. That is why we must now return. Tonight I will tell Conor to make the necessary preparations for our departure and in the morning we will begin our journey back to..."

The thought fled abruptly and she squinted out to sea in a moment of stunned disbelief. A horde of terrifying creatures had emerged from behind the tip of the far peninsula, riding on patches of cloud that propelled them along the surface of the water. They were stalking the curraghs. At first, Finola stood motionless, uncertain of what she was seeing. Then her hand flew to her mouth.

Sails! Norsemen!

Blood roared in her ears as she instinctively turned and fled toward Bray. Reason and logic deserted her, her mind and body governed by a single driving resolution.

Devlin! Must reach Devlin!

Finola glanced wide-eyed over her shoulder. Now she could make out the wooden hulls of the longships – dragons' heads charging for the small fishing boats. She stumbled and the world suddenly tilted as she was pitched face down on the beach. Desperately she scrambled to her feet, spitting the gritty sand from her mouth.

Must warn them – must get Devlin away!

The throaty shouts of men in battle, screams and the clash of steel blades now drifted to her from across the water. But Finola's attention was focused ahead on the thatched roofs and lime–washed houses of Bray. Then she sighted the lone figure that had emerged from the outskirts of the tuath and was running toward her.

"Vikings!" she screamed in a voice that she did not recognize as her own. Conor, sword in hand, caught her with his free arm as she grasped his tunic in despair, dragging him back toward the village. "My baby... the others... we must get to the horses!"

"Devlin is all right," he quickly assured her. "But the horses are gone; stolen by cowards who have already fled." He narrowed his eyes as he peered out at the sea battle for a moment, then grasped her arm and roughly pulled her along. "Come with me," he said urgently. "Hurry!"

Bray was in panic. People were everywhere, jamming the narrow avenues that led to the centre of the settlement. Women were dashing about with children, warriors running for the beach with weapons drawn. As Conor dragged Finola through the teeming crowds, she suddenly spotted a child standing alone, crying in the midst of the confusion. Without breaking stride, she scooped the youngster into her arms.

Conor led her to the chieftain's hall where most of the women and children had congregated. The scene inside was little different from the pandemonium which had seized the rest of the small community. Women were wailing and calling after missing children, infants bawled, strained voices barked urgent orders. After several minutes of searching, Finola and Conor found the others. Finola handed the abandoned child still in her arms to Morallta, then anxiously took Devlin from Muireen and clutched the innocently smiling baby to her breast. "Thank God you are safe," she gasped, affectionately stroking the fine wisps of his red hair and looking from one woman to the other. "Thank god you are all safe."

"We are until those savages are upon us," Muireen hissed.

"Aye," Conor interjected. "I have already sent my bodyservant to Naas for more warriors, but there is little hope that they will be able to reach us in time."

"Then we will have to fight," Muireen said. "I for one can wield a sword as well as any man."

Conor shook his head. "No. You and Finola must lead the women and children inland. If you leave now and move quickly you may be able to meet Bran and his warriors." He turned to Finola. "We will hold the foreigners here for as long as we can."

"You can't mean to stay here!" she shouted, aghast at the proposal. "You saw them! There are too many for – "

"I will not leave these people to face the Norsemen alone," he interrupted, his voice terse. "Bran would not. And neither will I." The tousled red hair and steady blue eyes suddenly reminded Finola of her husband, and she knew by the set of the young man's jaw that he would not be dissuaded from his decision. She leaned forward and kissed his cheek.

"Then Holy Mary watch over you until next we meet," she whispered somberly, knowing that she would never see him again.

Conor smiled back, then turned and embraced his sister. Finola saw the tears welling up in Muireen's eyes but knew that she would neither weep nor attempt to stop him.

"Keep to the main roads," Conor advised Muireen as he stepped back. "You will make better time than moving through the woods. Now go!" As he turned and pushed his way through the crowd, Morallta stepped to Muireen's side.

"Muireen," she stammered awkwardly. "I..."

Muireen threw her arms around the two women. "Come," she murmured, her voice choked with emotion. "There is little time."

CHAPTER EIGHTEEN

While waves of Viking swept onto the beaches at Bray, Bran and his warriors leisurely rode toward Naas, both horses and riders relieved that the hectic pace they had endured during the king's circuit of the southern clans no longer needed to be maintained on the journey home. For nearly two weeks they had raced from tuath to tuath, pausing only long enough to convince the local chieftain to send his clansman to Naas within a fortnight where a great army was to be assembled and readied for the anticipated Viking invasion. Although a few of the less heroic leaders had to be gently reminded of their obligations to their king and to Leinster, most of the chieftains had readily agreed with Bran's suggestion that it was more prudent to meet an enemy up the road than it was to wait until he stood at the door to one's home. He had also subtly pointed to the fact that no one clan had ever stood against the foreigners and that those who refused their cooperation now were likely to find themselves alone and isolated – easy prey for murderous raiders. Two weeks after he had began, Bran had ensured the loyalty and support of all the southern clans.

Now, as he journeyed home, Bran's thoughts turned to Finola and his family. *As soon as we arrive I must send for them,* he resolved. *With the army of Leinster as their guardians they will be far safer in Naas than anywhere else. And I have been too long without my wife.* Finola. His senses brought the memory of her back to him – the scent of her body, her eyes, her laughter, the creamy texture of her flesh.

Bran smiled.

An hour later, as they reached the highlands that surrounded the Liffey valley, the advance scouts suddenly appeared on the brow of the grassy knoll ahead of them and urgently signaled them forward. Bran glanced uneasily at the captain of the bodyguards, then both men kicked at their horses.

"It may be nothing, my lord," one warrior gasped excitedly as they reached the summit of the hill. "But I thought you should see for yourself." He pointed across the valley to the distant stone walls of Naas. Columns of warriors were positioned in the lush pastureland surrounding the ringed fortress.

Bran shielded his eyes from the sun and squinted. "Those are our men," he said peering across the valley. "But what is old Etach up to? It looks as if he has called out every warrior in the clanna Ui Faelain."

"Perhaps he means to welcome you my lord," the scout suggested.

"It is not us he is expecting," Flann said gruffly. "I can make out the banners of other clans, and see how they are assembled in battle formations."

"There is only one man who can explain what this is all about," Bran responded quickly, then lashed the reins across his mount's flanks. He led his men down the hillside and across the valley floor, their horses panting heavily as they galloped across the plain. As they drew near to the clusters of warriors, cheers erupted from the ranks, the formations suddenly bristling with the spears and swords of Leinstermen who excitedly raised their weapons in salute.

"It is the Ui Faelain! The king has returned!"

Etach and several officers raced along the front ranks, reining in their horses abruptly as they drew up in front of Bran. "Thank God you are here!" the old warrior sputtered breathlessly, grasping Bran's arm in greeting. "But I regret that we can only welcome you with bad tidings."

"What is it?" Bran asked quickly.

"A Norse fleet of some six score vessels has been sighted on the River Liffey, not ten leagues from here. So far they have left the villages along their route unmolested. It would seem clear that they intend to strike at us here. I have assembled what clansmen I could, but still I fear we will be badly outnumbered. Just this hour I have sent word to the Ui Muiredaig, for without their support I fear all will be lost."

"They will come," Bran said with certainty. "We have but to hold until they arrive." He glanced up and noted the position of the afternoon sun. "How much time do we have?"

Etach shook his head slowly. "No more than three hours, my lord. Even then we will have to wait until the bastards land before confronting them."

Bran squinted toward the west. "Perhaps we can make better use of our time. We cannot allow the heathen to choose their own ground. The Liffey curls around Naas and it would be an easy task for them to surround us. Before they accomplish that, they must be stopped on the river."

"The few small boats we have are no match for their longships," Flann interjected. "Surely you can't mean us to face the Viking in those!"

Bran turned to his bewildered captain. "The foreigners are a seafaring people and we would indeed be fools to confront them in their own element. But what we can do is bring them ashore at the point of our choosing and attack before they have a chance to organize. No more than a half hour's march from here, the Liffey narrows at a spot where the sandbars will make progress difficult for the Viking. Perhaps we can make it even more so."

"What is it you wish us to do, my lord?" Etach queried.

"When we reach the narrows, have your men fill the gaps between the sandbars with stones and felled timber so that no vessel may pass. Our warriors will be positioned on the opposite banks – Etach on the west and I on the east. We will remain concealed until the invaders attempt to come ashore. Then, we will attack."

"But what about Naas, my lord?" Etach asked. "We dare not leave it undefended."

Bran regarded him in silence for a moment, then moved his horse nearer him. "It is not just Naas but Leinster itself that we march to defend. Every sword, every warrior must be set against the invader if we are to succeed. Our future depends on it."

Two hours after they reached the River Liffey, the warriors of Leinster had succeeded in effectively blockading the shallow waterway. Thick tangled walls of jagged rock and sharpened tree trunks spanned the sandbars, lying just beneath the surface of the water, their presence concealed by innocent looking clusters of willows and leafy branches which had been thrust into the carefully constructed debris.

The task completed, Bran positioned half the warriors on the west bank of the river under Etach's command, while the others remained with him on the eastern shore. Concealed behind the densely thicketed forest that stretched along the shorelines, ranks of archers, slingers and spear casters were carefully posted at intervals and flanked by cohorts of heavily armed warriors. Once the ambush had been laid the men of Leinster crouched in silence, anticipating the arrival of the foreigners.

They did not have long to wait.

As the golden rays of the afternoon sun danced along the ripples of the gently flowing river, they came, their sails furled, the longships gliding forward. Rows of oars rhythmically dipped into the murky water, perfectly synchronized with the slow monotonous pounding of battle drums that gradually crescendoed like the rumble of distant thunder. Behind the round shields that hung on the gunwales of the sleek vessels, the fierce looking Vikings with their pointed beards and conical helmets grunted with the effort of each stroke.

Secure within the shadows of the wild woods that rambled along the banks of the Liffey, furtive eyes peered out at the unsuspecting fleet as it approached the hidden barricade. The warriors of Leinster clutched their weapons and listened for the signal that would send them charging forward.

From his vantage point on the eastern shoreline, Bran stared in awe at the foremost ship. The blood red sail of the *draken* was emblazoned with Oden's black ravens, foretelling the doom that the dragonship brought. Intertwined gargoyles leered along the entire length of the hull, from the dragon's head on the prow to the serpentine–like tail that curled into a spiral at the stern. Stem and stern posts had been chiselled into friezes of animals interlaced with rhythmic loops of ribbon bodies, human hands and gnome–like beards. The draken measured over fifty long paces from end to end – a nightmar-ish spectacle that raised the hackles on Bran's neck. His eyes came to rest on the intimidating figure who stood on the bow leaning against the forward halliards. The man was much taller and stockier than the fair–haired Norsemen who stood on the deck behind him, the contrast made all the more striking by the thick black beard that covered his jaw. His facial fea-tures were otherwise obscured by the nose and cheek pieces of his helmet and he wore a knee–length coat of dark chainmail.

"*Dubh–gall!*" Bran whispered to himself in astonish-ment as he stared at the black heathen, the Danes so named because of the dark colour of their distinctive body armour. *What is he doing leading the Finn–gall?* he wondered. *Either the Norse have resorted to using mercenaries for sea chieftains or this is a man that the white heathen hold in high esteem.* "Closer," he muttered to himself, his eyes fixed on the huge Viking. "Bring your death ships a little closer."

The Dane suddenly raised a brawny arm and in a strange guttural tongue bellowed what sounded like a com-mand, the captains of the other vessels in turn barking the same order to their respective crews. The drums ceased and oars plunged into the water, bringing the entire fleet to a gradual standstill within a stone's throw of the barricade.

Bran's muscles tensed as he reached for the hilt of his sword.

Saxulf peered uneasily at the eastern shore and stroked the matted beard that now covered his jaw. There was some-thing unnatural, out of place. But although his instinct warned him of imminent danger, his eyes could not discover the cause of his apprehension.

Much depends on our success against the Leinstermen, he told himself, mentally reviewing once more the details of the conspiracy he and Otta had undertaken months earlier at their meeting in the sacred grove. *Only if I return victorious to Lough Ree will Otta move to eliminate Thorgest. When he is dead, the Norse and Danes I have led from our homeland will rally to me, the triumph I will give them against the Gael still fresh in their memories. With their support, and that of the high priestess, none will dare challenge my claim to the place of honour in our firehall. Then I will become emperor of the Irish — with Otta ruling at my side.*

But what if I am defeated?

Saxulf frowned as he scanned the trees that bristled along the shoreline.

"What is it, lord?" one of the Norse jarls asked, stepping to his side.

"I do not know," he replied slowly. "Something is wrong. I can smell it." He tilted his head back and surveyed the sky. "The birds. Why have we seen no birds?"

"Perhaps the drums have driven them off," the jarl offered, grinning broadly. "As they soon will the Irish."

"Perhaps," Saxulf grunted, frowning as he glanced sideways at the man. He had never approved of the habitual vainglory that seemed characteristic of the Norse. A man was to be measured by his deeds — not his words. "Give the signal to move on. And pass the word to keep a keen watch."

The jarl's smile faded as he nodded. Grasping the silver inlaid horn that hung at his side, he raised it to his lips.

As the haunting blare rose in pitch and moaned throughout the river valley, oars sliced the water again and the fleet leapt forward.

"Helmsman!" Saxulf roared furiously, twisting to glare at the Norseman who manipulated the rudder. "Can't you see those shoals? Go between them, you sluggard – through the willows!"

The oarsmen had found their pace and Saxulf's ship knifed through the water, slipping into the gap between sandbars.

Suddenly there was a loud crackle of splintering wood, followed by a severe jolt that pitched Saxulf head first into the river.

"Now!" Bran shouted.

The sky above the startled Vikings hailed death as the Leinstermen sprang forward and launched their projectiles. Arrows, spears and rocks found their targets on the decks of the encumbered vessels and within moments scores of bodies littered the longships or drifted aimlessly in the gentle current of the river. Missiles which had been soaked in pitch then set afire arced through the air, leaving trails of black smoke behind them like long demonic fingers ruthlessly clawing at the crippled flotilla from both shorelines. Some fell short of their intended marks, plunging harmlessly into the muddy water and dying with a distinct hiss. But others found the weathered planking of the longships, setting dozens of small fires that desperate hands struggled to extinguish. The furled sails of several ships had been ignited and they blazed atop the masts like giant torches, sending showers of embers and burning strips of fabric onto the heads of alarmed de-fenders.

At first, panic seized the Viking fleet. In addition to Saxulf's ship, three others had struck barricades. Unable to reduce their speed quickly enough, the vessels behind had collided into them, shearing off oars and rudders. One of the stranded longships had been rammed broadside, leaving a gaping hole in the hull that quickly flooded, causing the ves-sel to list heavily to one side.

But despite the initial success of the Irish attack, less than a third of the fleet had been seriously damaged. The captains of the vessels that were still maneuverable quickly turned their bows to shore, lessening the effect of the deadly volleys that continued to streak through the air. Shield walls were formed to protect those who manned the oars and the longships crept toward the opposing river banks. When the keels began to scrape bottom, hundreds of Norse and Danish warriors leapt into the chest–deep water, screaming wildly and hurling insults at their adversaries as they hastily waded ashore.

For nearly an hour, the Leinstermen contained them. The first wave of Vikings had died as they reached land, the Irish warriors easily cutting them down as they struggled ashore. But the foreigners had kept coming, hundreds upon hundreds of them, howling like men possessed as they flung themselves at the steadily thinning ranks. Overwhelmed by the superior numbers of their assailants, the clans of Leinster gradually began to fall back under the force of the murderous onslaught, leaving countless dead and wounded in their bloodied footsteps. Driven to the edge of the forest, their backs against the trees, the warriors were crowded so closely together that they could scarcely swing their swords for fear of striking a comrade.

Some of the men in the rear ranks broke and ran, oblivious to the branches and thorns that rended their flesh as they fled back through the thickets in wild–eyed terror. The Viking, seeing their incipient victims hopelessly trapped, intensified the ferocity of their attack.

Suddenly a single deep–toned battle cry, like the deafening roar of the great bear, rose above the din of combat and reverberated throughout the river valley.

"Ui Muiredaig!"

On both sides of the river Ragallach's warriors charged out of the woodlands, falling upon the exposed flanks of the bewildered Viking. Heartened by the arrival of their ally, the clansmen who had been so hard pressed only moments earlier surged forward, counterattacking with renewed vigor.

Confronted by the Irish on three sides, several Norsemen turned and fled.

"Tur–aie!" they cried as they scrambled into the water, desperate to reach the safety of their ships. "Thor help us!"

Oblivious to the deep gash in his thigh, Bran led his warriors forward, swinging his sword with hatred as he stepped over the bodies of fallen Leinstermen. But he felt neither remorse for his dead warriors nor pity for the enemy who now fell before him. There was only the cold emptiness of revenge. His savage blows exacted a bloody retribution from those who had violated his land and slaughtered his people. Nothing else mattered.

Then, through the countless melees that cluttered the

riverbank, Bran saw him.

The huge Dane stood, his long–handled battle–axe poised high above his head, aiming a final death blow at the wounded Leinsterman who lay helplessly on the sand beneath him. As the steel whistled through the air, the defenseless warrior threw up an arm as if to ward off the blow. The finely honed blade neatly severed the extended limb at the elbow and cleaved into the screaming man's torso, his blood splattering the black iron of his murderer's chainmail. The Dane jerked his weapon free of his still twitching victim and turned, his teeth bared as he glared at Bran.

A primeval cry of anguish and outrage erupted from Bran's throat as he charged the Dubh–gall. The heathen quickly adjusted his grip on the bloodied axe and shifted to a defensive stance, his feet planted wide apart, bracing himself against the frenzied assault.

Casting his shield aside, Bran grasped the hilt of his broadsword with both hands and struck wildly at his adversary. The Dane easily parried the blow to one side, then swung his battle–axe in a wide circle above his head, directing the blade toward his foe's exposed neck. Bran instinctively dropped to one knee, the deadly wedge passing harmlessly overhead. The Dane twisted slightly with the momentum of the stroke and Bran pivoted, slashing at his unguarded midsection.

The steel blade rang off the iron rings of the heavy chainmail, vibrating in Bran's hand. As the Dane regained his footing, he stepped back and smirked contemptuously.

"You cannot destroy me, Irishman," he taunted in broken Gaelic. "The blood of Thor courses through my veins."

"It will not remain there much longer," Bran snarled, then lunged forward, thrusting at the heathen's naked throat. Dodging aside with remarkable agility, the Dane hooked the sword blade with the head of his battle–axe and wrenched it in a circular motion, tearing the weapon from Bran's grasp and sending it careening off into the air.

In the instant that Bran's eyes flickered upward his opponent's shoulder slammed into his chest. Caught off balance, Bran clutched the cheek–pieces of the Dane's helmet and toppled backward, dragging the Viking down with him. The two men crashed heavily to the ground. Before Bran could recover, the black–bearded Dane was upon him, choking him with the handle of his battle–axe.

Bran gripped the iron shaft and pushed, arching his back with effort as he strained to relieve the pressure on his windpipe. But he could not match the power of the stocky Dane and the muscles in his arms soon began to weaken, the weight on his throat steadily increasing until he hoarsely gasped for air.

"Can you hear the cries of the Valkryies?" the heathen mocked between clenched teeth, his eyes gleaming with sadistic delight. "It is you they come for!"

The swarthy face above Bran began to blur and the discord of the fray around him gradually faded into the distance, replaced by the frantic tattoo of his own heartbeat. The aching sensation in his chest changed abruptly to intense pain and his arms dropped limply to his sides, his fingers brushing the dagger that hung at his belt. Willing his hand to grasp the hilt, he fumbled to unsheathe the weapon. When the blade was clear, he summoned the last reserves of strength he possessed and thrust upwards.

Then all was darkness.

CHAPTER NINETEEN

"Are you with us, lad?" The familiar voice reached Bran from somewhere beyond the blackness, invading the serene peace of the world he had found. He tried to ignore it, but an invisible hand gripped his shoulder and shook him with gentle persistence. "Can you hear me, my lord?"

As Bran slowly coaxed his eyes open, his refuge was flooded with a brilliant light and he winced. An excruciating pain shot through his temples. When his vision cleared, he looked up into Etach's drawn face.

"He is all right," the old soldier announced with marked relief, glancing over his shoulder at the warriors who were gathered around him. "The king lives!"

While the clansmen of Leinster cheered, Bran caught the sleeve of Etach's tunic and weakly raised himself on one elbow. "The Norsemen?" he croaked.

Etach grinned triumphantly. "The battle is ours, my lord. When the Ui Muiredaig arrived we drove the foreigners back to the river. Those who were not killed fled in their longships. You have brought us a great victory."

"This time," Bran muttered groggily, massaging his bruised throat. The image of the man who had nearly succeeded in killing him flashed through his mind. "There was a Dane among them. Was he..."

"There," Etach grunted, his lip curling with disdain as he thrust his chin forward. Bran turned his head slowly and stared into the lifeless eyes of the black heathen who lay sprawled beside him. The hilt of his dagger protruded from the dead man's side, the blade fixed through the centre of one of the iron rings that made up the Viking's chainmail. Reaching out, Bran grasped his weapon and wrenched it from the pallid corpse. The blood of Thor oozed out of the open wound.

"Had the blade struck a rib, the blow may have been deflected," Etach observed with cold objectivity. "You are indeed fortunate, my lord."

"As are we all." Bran sheathed the bloodied dagger. "And once again we are indebted to the Ui Muiredaig. I must speak with Ragallach."

With Etach's help, Bran struggled to his feet unsteadily. The acclamation of the clansman roared in his ears, their smiling faces spinning dizzily around him.

"Help me," he murmured, leaning inconspicuously against Etach amid the press of warriors. Instantly he felt the seasoned campaigner's iron grip tighten around his bicep.

"This way, my lord," Etach loudly advised, waving men aside as he guided him through the jubilant throng. "Make way for the king!"

"Long life to you, Bran Ui Faelain!" one warrior cried.

"God's blessings on you and yours!" another shouted, clapping him on the back as he passed.

Today you hail me as victor, Bran mused as he smiled and nodded back at the lauding warriors. *God help me if ever I fail you.*

When they were clear of the jubilant mass, the troops behind them began to disperse and Bran eased his arm out of his companion's grasp. "I'm all right now," he said, frowning as he surveyed the aftermath of the battle.

The damaged longships that the Viking had abandoned

along the barricades still blazed on the river like funeral pyres, thick clouds of slate–grey smoke rising like gigantic plumes against the crimson horizon. Along the shorelines, parties of warriors hurried about collecting the Irish dead, carefully laying the corpses shoulder to shoulder in neat rows at the forest's edge. The men worked quickly, anxious to conclude their grisly task before nightfall.

"It's an orderly profession, this killing," Bran mused to Etach. The veteran remained silent.

The Ui Muiredaig captain who was obviously responsible for the burial detail approached them and bowed formally, his clothes reeking of death.

"I have no orders for the heathen, my lord," the officer complained to Bran. "And the men refuse to bury them alongside our own warriors. What shall I do with them?"

Bran's eyes narrowed as he inspected the hundreds of bodies that littered the battlefield. "If we leave them to rot, these bastards will plague us in death even as they did in life." He paused for a moment, staring without seeing. "Burn them."

"My lord?" the bewildered captain exclaimed, raising an eyebrow.

"You heard me," Bran said flatly, looking into the shocked warrior's eyes. "Heap their bodies with kindling and set them afire. They have already taken too many lives."

The officer bowed, then turned to execute his instructions.

"Where is your chieftain?" Bran called after him. "I would speak with him."

"He has been wounded," the captain shouted back, pointing to a congregation at the river's edge. "His son attends him there, by the barricades."

Bran and Etach made their way to the beach where several noblemen and senior officers of the Ui Muiredaig clan had gathered into a tight circle, their heads bowed. Bran noted their ominous silence as he tapped the shoulder of one of the warriors in the rear rank.

"Ragallach Ui Muiredaig?" he whispered cautiously. "Where is he?" The soldier muttered something to his comrades and the lines parted, allowing Bran to step between the grim–faced men.

Rowan was kneeling next to his father, his hands still pressing a piece of blood soaked linen to the chieftain's chest. The glazed expression in the once mirthful eyes told Bran that Ragallach was dead. He moved to Rowan's side and gently laid a hand on his shoulder. The young warrior sat back on his heels and looked up, his bemired face streaked with tears.

"He... he gave up his life for you," Rowan stammered, lips quivering with emotion.

Bran pushed back the guilt that gnawed at him. "For all of us," he said softly. "For Leinster."

Rowan stared at him blankly for a moment, then closed his eyes and slowly nodded his head. "He told me there is but one clan in Leinster and that we are all a part of it." Turning back to his father, he reached out and gently closed the dead chieftain's eyes. "That is what he died for."

"Rowan... I – "

The unexpected sound of an angry voice behind him startled Bran. A burly officer was tussling with a spindle–legged boy who was desperately endeavouring to pass his antagonist.

The grubby youth suddenly slipped out of his grasp and darted to one side, but the Ui Muiredaig clansman caught the shoulder of his soiled tunic.

"This is no place for beggars," he boomed through his tangled red beard, roughly shoving the freckled–faced lad to the ground. "Be off with you!"

"Please," the boy persisted, scrambling to his feet. "You don't understand. I must see the king. I have travelled for two days and nights without pause to reach here."

The irate warrior took a menacing step toward him.

"Wait!" Bran ordered, astounded to hear the voice of his younger brother's bodyservant. "Let him through!"

The tattered boy bolted forward and dropped to his knees. "You must come at once, my lord. Conor..." The youth paused abruptly, gasping.

Panic surged through every nerve in Bran's body and he grabbed the frightened servant's arms, savagely dragging him to his feet.

"What about Conor?" he demanded, shaking him violently. "Where are the others? Speak up lad!"

"The Norse, my lord!" the terrified boy blurted out. "The Norsemen are at Bray!"

Bran rode all night, the legion of warriors that followed in his dusty wake lashing the flanks of their frothing horses to keep up with him as he raced for Bray. Distraught by the report of the Norse raid on the coastal village, he had hastily selected a thousand of his finest men to accompany him, leaving Flann to lead the remainder of the army back to Naas in anticipation of a possible counterattack by the defeated Vikings. Now, as he frantically galloped through the darkness, the haunting faces and voices of his loved ones flooded his memory, urging him on.

I was only trying to protect them, Bran agonized, regretting the decision that had placed his entire family in jeopardy. *With the heathen approaching Naas, I thought they would be safer in Bray. But fate has found a way to twist my intent and threaten the lives of those who are the very core of my existence. My family is my life. What will I do if they are... taken from me.*

God let them be safe, he prayed fervently as his heels hammered against his horse's ribs.

The following morning, as the rising sun slowly emerged from the aquamarine depths of the calm sea and bathed the deserted coastline in the resplendence of dawn, they reached the smoldering ruins that had been Bray. Reining their mounts in as they reached the outskirts, the warriors cautiously moved into the ravished village, the charred and gutted buildings silhouetted against the magenta of the morning skyline. Scenting blood, the horses pawed nervously at the ground and whinnied, their warm breath vaporizing in the chill air of daybreak while hazy tufts of steam hackled along their glossy, overheated hides.

Any hope that Bran had harbored of finding his family alive began to wane as he gaped in shock at the scene of the massacre. The twisted and mutilated bodies of Bray's wretched inhabitants, most of them women and children, lay strewn in disarray in the mud and turf, the stench of their rotting flesh pervading the air. Many of the corpses had been decapitated and the heads mounted on bloodstained poles, their glazed eyes grotesquely staring down at the spectacle beneath them. Bran fought back the bile he felt rising in his throat as he turned to Etach.

"There are few men among the dead," he said "Order the warriors to dismount and search the area. I want to know what happened to the men." He paused for a moment, then looked away. "And... the others," he quietly added, his voice constricted.

Before Etach could reply, Bran savagely kicked his horse forward, anxious to conceal the grief that threatened to overwhelm him. *They cannot be dead,* he thought, his mind resisting the jarring reality that his senses continue to thrust upon him. *God in his infinite mercy cannot have taken them from me!*

When he reached the chieftain's hall he reined in alongside the entrance and dismounted. The stone and mortar of the gathering place was still intact but the lime–washed walls had been stained a dirty grey with smoke and soot. A pile of ashes and partially incinerated bundles of kindling lay at the entry and the charred oak doors hung obliquely on their hinges, the surface of the carbonized wood scored in several places where it had been repeatedly struck with a battering ram. Bran stepped inside then doubled over and vomited, leaning against the wall for support as spasms of nausea racked his body.

Chairs, tables, anything that would burn had been stacked into the hearth in the centre of the chamber and put to the torch. Several corpses lay mangled among the ashes, blackened carcasses distorted beyond recognition. Those who had been spared the fate of being burned alive had been slaughtered where they stood and scores of bodies sprawled in bloodied heaps across the floor of the hall.

When the convulsions subsided, Bran drew himself weakly to his full height and filled his lungs with air, instinctively breathing through his mouth in an effort to shut out the sickly sweet malodour of roasted flesh. Moving from one corpse to the next, he set about the ordeal of searching for his loved ones among the dead. But the pallid faces he examined were unknown to him, their tormented features frozen in the pain and anguish of their final moments.

And then he saw her.

A few paces ahead of him the woman lay face down on the stone floor, the white bronze of her hair fanned out around her head like an angel's halo. The tip of a Viking spear protruded obscenely from her back, the broken haft of the weapon beside her.

For an instant Bran could not bring himself to move, his unblinking eyes fixed on the familiar silken tresses.

"Finola," he unconsciously muttered to himself, then staggered forward and knelt beside the woman's head. His hand shaking, he grasped her shoulder and gently eased her onto her back. To his horror he discovered that she had died while clutching her infant to her breast, the spear having passed through both mother and child, pinning them together. But their faces were those of strangers and Bran sat back heavily on his heels, his chest heaving with emotion.

"Thank God," he signed, but the relief of his own suffering was quickly replaced by a profound sense of anger and guilt, and he slammed his fists into the ground in fury.

I am not worthy to be king, he thought bitterly. *I rejoice at finding a lady and child such as this murdered along with hundreds of my innocent subjects. My joy is for my own kindred, without regard for those who entrusted themselves to my protection. If I had…*

"My lord," a deep–toned voice beckoned him from the doorway. "Your brother has been found."

Springing to his feet, Bran dashed over to the warrior and clutched the front of his tunic. "Where? Is he alive?"

"I know not, my lord," the startled man replied. "Etach is with him now at the water's edge."

Roughly pushing the man aside, Bran charged out of the chieftain's hall and through the village. As he reached the edge of the beach he saw Etach stooped over the prostrate figure in the sand. Oblivious to the hundreds of bodies that lay about him, Bran slowed his pace to a cautious walk.

"He is dead, my lord," Etach said solemnly, his grey eye glistening.

Bran squatted beside his younger brother, staring. Conor lay with his head to one side, his skull cracked and his brain spilling out onto mother earth. All that had been the younger son of Crimthan Ui Faelain – the imagination, the dreams, the love – was gone, terminated with the single blow from a Viking club.

Bran tilted his head back and screamed, then threw himself across his brother.

"No! No!" he lamented, cradling the limp body in his arms.

"You must come away from here, my lord," Etach begged, pulling him to his feet. "There is nothing you can do for him now. You must think of your wife and child."

"You have found them?" Bran asked anxiously. "Are they safe?"

Etach shook his head. "Neither they nor your sister have been found among the dead. But there are signs of a struggle just beyond the village. We can but assume they have been taken as slaves."

It was well known how the foreigners treated their female captives, and the thought tortured Bran. He turned and paced away from Etach, his head lowered. He had always been able to view the Viking atrocities with a certain degree of detachment; as reprehensible crimes against the other peoples of Erin that nevertheless had left the clans of Leinster unscathed. Now the heathen had shattered his world, killing and abducting members of his own family. Now, the war with the Viking took on a new perspective and his soul called out for blood.

"Hear me!" he cried, pivoting to face his warriors. "All of you! My obsession with peace has cost the lives of these good people, my own brother among them. And my wife and son have been taken by the Viking, lost to an unknown fate. Until now we have been secure within our borders and have idly looked on while the rest of Erin has been systematically butchered by the heathens. But no more!"

He grasped the hilt of his sword and drew it out of its scabbard, brandishing the gleaming weapon.

"Norse and Danish blood shall be the eraic for the foul murders of our countrymen and it shall be exacted until the foreigners have rendered every drop unto us! From this time forward, the clans of Leinster will not rest until every trace of the invader is driven from our homeland!"

The eyes of the wolf gleamed in the hilt as Bran swung his father's sword above his head.

"Death to the Viking! Ui Faelain Abu!" he roared, his voice quivering with fury.

A hundred blades flashed in the afternoon sun as the warriors of Leinster took up the chant.

"Ui Faelain Abu! Victory to the Ui Faelain!"

CHAPTER TWENTY

Four days later, word of the Viking incursions into Leinster reached Cashel and that same evening the great hall resounded with drunken jubilation as the men of Munster celebrated the misfortunes of their long–standing enemy. Goblets were raised in salute to the foreigners, men calling them comrades and allies, and the warriors excitedly speculated among themselves how such an alliance could easily lead to the defeat of their common foe. Little more than a year had passed since they had been caught between the combined forces of Niall Caille and Crimthan Ui Faelain, and the subsequent tribute that Munster had been compelled to render to the tanaiste of the slain king had served as a constant reminder of the bitter defeat they had suffered. But even as they cursed the man responsible for their disgrace, great care was taken not to abuse the name of the Ui Faelain, for fear of offending the outsider who had so quickly come to be a power in the court of Cashel.

Kenan sat at Feidlimid's right hand and drank to the invasion of Leinster. His stay in Cashel had not yet seen the passing of one moon and yet in that time Feidlimid had taken him into his confidence, at least to a limited degree. In addition to being given all the rights and privileges normally afforded his rank, the king of Cashel had entrusted him with the task of collecting and accounting for the tribute which all landholders and merchants were required by law to submit, a gratifying chore which Feidlimid had previously attended to himself with great relish. But as Kenan had suspected, his preferential treatment rankled many of the warriors and noblemen who had faithfully served their king for years and found it strange that he would entrust a position of such prestige and responsibility to a man who only weeks earlier had been their sworn enemy. Though Kenan himself had not fully understood Feidlimid's reasoning he had ignored the disapproving frowns and the dagger eyes, graciously accepting the honour which had been bestowed upon him, reasoning that the rejection of Feidlimid's generosity would seriously jeopardize his future ability to lay claim to the throne of Leinster. Now as he surveyed the faces around him in the great hall, he looked into the eyes of those he knew to be his enemies and smiled.

Never before have I felt such contempt and hatred, he thought. *Not even from my brother's lackeys back home in Leinster.*

Leinster. Home.

As the Munstermen around him made sport of the massacre at Bray, Kenan felt himself beginning to withdraw, raising his goblet less frequently as the toasts became more outrageous and obscene. *What is it?* he asked himself, perplexed by the unexpected wave of emotion that was sweeping through him. *Why is it I feel such an affinity for the people they mock? It is not I but my brother who is responsible for their deaths. Had he negotiated a treaty with the Viking there would not have been a raiding party and their lives would have been spared. Such is the price of ill-advised loyalty.*

But they were Leinstermen, the voice inside him whispered.

"Why are you not drinking, my friend?" Feidlimid drawled, leaning unsteadily on the armrest of his chair as he peered at Kenan with bloodshot eyes. "It would seem the heathen have found some way to read our thoughts, for they have done the very thing we would have petitioned them to do. Soon, Leinster will be ours."

Kenan held out his goblet to be refilled by a passing servant. "I do not think it would be prudent, my lord, to dismiss Leinster or my brother too hastily. The village that these fearsome Norsemen raided had few or no warriors, and those who met with resistance near Naas were quickly routed. I mean no insult to you, but the Viking accomplished nothing for us."

"Perhaps we misjudged your brother's strength," Feidlimid agreed, nodding his head slowly. "Some of the reports I have received suggested that he would have been defeated had it not been for the support of the clanna Ui Muiredaig. And yet the woman from Mullaghmast assured us they would not ally themselves with Bran against the Norsemen." He raised his thick, dark eyebrows and leaned forward. "Could she have been... mistaken?"

"No, your grace," Kenan answered with stiff formality. "I have no cause to doubt the lady's word. I think it more likely that the Viking fleet found themselves less capable of dealing with armed warriors than they are defenseless women and children."

Feidlimid studied him in silence for a moment, then leaned back and grinned wryly. "You underestimate Thorgest, my friend. What you perceive as an invasion is little more than a test and this so—called defeat has only served to whet his appetite for conquest. When he is ready, Thorgest will return. And I promise you, he will not stop until your brother is destroyed."

Kenan drained the contents of his goblet and set it heavily on the table. "And once this barbarian has conquered Leinster, I suppose he will simply hand the crown over to me?"

Feidlimid eyed him in silence. "I feel the need for some air," he said suddenly, rising with cumbersome purpose from his seat. "Attend me."

Kenan followed him through the great hall and down a long passageway at the end of which a stone-faced sentry guarded a single door. As they approached, the warrior saluted stiffly, then opened the door and stepped briskly aside. Striding past him, they stepped out into the cool night air.

The king's garden was surrounded by a towering stone wall that encompassed the grounds in one continuous circle but for the iron gate on the far side of the enclosure at which another guard was constantly posted. Iron torch brackets had been set into the mortar between the stones so that even at night Feidlimid's private retreat was well illuminated.

Having only admired the conservatory from a distance, Kenan was awed at the diversity of flowers and the manner in which they had been arranged into a series of elaborate geometric patterns. Violets, primroses and numerous other species of wildflower formed the loops and spirals of traditional Celtic design, covering the ground like an intricate woven tapestry.

"How sweet their fragrance," Feidlimid sighed, taking obvious delight in the aromatic scents that filled the air as he escorted Kenan along the cobblestone walkway that had been unobtrusively incorporated into the device.

"You still have not answered my question, your grace," Kenan said irritably, annoyed by Feidlimid's apparent complacency. "How can I be certain that the Norse will respect my claim to the throne once they have invaded Leinster?"

Feidlimid shrugged. "Thorgest already knows that it will be to his advantage to do so, for he has come to understand that the Irish will never bow to a foreign overlord. He will rule the kingdom by proxy, through a Leinsterman of royal blood. And so you see, your concern is unfounded. In time, you will ascend the throne and rule as king of Leinster. But you will also be Thorgest's vassal – or so we shall allow him to think."

"What are you talking about?"

Ignoring the question, Feidlimid walked ahead a short distance then turned and gestured expansively.

"My garden is exquisite, don't you think? See how the flowers are combined to form a singular design, a pleasing contrivance comprised of numerous individual blossoms. Each one has been precisely positioned where I have chosen it to be, so that it enhances rather than contradicts the overall beauty of the arrangement."

He squatted and gently cupped the delicate petals of a primrose in his pudgy hands. "I planted and nurtured these myself," he remarked, smiling up at Kenan. Abruptly, he seized the stem of the plant and viciously uprooted it. "But each may be just as easily removed, without significant loss to the conception as a whole."

Struggling to his feet, Feidlimid sniffed indifferently at the flower, then casually tossed it aside.

"So it is with you, my friend. It is I, not Thorgest, who

is placing you on the throne of Leinster, where you will remain for as long as I can depend on your loyalty. There are others like yourself, men of royal blood in Meath and Connacht, that we will assist in attaining their... rightful claims. In time, with four of the provinces controlled by Cashel, Niall Caille will be forced to concede Ulster and acknowledge my authority as Ard–Ri." He suddenly clapped Kenan on the shoulder and grinned seditiously. "In the meantime, let us cater to Thorgest's inflated ego a little longer."

Kenan grinned back at him. *And for now I will have to tolerate this bloated swine a little longer*, he thought. *But the day will come when he finds that it is a king he has placed upon the throne of Leinster – and not a pawn.*

"Your stratagems astound me, my lord. But surely Thorgest will not present Leinster to me merely on the strength of your recommendation. I have never even met Thorgest."

Feidlimid winked. "Oh, but you will. Tomorrow you will lead the trader's caravan to his base at Lough Ree. He will be expecting you."

Although Kenan was well aware that Feidlimid was in constant communication with Thorgest with regards to commerce, he found it unnerving to think that he himself had been a subject for discussion between the two leaders.

"Suppose he does not favour your proposal and flatly rejects my petition?"

"I assure you he will not. Thorgest is nearly as shrewd a merchant as he is a soldier, and as such will not risk disrupting trade by insulting my representative. Besides, I have arranged for you to personally present him with a gift that will place him in your debt – and mine."

Kenan frowned, puzzled by Feidlimid's confidence. "What prize in all Erin would compel Thorgest to such gratitude?"

"Not what – who," Feidlimid whispered in a conspiratorial voice. "When you arrive at Lough Ree, you will deliver Forannan into Thorgest's hands. His wife has long been obsessed with capturing the archbishop of Armagh, insisting that he be brought to her alive." He clasped his hands behind his back and shook his head in mock solemnity. "But it is my understanding that he will not remain so for long once that she–devil has her hands on him."

In spite of himself, Kenan could not help but admire the meticulously woven intrigues that Feidlimid's intellect had spun. "And with Forannan disposed of, you will naturally take his place as head of the church in Erin," he said admiringly. "You have moved with the agility of a master swordsman, your grace. In one motion, you have eliminated a dangerous rival, strengthened your alliance with the Norsemen, and ensured that the crown of Leinster will be mine."

"Such is the nature of trade," the king of Cashel responded haughtily. "In any venture, the acquisition must always be greater than the initial investment."

Kenan nodded appreciatively as he stared at the ground, scuffing his sandals across the smooth cobblestones. "Aye. There is much that I have yet to learn from – "

"My lord! My lord Kenan!" a strident voice called out from the gate at the opposite end of the garden. Illuminated in the jaundiced glow of the flickering torchlight, a buxom maidservant jumped up and down repeatedly, waving at him from behind the brawny sentry who barred her path.

"Let her pass," Feidlimid ordered, waving the guard aside. As the warrior stepped back, the flustered maidservant scurried to Kenan's side and grasped the sleeve of his tunic.

"You must come at once, my lord!" the plump–faced matron wheezed. "Your lady is grievous ill and has taken to bed!"

"Calm yourself," Kenan insisted, pulling his arm free of the fretting servant's hold. "That is not uncommon for a women whose belly is swollen with child. Why do you bother me with this?"

The anxious woman shook her head insistently. "It is more than that, my lord. Please... the physician is with her now and she is asking for you."

The desperation in the old servant's voice alarmed Kenan and he glanced quickly at Feidlimid.

"Do not await my permission," the Munster king grunted. "Go to her, man! Were she my woman, I would this moment be as her shadow."

Kenan bowed curtly to him, then turned and followed the portly maidservant across the garden. When they reached the courtyard, she hiked her skirts up above her ankles and scuttled on ahead, shouting back at him over her shoulder.

"Hurry, my lord! There may be little time!"

Kenan broke into a run, darting past the puffing maid-servant. Panicked by the prospect of losing the only woman he had ever truly loved, he charged ahead blindly, fear twist-ing at his insides.

Taillte had arrived in Cashel less than a fortnight ear-lier, throwing herself at his feet and begging forgiveness for having spurned his love. "I never truly realized what we had together," she had told him, her eyes brimming with tears. When she described in minute detail the beatings and abuse she had suffered at Rowan's hands, Kenan had become furious and swore that her tormentor would pay for his cruelty with his life. Her voice quivering, Taillte had explained how she had longed to escape but chose instead to remain until she had managed to convince Rowan that an alliance with Bran Ui Faelain against the Norsemen would ultimately jeopardize the future of the Ui Muiredaig. Only after she was certain that she had fulfilled Kenan's request had she fled and sought him out.

Her sincerity had moved Kenan deeply and as he had taken her in his arms, he wished for nothing more than to love and protect her. The fact that she was pregnant with Rowan's child had not mattered. He would raise the child as his own. Soon the dream that had sustained him all his life would be fulfilled, he would reign as king of Leinster with Taillte by his side as queen.

But now, as he ran through the darkness toward his chambers, Kenan felt his destiny slipping away. Without Taillte, there was no future.

The wind picked up suddenly, howling between the stone and mortar houses like an abandoned hound baying for its master. The rain began to fall in a light drizzle, then moments later descended in relentless torrents that quickly soaked through to Kenan's skin, making his garments cling to his flesh. When he reached the door to his quarters he was outraged to find it bolted from the inside and he hammered furiously against the sturdy oak with the palm of his hand, loudly cursing the downpour.

Almost immediately the door swung open and a tall, hawk–faced man with delicate features stepped outside placing one hand against Kenan's chest while the other gently eased the door closed behind him. There were few men in Cashel who could have restrained Kenan at that moment, but Cormac was one of them. He had gained Kenan's respect. From the first day of his arrival, when the quiet physician had attended to his retainers' wounds, Kenan had developed an instant liking for this man whose humanity was not clouded by tribal boundaries or loyalties.

A jagged bolt of lightning flashed overhead and Kenan stared at the splotches of blood on the physician's tunic.

"She has lost the child," Cormac said.

Thunder rumbled across the distant hills.

"Is she all right? Kenan asked nervously, wiping the rain from his face. "What in the name of God happened?"

"The infant came too soon," Cormac explained softly, "She kept muttering something about a riding accident back at Mullaghmast."

Kenan remembered all too well Taillte telling him how Rowan had caused her mount to rear and throw her the day before she left Mullaghmast. Now, hatred seethed within him.

"And would the child have been..."

"It would have been a boy," Cormac answered softly.

"I must see her," Kenan uttered, pushing Cormac aside.

The physician caught his arm as he passed. "Do not stay long. She has lost much blood and I know that you do not want to bear the weight of her death upon your shoulders."

Kenan stared at Cormac in dismay.

"Will she live?"

The lightning flashed again, reflecting in the physician's eyes. "I do not know," he answered quietly.

Kenan pushed past him and flung the door open. The tallow candles in the far corners of the small chamber flickered in the sudden draft, the ghostly shields of iridescent light wavering along the mortar walls while shadows thrown by the furniture mysteriously pulsated along the floor. His eyes fixed on the huge bed which dominated the centre of the room, Kenan eased the door closed behind him then slowly moved across to the maidservant who stooped near the delicately carved headboard, gently sponging the face of the unconscious woman who lay before her.

"Out," he croaked hoarsely, choking back his grief as he took the moistened cloth from her. The servant looked up at him sympathetically, then nodded and hurried from the room. His eyes brimming with tears, Kenan reached out and touched the long black hair that he had so often dreamed of caressing again.

Taillte lay with her cheek resting against one shoulder, her raven tresses twisting into wet tendrils that spilled over the ivory flesh of her shoulders and bosom. Perspiration beaded her forehead and upper lip, the tiny rivulets that trickled down her temple glistening bronze in the candlelight, her creamy breast heaving irregularly with each shallow breath.

"Even though death threatens to take you as his mistress," Kenan whispered softly as he pressed the linen to her brow, "you remain as beautiful as when first I saw you."

Taillte moaned and passed her tongue over her pale,

chapped lips. The long dark eyelashes fluttered slightly and she slowly opened her eyes, the corners of her mouth curling into the hint of a smile as she drowsily looked up at him. "You came," she murmured weakly.

"How could I not?" Kenan took her delicate hand in his. Her flesh was cold and he knew that she lay within death's icy embrace. "You know I have never been able to deny you anything."

Sorrow suddenly flooded Taillte's emerald eyes and she squeezed his hand tightly. "Forgive me, my lord... the baby..."

"The fault is not yours, lady," Kenan interrupted, touching his fingers to her lips. "There will be other children. We have the rest of our lives together to raise a family of our own."

Taillte abruptly turned her head away from him, sobbing in anguish. "You do not understand – there will be no more children! How can I ask you to spend your life with a woman who cannot bear your sons and daughters?"

Kenan gently lifted her chin, drawing her face toward him. "It matters not. I have you in my life and that's all the love I have ever needed. Without you, I am less than nothing."

"I made the mistake of leaving you once," she whispered. "I will not do so again."

Kenan bent down and lightly kissed her forehead. "The pain of this night's misery will fade and disappear amidst the joy that awaits us in the days to come. But we will talk of that later. For now, you must rest." He turned to leave, but Taillte held his hand firmly.

"I will never rest," she gasped weakly. "Not so long as

the man who did this to me lives. Promise me, Kenan. Promise me that my dead son will be avenged."

Kenan took her in his arms and buried his face in her silken hair. "I promise you, my love," he muttered in a voice that vibrated with constrained hatred and fury. "Rowan Ui Muiredaig will pay for his crime in blood."

CHAPTER TWENTY-ONE

Five days later Kenan left for Lough Ree. When he had expressed his concern for Taillte's condition, Feidlimid had agreed to delay the departure of the trader's caravan. Kenan had then remained at Taillte's side throughout the day and night, insuring that she was continually attended by her maidservants and insisting that Cormac, the physician, look in on her every few hours. Within a few days, the colour had begun to return to her face and although he noted that she was still weak from her ordeal, Kenan knew that the worst of his fears had been allayed. He rode out of Cashel confident that the life they had begun together would be restored to them upon his return.

The foothills of the Ardagh mountains gradually gave way to the Nor valley and from there Kenan led the caravan north along the grassy heaths that fringed the banks of the River Shannon.

As they drew nearer their destination, the prospect of willingly entering the Viking stronghold gradually became less appealing to Kenan. He had never actually seen a Norseman or a Dane. His knowledge of them was restricted to the terrifying stories that recounted their savagery and ruthlessness. He wondered with uncertainty how a civilized man would fare among such barbarians. In the end he concluded that despite his fears there was no other option; his entire future depended on the outcome of his meeting with Thorgest.

On the third day of their journey the caravan reached Lough Ree and Kenan was far less impressed with the beauty of the woodlands surrounding the picturesque lake than he was by the proportions of the Norse fleet. Hundreds of ships of every size, some of them large enough to carry a small army, were anchored in the tranquil harbour as testament to the Viking's power.

Beyond the waterfront lay Thorgest's stronghold. Although larger than the dun at Naas, Kenan thought it crude by Irish standards for little mortar and stone had been used in its construction. Palisades and watchtowers of rough-hewn timbers surrounded scores of tightly clustered buildings, most of which appeared to be constructed of wood planking. He could not help but speculate how easily the entire garrison would be consumed by fire.

As they approached the main gate, several fair-haired warriors in conical helmets emerged and stood barring their entry, shields before them and weapons drawn. Kenan signaled the caravan to halt, then rode forward. As he reined in his horse before them, a huge Viking in a leather vest stepped forward, the muscles in his tanned arms rippling as he shifted his battle-axe from one hand to the other.

"What is it you seek, Irishman?" he grunted in broken Gaelic, scowling behind his neatly pointed beard.

Kenan ignored the insulting tone and gestured to the carts behind him. "We bring all manner of goods from Feidlimid of Cashel, to trade at your chieftain's pleasure."

The Norseman cocked his head and eyed him dubiously. "I have not seen you before. Where is the man who usually leads the merchants?"

"I have come in his stead," Kenan explained, "as a special envoy from the King of Munster to deliver a gift of great value to the mighty Thorgest."

The man hesitated as if unwilling to take responsibility for whichever decision he made. "Wait here," he ordered, then turned and ran back through the main gate. Kenan shifted uncomfortably under the watchful eyes of the remaining Vikings who stood poised to strike should he be foolish enough to move in a threatening manner. To his relief, the Norseman returned a short time later and waved him forward.

"Follow me," he shouted from the gate.

Signaling to the carts behind him, Kenan kicked his horse forward. Within the palisade walls, the town bustled with activity. Children were playing, people arguing, merchants hawking their wares, all in a tongue that sounded like guttural gibberish to him. The narrow street was a sea of mud and fresh dung and their progress was slow, for they had to stop periodically in order to free carts that had become stranded in the mire. The air reeked of manure, the stench further compounded by the rotting flesh of animal carcasses that hung from projections above the doors of the wooden houses.

As they made their way toward the centre of the town, Kenan wondered how so barbarous a people had come to be the masters of nearly half of Erin.

After a time they reached the hub of the community and Kenan's guide pointed to the large building which commanded the area. "Thorgest's firehall," the man grunted.

Kenan nodded and dismounted, following him to the iron–studded doors at the entrance. The Norseman pivoted suddenly, slamming his open hand into Kenan's chest.

"You will not need that here," he said, his eyes moving to the sword that hung at Kenan's side. Unfastening his sword belt, Kenan handed him the weapon, then stepped into the firehall.

Warriors in various stages of drunkenness slouched at tables around the blazing open hearth in the centre of the room drinking, singing, and hurling insults along with the occasional piece of crockery at the miserable juggler who was still struggling to entertain his unappreciative audience. Some of the jarls had fallen into wine–induced slumber, snoring loudly as they slept beneath or on top of the tables, oblivious to their comrades who precariously danced around them. In the midst of the pandemonium, two Vikings who had stripped to the waist wrestled each other on the floor, blood streaming down their faces as they rolled dangerously close to the crackling flames.

Kenan was led through the mayhem to the opposite end of the hall where two warriors, apparently unconcerned with the uproar around them, sat quietly talking at a table that had been set apart from the others. The Norseman who had escorted Kenan stooped and spoke briefly to one of the men, a blond giant whose curt manner bespoke authority. From Feidlimid's description Kenan knew that he was looking at the Viking leader who had organized the systematic rape of Erin.

Dismissing Kenan's escort, Thorgest leaned forward and casually skewered a piece of meat from the platter in front of him and stuffed it into his mouth, washing it down with a draught of wine. He wiped his lips with the back of his arm and leaned back in his chair, his feet propped up on the table.

Only then did he raise his eyes to Kenan.

"You are late," he stated in flawless Gaelic. The dark–haired Viking beside him leaned forward and peered at Kenan, his black eyes like those of a hawk.

"Our delay was unavoidable, Lord Thorgest," Kenan replied, trying to control the quaver in his voice.

Thorgest nodded and sucked his teeth loudly. "So you are the would–be king of Leinster." Several of the men around him snickered.

Kenan's face flushed. "I am called Kenan, eldest son to Crimtha –"

"I know who you are," Thorgest interrupted. "And why you are here. You wish to steal the crown from your brother, do you not?"

"My brother is a usurper who..."

Thorgest waved the remark aside. "You need not tell me of your brother. I lost many good men to him on the banks of the Liffey. Those who escaped with their lives already speak as if he were a great warrior–king, a legend; calling him 'Wolfblade' and swearing that they heard his broadsword howl as it sliced through the air towards its victims." As the firehall grew abruptly silent, he glanced at the dark Viking beside him, then turned back to Kenan. "Some say that the Leinster king was slain by Ragnar's own brother, but that this – this Wolfblade returned from the underworld and fought Saxulf again. Our comrade did not return with the others and it is said that he now sits at Oden's right hand in Valhalla."

"You speak of Bran as if he were a god or demon," Kenan said, bemused by the superstitious yarn. "I assure you, lord Thorgest, my brother is naught but flesh and blood."

"I would welcome the opportunity to determine that for myself," Ragnar interjected. "Saxulf's spirit will not rest until his death is avenged."

"You will have your chance, my friend," Thorgest told him. "The next time we face the Leinsterman there will be little doubt as to the outcome." He turned to Kenan. "And with your brother dead, the path will be clear for you to seize the crown – providing your countrymen agree to pay tribute to us."

Kenan shook his head emphatically. "The people of Leinster will never pay tribute to Norsemen. I will have to collect it on your behalf. They will not object to rendering the king what is rightfully his. What amount do you propose to seek each year?"

"Fully one half of the kingdom's wealth."

"Lord Thorgest!" Kenan exclaimed, staring at him in astonishment. "Not even the high king commands such tribute from his provinces. If we are to succeed at all, you must allow me to extract such tribute gradually, and over a period of years it may be steadily increased. We would begin the first year with a quarter, increasing that to a third the second year and so on. After all, we cannot drag the people down into the very depths of poverty. The highest percentage of a kingdom that is not prosperous is worth little."

Thorgest stroked his golden beard thoughtfully. "Agreed. But how can we be certain that your chieftains will ultimately be prepared to negotiate with us?"

"It is the council of elders in Naas and not the clan chieftains that will make such decisions. And once they are convinced war is the only alternative, I am certain that they will be anxious to consent to any solution which will restore peace to Leinster."

"But will they follow you?" Thorgest asked insistently, frowning. "Will they make you king?"

"They will have little choice," Kenan replied, smiling confidently. "As I am the only nobleman of royal blood who will be in a position to negotiate with you, they must be prepared to pay the price of insuring that their land and its people are not destroyed." Kenan paused, savouring the moment. "And my price is the crown of Leinster."

Thorgest shifted in his seat, his eyes narrowing. "I find it difficult to believe that a man who can so callously plot his brother's death and betray his own people can be loyal to anyone other than himself. Can such a man be trusted?"

"We must trust each other," Kenan retorted. "Without you, I have no hope of reclaiming my birthright. Without me, you face a long and bloody war against a people who, though they be conquered, will never yield to you." Kenan paused to allow the weight of his words to take effect. "I know my people, Lord Thorgest, and they will never allow anyone other than a Leinster king to govern them."

Thorgest studied him in silence for a moment, then threw back his head and laughed. "I see now that Feidlimid's confidence in you has not been misplaced," he said smiling. "You will indeed make a capable king."

"You honour me when it is I who have come to pay homage to you," Kenan replied, bowing deeply. "Allow me to return the compliment by presenting you with a token of my gratitude, along with the regards of Feidlimid Ui Owenachta, King of Munster."

He marched across to the main doors and signaled his retainers, then strode back to stand at Thorgest's side. A few moments later two stocky warriors entered the firehall, escorting an old man in tattered clothes between them. As he was brought to stand before Kenan the patriarch's eyes widened and he launched into a tirade of colourful maledictions.

"Your black heart will burn for all eternity in the fires of hell, Kenan Ui Faelain! Satan himself has his paw on – "

The backhanded blow that Kenan delivered to his temple sent the old man reeling backwards, and he fell unconscious to the ground.

Kenan pivoted on his heel and grinned. "Lord Thorgest, may I present Forannan, Archbishop of Armagh."

Thorgest rose abruptly from his seat and stared dumbfounded at the crumpled heap. He gazed back at Kenan. "My wife will indeed be pleased. For many months she has longed to... make this holy man our guest. Einar! Fjolnir!" he called out, summoning two of his warriors. "Take this grey beard to the sacred oak and guard him well until morning. Otta will doubtless wish him to... participate in the festival of Uppsala tomorrow."

As the two burly Norsemen dragged the limp archbishop away, Thorgest whispered to Ragnar, who grinned, then hurried after them.

"Come, share my table," the Norse leader told Kenan, guiding him into Ragnar's place. When they were seated, he filled their goblets with wine. "I have sent Ragnar to prepare quarters for you and your men. As is our custom, I am obliged to render onto you a *heriot* in exchange for your oath of allegiance. But rather than merely providing you with the horses and armour that are your legal due, I have arranged for a special gift that I hope you will find... more pleasurable." He tilted his head back arrogantly, squaring his shoulders. "Like the Irish, we too pride ourselves on our hospitality."

Kenan raised his goblet in salute. "I am overwhelmed by your generosity, Lord Thorgest. I swear that from this day forward I will serve you as a loyal ally."

Thorgest smiled, his blue eyes sparkling. "It would be foolish to do otherwise."

Two hours and several flagons of wine later, Kenan staggered slightly as he followed Ragnar through the moonlit streets of the Viking settlement, the light from the Dane's torch waving erratically along the walls of the wooden buildings as they made their way to the cluster of *shielings* on the outer perimeter of the town. The shutters and doors of the small houses were barred from the outside and at first Kenan assumed that the simple structures were either pinfolds or storage sheds. But Ragnar suddenly stepped to the entrance of one such dwelling and began to lift up the thick timber which secured the door.

"What are you doing?" Kenan asked in amazement. "Does your chieftain usually insult his guests by providing them with such paltry accommodations?"

Ragnar laid the heavy beam against the wall and chuckled. "These are not your quarters – these are *thralls'* quarters. Your chambers are on the other side of the compound. Lord Thorgest ordered that your heriot be brought here where you may find it somewhat more manageable." Lifting the latch, he opened the door and smiled at Kenan. "I envy you, Irishman. Gladly would I surrender my own quarters to be in your place for but an hour this night." Offering him the torch, Ragnar motioned him inside. "I will return for you at dawn."

Kenan hesitated, a strange sense of foreboding sweeping through him. Even so, he knew that he could not risk offending Thorgest by refusing his hospitality. He accepted the torch from Ragnar and stepped inside.

Instantly, the door slammed shut and panic engulfed him as he heard the heavy timber drop with a thud into place. He threw his weight against it in a frenzy to escape, but it would not budge.

"Enjoy yourself, Irishman," Ragnar called to him. Kenan pressed his ear against the thick wood and listened until the Dane's footsteps faded into the night. Then, but for the crackling of his torch, there was silence.

Kenan leaned his forehead against the door. *Am I a prisoner?* he wondered. *A hostage? For what purpose? It does not make sense for them to hold me when there is no one who would pay for my release. I knew something was wrong. I knew I shouldn't have come to Lough Ree.*

A sudden noise in the far corner of the room startled him and he spun about sharply, reaching for his sword. But his scabbard was empty. He remembered relinquishing his weapons to the Norseman before entering the firehall. Holding the torch high above his head, he peered into the darkness. Across the room, a figure moved within the shadows.

"Who's there? Show yourself!"

An ominous shape moved forward, gradually taking the form of a woman as it drew near to him. She wore a shift of blue linen that fell to her feet but the back of the robe was longer, trailing in pleats and folds behind her. A knotted girdle held the dress in place at her waist and she wore tortoise brooches on both collar bones which were linked by festoons of silver chains. Her hair was pulled into a knot at the nape of her neck and hung loosely down her back, mingled with ribbons. As she stepped out of the darkness the torchlight shimmered along the white bronze of her flowing tresses.

"Finola!" Kenan uttered, taken aback at the apparition before him. "How the devil did you get here?"

Finola jerked her head up, her violet eyes widening. "Kenan!" she proclaimed excitedly, rushing forward and embracing him. "I never thought to see any of you again!" Then she looked up at him. "We were in Bray when a raiding party attacked and took us captive," she said quietly. "Conor is dead. But Muireen and I, along with Morallta and young Devlin, were spared and brought to this place." Abruptly, Finola touched her fingers to her lips. "Merciful father! Then you are also a prisoner. Tell me, what has become of Bran? Don't tell me he's – "

"Dead?" Kenan asked, raising his eyebrows. "Oh no. The whore–son still lives. But that oversight will soon be corrected."

Finola backed away from him nervously. "Can it be you hate Bran so much that your obsession pursues you even now? Here?"

Kenan wedged the torch into a gap between the wood planing on the wall then slowly paced across the room, moving behind her. "You still don't understand, do you?" he whispered in her ear. "With Feidlimid of Munster and the Norsemen as my allies, Bran is all that stands between me and the throne." He laid his hand on her shoulder. "And that means he is not long for this world."

Finola whirled and slapped at his face, her arms flailing wildly. "Traitor! Coward!"

Kenan caught her wrists and she struggled in his grasp, kicking at his legs. "You are indeed a woman of spirit," he murmured, leering openly at the curves of her body. "What pleasure you must have brought to my brother's bed each night! I must remember to thank Thorgest for so fine a gift."

Finola spat in his face. "Only a mud–sucking pig would ally himself with murderers and thieves!"

Restraining her with one hand, Kenan slowly wiped the spittle from his cheek. "What has become of your courtly manners? Such behaviour does not befit a woman of your noble bearing. No more than those Norse rags you wear." In one deft motion, he reached out and tore the front of her robe open.

Breaking free of him, Finola cautiously backed toward the door, her arms covering her exposed breasts.

"They took everything!" Kenan bellowed. "Your husband and your brother took everything that was mine!" He began to stalk her. "Tonight I will repay them in kind."

"Bran will kill you for this," Finola whimpered, trembling.

"I don't think so," Kenan replied, smiling maliciously. "But before I kill him, I will make a point of telling him how much I enjoyed this night."

Finola turned and frantically hammered on the door, crying for help.

Then Kenan was upon her. As he grabbed her she

twisted around and raised her hand to slap him.

Kenan struck her repeatedly, pummeling her with his fists, his hatred and fury rushing in a floodtide that would not be checked. Beating her, stripping her, in a frenzy of revenge.

Wrestling her to the floor, Kenan pinned her beneath him, his fingers cruelly pinching and prodding her tender flesh.

"No!" she pleaded, gasping for air. "No!"

Forcing her legs apart, Kenan fumbled with his clothes, then lowered himself onto her.

Finola screamed again and again.

CHAPTER TWENTY-TWO

The next morning dusty beams of sunlight squeezed between the wooden planking of the shieling and stabbed through the gloomy interior. Finola woke with a start on the hardened dirt floor, wincing and sucking in her breath sharply at the throbbing pain between her thighs. Furtively she glanced about the confines of the room, fearful that she was still at Kenan's mercy. But a quick appraisal of her squalid surroundings convinced her that she was alone. She shuddered involuntarily.

Several moments elapsed before she was able to sit up, moaning softly with the agonizing effort. She touched her swollen lip, then stared blankly at the blood on her fingertips. Gently massaging her bruised cheekbone, she gazed down with revived horror at the scraps of fabric that lay strewn about her. Slowly she collected the remnants of her torn robe and clutched them to her naked breast.

Burying her face in tightly clenched fists, Finola doubled over and wept.

How can I explain this to Bran? she thought in anguish. *What did I do to bring this shame upon myself – upon my husband?*

Finola shivered with revulsion, recalling Kenan's stinking breath in her face; his hands, his mouth exploring her body.

"No!" she cried aloud, pounding the floor with her fists. She would not be taken again, not by him nor any other man. Her eyes frantically darted around the room, seeking another means of escape. Her gaze came to rest on a pile of kindling that was neatly stacked in one corner and she scrambled across to it, crawling on all fours. Rummaging through the dried branches, she selected a bough which she guessed to be about the same thickness of the shaft of a throwing spear. With all her strength, Finola flexed the branch and snapped it in twain, then cast the smaller portion aside.

"I will not be dishonoured again," she promised herself, testing the splintered tip of the stake against the palm of her hand.

Rising to her feet, she held the blunt end of the branch to the wall and leaned forward slightly, the jagged point to her breast.

"Lord, give me strength," she whispered, closing her eyes. Her grip on the wooden stake tightened. Summoning the last reserves of her will she inhaled deeply and held her breath, the muscles in her legs and arms braced to hurl her into oblivion.

Devlin. Abruptly she opened her eyes, exhaling loudly as she tried to focus on the reality of the world she had almost forsaken.

"What is to become of my son if I..."

Finola started at the sudden noise outside the door and she dropped the stake, hastily collecting her tattered clothes in an effort to cover herself.

The door swung open and a stout Norseman stood at the entry, beckoning her. As she stepped out into the blinding sunlight he caught her wrist and dragged her along behind him to a nearby shieling. Lifting the bar with one hand, he threw the door open and flung her inside.

"My lady!" Morallta shrieked as Finola collapsed to

the floor, the heavy door slamming shut behind her.

"Get her something to wear!" Muireen curtly ordered. "And bring some water!" She stooped over Finola, examining the marks on her face. "Dear Lord! What happened?"

"It was Kenan," Finola answered between sobs. "He is here – with the Norsemen and he... he..." Finola's shoulders convulsed as she turned away from Muireen.

As Morallta returned with a water basin and clean shift, Muireen leaned forward and embraced Finola, tears glistening in her own eyes. "God's curse on him, for he has shamed us all," she muttered in a husky voice. She picked up the sponge from the water basin and gently swabbed at the dried blood on Finola's face. "I beg your forgiveness, sister, not for his sake but for that of the clanna Ui Faelain."

Finola held Muireen's face in her hands. "I cannot give you my pardon, for you have not wronged me, Muireen. But I will gladly give you my gratitude. Through all that we have endured together you have been my friend and I have drawn heavily on your strength." Rising to her feet, Finola pulled the ankle length shift over her head.

"We have both depended on you," Morallta told Muireen. "Without your stamina, neither one of us would have survived this long."

Devlin, who had been peacefully sleeping on a straw pallet in the corner, suddenly began to cry. Finola had just bent over to pick him up when the door burst open and several heavily armed Vikings stormed inside. She barely had time to snatch up her child before she was dragged outside with the others. All around them thralls were being gathered into the tightly packed group that was surrounded by dozens of guards.

"What's happening?" Morallta fretted nervously.

Finola glanced apprehensively at Muireen. "I do not know. It is the first time since we were brought here that they have assembled all the slaves at once. Perhaps they mean us all to work in the fields today."

One of the jarls barked a command and the Norsemen began herding them forward, prodding the stragglers with spears and swords as they drove the frightened group through the town. They were taken through the main gate and as they marched out into open country, Muireen looked at Finola and raised her eyebrows quizzically.

"We dare not try to escape now," Finola replied in answer to the unspoken question. "There are too many guards." She grasped Muireen's hand. "Don't worry, sister. Our chance will come."

Sometime later, they were halted near an expansive oak grove. Finola had often heard the other slaves speak of it with fear in their eyes, but until now she herself had never seen it. The huge oak that the foreigners called sacred stood isolated in a small clearing with numerous carcasses still suspended from its branches where animals had been hung by their necks and impaled as they struggled. The grass at the base of the ancient oak glistened with freshly spilled blood.

Hundreds of Norsemen and Danes, including women and children, had collected around the fringe of the clearing and from the general mood that seemed to prevail, Finola guessed that they had assembled to observe some festival or religious rite.

A huge altar of polished wood stood beneath the sacred tree, its surface gleaming with gilded adornments. A solitary woman stood before the altar clutching a long hawthorn staff mounted with a brass representation of a war hammer. Her head was covered with black lambskin and she was dressed in a robe of deep indigo that was girded at the waist with a thick belt of embossed leather. The cloak of blazing scarlet that fell to her ankles was pinned at her collarbones with tortoise brooches and she wore a silver chain inlaid with precious stones about her neck.

As the woman turned around, Finola recognized the harsh features and thin colourless lips.

"Otta," she whispered to herself.

Thorgest's wife strode across the clearing until she stood before the cluster of thralls.

"Hear me!" she commanded in heavily accented Gaelic, raising her arms dramatically over her head. "I will speak to you in your own tongue so that you will know the significance of this day."

As she lowered her arms, a deathly silence descended over the grove.

"This is the first of the nine days in the festival of Uppsalla and I, as high priestess to Thor, have called you here to witness the gift we offer to the mightiest of all gods."

Otta walked back to the altar, then turned and tilted her head. "Bring the sacrifice forth!"

Finola gasped as she watched Forannan dragged through the cheering throng to the trunk of the sacred oak. "You cannot slay him!" she protested, pushing her way through the crowd. "He is a man of God – a holy man!"

"He is a blasphemer!" Otta screamed back to her. "He

preaches that there is but one god! What of Thor or Oden or Freyja?"

"But those are your beliefs," Finola argued. "We worship the one true God. You cannot destroy our faith by killing one man."

"Perhaps you are right," Otta replied, smiling malevolently. "A woman would add much greater meaning to our sacrifice." She pointed her staff directly at Finola. "Seize her!"

As the Norse warriors shouldered their way through the dense crowd, Morallta stepped forward. "She is right, you sodded whore! To destroy our faith you will have to kill all of us!"

Otta looked at her in astonishment. "Are all you Irish so anxious to die? Very well, my young one. You shall go in her place."

Morallta turned to run, but a red-faced Norseman caught her hair and pulled her toward him. The panicked maidservant screamed and threw herself upon the ground in an attempt to postpone her fate. But the Norseman grasped her wrists and dragged her, kicking wildly, into the clearing.

"Take her to the sacred oak and prepare her," Otta commanded.

Finola tried to break through the line of guards that surrounded the thralls, but Muireen held her back. "Don't be a fool. There is nothing you can do."

Helpless to do anything but watch, Finola looked on as Morallta and Forannan's hands were bound behind their backs. Nooses were placed about each of their necks and the ropes thrown over a tall branch to warriors who caught them on the other side. The hapless pair stood together, leaning on one another as Otta circled about them like a bird of prey, chanting and mumbling invocations.

Forannan's face seemed strangely peaceful, but Morallta's eyes were those of a frightened doe. "Forgive me," Finola softly whispered.

Otta suddenly thrust the staff above her head and the two victims were propelled upward, their legs jerking spasmodically as they began to strangle.

"THOR!" Otta screamed. As a score of warriors armed with spears moved in beneath them, Finola turned and buried her face in Muireen's shoulder.

"It's over," Muireen stated quietly a few moments later. Suddenly she caught Finola's shoulder and shook her in frustration. "Listen to me! We must find a way to flee from here or we will end up as they did."

Finola's body trembled with emotion. "I wish I could squeeze the life out of that demon's whore with my own hands!"

"Forget Otta! Even if you have the chance, slaying her would not gain our freedom. If ever we are to see Naas again, we must find a way to escape from here before it is too late."

Finola glanced at the dangling corpses, then looked down at the infant that squirmed in her arms. Abruptly, Devlin reached and caught the gold Celtic cross she wore in his tiny hand. The visions of Naas, of home, of Bran suddenly flashed across Finola's mind and she clutched her child to her breast.

"Aye," she murmured. "We must escape."

CHAPTER TWENTY–THREE

Six weeks after the Norse raid on Bray, as the rising north wind rolled dark rain–laden clouds over Naas and robbed the midsummer afternoon of its warmth, Etach paced along the stone ramparts of the ringed fortress and gazed down at the hundreds of brightly coloured pavilions that had been pitched in the open plain below. In accordance with the king's command, warriors from every clanna in Leinster had assembled at the royal dun and the variegated standards that marked their respective positions in the camp flapped noisily in the chill breeze like the beating of eagles' wings. On the well–trampled pastureland that lay beyond the encampment, scores of swordsmen were paired off against one another, the air filled with clanging and grunts as they honed their skills in mock combat. Further south, a group of slingers and spearcasters laughed and mocked each other as they hurled their missiles at targets which had been positioned across the field.

Etach critically eyed the ranks of warriors who marched across the lush river valley, raising and lowering their shields on command and smoothly changing into formations which weeks earlier had been unfamiliar and awkward. Many of the men wore helmets and shirts of mail, and several units bore long–handled axes in place of the broadswords with which they had been accustomed.

There is no honour in this, Etach thought, frowning. *Our men should not be herded into battle like a gaggle of tamed geese and constrained to fight as the foreigners do. A warrior must stand alone against his enemies, and live or die on the strength of his own abilities rather than depending on that of his comrades.*

But even though he had disagreed with the reorganization of Leinster's army, Etach's loyalty and devotion to Bran had compelled him to silence and he had continued to execute his orders with the disciplined expedition of a professional soldier. As he stared across the valley floor to the deep blue ribbon that was the River Liffey, Etach's mind wandered back to the tempestuous night when they had returned from Bray, plodding blindly toward Naas through the driving rain that mercilessly pelted the weary horsemen like a flurry of pebbles. Even before they had reached the main gate, Bran had sent riders ahead to summon the clan chieftains and his own senior officers to a war council in the great hall. A short time later, he had stood before them, water dripping from the drenched tunic that hung loosely from his muscular frame as he described the scene of the massacre in explicit detail. His voice had quaked with fury as he spoke and when he was finished he paused for several moments, then shook a white knuckled fist at his mute audience.

"If ever we are to drive the heathen from our island we must first learn to think – to fight as they do," he had told them, his words filling the hall. "Our warriors must learn to move as one and they must be equipped with weapons that will match those of the Viking. Let our blacksmith's fires burn through day and night, forging the chainmail and battle–axes that will bring us victory! Let our ranks become as walls of steel!"

His eyes had blazed with the zeal of a fanatic, but Etach had seen the pain that lay beyond and knew that the king was a man whose soul was tormented by the loss of his family. In the weeks that followed, the aging warrior repeatedly tried to distract him from his misery but Bran gradually became more remote and reclusive, often remaining in his chambers for days at a time while his servants were forced to neglect their regular duties in order to run messages between him and his military commanders.

Staring past the mist shrouded hills that faded into the distant horizon, Etach remembered how he had once carried the shy, freckle–faced boy upon his shoulders. He had loved Bran as a son, guiding him into manhood with a patience and dedication born out of true affection, sharing the triumphs and pain that always accompanied the cruel passing of youth. But now, for the first time in his life, he felt genuinely help-less for he knew that only Bran could purge himself of the demons that raged inside him.

The old warrior wistfully shook his head and slowly trudged on along the rampart.

Later that afternoon, as the chieftains and noblemen began to assemble in the great hall for the evening meal, Etach was summoned to the king's private chambers. He strode briskly across the cobblestone courtyard, then abruptly checked himself and changed direction, recalling that Bran had taken up lodging in the spartan quarters which had once belonged to his father. There were those who said it had been the lingering memories of his wife and child which had driven him out of his own residence. But Etach sensed some deeper purpose for the transfer, as if Bran were trying to draw strength from the memory of his father.

With this last thought still in mind, Etach stepped to the entrance of Bran's quarters and knocked loudly.

"Come," a gruff voice from inside curtly ordered.

Stepping into the dimly lit room, Etach suddenly froze, his hand still on the latch as he gaped at the apparition before him. In that one terrifying instant, he fully believed that he was looking at the profile of Crimthann Ui Faelain.

Preoccupied by the scroll he was stooped over, Bran knelt in the centre of the sparsely furnished chamber, his father's mantle draped over his shoulders. With the tangled thicket of coppery whiskers that now bearded his jaw, he bore such a striking resemblance to the deceased king that Etach had thought him to be a specter.

"You sent for me, my lord?" he inquired, silently chiding himself as he recovered and closed the door.

"How much longer must I wait before our troops are ready for battle?" Bran asked irritably, sitting back on his heels. Sheets of parchment and several large maps carpeted the stone floor in front of him, illuminated by the stub of a tallow candle which flickered uncertainly in the final stages of its life, it's hardened drippings caked onto the bronze holder in which it rested. "When in God's name will they be ready to march?"

"They were almost ready more than a fortnight ago," Etach replied brusquely, annoyed at the condescending tone in Bran's voice. "But now I fear that much more time must pass before they are again as well prepared."

"I have no time for riddles," Bran snapped, frowning. "Speak plainly, man."

"Very well, my lord," Etach answered evenly. "This... new way of fighting is as unnatural to our warriors as chastity is to an old harlot. Oh aye, they have learned to march and drill together well enough, but they will need to be capable of much more than that before we dare send them into battle.

In the time that a man takes thinking about what he is supposed to be doing, he could well be dead. You yourself know
that a warrior's survival in combat often depends on his in-
stincts and I am afraid that it will be some time before our
men are able to develop these techniques to that extent – if
ever they do."

Furrows slashed across Bran's forehead as he raised his
eyebrows. "I take it that you do not agree with the changes
that have been made?"

"I do not," Etach answered. "You have some of the finest warriors in all Erin at your command, but you have chosen to ignore their training and experience by ordering them
to adopt the tactics of the heathen. They are not Norsemen,
nor can you make them so. They are Irishmen who have always honourably fought and – "

"Died!" Bran exploded, leaping to his feet and thrusting his face forward. "At the Liffey they fought and died as
Irishmen by the hundreds! Linen tunics against armour; where
was the honour in that? It was only by the grace of God, and
the Ui Muiredaig, that our defeat was turned into a victory.
Even then, it was we, not the Viking, who suffered the most
casualties." Bran squared his shoulders and raised his chin,
his blue eyes gleaming with the intensity of his resolve. "I
swear on the blood of those who fell that day, the mistakes
that were made in our first encounter with the foreigners will
not be repeated in our next attack."

"Attack?" Etach exclaimed, drawing back in astonishment. "But at the war council all of the chieftains agreed that
it would be best to wait until the heathen crossed our borders
again before acting."

"I have since decided otherwise," Bran retorted, as he squatted and began to collect the manuscripts and scrolls. "We cannot afford to simply sit back and wait for them to hack their way through Leinster as they did Ulster. We have already seen the fruits of Viking ambition; we need not look upon those horrors again to be convinced of the heathen's determination to conquer us all." He paused for a moment, then slowly lifted his eyes to Etach. "That is why I have decided that we will strike the first blow, before Thorgest has an opportunity to emerge from his lair. Within a fortnight's time, we will lay siege to his stronghold at Lough Ree."

Etach shook his head. "With all due respect, my lord, such a plan would be disastrous. The forces that Thorgest hurled against us at the Liffey were but a fraction of the larger contingent he maintains at Lough Ree to protect his fleet. While we may be able to contend with a large scale invasion, it is madness to suggest that we confront Thorgest where his entire strength has been consolidated."

"There is no other way," Bran muttered as he slowly rose and crossed the chamber to the large storage chest which rested in the corner. Etach continued to stare at him incredulously as he lifted the lid and carefully deposited the scrolls.

"But we will need more men; more time to..."

Bran abruptly slammed the lid closed and pivoted. "Don't you understand, you doddering old half-wit?" he shouted, his cheeks flushing scarlet as he glared back at him. "There is no more time!"

Etach clenched his teeth, swallowing his anger. His love of the man before him checked the impulse to draw his sword. Such an insult from another would have otherwise demanded an immediate response in bloodshed. He had never before known Bran to be given to fits of anger and in all their time together a harsh word had never once passed between them. Across the awkward silence that now separated them, Etach saw the deep-set lines in Bran's face and the dark smudges of fatigue beneath his eyes and understood.

His fury spent, Bran's eyes softened, the hint of an apologetic smile curling one corner of his mouth. "Forgive me, old friend," he said, sighing deeply and passing a hand over his face. "I have been much distracted since we returned from Bray. From the moment we laid Conor to rest on that Godforsaken beach, I have been tormented by the question of what fate has befallen the rest of my family. When they were not found among the dead I was overcome by an inexplicable feeling that convinced me they were still alive. But if they had been captured, how would I find them? Where would I begin to look? Then, as we rode back to Naas, I suddenly realized there was only one place they could have been taken – Lough Ree."

Hope sparkled in his eyes like flecks of sunlight on a wind rippled lake and Etach already regretted what he was about to say. "Is it not possible they were taken north, to Lough Neagh?"

"I think it unlikely," Bran replied. "A mere raiding party would not have dared to attack Bray, and dispatching a larger fleet would have left the garrison there poorly defended; an opportunity I am certain Niall would not have hesitated to exploit. Besides, the attacks on the Liffey and at Bray were too well coordinated to suggest they originated from separate bases." He clasped his hands behind his back and began to pace back and forth in front of Etach, his head bowed with concentration. "No, I am convinced that the ships either came from Lough Ree or were part of a larger incoming fleet."

"Reinforcements?" Etach pondered aloud, scratching his head. "Then Thorgest may well have even more men than we suspect."

Bran nodded slowly. "Perhaps. But if indeed Finola and the others are still alive, I know that I will find them at Lough Ree."

His voice was tinged with the passion of one whose conviction had already begun to blossom into obsession and Etach suspected his judgment was blurred with sorrow and self-recrimination. He reached out and gripped Bran's arm, willing him to look past his own pain.

"Listen to me, lad. I know what you are feeling and I cannot say that I myself would not be doing the same in your place. But it is your heart and not your brain that is governing your thoughts. If we are defeated at Lough Ree, Leinster will surely fall to the Viking. As much as you love your family, you cannot risk sacrificing an entire kingdom for the sake of a few."

"Etach," Bran said quietly, smiling. "You have always been my friend and comrade. Yet despite our years together you still have not come to know my thoughts. It is not just for myself and my loved ones that I must go to Lough Ree; it is for all Leinster. You remember the women, the babies we found butchered at Bray, and how the heathen left them as carrion for the ravens and wild beasts. If we are to prevent that carnage from being repeated throughout Leinster and the rest of Erin, Thorgest must be crushed and his followers driven back into the sea that spawned them."

"Aye," Etach grunted, glancing down at his feet. "But a righteous cause in itself will still not bring us victory over superior numbers. You do not seem to realize that Thorgest can field at least three warriors, probably more, for every one of ours. With such odds against us, the attack you propose will be more of a slaughter than a battle."

"Not if we attack at night," Bran explained, his eyes glistening in the firelight. "We will lay siege to their fortress, burning their ships and farmsteads, even as they have put so many Irish villages to the torch. With their food and water cut off, it will only be a matter of days before their supplies are exhausted."

"But that is certain to drive them out into the open where the advantage will be theirs."

"They will have no advantage," Bran assured him. "By then, the odds will be even."

"And how in the name of God do you plan to arrange that?" Etach blurted out, waving his arms in exasperation. "Every warrior in Leinster is already rallied to us. There are no more men to be had from the clans."

"That is why I intend to petition Niall Caille to lead his army to Lough Ree."

Etach allowed himself a derisive grin. "I think you will find that the Ard–Ri cares little for travel these days," he scoffed. "The instant he leaves Ailech, Niall will be caught between Thorgest and the foreigners from Lough Neagh and Ulster will be overrun."

"He is already a captive in his own domain and will remain so until we stand united against the Viking." Bran gazed past Etach, his eyes focused on some point beyond him and the confines of the small chamber. "My father thought Niall Caille a sort of man worth dying for; a man of honour and duty. He will come."

Etach suddenly remembered another time, a time he had almost forgotten, when another king of Leinster had stood before him in that very room and outlined a plan for the unification of the clans. On that occasion he himself had laughed at what he considered to be a preposterous notion which he had known would never come to pass. But the will and perseverance of Crimthann Ui Faelain had proven him wrong and after years of inter–tribal warfare an enjoined peace had been brought to Leinster.

Now another young king stood before him, outlining a plan that would have Ulster and Leinster put aside their individual concerns and fight side by side to drive a foreign invader from their land. *Their land*, Etach silently mused. *Why not? If clan chieftains could be brought together under one standard, why not the provincial kings? One Erin – a united Erin.*

He smiled proudly at Bran. "You have more of your father in you than I realized, and you have learned much since the day the gold was first placed upon your brow. I have no doubt that the Ard–Ri will be hard pressed to refuse whatever petition you set before him." The old soldier adjusted his mantle about his shoulders, then smartly came to attention. "When do you plan on leaving for Ailech, my lord?" he added formally.

"Tomorrow morning," Bran replied. "I will need my horse saddled before dawn and packed with a fortnight's supplies."

Etach nodded. "I will attend to it myself. As you will no doubt wish your personal guard to accompany us, I will – "

"I cannot drag an escort through Meath and Ulster like a clatter of dogs," Bran interrupted. "Nor can I take you along with me, old friend. You are the only one I can trust to take command should the Viking act before my return. Besides, I will have a better chance of passing unnoticed if I travel alone."

"I will not hear of it!" Etach blustered. "I have been responsible for you ever since you were but a cub in the cradle and I will not – "

"Very well," Bran conceded, raising his arms as if to shield himself from Etach's protests. "I will ask Rowan Ui Muiredaig to accompany me. Next to yourself, there is no finer warrior in all Leinster."

Grunting his assent, Etach marched to the door, then paused and glanced over his shoulder. "And what if Niall does refuse you?"

The steady blue eyes that gazed back at him revealed no hint of uncertainty. "With or without his help, Thorgest must be stopped. We can choose no other path."

CHAPTER TWENTY–FOUR

Three days later, Bran and Rowan reached the Ulster border. Clad in the simple woolen tunics and hooded brats of freemen, their weapons concealed on the stubborn little packhorse that Rowan hauled behind them, they had journeyed without incident along the main roads that wound north between the treeless hills and limestone outcrops that covered the rich pastureland of Meath. Although they had sought food and shelter each evening at the bruideans that conveniently awaited travellers at major junctions and crossroads, the other patrons of the hospitality houses had taken no notice of them, allowing them the luxury of hot food and comfortable beds without fear of exposure or provocation. But as they entered Ulster, they left the high road and guided their horses cross country along the drumlin driftbelt of the province's central lowlands, skirting the Norse garrisons and settlements that marred the sorrowful landscape. The sight of the charred villages and deserted farmsteads sickened Bran and filled him with a terrible foreboding. *Am I looking into Leinster's future?* he silently asked himself, gazing beyond the scenes of destruction which now seemed more a product of insight than reality. *It is I who am responsible for the destiny of my people. The course I have chosen will either spare them from this dark fate or plunge them into the terror of a living nightmare. I know not which, but pray that God has mercifully guided my decision.*

That evening, as the last rays of sunlight crowned the surrounding hilltops with laurels of gold, they sought shelter amidst a small cluster of evergreens interspersed with bracken and willows, reasoning that the dense foliage would provide them with at least some measure of security. No sooner had they dismounted than Rowan disappeared into the brush, leaving Bran to unload the packhorse, then set about collecting kindling for the fire. The Ui Muiredaig chieftain returned a short time later, grinning triumphantly as he strode into the small clearing, a large hare in each hand. Without a word, he promptly proceeded to clean and spit his catch, then carefully roasted the carcasses over the open fire.

After they had eaten, Rowan leaned back and sighed heavily. His deep brown eyes captured the glow of the wavering flames as he stared into the fire in silence, then he began to smile.

Bran glanced at him inquisitively. "What is it that amuses you?" he asked.

"I was only recalling the occasion of our first meeting," Rowan replied, turning toward him. "Do you remember?"

Bran smiled and nodded. "The day our fathers made peace with one another. Were it not for their wisdom, we might well have come to face each other as enemies rather than friends."

"Our fathers," Rowan mused, tilting his head back to gaze up at the stars. "Does it not seem strange to you that we are now as they once were; chieftain and king, with the lives of thousands dependent on our decisions and actions?" He shook his head slowly. "When did we lose our youth, Bran? I can still see myself as a child, weeping with anger and frustration because I lacked the strength to lift my father's sword. And I remember how serious his face became as he took me upon his knee and wiped the tears from my cheeks. 'You must pray for the time when you will not need to raise the sword, little one,' he told me. 'Only then will you and the rest of Erin have discovered the true nature of your strength.' It wasn't until years later that I understood what he meant. When you and I first met, you spoke of the clans being united under one banner, one standard. I see now that it was not just the clans of Leinster that you were referring to, but those throughout all of Erin." Rowan brushed a wisp of red hair from his eyes and leaned forward, his arms resting on his knees. "Think you such a time will ever come to pass?"

"I do not know," Bran replied slowly as he tossed another piece of kindling onto the fire. The dry wood crackled loudly as it ignited, then popped, sending a spray of glowing sparks up into the darkness. Bran's eyes followed their paths as they flickered for an instant against the sable of the night sky, then died. He glanced back at the hope and expectation that shone on Rowan's face. "I once had many dreams," he continued quietly. "After Devlin was born I thought that my personal designs were within reach; the future seemed so clear, so certain to me. Now it is as if a shroud has descended between me and my destiny. I dare not consider what will or will not be, for I can no longer see tomorrow."

"But there will be a tomorrow," Rowan contended. "Then another and another. And with the dawning of each new day we are all given the opportunity to try again; to attain our dreams — or rescue those we have lost."

The warmth from the fire felt suddenly strange upon Bran's face, a gentle caress that was at once soothing and familiar. The wind that teased the waggling flames rose abruptly and whispered to him in the voice he had so often yearned to hear.

"Come," the night breeze sighed. "Come to me."

Bran closed his eyes and drifted into Finola's embrace. She drew him closer, her delicate arms encircling his neck, her lips soft and warm upon his throat. The lavender eyes that gazed up at him shimmered with the promise of love and peace; a refuge from the pain and loneliness which had tormented him. Bran bent down and kissed her. But as their lips met, the image of the woman he loved suddenly began to waver, dissolving in his arms. Bran frantically tried to hold her fast, but there was nothing of substance for him to secure and slowly Finola began to fade.

Then, she was gone.

The emptiness to which Bran had become accustomed had been only momentarily appeased and as he opened his eyes to focus on Rowan's troubled face he felt the familiar desolation beginning to seep back into his soul.

"You have been a good friend, Rowan," he said sincerely. "And I know that your words come from your concern for me and love of your sister. But do not ask me to trust the lives of my family to fate."

In one deft movement Bran snatched up his scabbard and unsheathed his sword, flames reflecting along the polished blade as he rested it in the palm of his free hand.

"This is where I have placed my trust," he said emphatically. "This is what will bring them back to me. And know this, Rowan Ui Muiredaig, I will not stop until they are found."

Rising to his feet, Rowan crossed the short distance between them and stood for several moments staring down at him in silence. Abruptly he dropped to one knee.

"You are my king and my friend," he said firmly as he reached out to touch the gleaming steel. "No matter how long the path stretches out before you, I swear you shall not have to make this journey alone. My sword and my clan are yours to command."

Bran nodded.

Four days after entering Ulster, Bran and Rowan came within sight of Ailech, the royal residence of Niall Caille, chieftain of the northern Ui Neil and Ard–Ri of Erin. Built in the rocky highlands north of Derry, the circular stone fortress commanded the area between Lough Swilly and Lough Foyle, and Bran guessed that its strategic location accounted for how Niall had been able to fend off the incessant attacks of the foreigners. But even at a distance, he could make out the black stains on the stone where pitch fires had been set and there were several irregularities where the walls had been breached, then hastily repaired. He wondered how many times the Viking had laid siege to the fortress and how much longer the high king would be able to hold out against the continued strikes.

As they crossed the gently rolling plains south of Ailech and came within earshot of its ramparts, several dozen mounted warriors suddenly emerged from the stronghold and galloped toward them. Rowan quickly drew the packhorse alongside his own mount and frantically groped among the bundles for his sword.

"No!" Bran commanded, touching his free arm. "We will have no need of weapons here." The anxious chieftain looked at him uneasily while the body of warriors drew up in front of them, unsheathing their weapons as they reined in their horses.

Bran's eyes moved along the line of grim–faced men before him. "Which one of you leads these warriors," he demanded loudly.

"I do," came the throaty reply. The huge man with a sand–coloured beard wore the royal blue of the Ard–Ri's personal guard. He clucked his horse forward and positioned himself directly in front of Bran, glowering down at him.

"I am Turloch Ui Neil, captain in the amhuis of the high king. Who might you be?"

"You may tell the Ard–Ri that it is Bran Ui Faelain, king of Leinster, who has come to seek his counsel on a matter of great urgency."

"How do I know you are who you say?" Turloch asked slowly.

"Your king will remember me," Bran replied firmly. The stocky warrior hesitated for a moment, then abruptly turned and rejoined the ranks of his own men. Leaning forward in his saddle, Turloch conferred with two of his companions, their voices lowered to husky whispers. When he returned, his face remained implacable.

"Your man will be escorted to the great hall and given food and drink," Turloch informed Bran. "You," he added, jerking his horse's reins to one side, "come with me."

Bran glanced reassuringly at Rowan, then urged his horse forward, galloping after Turloch as he was led to the shock of trees that bordered a small stream paralleling the western wall of the stone fortress. Guiding their horses between the sparse evergreens, the pair wound their way through a maze of boulders and fallen tree trunks which were covered with liverworts, heavy mats of tall grass and filmy ferns. Ivy and honeysuckle clung stubbornly to the bases of the trees and the rich scent of damp moss hung heavily on the air.

A solitary figure sat on the moss that fringed the water's edge, his back propped up against the thick trunk of the tall evergreen. Bran smiled to himself as he recognized the grey-flecked beard and lean muscular frame that somehow continued to defy the passage of time. Niall's hands rested comfortably in his lap, clutching the end of a line that spanned the air, then disappeared beneath the surface of the rippling stream. With his eyes closed and his chin drooped onto his chest, the high king appeared to be asleep, apparently oblivious to both their approach and the flock of rooks that hoarsely nattered at each other in the branches above his head.

Following Turloch's example, Bran dismounted a short distance from the stream and tied his horse's reins to the branch of a decaying log. But as he started toward Niall, a large meaty hand gripped his shoulder and held him fast.

"Are you armed?" Turloch asked gruffly.

"You can see that I am not."

The heavyset warrior released his grip, but his eyes moved down to the large leather pouch that hung at Bran's belt. "What is it you carry? It cannot be a purse, for even a king would not dare to openly flaunt such wealth."

"It is not gold or gems," Bran attested as he unfastened the leather thongs and handed the pouch to him. "Nor is it a weapon."

Turloch examined the contents of the sack then looked

up at Bran, drawing his eyebrows together into a perplexed frown. "Forgive me, my lord, but... what are they?"

"A gift for the Ard–Ri," Bran answered, retrieving the pouch and fastening it to his belt. "Have I now your permission to present it to him?"

"Follow me," Turloch snorted, turning on his heel and walking on ahead of him. As Bran trod after him, he could not help but think how often he had seen the same protective loyalty in Etach and he knew that this was a man who would willingly lay down his life to protect that of Niall Caille. When they reached the high king, Turloch dropped to one knee beside him.

"My lord," he called softly, his inflection like the reverent whisper of a prayer. "My lord. This... chieftain would speak with you. He says it is urgent."

Niall tilted his head and opened one eye to look up at him. "It is always urgent," he sighed. "What is it this time?"

Bran stepped forward, grinning broadly. "I was led to believe that the war with the Norsemen has left the Ard–Ri with time for little else." He nodded to the half dozen trout that had been neatly arranged on the moss alongside Niall's sword. "I see now that I was misinformed."

Pivoting toward the source of the sarcastic remark, Niall opened his other glowering eye. Almost instantly his expression changed as recollection spread across his face. "Bran?" he murmured dubiously, his lips forming the name slowly as he rose to his feet. Suddenly, his face beamed with affable recognition.

"Bran! Bran Ui Faelain! By my soul, you are the last man I ever expected to see here." He took and released Bran's arm in greeting, then thrust his own hands onto his hips and glanced at Turloch. "The man who stands before you is not merely a chieftain – but king of all Leinster and my most valued ally."

Turloch met Bran's smile, then turned to Niall. "With your permission, I will attend to the horses." As the high king nodded, the warrior bowed formally, then turned and strode quickly back through the trees. Niall's eyes followed him. "He is a good man," he told Bran. "With a thousand more like him I would have driven the heathen from Ulster long ago. But as it is, our ranks are plagued with desertions and with each passing day we become a little weaker. Even as our enemy grows stronger."

"Has Malachy offered you no assistance?" Bran queried. "As Ri–Ruirech of Meath he must realize that it is his kingdom the Viking will descend upon next should Ulster fall."

Niall shrugged. "His chieftains war among themselves as they always have and Malachy himself is not without enemies. He dare not leave his throne undefended so long as there are those eager to lay claim to it. In the meantime, my own men have grown weary of defeat and many have come to accept it as inevitable. If I do not give them a victory soon, there will be no army left to oppose Thorgest and he shall have his 'kingdom of the north'."

"Then you must give your warriors a victory," Bran told him, carefully noting the tone of futility in Niall's voice. "Give all Erin a victory."

"My chieftains and officers have yet to develop a plan to accomplish that," Niall replied a trifle sardonically as he sat down at the base of the evergreen, his back propped up against it. He picked up his fishing line and began winding it around his fingers. "I am afraid that such a thing is not quite as simple as you imply."

Bran squatted beside him. "It could be – if we stood together, as we once did against the Munstermen."

Niall stared at him curiously, "What is it you need?"

Choosing his words carefully, Bran began to describe in detail his plan for the attack on Lough Ree. He explained how the clans of Leinster had adopted and become proficient in the tactics of the Viking and how the new formations would be brought into play once the besieged Norsemen were lured out into the open – and the ambush that would be awaiting them. As he spoke he watched Niall's face, but the high king's expression gave no hint of either endorsement nor disapproval. When he concluded, Bran sat back on his heels and waited in silence for the man's reaction.

Crossing his arms over his chest, Niall leaned back and gazed out across the stark landscape. "There is much risk in your plan – for both Ulster and Leinster. I cannot spare enough warriors to be of any use to you. Even if I sent the entire army to Lough Ree, we would still be badly outnumbered. The ambush you propose would be but a momentary shock to the Viking. Once they recover, their superior numbers will compel us to take the defensive; a posture from which no battle has ever been won."

"What you say is true," Bran commented, nodding slowly. "But you are assuming that the entire battle will be fought on foot. I intend to use mounted warriors for the ambush."

"Cavalry?" Niall uttered skeptically. "Battles have always been won by the wielding of spear and sword in close–ordered ranks. Any such mounted support as accompanies them has always been used to scout or harass the enemy's flanks. And to that extent they have proven effective. But to suggest that they be used as the main thrust at the critical point in a battle would be an unacceptable gamble. Besides, a mounted warrior is easily put off balance and therefore cannot use his weapons as freely as one on foot."

Bran reached into the leather pouch that hung at his side and withdrew two triangular shaped pieces of steel. He handed them to Niall. "These will give our mounted warriors the balance they need."

"What is god's name are they?" Niall pondered aloud, turning the objects over and over as he examined them closely.

"That is what will defeat the Viking," Bran replied. "The Franks took the concept from the Magyars who raided them and used it to build an empire. They are fastened to the saddle by leather straps, each hanging down on either side of the horse's belly. By placing his feet in them, an experienced rider immediately resolves the problem of balance, in essence becoming one flesh with his war horse. A battalion of mounted warriors similarly equipped and armed with long thrusting spears would wreak havoc on Thorgest's foot soldiers."

Niall winced with uncertainty. "The idea has merit," he agreed hesitantly, "but the use of offensive cavalry on such a scale has never before been attempted and we have no way of knowing whether or not such a tactic would prove effective. Neither one of us can risk defeat merely to test your theory in combat."

"It is more than a theory, my lord," Bran insisted. "I have studied copious detailed accounts of how these same tactics were not only employed – but were repeatedly proven successful over a numerically superior adversary. In a time before your father was crowned Ard–Ri, Charlemagne used such cavalry to repulse the Norsemen from the frontiers of his Holy Roman Empire. His mounted warriors not only matched the speed of the longships, they frequently broke Viking shield walls that had previously been impervious to the attacks of his somewhat more poorly equipped retainers. Do those situations not parallel our own?"

"Aye," Niall sighed wearily. "But the Franks were well trained in the art of fighting from horseback. By the time our warriors develop the requisite skills, it will be too late."

Bran glanced down at the ground, then slowly raised his eyes to Niall. "These past six weeks, five hundred of my finest warriors have been training in secret in Leinster to accomplish just that. They need no more time."

Niall paced to the edge of the stream, his back to Bran. Bending down, he picked up a small rock and flipped it out into the water. The stone skipped thrice along the rippling surface, then disappeared. As he turned around, his expression told Bran that his journey had been made in vain.

"Forgive me, my friend. I cannot leave Ulster without–"

"Damn you, Niall!" Bran exploded. "They have taken my family!"

For an instant shock flashed in Niall's eyes, then he frowned. "I did not know," he said. "Tell me."

As Bran related the events leading up to his discovery

of the massacre at Bray, Niall paced before him, head bowed and hands clasped behind his back, pausing occasionally to question the Leinster king on certain details of the Viking raid. When at last Bran fell silent, Niall stopped and peered out across the Ulster landscape.

"Forgive me, my friend," he muttered finally. "For the moment, I cannot help you."

"It is not I to whom you will have to apologize," Bran protested. "When I became Ri–Ruirech of Leinster I swore an oath before God to protect and defend my people. To deny my duty to them is to forswear those sacred vows. With or without you, I will do what I must."

Bran turned to walk away, his hopes shattered. *I will fight alone if I must,* he told himself. *So long as I have strength enough to lift my sword, I will never surrender my family and my country to the Viking.*

"Wait!" Niall's voice boomed behind him. Bran hesitated, then spun about. "You have yet to learn the patience that is required of a king," Niall reprimanded him. "Were you in possession of that illusive virtue, you would now understand that Leinster must first come to my aid before I am able to render assistance to her."

"I do not understand," Bran said suspiciously.

"The foreigners at Lough Neagh must be defeated before I can divert my forces south," Niall explained. "And in order to accomplish that I will need your Leinstermen. Once we have lured the Viking from their fortress, we will have an opportunity to test your plan – and your cavalry."

"They will not come out into the open to do battle," Bran pointed out. "Especially when they find themselves confronted with two armies. And if we besiege their stronghold, they have but to send word to Thorgest and wait. Only when he arrives will they emerge, then we will both be caught between them, as we would have if we attacked Lough Ree."

Niall grinned, the creases at the corners of his eyes deepening. "The wise fisherman always knows which bait is best. If I ride at the head of my warriors to Lough Neagh, Bothvar will not be able to resist the opportunity to take me alive and crush the last of the resistance in Ulster. When he attacks, we will fall back to a point where you and your Leinstermen will lie in ambush. While your warriors attack the Viking flanks on foot, your cavalry will cut off their retreat back to the fortress. When we have eliminated the heathen in Ulster, we will turn our attention to Lough Ree."

Bran suddenly felt ashamed that he had doubted the integrity and courage of the man who stood before him. "Leinster will stand beside you," he promised. "But you risk much, my lord. Erin does not need to lose her Ard–Ri."

"If we are defeated, Erin will be no more," Niall replied matter–of–factly. "We will meet in Dungannon in a fortnight's time. I will send word to Malachy, petitioning him to grant your warriors safe passage through Meath. Perhaps Leinster's courage will shame his chieftains into putting their differences aside and taking up arms against the Viking." Uncertainty and apprehension suddenly clouded his eyes and he reached out and caught Bran's shoulders with both hands. "Do not fail me, Ui Faelain. If you are late, we shall not be able to hold them alone."

In that instant Bran realized that he would lay down his life for the Ard–Ri and what he stood for, even as his father had. "There is no power on this earth that will prevent me from fighting by your side at Lough Neagh," he vowed.

CHAPTER TWENTY-FIVE

Ten days after Bran had left Ailech, Niall stoically rode at the head of his ragged warriors as he led them out of the battered stone dun, marching southeast into a thick morning fog that still clung to the rock studded meadows and created the illusion that it was more an integral rather than a separate part of the spectral landscape. The eerie mist seemed to part before them, beckoning them forth, away from the women and old men who stood huddled about the main gate, staring in grim-faced silence as rank upon rank of their loves and hopes paraded past them into the unknown fate that lay beyond.

The scene was one which Niall had witnessed many times before. He glanced back once more at the solemn assemblage then kicked his horse forward, the mist creeping in behind his warriors as they trudged on. Its last remnants had been burnt off by the time they reached the banks of the River Foyle at midday. Opposite the point that Niall had chosen to ford the river, the expansive plains of Magh Itha stretched out for several league in all directions, bordered along the south by the gently rolling foothills that gradually rose to the Sperrin Mountains, and on the north by a densely thicketed forest which cut across the open ground like a massive wedge.

The advance scouts crossed the slow moving river first, briefly reconnoitering the landscape beyond before signaling the remainder of the army to follow. With columns of Ulstermen strung out behind him, Niall guided his mount through the chest-deep water. Once he had reached the other side, he dispatched the scouts to survey the surrounding foothills and forest. As they galloped off he rode back along the riverbank, abruptly reining in his horse beside Turloch who was still supervising the crossing. For several moments, he watched with deep admiration and pride as his poorly equipped men filed ashore. Their tunics were threadbare, their sandals worn thin, and the pale scar tissue of old wounds contrasted with the bronze of their deeply tanned limbs.

"We have been deceived, my friend," Niall said pensively to Turloch, his eyes still focused on the long columns of men. "How many times have the bards and seanachies enchanted us with tales of glorious deeds and the great men who accomplished them? There," he added, nodding at the warriors, "there are the true heroes of Erin. Men of flesh and blood, not legend."

"Even so, the bards may sing their praises sooner than we expect," Turloch commented wryly.

Niall turned in his saddle to face him. "What do you mean?"

"We risk much in this battle," Turloch replied gravely. "Perhaps too much to depend on the Leinsterman for our victory. I fear our alliance with him is ill-fated."

Niall frowned. "Your fear would be better spent on the Norsemen."

"Treachery is the only enemy I fear," Turloch answered gruffly. "And I am not alone in that. We all heard the Leinster king in the great hall; speaking of the loss of his family and how he believes they are being held captive in Lough Ree. What if he is merely using us as a diversion to lure Thorgest north so that he may attempt their rescue?"

What if indeed, Niall thought to himself, recalling the

flicker of obsession in Bran's eyes. "His position is much the same as ours – together as allies we have a chance, alone we do not. Should he leave us to face the Viking alone, he must realize that we will surely be defeated. Then Thorgest will turn on him."

"A man in his position will sacrifice much for the love of his family. Many of the chieftains feel that such a man is unreliable."

Niall gazed out thoughtfully across the open plain. "We will camp here tonight," he told Turloch. "By now Bran should have crossed our border. Tomorrow morning, I will dispatch our scouts to verify that he has done so."

"And if he has not?"

Niall turned and stared at him in silence for several moments. "Then we will have no choice but to return to Ailech," he said finally. "Until then, we will wait here. See to it that the chieftains are informed."

"Aye, my lord," Turloch grunted, then roughly jerked his mount's reins, galloping along the length of the column. As Niall watched him ride off, he wondered which of them had truly misjudged the Leinster king.

Within an hour, nearly all the chieftain's pavilions had been erected and hundreds of warriors lounged about on the soft spongy moss that was as comfortable as any bed, laughing and talking among themselves as they awaited the preparation of the evening meal. Although Niall had forbidden the use of campfires for fear of drawing attention to their position, hundreds of hungry eyes anxiously looked on as the raw carrots, leeks and potatoes were hastily unloaded from the carts and packhorses. As he had expected, his command had evoked few complaints for it had been his experience that a growling stomach tended to be far less discriminating than a full one.

As he rode about the perimeter of the camp inspecting the guards who had been posted, one of the scouts he had sent out earlier suddenly exploded out of the distant forest, lashing the flanks of his lathered mount as he galloped toward the encampment. When at last he reached Niall, the warrior halted his horse so quickly that he was nearly unsaddled.

"Vikings, my lord!" he gasped as he recovered himself. "Three... maybe four leagues north... along the river."

"How many?" Niall asked quickly.

"I do not know, my lord, I saw but three of their longships."

Niall sighed heavily, making no attempt to conceal his relief. "A small raiding party. Probably bound for Derry." *But what if they have already seen us?* he asked himself, then spoke aloud. "In which direction were they sailing?"

A puzzled expression washed over the warrior's face. "In no direction, my lord. They lay at anchor in a small cove just beyond the elbow of the Foyle."

Niall nodded slowly. "Then the heathen are still unaware of our presence." He flashed the warrior a reassuring grin. "So long as they remain ignorant of our intentions, the odds will be in our favour."

That evening, less than seven hours after Niall's scout had spotted the Viking raiding party, the sea chieftain of the longships that had fled at the sight of the Ard–Ri's army stood before Bothvar in the firehall at Lough Neagh. The golden–haired Norseman listened to his jarls without interruption, his face expressionless as the light from the hearth cast shadows across his ruddy face. When they had finished, he slowly leaned back in his place of honour and scratched his tangled beard.

"So," he grinned, his small eyes gleaming. "The Irish rabbit has at last ventured out of his hole..Now, we must see if we can snare him."

Einar, the heavyset Norseman who had led the raid, smirked back at him. "It should not be too difficult, lord. By positioning himself between us and the fleet at Lough Ree, the Irish king will be crushed between us. We have but to cut off his line of retreat back to Ailech. Lord Thorgest will be pleased."

"He will be even more pleased when we defeat that whore's–son ourselves," Bothvar replied. "If I present him with the head of Niall Caille myself, along with the kingdom of the north, Thorgest will no doubt wish to express his... gratitude. Indeed, granting me a portion of his newly acquired territory would not be considered an inappropriate award."

Einar glanced anxiously at his comrades. "It is dangerous to tempt Skuld, for he is a mischievous Norn who delights in twisting men's destinies. We have long awaited an opportunity such as we have now, let us not squander it recklessly by attacking alone. With Lord Thorgest's support from the south our triumph will be certain."

"Your words are womanly," Bothvar growled. "Our warriors already number twice those of the Irish king. We need no more men." His lips parted into a yellow–toothed grin as he leaned forward, his voice lowered to a conspiratorial whisper. "It is well known that a victory shared does not taste as sweet. Soon Thorgest will realize that those of his own blood are of more value than the likes of the Dane who now sits at his right hand." He quickly cast his eyes about the room to insure that his remark had not been overheard, then raised his eyebrows as he peered back at Einar. "Is this not so?"

"I doubt not your wisdom, lord," Einar said nervously, glancing over his shoulder at the swarthy Danes behind him. "Nor do I question the courage of my comrades. But if we do not have enough men to contain the Irish at Magh Itha, they will surely escape back to Ailech."

"You seek problems where none exist," Bothvar sneered. "We will cut off their retreat by blockading the River Foyle, half our fleet attacking the Irish from the north, the rest slipping past their position under cover of darkness and striking from the south." Bothvar raised his arm and slowly clenched his fists. "Then we will squeeze the life out of those Gaelic pigs."

"But to do that, we will have to leave Lough Neagh undefended," Einar protested. "And the Irish – "

"Enough talk!" Bothvar roared as he rose to his feet. "Have the captains make ready to sail within the hour. Our ships must be in position before dawn or the Irish will escape our snare." He stared beyond the confines of the firehall to the victory that he knew lay within his grasp.

"After tomorrow, the people of Ulster shall have a new master."

The next morning, as the first beams of sunrise glistened on the dew–laden plains of Magh Itha and the song of the lark replaced that of the nightingale, Niall Caille sat atop a treeless hillock gazing beyond the still dormant camp to the gently rippling waters of the River Foyle. His concern for the incipient attack on Lough Neagh had kept sleep from him throughout the night, his mind turning over every detail of the plan, searching for some unforeseen flaw that could culminate in tragedy. But no matter how many times he examined the various aspects of the strategy, the conclusion always remained the same – his victory, and ultimately Erin's, would depend on Bran and his Leinstermen. The fact that the scout he had dispatched the day before had not yet returned, only intensified his uneasiness.

"God forgive me if I have misjudged you, Bran Ui Faelain," he murmured pensively. "If that is so, generations yet to come will curse us both." Lowering his eyes to the encampment below, Niall gazed with affection at the hundreds of warriors who lay huddled on the moss. *Rest on, my sons*, he thought. *There will be much for all of us to do soon enough.*

Suddenly, a Viking horn blared faintly in the distance. Scrambling to his feet, Niall stood motionless and listened. The sound had come from somewhere along the southwestern stretch of the river and he felt suddenly chilled.

"Thorgest!" he whispered.

A second horn wailed into the stillness of the morning air, this time further upriver. Niall pivoted quickly and stared toward the mist shrouded elbow of the River Foyle that faded into the distant horizon. Tiny squares began to appear intermittently between the patches of fog, the golden rays of dawn highlighting their varied colours against the somber grey of the sky.

Longships!

"Mother of God!" he cursed aloud. "We are caught between them!" Charging down the steep embankment, he raced past the bewildered pickets. "To arms!" he bellowed with all the power his lungs could muster. "The Viking are upon us! To arms!"

Still groggy with sleep, hundreds of warriors fumbled with their weapons and tunics as they staggered blindly to their feet, rubbing their eyes and wincing at the dull ache of muscles which had stiffened overnight. Confused and disoriented by the alarm, they collided with one another as they frantically dashed through the chaos to their positions, their equally flustered officers screaming orders and profanities as they feverishly attempted to form the disorganized mass into defensive lines about the camp perimeter.

By the time Niall reached his tent, his bodyguard and several of his senior officers were already waiting for him, their faces tense as they greeted him with a battery of questions. "Come," he commanded gruffly as he brushed past them and stepped into his pavilion. Once inside, he picked up the sword and buckler that lay across a small table and hastily belted it about his waist.

"We have not much time," he announced to the assembly of officers. "It would appear that Thorgest and Bothvar have somehow managed to position their fleets on either side of us, obviously to prevent us from crossing back over the River Foyle and fleeing to Ailech. Now that they have us in the open, this is where they intend to keep us."

"How do we know that it is both fleets," a beardless young officer queried. "Could not one or the other have somehow maneuvered themselves into the same position?"

Niall nodded slowly. "It is possible that they slipped into position under cover of darkness. But that is of little consequence. Either fleet poses a serious threat to us. Without the Leinstermen we will be sorely outnumbered."

"Then why are we wasting time here?" one of the senior officers demanded. "We have no option but to march east until we rally with the Leinstermen."

"It is too late for that," Niall quickly pointed out. "If the Viking catch us strung out on the march, we will be utterly defenseless. The only chance we have is to form our lines here and send word of our situation to the Ui Faelain. We have no choice but to hold until he arrives."

"Aye," the chieftain stated contemptuously. "*If* he arrives."

An uneasy hush filled the pavilion as Niall looked up. "One of us will soon be proven wrong," he said quietly, then glanced at the faces crowded about him. "Go back to your men and have them make ready. Remind them that they are Ulstermen and that it is their homeland they are about to defend."

When they had filed out of the pavilion, Niall summoned Turloch, then paced back and forth across his quarters as he awaited his arrival. A short time later the burly warrior stooped between the tent flaps, then stood reticently just inside the entrance, the tip of his huge broadsword resting on the ground between his feet. "You sent for me, lord?"

"Aye, Turloch," Niall replied. "I want you to fetch the

swiftest mount you can find and make haste to Dungannon. Tell Bran I beg him to come to Magh Itha before this day's sun is gone; and all of us with it."

Turloch shook his head. "I beseech you send another, lord," he implored. "I am champion of the Ui Neil and captain of your bodyguard. If we are to go into battle, clearly my place is at your side."

"Too many lives depend on the success of this mission," Niall explained, looking up at him. "I cannot entrust it to any other than my finest warrior. Now, go quickly. The passage through the mountains will be difficult, but with the grace of God you should reach them by midday."

"And if he is not there?"

Niall silently prayed that the man's fear was unjustified. "Then you need not return, old friend," he softly replied. "For there will be nothing left of us or Ulster."

CHAPTER TWENTY–SIX

As Turloch galloped east toward the hazy peaks of the mountain range that stretched across the far horizon, Niall set about hastily preparing his warriors for the impending battle. Those who bore sword or thrusting spear were positioned along the outer perimeter of the camp in four ranks of concentric circles, their shields and bodies forming a protective wall for the spear casters, slingers, and archers who stood behind them. Anticipating that the heathens would continually shift the focus of their attack in an attempt to breach the formation, Niall organized his finest warriors into a separate detachment that he himself would lead in support of any weaknesses or gaps as they occurred in the defensive line. Though confident that the stratagem would be effective to a point, he had no illusions that the outer buffer would eventually be penetrated. Once that had occurred, he knew that they would be quickly outflanked and overrun.

Niall glanced up at the position of the sun in the morning sky and silently prayed. Over an hour had elapsed since he had first sighted the longships and he had already concluded that the Norse had no intention of consolidating their fleet and launching a river–bourne assault. *They have marched inland and intend to strike simultaneously from both directions*, he told himself as he surveyed the expanse of the grassy plain around him. *They are out there somewhere, positioning themselves to insure that we are completely surrounded. So much the better. Anything that wastes time is a blessing to us now. The longer the foreigners wait to attack, the greater the chances of Bran reaching us before it is too late.*

Niall pushed the uncertain consequences of the thought out of his mind and kicked his horse forward, circling the perimeter of the camp as he focused his concentration on inspecting the lines of stone–faced men who mutely waited the arrival of the Viking.

A quarter of an hour later they came.

Without warning, the heathen charged out of the surrounding hills and woods, their individual battle cries mingling into a single uproar that seemed to be everywhere at once. *Beserkers* clad in animal skins, their naked bodies brightly painted in bizarre configurations, leapt wildly in the air and rushed ahead of their comrades, their blood frenzy erupting into fits of screaming and howling. Behind them, groups of Norsemen and Danes in leather tunics or chainmail advanced in loose formations, the rattle of their weapons and armour adding to the already deafening cacophony. As they advanced, the formations gradually dissolved into lines that linked up as they drew nearer the Irish, effectively containing them on all sides.

Niall quickly dismounted and stood alongside his flying column, his eyes moving constantly as he carefully gauged the rate of the Viking advance. When the heathen were less than a hundred paces away, he drew his sword and raised it high. Beads of perspiration trickled down his brow as he watched the interval between the two factions gradually diminish. Sixty paces, fifty paces, forty paces. Niall's mouth went suddenly dry as he filled his lungs with the cool morning air, then held his breath for an instant.

"Down!" he bellowed, his voice rising above the crescendoing din. The swordsmen in the outer four ranks immediately dropped to their knees; the archers, slingers and spear casters moving into position behind them, their weapons held ready. Niall's sword slashed through the air.

"Fire!" he roared.

Arrows, stones and spears streaked through the air and found their marks. Scores of foreigners crumpled before their fellows, the momentum of the Viking advance broken as they stumbled over the dead and wounded. But the heathens recovered quickly and responded by hurling back short handled throwing axes and spears with deadly accuracy.

"Forward!" Niall yelled when they were less than twenty paces away. The swordsmen sprang to their feet and the outermost rank surged forward, the warriors screaming the battle cries of their respective clans as they met the Viking with a tremendous crash of shields and steel.

As the two lines came together the foremost Norsemen suddenly found themselves encumbered between the Irish and the press of the Danes at their backs. Blades of battle—axes and broadswords gleamed like molten silver in the morning sunlight, fountains of blood spraying upward wherever they connected with unprotected flesh. Dead and wounded from both sides soon littered the ground, their blood spilling into slippery red patches on the trampled moss that caused many a warrior to lose his footing.

For three hours the battle raged without noticeable advantage to either side. But the superior numbers of the Norse and Danes began to take its toll as the outer line was breached time and time again. Although Niall's flying column had managed so far to patch the gaps, by midafternoon the Irish defenses had begun to weaken as the Viking incursions became more frequent.

Suddenly the low drone of a Norse battle horn wailed across the plain and the heathen began to withdraw, retreating back toward the security of the surrounding woods and hills. Cheering, several of the chieftains began to move their warriors in pursuit, but Niall galloped in front of them waving them back.

"It's a trap!" he shouted frantically. "Return to your positions!"

"But the bastards retreat, my lord," one chieftain protested indignantly. "Now is the time to finish them off!"

"Have you eyes to look beyond the hills and trees?" Niall challenged. The Viking attack had been much weaker than he had anticipated and he wondered why they had not committed all of their warriors and destroyed them in a single stroke.

The chieftain opened his mouth to reply, then hesitated for a moment as he gazed past Niall, his eyes widening. "God help us," he muttered under his breath, his lips quivering.

Glancing over his shoulder, Niall stared in awe at the solid wall of chainmail and shields that was advancing toward them. The Viking had not retreated, merely regrouped. This time there would be no frenzied assault, only the slow methodical tightening of the noose. They advanced in deadly symmetry, the rhythmic tramping of their feet like the heartbeat of a single monstrous entity.

Glaring down at the advancing foreigners from his position atop the hills that fringed the southern edge of Magh

Itha, Bran clenched his teeth, the muscles in his jaw flexing involuntarily as he reached for his sword. Drawing the weapon from its scuffed leather scabbard, he slowly raised it overhead, then glanced over his shoulder at the mass of grave-faced warriors whose gaze was focused on the gleaming blade that would signal them forward.

Bran peered back down at the battlefield, looking beyond the blood and death below, into the soft violet eyes that haunted him. Her eyes, entreating and sorrowful, beckoning him.

"Finola," he whispered softly as he tightened his grip on the hilt of his sword. Abruptly, the steel blade flashed through the air in a narrow arc as he kicked his horse forward.

Pouring over the deep green of the mossy slopes, Bran's cavalry charged down into the open plain like a dark wave, ominous and silent, the dull pounding of hooves across the soft turf drowned out by the din of the battle that raged before them. Bran rode abreast of Rowan and Turloch as he led the irruptive mass of muscle and steel diagonally across the valley floor. His flaming hair and black bear skin mantle flowed out behind him as he repeatedly slapped his galloping mount's hind quarters with the flat of his broadsword. Behind him, the surging ranks of his mounted Leinstermen bristled with the long thrusting spears he had armed them with, sunlight glinting off the upraised steel tips as the warriors swept toward the unprotected flanks of the Viking. Tight lips and clenched teeth stifled the blood chilling battle cries that their aching throats yearned to release, for the king himself had sworn to take the head of the first man to utter a sound.

On the opposite side of the battlefield, some of the Norsemen who had begun to press Niall's Ulstermen along the northern perimeter of their defensive lines gaped in terror at the approaching horsemen, then waved frantically and screamed warnings across the Irish formations to their unsuspecting comrades on the other side. But their efforts were futile, their panicked shrieks of alarm swallowed by the uproar of the fray around them. Helplessly they watched as the oncoming cavalry lowered the shafts of their weapons, directing the glinting spearheads at the exposed backs of the heathen before them.

The Leinstermen struck and hundreds of agonized voices erupted into a collective scream, the narrow steel—tipped spears piercing the soft flesh that lay beneath the wide rings of foreigner's chainmail. The rear ranks of the Viking formation collapsed. Those not killed outright were trampled to death beneath a flurry of hooves as they writhed in pain upon the ground, clawing at the wooden shanks that protruded from their backs. The battered and pulpy heaps left behind bore little resemblance to the men who had stood only moments before.

Alerted by the shrill death screams of those behind them, the startled Norsemen in the front ranks frantically jostled against one another as they strove to swing about and bring their shields to bear against the wave of death that threatened to overwhelm them. But the Irish cavalry had not broken stride, the momentum of their attack carrying them through the panicked formations with such speed that few defenders had time to turn before they were set upon by a swell of flashing steel.

Their spears abandoned in the impaled corpses behind them, many of the Leinstermen had already drawn their broadswords and had begun to hack swaths through the tightly packed mass of Danes and Norsemen. To the complete astonishment and confusion of the Viking, many of the mounted warriors were clad in chainmail and clutched shield and reins in one hand while the other swung wide bladed axes in wide sweeping arcs on either side of their mounts, sending up sprays of blood that spattered both horse and rider.

Then, as the panicked ranks before them disintegrated into a scattering of confused melees, the main contingent of the Leinster cavalry abruptly changed direction. Veering off in a wide semi circle, they swept around behind the tightly packed formations until the Viking were effectively contained on three sides, their line of retreat back to their longships severed. While the horsemen savagely wielded death along the length of the terror–stricken rear ranks, Niall's warriors found new strength and laid on with the fury of men who only moments earlier had looked into the face of defeat. Gradually, they drove the heathen back, forcing them into a congested press where they could scarcely raise their weapons to defend themselves.

Bran was deep in the throng of skirmishing warriors, the scent of sweat and freshly spilled blood assailing his nostrils. The incessant clanging of metal on metal pealed out above the creaking of leather and the rattle of iron chainmail, deafening him to the clamouring shouts and anguished cries. Lost in the rhythm of battle he felt nothing – no fear, no pain, the oozing blood from the wounds on his shield arm and thigh smearing unnoticed against his glistening skin.

Skillfully maneuvering his mount among the host of men locked in mortal combat, he methodically advanced from one opponent to the next, consumed by a killing lust that knew neither compassion nor remorse. Hack, thrust, move forward. Each blow exacted a lethal retribution for the loss of his family. Each gory step somehow led him closer to them.

As he ruthlessly dispatched another Norseman to Valhalla, an ominous blur of movement to his left caught Bran's eye and he quickly twisted above in his saddle, instinctively angling his shield to fend off the anticipated blow. In the instant that he glimpsed the snarling face of the golden thatched Viking who had stepped alongside him, the broadheaded axe crashed into his shield then glanced off the iron boss, the keen–edged blade slicing across the velvety hide at the base of his horse's neck. Whinnying in agony, the panic–stricken mare reared up on her hind legs, her widened eyes rolling back in their sockets as her front hooves pawed at the air.

Caught off balance, Bran grabbed at his horse's flowing mane, leaving his shield dangling uselessly from his forearm. The Viking stepped forward, drawing his weapon back to strike again.

Suddenly, Rowan was galloping toward the Norseman, his sword at the ready. Reining to one side he leaned forward in his saddle. Steel flashed through the air and the blond head careened off the Viking's shoulders amid a fountain of blood.

Regaining control of his frightened mount, Bran quickly inspected the narrow gash on its neck. Satisfied that the wound was only superficial he stroked the animal reassuringly and glanced sideways into Rowan's blood–streaked face.

"Ui Muiredaig Abu!" he yelled at the leather clad warrior who grinned back at him. Rowan touched the crimsoned blade of his sword to his forehead in salute, then both men kicked their horses forward to meet their next opponents.

Throughout the long afternoon and into early evening, the Irish gnawed at the steadily crumbling lists of the Viking formations that struggled to hold their positions, too engaged in the urgent task of defending both front and rear to initiate any kind of synchronized counterattack. By sunset, any semblance of organization within their ranks had completely disappeared, discipline forsaken as the instinct for self–preservation governed each man's actions.

With the Irish offensive gathering momentum, Bran left his position briefly and guided his horse south to a grassy knoll overlooking the bloodied plain. From his vantage point he critically eyed the battlefield, assessing the after effects of his charge and seeking potential weaknesses in the plan that was still taking shape beneath him. Caught in the vice created by the Leinster cavalry and Niall's Ulstermen, the harried Viking had already begun to flee in the direction of the only escape route left open to them – west toward the Sperrin Mountains and the fortified sanctuary that lay beyond at Lough Neagh. Suddenly, the northern and southern most wings of the Norse and Danish lines collapsed, the foreigners trampling their slower comrades as they turned and swarmed through the narrow gap in full retreat.

"Now Ulster!" Bran muttered hoarsely, rising in his saddle. "Now is your time!"

As if in response to the inaudible command, Niall's

warriors surged forward, driving the remnants of the Viking centre before them. Scores of men fell before the ruthless on-slaught, speared or hacked down from behind as they desperately scrambled for open ground. Dogged by the clamouring Irish, the ravaged heathen army spilled across the plain, a tumultuous swell of frenzied humanity whose sole aim was to evade the death that now stalked them.

Abruptly, the contented grin dropped from Bran's face. The Ulstermen were breaking off their attack, the front ranks' progress arrested by the chieftains and officers who rode along the line barking orders and reforming the warriors into neatly arranged companies.

"What in God's name...," he fumed, savagely kicking his mount while his gaze remained fixed on the steadily widening gap between the fleeing Viking and the now static Irish. Scarcely able to contain his fury, he galloped back across the corpse littered battlefield to the clamouring warriors whose lilting songs of victory drifted across the plain on the gentle breeze that was already heavy with the stench of rotting flesh. Oblivious to the cheers that greeted him, Bran impatiently forced his way through the crush of rejoicing soldiers, slowly working his way toward the Ard–Ri's standard.

"Ui Faelain!" Niall shouted heartily as their eyes met, then urged his mount forward to meet him, Turloch dutifully riding at his right knee while the Ulster chieftains followed along closely behind. When he reached Bran, the Ard–Ri reined his horse in and smiled, relief washing over his besmudged face. "Thank God you are alive!" he exclaimed as he passed the back of his swordhand over one crimson stained cheek. Beneath the gold circlet that had saved his life, blood still oozed from the ugly gash on Niall's brow. "I feared that our victory had been gained at the expense of my most valued ally."

"You have gained nothing!" Bran snarled, his voice quaking with anger. "It is the Viking, not us, who are winning the battle for Ulster."

Cheering in the ranks that surrounded the party of horsemen quickly subsided as the puzzled warriors nearest to Bran compelled their comrades to silence.

"You speak in riddles, my lord," Turloch remarked flatly, his bushy eyebrows drawn together as he frowned at Bran and pointed to the retreating swarm in the distance. "The heathen flee before us like frightened hares."

"Aye," Bran grunted derisively. "They escape to Lough Neagh while you all stand here congratulating yourselves. Can't you see that by not pursuing him, you have given Bothvar all the time he needs to consolidate his warriors and prepare his defenses. Once the Vikings are barricaded within their fortress, it will be both difficult and costly to root them out."

"Then we shall lay siege to them," Niall interjected, "as we originally planned. But now, rather than attempting to lure the Viking into ambush, we need only blockade them. When their reserves of food and water are expended they will be compelled to yield, and we will have accomplished our task with far less Irish blood spilled than might have been otherwise." He paused and smiled, his steel blue eyes not unlike those of Bran's own father, reflecting both the ferocity and compassion that lay within. "Be patient, my friend, and together we will bring Bothvar and his pagan rabble to their knees."

"I doubt that will be accomplished before Thorgest arrives," Bran said grimly, "as he inevitably will."

"Thorgest?" Turloch scoffed loudly. "Your concern is unwarranted, my lord. That serpent is either dead or slithering alongside his minions to Lough Neagh. Every man here knows that only Thorgest could have attacked us from the south with such a sizable force."

"Then you are all fools," Bran countered wryly. "If Thorgest had acted jointly with Bothvar, none of us would be alive to speculate on his whereabouts."

Turloch leaned forward in his saddle and opened his mouth to speak, but Niall gestured him to be silent.

"It is not Thorgest we need concern ourselves with," Bran continued, shifting his gaze back to Niall. "Although Bothvar's warriors have suffered heavy losses and withdrawn in panic, their numbers remain greater than ours. If they rally and turn on us, we will be hard pressed to hold our own against them."

"Your mounted warriors have already tipped the scales in our favour once today," Niall replied confidently. "If the need arises, they will do so again."

Bran shook his head. "They were only effective as shock troops because they were unexpected. Now that Bothvar has encountered my horsemen, I doubt he will be caught off guard a second time. Once he realizes that my cavalry are your only reserves and not part of some larger contingent, their presence will do little to deter him."

"What of the remainder of your warriors?"

"They await us at Dungannon," Bran explained. "If

Bothvar is allowed to regroup and counterattack on this side of the Sperrin Mountains they will be of no use to us."

"And if he doesn't, your Leinstermen will be caught between him and Lough Neagh."

Bran nodded slowly.

"What do you propose we do?" Niall asked, concern in his face. Behind him, the Ulster chieftains remained silent and Bran paused for a moment, choosing his words carefully.

"A messenger must be sent to alert my warriors at Dungannon. Then we must keep our swords in Bothvar's back — prevent him from consolidating. If he can be driven across the Sperrin Mountains he will be trapped in the open between both our armies." Bran glanced up at the patches of scarlet rimmed clouds that were the harbingers of nightfall. "But it will be dark soon and we must act quickly."

Niall shook his head. "My men are exhausted and their bellies empty. I cannot expect them to march all night without food or rest."

"They are warriors," Bran answered coldly. "They will do what they must."

"And what would you have me do with the wounded?" Niall queried, his voice rising. "Many will die if they are not attended to."

Bran hated himself for what he was about to say, but knew it to be the only answer he could give. "Many more will die if we delay for their sake. We have no choice but to leave the serious casualties behind. Those who can still walk and fight will come with us — so long as they keep pace."

"The Leinsterman goes too far!" Turloch blurted as he turned to Niall. "You cannot expect us to desert our comrades and friends, lord. The Ui Faelain would have us dishonour ourselves to save his own!" As grumbled agreement rippled among the Ulster chieftains and through the ranks of their warriors, Bran noticed Rowan and several of his own men edging closer to him. "We have listened to the Leinsterman long enough!" Turloch added, shaking his fist. "We do not need him to – "

"Turloch!" Niall's voice rose clear and cold. "You dishonour yourself and all of us by insulting the man to whom we owe our lives. Were it not for the Ui Faelain and his warriors, the ravens of battle would this moment be feasting on our corpses. Are we now to ignore our debt to the men of Leinster?"

The startled warrior hesitated and cast about the others who had fallen abruptly silent. Turning to Bran, Turloch lowered his eyes. "Forgive me, my lord," he muttered as he bowed his head. "I – "

"Your concern for your comrades cannot be faulted," Bran interjected. "I have no more wish to leave the wounded behind than you. But understand this – they are also my comrades. We did not come here to fight at your side because of which clan or province or king you swear allegiance to. We came because you and I and every other man who takes up arms against the invader belongs to one clan – Erin."

"Look not to the past, but to the future, Turloch," Niall told him. He glanced at Bran then surveyed the haggard faces of his chieftains. "Make ready to march," the Ard–Ri commanded them. "We leave within the hour. God willing, tomorrow the sun will set on a free Ulster."

CHAPTER TWENTY–SEVEN

Throughout the night, the Irish swept southeast across the plains of Magh Itha like a wave of fire, the long formations of men carefully aligned so that the torches they bore alluded to a much larger contingent than daylight would ultimately betray. Wavering pools of amber light danced along the ground ahead of the advancing warriors, periodically illuminating the shields and equipment which had been hastily discarded by the retreating foreigners. Strident voices rose above the monotonous tramping of feet as the Ulster soldiers bickered among themselves over the ownership of each newly commandeered trophy. To the north of their steadily filing ranks, the torches of scouting parties flickered between the trees like a friar's lanterns while the Viking deserters and stragglers who had fled into the woods were systematically hunted down.

For several hours the leagues passed beneath the well–worn sandals of Niall's army, the level plain gradually rising to the highlands of the heather–clad moors. Near midnight they reached the base of the Sperrin Mountains and began cautiously winding their way along the narrow pass that meandered between the granite giants. Veils of cloud glided ethereally across the pale moon overhead, animating the shadows which clung to the jagged ridges so that strange, foreboding shapes lurked and moved in the darkness behind every rock. The raw wind crooned and howled along the snaking corridor like a lost soul, chilling both flesh and spirit and adding another dimension to the fear that already knotted in each warrior's belly.

The ghostly terrain was well suited to ambush, and

those at the head of the long column rounded each fresh bend in the path warily, their clammy palms tightly clutching readied weapons. Eyes that already burned with fatigue scanned the night for the one aberrant movement or glint of metal that would herald death's arrival.

Watching. Waiting.

Anticipating the searing pain of cold steel.

But with the passing hours it became evident that the fleeing heathen had not thought to leave a rear guard to protect their withdrawal. As darkness reluctantly surrendered to the incipient light of day, the exhausted Irish gradually made their way down the gentler grade of the eastern slopes to the moss and heather blanketed foothills, the men fanning out into long lines that undulated rhythmically across the irregular landscape.

Then, as the rising sun banished the last vestiges of night, several of the warriors in the vanguard shouted excitedly and pointed to the far side of the glen that stretched out before them. In the distance, the Viking oozed across the valley floor like a stain toward the tranquil waters of Lough Neagh that lay beyond. But the fact that the heathen were retreating did little to augment the confidence of the Ulstermen. In the daylight they could see how severely they were outnumbered. Still, they continued to press on, their love of Niall and hatred of the foreigners propelling them forward.

Near midday, Niall abruptly signaled the long lines of men to halt, reining in his mount as he turned to Bran and pointed east to the large contingent of warriors that had suddenly emerged from beyond the outlying hills. Even at a distance, the conical helmets and chainmail were clearly discernible as a body of troops marching to meet the fleeing heathen.

"It is exactly as we feared," Niall muttered grimly. "Thorgest has landed with reinforcements for Lough Neagh."

Bran squinted at the dark legions which continued to move north toward the Viking stronghold, apparently oblivious to their presence. "I do not think so," he said slowly, a broad smile gradually spreading across his face as he peered at the familiar banners that fluttered above the columns. "Not unless the Viking have adopted the wolf as their standard."

"What?"

The chilling drone of a war horn suddenly erupted from the distant ranks and as it moaned across the rolling landscape, Bran recognized the signal to attack.

"Christ, Niall!" he exclaimed, catching the Ard–Ri's sleeve. "Those aren't Vikings – they're Leinstermen! Flann has brought up the infantry from Dungannon!" He released his grip and wagged his head in astonishment. "God bless that bastard. He's marched those lads all night to get here."

"Then we have a battle to win," Niall declared. "Come on, Ulster!" he called back to the chafing warriors. "Now's your time!"

The armies of Leinster and Ulster gradually converging, the Irish pursued the Viking relentlessly, gaining ground so rapidly that they were little more than a league behind when the harried foreigners reached the gates of their fortress at Lough Neagh. They were close enough to hear the bellowed orders of the jarls and panicked shrieks of women as the occupants of the farmsteads which surrounded the settlement clamoured alongside the warriors who poured through the main gate, seeking refuge within the towering palisades. Once inside, the alarmed heathens had scarcely enough time to bar the massive oak doors before the screaming warriors of Ulster and Leinster descended upon them.

On Niall's orders, timbers were cut down from the nearby woods and used as battering rams, the Irish frantically labouring to smash through the entry. Even though the walls of the stronghold had been set afire, the thick billowing smoke affording them some measure of cover, the Vikings on the ramparts above cast spears and poured hot pitch over the heads of the defenseless men below. But each time a warrior fell, another took his place until at last the gate gave way, the wood crackling loudly as it splintered. Pouring through the breach in a great torrent, the army swept along the dirty wood–paved streets driving the heathen before them, putting the torch to the wooden sheilings which blazed like tinder and filled the enclosure with dense, choking smoke.

Gradually the Viking began to fall back, retreating toward the longships which lay moored in the harbours behind them. They had almost reached the beach when Niall's archers began to launch volley after volley of arrows which had been soaked in pitch and ignited, the flaming shafts arcing across the sky to the wooden decks of the vessels. Before the Viking could react, the bulk of the fleet was ablaze. With their only means of escape rapidly becoming a raging inferno at their backs, some of the Norse and Danish warriors threw themselves at their antagonists, screaming wildly until they were overwhelmed and silenced. Many more turned and ran, discarding their weapons as they dashed into the water, then clawed frantically at the hulls and oars as they tried to pull themselves aboard the vessels which remained intact. Others that followed were pushed back into the water or slain by their comrades already aboard. Only those fortunate enough to reach the longships first found a place for themselves.

Of the scores of ships that made up the fleet, a few escaped to the middle of the lough, moving south to the mouth of the River Bann, the men who strained at the oars oblivious to the cries of the comrades they had left behind on the shore. The stranded men fought on with the ferocity of the doomed, their ships blazing in the harbour behind them. Some laid down their arms and begged for mercy – only to be cut down in droves until the water that lapped at the shoreline ran red with their blood and the beach was littered with the dead and the dying.

Their bloodlust only whetted by the slaughter at the harbour, the Irish turned their fury back upon the settlement. Then, the killing began in earnest. Old men, women, children were put to the sword as the delirious warriors baptized their vengeance with blood, venting their hatred on the foreigners who had ravaged their country and their lives.

Helpless in the swell of destruction that now swept into the town, Bran guided his mount through the frenzied horde, imploring Irish warriors to halt the senseless butchery.

"For the love of Christ – No!" he screamed hoarsely, trying to make himself heard above the war cries of the warriors and the terrified shrieks of their victims. "Put up your weapons! The heathen are defeated!"

But his pleas went unheeded. One chainmail clad Leinsterman dashed out into the street from a burning shieling just as the roof collapsed, a golden–haired infant in his arms.

He smiled broadly as he glanced up at Bran, then suddenly tossed the child high into the air. In that instant Bran realized the atrocity had been borrowed from the Norse, and before he could act, the warrior savagely thrust his weapon upward as the wailing baby fell, impaling the tiny body on the blade of his sword. Bran slew the man, then kicked his horse forward.

This must be stopped, a voice inside him screamed as he looked around for Niall's banner. *This must be stopped.*

As he turned down a side street between two rows of burning buildings, a young girl suddenly cut in front of him, running from one of the houses, a stocky Ulsterman in pursuit. Catching one of the golden braids that flowed out behind her, the warrior threw her violently to the ground. As she screamed and writhed beneath him, he tore open the front of her dress, revealing her small breasts. She struggled to kick herself free of him, but the warrior pulled up her *skyrta* and cruelly forced her legs apart.

Diving from his saddle, Bran landed on the Irishman's back, knocking him sideways. Before he could recover, Bran was upon him, smashing the hilt of his sword into the warrior's face.

"No more! No more!" Bran raged as he struck repeatedly, oblivious to the man's yelps for mercy. Here in his grasp twisted the entity who had killed his father and brother, taken his family from him, and glutted itself on the misery it had brought to the people of Erin. Now, his free hand locked on the beast's throat, it would not escape. He would crush the evil that was the demon's soul and put an end to its unholy reign of terror.

Even after the Ulsterman had ceased to struggle, Bran continued to bludgeon him.

"Bran!" a voice called out to him from somewhere beyond the fury that roared in his ears. "Ui Faelain!"

Bran paused, his bloodied sword hand in midair. Looking up through the veil of red mist that obscured his sight, he peered at the silhouetted figures who stood over him. As his vision gradually cleared, he saw that Niall and Turloch were among them and he slowly rose to his feet, his chest heaving.

"You can stop now, Bran," he heard Niall say, the high king's voice barren of feeling. "He's dead."

Bran glanced down at the pulpy abscess that had been the Ulsterman's face. Beside the bloody corpse, the Norse girl looked up at him, her eyes widened in terror. Lifting his head slowly, Bran stared past the Ard–Ri and his bodyguards, scanning the carnage that surrounded them.

Few buildings had escaped the torch, and thick chalky smoke swirled throughout the compound, stinging Bran's eyes and filling his nostrils with the acrid scent of burning timber. Through the ghostly smother he glimpsed the few remaining pockets of resistance, the ill–fated defenders cursing and taunting their antagonists as they fought back to back in small clusters, surrounded by the sea of Irish warriors. Seeking refuge from the murder and lust that stalked them, Norse and Danish women ran erratically about the settlement, their high pitched screams punctuating the battle cries and the clanging of weapons.

Abruptly, Bran reached out and caught Niall's tunic, his voice cracking with emotion. "Please," he pleaded, tears welling in his reddened eyes. "You must... stop this."

Niall waved back Turloch and the guards who had moved in to protect him. "I cannot," he told Bran in a husky whisper. "No more than I can contain the wind. These men have sworn to avenge their own and their wrath will not now be harnessed. The heathen brought terror to our shores and unleashed it upon our people. Now, like a rabid hound, it has turned upon its master."

"But there has been enough killing," Bran began wearily, then glanced over his shoulder at the young Norse girl who still lay cowering in the dirt behind him. Sheathing his sword he turned toward her and smiled reassuringly as he stooped down and offered his hand. The girl drew back from him warily, clutching her torn robe to her breast. "Come," he entreated her softly. "You will be safe now." Cautiously she took his hand. Bran helped her rise, then wrapped his blood stained arm about her shoulders and stared back at Niall. "Grant her the protection of your guardianship."

Niall opened his mouth to reply, then caught himself and shrugged resignedly. He spoke briefly to Turloch who nodded curtly, then gestured one of the bodyguards to follow as he stepped forward and relieved Bran of his charge.

"You take too much upon yourself, my friend," Niall offered. "Do not add the sins of other men to the burden of the gold that already weighs heavy upon your brow."

Bran adjusted the bearskin mantle that was draped over his shoulders. "I have no choice," he replied evenly. "That burden was mine – and yours from the time when men first called us king."

Niall scratched his beard as he studied him. "Come," he said. "Let me show you something that will relieve your guilt and temper the madness you have witnessed here this day with reason."

The sun had already begun to yield to the half light of dusk as the two men slowly wound their way toward the hub of the settlement, stepping over the corpses that lay where they had fallen along the narrow street. Bathed in the lurid glow of the fires that continued to consume the buildings on either side of the blood–drenched lane, the dead stared up at Bran, their unseeing eyes haunting him.

Abruptly, the image of the Ulsterman he had slain, the battered face no longer recognizable, flared within his mind's eye.

What demon possessed my hand to slay that man, he wondered with remorse. *It was not necessary, for I had prevented his attack on the girl and he was restrained. Yet, that was not enough. A temporary madness drove me to vengeance, and in so doing I became a victim of my own violence. I cannot sit in judgment of others without likewise condemning myself. Concealed beneath a facade of righteousness, my anger and thirst for revenge has lurked in the depths of my soul like an assassin, awaiting the moment it could leap forth and strike. God forgive me, for I no longer had the will to suppress it.*

Bran suddenly realized that the screams and clash of arms that had filled his brain earlier had been mysteriously silenced, replaced by the cheers and drunken uproar of the Irish warriors who thronged the open area surrounding the Viking hall. As he strode among them at the Ard–Ri's side, their voices rose to a deafening clamour.

"Long life to you Niall Caille!"

"Lord love you both – saviours of Erin!"

"God's blessings on the wolf of Leinster!"

Following the bodyguards who quickly forged a path through the press of exhilarated warriors, Bran and Niall finally reached the charred entry to the Viking hall, around which numerous sentinels had already been posted.

While nearly all the other buildings at Lough Neagh had been put to the torch, the firehall had sustained only superficial damage. Judging from the number of warriors who had been allocated to cordon off the area, it was obvious to Bran that the Ard–Ri intended it to remain intact. As the guards closed the heavy oak doors behind them, Bran squinted at the shadowy figures who sat huddled about one of the tables at the opposite end of the dimly lit hall.

"Who are they?" he asked Niall in a throaty whisper.

"Look well, my friend," Niall replied as he removed a torch from the bracket on the wall beside him. "They are the future that the heathen would thrust upon Erin. Come."

Gradually the two men wended their way through a disarray of tables and overturned chairs until finally the wavering torchlight washed over the faces of the small congregation. Affording Bran and Niall little more than a cursory glance, they sat in silence, greedily devouring the bowls of stirabout that had been set before them. Most were spindle–legged boys, hollow cheeked and pale, their movements quick and feral as they gorged themselves. Two young girls, their budding breasts ill–concealed beneath their flimsy shifts, sat isolated at one end of the table. Aged by their powdered faces and stained lips, they looked up at Bran with old young eyes that had seen and endured too much.

"Christ, Niall," he muttered, glancing sideways.

"Where did all these children come from?"

"They were taken in raids and brought here by the heathen to be used as slaves and concubines," he answered. "Those who resisted were either killed outright or... disciplined." Walking to the side of one curly-haired boy who had not yet touched his food, Niall handed his torch to one of the guards and caught the lad up in his arms, then handed him to Bran. "Show him," he said quietly.

Hesitantly, the little boy opened his mouth. Bran winced at the sight of a pulpy stub. The child's tongue had been cut out.

"I am told he screamed when he was forced to submit to his master's desire," Niall explained as he gently took the boy from Bran and eased him back onto his seat. "He is but one of many. These are only a few of the Irish prisoners we found."

Bran felt suddenly cold and he shuddered. "What of the others?" he heard himself ask.

"Their bodies surround the altar to the heathen's pagan god," Niall told him. "Slaughtered only hours before we arrived."

Bran started to turn away but Niall caught his arm. "Your family was not among them." In the soft light of the torch, the creases on the high king's forehead deepened. "If they live, we will find them at Lough Ree."

"Then you do intend to march south?" Bran asked quickly.

Niall nodded. "Aye. But not before we have cut off the head of the serpent. Once that is accomplished, we need not fear his coils."

"I do not understand."

"Thorgest must die," Niall replied, his voice laced with hatred. "And die he will when Malachy delivers him into our hands."

"How?" Bran shot back, startled at the suggestion that the King of Meath could accomplish such a task.

"Ever since you defeated the foreigners on the River Liffey, Thorgest has been wooing Meath even as he did Munster, anxious to establish a treaty that would drive a wedge between Leinster and Ulster. Though he has remained neutral, Malachy has kept me informed of Thorgest's proposals and now, at my request, has arranged to meet him in secret to discuss the terms of an alliance. In a fortnight's time they will meet at one of the small garrisons Thorgest maintains within Meath – on the banks of Lough Owel."

Bran frowned. "I do not trust Malachy. Why is he so anxious now to commit his warriors to fighting the foreigners when he would not do so before?"

"It would appear that the Viking have accomplished what Malachy himself could not," Niall told him. "After Armagh was destroyed, Thorgest's wife, who is some kind of priestess or witch, desecrated that ancient holy place by offering her pagan sacrifices on the same altar that was once used by St. Padraic. So insulted were the clans of Meath by that vile act that they are now united in their outrage and clamouring for revenge. Yet, Malachy dare not call his men to arms for fear of alerting Thorgest to his plan and facing the full brunt of his fury alone."

"Then we must march to Lough Owel to spring the trap ourselves," Bran urged.

Niall shook his head. "To do so would likewise alert Thorgest to our own intent. Malachy's neutrality has given Thorgest many eyes in Meath and an army on the move cannot be concealed. The task therefore must fall to you and your Leinstermen."

"My men are no less visible than yours," Bran replied. "Thorgest will be expecting us to march south for those who fled will no doubt inform him that a contingent of Leinstermen fought at your side at Lough Neagh."

"Exactly," Niall agreed. "And his eyes will be on them, not the warriors you left behind in Naas." He slowly stalked across the room then turned abruptly to Bran, his steel grey eyes catching the light from the flickering torches. "Less than a full day's march east of Lough Owel is the royal *crannog* of Tigerhnach, one of Malachy's most trusted chieftains and a man well known for his loathing of the heathen. Were you to send word back to the rest of your men, they could be marshalled in secret at his island fortress. Together with Tigerhnach's clansmen, they would have little difficulty in overpowering the garrison at Lough Owel and preparing an ambush to greet Thorgest when he arrives."

"But what of the warriors I brought here, to Lough Neagh?" Bran asked. "Surely they would be of better use to us positioned nearer the Meath border, to be sent in as reinforcements should the need arise."

Niall waved the suggestion aside. "We must lead them and the army of Ulster back to Ailech," he replied. "Thorgest must be convinced that I am content to remain in the north if our plan is to succeed."

"You ask me to leave my people undefended," Bran

said uneasily. "Even if the ambush succeeds, the heathen will look to Leinster for retribution. And with our warriors scattered all over Erin, there would be little to stop them."

"Not if we strike first," Niall pointed out. "Once the foreigners are without a leader, Malachy will march west on their stronghold at Lough Ree while we attack from the north. United, the warriors of Ulster, Leinster and Meath will finally drive the Viking back into the sea that brought them."

"It would seem that Malachy has already agreed to your proposal."

"He has," Niall affirmed, grinning. "But it is your commitment we need if victory is ultimately to be ours."

Bran glanced back at the ragged children who were cluttered about the table. *The future the heathens would thrust upon us*, he thought, recalling Niall's words. When he looked back at the Ard–Ri his decision had been made.

"In the morning I will send a messenger to Naas, summoning my warriors to Tigerhnach's crannog," he said with conviction. "But I myself will meet them there."

Niall frowned. "Such a risk is unwarranted," he said disapprovingly. "The journey is not without peril. Should you fall into the hands of the foreigners, Leinster will be left without her king at a time when he is needed most."

"Rowan and a small escort shall accompany me," Bran said firmly. "As for Leinster," he added, his voice softening, "the crown I bear is but a part of my life. The other part awaits me at Lough Ree."

CHAPTER TWENTY-EIGHT

Five days after the massacre at Lough Neagh, Thorgest listened with mounting fury as Bothvar stood before him in the firehall at Lough Ree, outlining the details of his defeat and subsequent narrow escape. His face haggard and drawn, Bothvar spoke in a guttural voice weakened by his obvious fatigue, the dried blood on the sleeves of his *kirtle* and tattered breeches attesting to the rigors of his ordeal. Surrounded by the jarls and sea chieftains who sat at their tables, Bothvar's eyes darted nervously between Thorgest and the dark haired Dane at his side. When at last he paused, Bothvar lowered his gaze to the floor.

"And the rest of the fleet?" Thorgest demanded wrathfully, leaning forward in his chair.

"Gone, my lord," Bothvar answered without looking up. "Destroyed. The ships that brought us here are all that remains of the fleet."

Thorgest glared at him. "Your folly and ambition have cost us much. Only a thickwit could convert such an opportunity to disaster. How many times have we tried, without success, to draw Niall out into the open so that we could confront him with all our strength. When he left Ailech you had only to send word to me and by now his head would be decorating our roofposts."

Bothvar raised his eyes fearfully. "I did not think it necessary, lord," he stammered helplessly. "Our numbers were far greater than those of the Irish king. The battle would have been ours had they not been reinforced by the Leinstermen."

"Leinstermen?" Thorgest snarled. "More likely you

underestimated Niall's strength. The Leinster king would dare not leave his own territory to march so far north."

"It's true, lord," Bothvar protested. "I swear. I saw him myself – the one they call Wolfblade. He came from nowhere, leading a host of mounted warriors who were armed with battle–axe and clad in chainmail even as we ourselves were."

"He lies!" one of the older jarls exclaimed, rising from his seat. "No man can manage his mount and wield an axe in combat without being unhorsed."

"I know what men can do!" Bothvar exploded, turning to face the man. "I was there! I saw them! Rider and horse were as one... demons... half man, half beast who trampled out comrades beneath their cloven hooves. And even as we fled through the night they hunted us; even darkness could not conceal us from their eyes. We no sooner came within sight of our *longphort* when another host of warriors appeared, as if the dead had risen up out of the ground to avenge themselves upon us."

"I fear no man," a stocky sea chieftain growled. "But only a fool does battle with the evil one."

Bothvar's head bobbed on his thick neck. "It is true... I have fought them and I can tell you; they are not men but the spawn of the darkworld and they will not be stopped. To stay here and fight such creatures is to die."

"He is right," another jarl blurted out. "Let us return home in our longships or seek out some other place where – "

"Enough!" Thorgest bellowed as he sprang to his feet and pointed an accusing finger at Bothvar. "We have already spent too much time listening to your superstitious rambling. We are not women or children to be frightened off by tales of fiends and goblins." Dropping his arm to his side, he scanned the faces of the warriors who looked up at him. "Hear me – all of you. The warriors of Leinster are naught but men who will bleed as any others when our swords bite into their flesh. And face them we will. The slaughter of our countrymen at Lough Neagh cannot go unavenged. Until that time, if your fear needs substance look to Niall Caille, for there can be little doubt he will be looking to us. And if we are to believe our comrade, Bothvar, he will not be coming alone. Go now, each of you, attend to your warriors. Make certain they sleep with their weapons at their sides. Double the guard on the fleet and see to it that the other sentries are rotated no less than every hour. And tell them I myself will cut the throat of any man I find asleep at his post. If Niall does attack he will not find us unprepared."

While the jarls rose from their tables, muttering among themselves, Thorgest eyed Bothvar who glanced about uncertainly as he stood isolated near the firepit. "Fjoinir," he called out, gesturing to one of his warriors. "See to it that quarters are provided for Bothvar and his comrades. Have food and drink taken to them immediately along with whatever else they require for their pleasure. I have no intention of neglecting these heroic men now they are in my care." He grinned at Bothvar.

The ragged Norseman smiled nervously back at him, then shuffled after Fjolnir. Thorgest watched until the last of his men had filed out of the firehall, then turned to Ragnar. He saw the disapproval in the cold black eyes that stared back at him and frowned.

"I have seen that look before, my friend, and I know it

well," he told Ragnar. "What troubles you?"

"It is a mistake to wait," came the blunt reply. "With Wolfblade in the north, Leinster lies before us ripe and unprotected. You yourself said that we must face them eventually, so why should we not be the one to strike the first blow?"

"And repeat Bothvar's mistake?" Thorgest shot back. "Until I know Niall's intentions I will not split our strength and leave Lough Ree only partially defended."

"To hesitate is to give him time," Ragnar protested. "Time to seek out allies, to build his strength."

Thorgest grinned. "We are not without allies of our own. And in less than a fortnight we may be able to include Meath among them."

"Surely you do not still intend to meet the Meath King at Lough Owel, lord," Ragnar exclaimed. "The journey now will be even more hazardous for news of the Irish victory will have spread quickly. Perhaps Malachy has already joined them."

"Malachy is an old man whose crown is threatened by feuds between his own chieftains," Thorgest answered, shrugging. "Until now, he has long refused to ally himself with our enemies for fear that Meath herself would be subjected to the same fate as Ulster. He has therefore tolerated periodic raids and even the establishment of our garrisons in his territory. No Ragnar, I think we can continue to rely on his fear."

"And if Niall marches south through Meath?"

"We shall know of it," Thorgest replied confidently. "The combined armies of Ulster and Leinster on the march will not be easily secreted. In the meantime, it is we who shall gather our strength. Send word to Feidlimid of Munster instructing him to send all the warriors he can spare to Lough Ree immediately. With our forces thus combined, Niall's rabble will be no match for us."

"But will the Munster king be willing to commit his warriors to fighting our battle?" Ragnar wondered aloud.

"He has long been anxious to avenge himself on both Niall and Bran Ui Faelain," Thorgest assured him. "And apart from the personal satisfaction of revenge, defeating Bran Ui Faelain will put an end to the eraic he has been compelled to render to Leinster for the slaying of the old king. Indeed, his greed will guarantee his cooperation." He paused a moment, thoughtfully stroking his golden beard. "And have him send along Kenan Ui Faelain. I would know more of his brother – the one they call Wolfblade."

"As you wish, my lord." Ragnar turned to leave, but Thorgest caught his arm and held him fast.

"The two qualities in a man that I will not abide are incompetence and cowardice," Thorgest said quietly. "Bothvar has brought shame and dishonour on both himself and his comrades. It will not be thought unusual that his life be taken by his own hand." Releasing his grasp, Thorgest met the Dane's dark eyes. "I do not wish to look upon his face again. See to it."

Ragnar grinned and nodded.

Clutching his cloak about him against the chill of the morning air, Kenan led the small contingent of nearly two hundred Munstermen north along the grassy heaths that occupied the lowlands surrounding the River Shannon; the rich, fertile landscape interrupted only occasionally by the farm-

steads which were nestled between treacherous bogs and scattered ranges of peat–clad moors. An hour later, the beauty of
the pastoral terrain was marred by the skeletal ruins of
Clocnamaise. As they passed by the charred remains of the
once sublime monastery, Kenan continued to wonder with
growing uneasiness why Thorgest's message had included a
stringent request that he himself accompany the reinforcements.

The Norse leader's envoy had reached Cashel three
days earlier and though irritated by the brusque tone of
Thorgest's demands, Feidlimid had finally yielded to the counsel of his advisors and ordered that a token force be dispatched
to Lough Ree. But rather than delegating any of the professional soldiers he retained, the Munster king pressed into service only men of the worst quality, brigands and thieves who
readily volunteered once informed that refusal to comply
would be worth their lives. When Kenan suggested to him
that Thorgest would surely be insulted by both the diminu-
tive size and questionable worth of the ragged band, Feidlimid
had only laughed.

"They are all I can spare," he wheezed between the
guffaws that shook his corpulent body. Recovering, he dabbed
at his tearing eyes then looked down at Kenan ruefully. "Forgive me, my friend," he begged, affecting a pout, "but it amuses
me that my precise compliance to Thorgest's directive, that
tender appeal so eloquently phrased, has also enabled me to
relocate the larger percentage of Cashel's vermin to Lough
Ree. Of course, you will have to take along your own bodyguards to insure that your fellow travellers do not... get lost
enroute to their destination. But they will no doubt be hap-

pier in their new home, don't you think?"

Kenan frowned. "I think Thorgest will take offense at your interpretation of his summons," he answered. "Taunting such a man, my lord, is a dangerous gamble."

Feidlimid's rounded shoulders hinted a perfunctory shrug beneath the voluminous folds of his robe. "From what I have been told, Thorgest will soon be preoccupied with matters much more pressing than his wounded ego." He grinned balefully, the dimples in the fleshy pouches of his mottled cheeks deepening. "If he feels slighted, perhaps Niall will consent to adjudicate his grievance against me."

"I think it more likely he will take up his complaints with me," Kenan uttered sourly, annoyed by the king's flippancy. "You can well afford this little jest at Thorgest's expense for it is not you who will stand before him at Lough Ree. I fear this outrage may well influence his disposition toward me and my claim to the throne of Leinster."

Mirth suddenly fled Feidlimid's countenance, leaving only indifference. "What passes between you and he is not my concern." He ponderously struggled to his feet. "I opposed Ulster and Leinster openly once before and shall not make the mistake of doing so again. Thorgest may well succeed where I did not and, if he honours his pledge to you, the crown of Leinster will be yours. In that event, you will both find Munster a valuable ally and a willing partner in trade. But until then, we wait."

With that, Feidlimid had turned his back on Kenan and ambled out of the great hall, leaving him alone to contemplate his hatred of the Munster king. The abrupt withdrawal of his patronage had not surprised Kenan. Through-

out his stay in Cashel he had frequently witnessed the calculated unfolding of Feidlimid's intrigues and his skillful ma-
nipulation of the clan chieftains, playing one off against another while he himself remained innocently aloof. Gradually
Kenan had come to realize that behind the lies and deceit
which were the essence of his potency cowered a weak and
selfish man, with love and loyalty to nothing beyond his own
avarice. Here was not a powerful warrior king such as his father had been, but rather a petty despot whose greed steadily
sucked at the lifeblood of Munster and Kenan had grown to
despise him.

His hatred had been further aggravated by Feidlimid's
steadily increasing interest in Taillte who seemed to flourish
in the light of his attentions. Overcome with anguish at the
loss of her child, she had become withdrawn and reclusive in
the days immediately following her miscarriage, and despite
his frantic efforts to reach her, Kenan had not been able to
distract Taillte from her misery. But as she recovered in the
weeks that passed, Taillte had gradually begun to change, attending with increasing frequency the nightly festivities in
Feidlimid's great hall where she quickly became a favourite,
basking in the attentions of the warriors and noblemen who
fawned upon her, including the Munster king. And much to
Kenan's dissatisfaction, it was Feidlimid who had somehow
managed to rescue Taillte from her anguish, a feat which he
himself had been unable to accomplish.

Initially, Kenan had considered her excesses a mere
distraction from the trauma of her miscarriage, the flamboy-
ant behaviour concealing a true agony within. But as time
passed he came to understand that the flattery and love she

craved was an obsessive appetite that he alone would never be able to appease. Gradually she began to draw away from him, preferring the company of others. Kenan was often left to lie alone at night and ponder what had become of the woman who had once so enthusiastically shared his bed.

Prompted by the jealousy and inadequacy that tormented him, he had therefore insisted that she accompany him to Lough Ree. At first she had refused, and it was only when he had fully outlined his agreement with Thorgest that she had finally acquiesced. Even so, the two day journey had been long and trying, made all the more so by her remoteness. Now as she rode alongside him in silence he wondered whether it was the love she had confessed so passionately or the prospect of the crown of Leinster which had first brought her to him.

Two hours later they reached the Viking stronghold at Lough Ree and were immediately taken to the firehall where Thorgest and his jarls awaited them. As they stepped through the massive oak doors, Taillte paused to remove her riding cloak, revealing a lena of scarlet silk which had been masterfully designed to accentuate her voluptuous curves. Gracefully, she laid her hand on Kenan's arm and smiled knowingly. A hush then fell over the boisterous assemblage of warriors and Kenan sensed their hungry eyes rudely appraising her as he escorted her across the room to stand before Thorgest. Attired in the long flowing robes of the high priestess to Thor and clutching the staff of her office, Otta was poised at her husband's side, her stern features made all the more severe by the icy gaze she had fixed on Taillte.

"The king of Munster sends you greetings, Lord

Thorgest," Kenan announced as he stepped before the Norse leader, raising his hand in greeting. "At your request we have – "

"I am told that you have brought only two hundred men with you," Thorgest interrupted loudly in Gaelic. "And that most of those would serve us better as rowers in our slave galleys than bearing arms against Niall. Were my instructions to Feidlimid not clear?"

"I cannot answer for him, lord," Kenan replied quickly. "As for myself I have accompanied these men at your request. But I can assure you of Feidlimid's support, for I know he holds you in high esteem."

"Do not intensify the insult with flattery," Thorgest snorted, shifting his gaze to Taillte. "What is the woman doing here?" he asked, the question obviously directed at Kenan, though his eyes remained fixed on the woman before him. "Is she yours?"

"Aye, my lord, she – "

"I have a tongue of my own," Taillte interjected, glancing at him peevishly. Then she bowed and smiled at Thorgest. "I am called Taillte."

"The journey could not have been a pleasant one for you," Otta suggested, her voice carefully neutral and her eyes cold. "Your devotion to your husband is to be commended."

Taillte grinned back at her as she straightened. "We are not man and wife. But when Kenan told me of his journey to Lough Ree my curiosity prompted me to accompany him for Lord Thorgest's exploits are well known at Feidlimid's court. I must confess lady, I could not resist the opportunity of meeting the conqueror whose name has already become a legend among our people."

Thorgest nodded. "I hope that seeing me in the flesh has not tainted your expectations."

"I have not yet been disappointed, my lord," Taillte replied softly. "I am certain that my stay here will be a welcome relief from the tedium of court life at Cashel."

Kenan caught the disdain that flickered for an instant in Otta's eyes. He watched with uneasiness as her mouth curled into a shoddy imitation of a warming smile. "I am certain that you will find our ways different in many respects from your own customs," the high priestess said to Taillte. "But you and I will speak of these things later. I fear we have already been inconsiderate hosts by contributing to your obvious fatigue." Otta frowned and clucked her tongue disapprovingly. "How pale and toil–worn your complexion seems for one so young – no doubt the consequence of so tiresome a journey. Come," she added, gliding forward. "Let me show you to your quarters that you may rest and recover yourself before the evening meal."

"I am moved by your gracious concern, lady," Taillte replied flatly as Otta came to her. "In truth, I have never experienced such hospitality."

As Otta turned to lead, Taillte started to follow, then stopped abruptly and turned back to face Thorgest. "I will look for you tonight, my lord – at the evening meal." Kenan felt the fury building inside him as her lips parted in the full inviting smile that left no margin for interpretation. "You do intend to sup tonight, do you not?"

Thorgest grinned and nodded slowly. "I do."

"Then I will take my leave of you," Taillte replied bowing formally. When she turned back to Otta, Kenan noted the expression of wicked delight on her face. "Now I will follow you," she told the high priestess. Kenan glimpsed the fire in Otta's eyes as she pivoted and strode across the firehall.

"That is a fine woman," Thorgest muttered under his breath, his eyes following her. When the women were gone, his gaze veered back to Kenan, the tone in his voice one of aggravated wonderment. "How came she to be with you?"

"Of her own choosing, my lord," Kenan replied shrugging. "It has always been Taillte's way to do only that which pleases her."

"I can well believe it." Thorgest refilled his goblet then leaned back in his chair. "Now, Leinsterman, to the reason I summoned you here. What can you tell me of your brother, the one you would usurp?"

"Bran?" Kenan grunted, caught off guard by the nature of the question. "Very little I'm afraid. I have neither seen nor heard from him since he banished me. But he can be of little concern to you, lord, as I will soon be taking his place upon the throne."

Thorgest narrowed his eyes. "Your brother would appear to be a man of considerable significance. It was he who assisted Niall in destroying our settlement at Lough Neagh. On their own, neither Ulster nor Leinster are capable of opposing us. But together they do present a serious threat." He leaned forward. "What I need to know from you is how committed your brother is to this alliance with Niall Caille. Is it possible that he could be distracted from it, perhaps by gold or territory?"

"Men such as my brother are incorruptible," Kenan

sniffed. "He is a man preoccupied with honour, whose loyalty to the Ard–Ri is only surpassed by his devotion to his wife and family."

Thorgest raised his eyebrows. "Would such a man perhaps reconsider his position in order to save his brother's life?"

"Bran places no value on my life," Kenan assured him nervously, his throat suddenly feeling dry and constricted. *Now is the time*, he told himself. "But my brother can be influenced," Kenan said, smiling. "And you already possess the means to accomplish that – right here at Lough Ree."

"Don't talk to me in riddles!" Thorgest snapped, slamming his goblet down on the table. "Speak plainly."

Kenan remained unruffled. "You may recall when we first met you gave me a gift," he said slowly, savouring the words. "A gift the value of which you did not know. Now, in exchange for your promise that the crown of Leinster will be mine, I will return it to you so that you may realize it's full worth."

"You try my patience, Leinsterman," Thorgest growled. "What is it you desire?"

"Why, reassurance, my lord," Kenan answered smugly. "Your guarantee that your word to me will not be broken and that once Bran is dead you will help me regain my rightful place upon the throne of Leinster."

Thorgest pulled at the yellow gold of his beard and scowled. "It is agreed," he said finally. "But if you are wrong about the value of this gift, Leinsterman, you will answer for it with your life."

"Agreed," Kenan replied confidently. "There is a slave here, taken on a raid, that matters a great deal to Bran." He grinned. "Her name is Finola. She is wife to the king of Leinster."

"Why did you not tell me this before?" Thorgest demanded as he sprang to his feet. "With such leverage we could have brought Wolfblade to his knees long ago!"

Kenan's voice remained steady and calm. "Aye, you could have brought Bran to his knees – but not all of Leinster. Even if you had used Finola as bait to capture or kill Bran, his elimination would still not have provided you with any measure of control over the individual clans. Needless to say, they would have strongly opposed any attempt on your part to govern them." Kenan paused and smiled. "No," he added, "if you wish to rule Leinster you must do so from within – by placing someone on the throne who will be both acceptable to the chieftains and sympathetic to your... objectives. Let us just say that I wanted to be certain that you had decided to support a suitable candidate before contributing to your endeavours."

Thorgest's scowl gradually faded into a grin, then he threw back his head and laughed. "Feidlimid has indeed taught you well," he said at last. "You are a dangerous man Kenan Ui Faelain. Even as an ally you will warrant my vigilance."

CHAPTER TWENTY–NINE

While Thorgest and Kenan considered the threat that Bran posed to them both, dozens of thralls laboured in the huge fields of leeks, corn and potatoes that stretched north from the palisade walls of the stronghold to the tangles of bracken and hawthorn which lay beyond. It had not rained that day and for once the sun glared down at them from a cloudless sky, their gangly shadows sprawling before them on the rich, black soil between the uniformly arranged rows as they sweated to cultivate the abundant crops. The handful of guards who oversaw them were congregated at the lakeside perimeter of the fields, casting lots to pass the time, their strident voices occasionally rising to mimic the gabbling of the ducks and wild geese that scrimmaged for food among the rushes which bristled along the shoreline of Lough Ree. On the opposite side of the settlement, herds of cattle and sheep grazed contentedly in the lush meadows that extended to the woodlands on the southern end of the lake.

With the exception of a few greybeards and young boys, most of the slaves were women, some with children old enough to toil at their mother's side. Others, the victims of their captors' lust, worked with swollen bellies or with bawling newborns tied to their breasts with dingy folds of coarse-grained homespun. All had been captured in Viking raids upon villages and farmsteads throughout Erin; the fathers, husbands and older sons who had futilely attempted to defend them, murdered before their eyes. Their families destroyed or torn asunder, the lives of the women had become little more than a recurrent trial to survive, if only for the sake of the children who had temporarily been allowed to remain with them. Those too weak or too sick to work were quickly taken away. They were not seen or heard of again.

As she had every day for the past several months, Finola hoed at the persistent weeds which had returned yet again to throttle the stalks of the shoulder high corn, moving with the practised rhythm of one who had grown accustomed to performing the same task repeatedly over a long period of time. She worked alongside Muireen in silence, for talk among thralls was forbidden. On the ground between them, Devlin lay wrapped in the filthy sackcloth that was his swaddling blanket, gurgling happily as he grabbed at the butterflies that flitted above him between the plants.

The first few days of her servitude had been the most difficult for Finola, a seemingly endless nightmare of blisters, aching muscles and hunger. But in the weeks that followed, her hands had calloused until they had become as leather, her fair complexion darkened, and her delicate skin had become accustomed to the rough woolen frock and ragged shawl which were now her only possessions.

In the arduous months following her capture, Finola had watched many succumb to the cruelty and abuse of her taskmasters, the flesh vanquished as their spirits died. But as her own ordeal wore on, a single persistent notion gradually evolved, firing her endurance and will to survive.

Escape.

From the time they were taken at Bray, Finola's dreams each night had been filled with glorious visions of Bran leading the warriors of Leinster to rescue them. But as the months dragged on and the changing leaves on the trees hinted at the approach of autumn, she began to accept the stark reality of her situation. Bran could not know what had happened to them, where they had been taken, or even whether they were still alive. Soon harvest time would be upon them, then winter. And even if in the course of that time Bran somehow discovered they were prisoners at Lough Ree, it would be spring again before he could mount any kind of attempt to free them. It was then Finola had decided she – they could not wait, and set about devising a plan for their escape.

Now, beads of perspiration rolled down her forehead, stinging her eyes as she tilted her head back slightly and glanced at the guards who were gathered on the far northwest edge of the cornfield. Engrossed in their gambling, they were looking up only occasionally in the direction of the thralls. It had not escaped her attention that the number of warriors allotted to watch over them had gradually diminished as the months passed, the Vikings apparently confident that the precautions and deterrents they had established were more than adequate.

Finola suddenly shuddered as she remembered the woman who had been caught in a bid to flee less than a week after she and the others had been brought to Lough Ree. At sunset, the heathen had assembled the thralls in the meadows outside the settlement to witness her punishment. The woman's agonized screams had lasted throughout the night, interrupted only by her whimpering pleas to be killed. Mercifully, she had died the following morning. There had been no further escape attempt since.

"Muireen," Finola whispered cautiously out of the corner of her mouth while her eyes remained fixed on the guards.

"Muireen."

"What?" came the cautious response.

"This may be our only chance," Finola said quickly. "I think we can slip away without being seen. But we must move closer to the woods."

"Don't be a fool, Finola," Muireen warned. "The guards would have to be blind not to see us."

"Not if we drop to our bellies and crawl between the corn."

"But it is broad daylight. They – "

"The guards are preoccupied with their wagering," Finola broke in. "And there will not be a head count again until they return us to our sheds."

"But what of Devlin?" Muireen insisted. "Even if we do make it through the woods, his cries will bring the whole of the guards down upon us."

"I will keep him silent," Finola assured her. Picking up Devlin, she hastily secured him to her breast with her shawl. "Now watch my shadow and follow me. When I give the word, drop to the ground and make for the woods."

Her eyes still focused on the distant sentinels, Finola began to shuffle backwards as she pretended to continue working. On the ground beside her, Muireen's shadow paralleled her course. With each furtive step, she strained to hear the angry shout that would challenge them. But there was only the rustle of leaves and the gentle breeze, the distant bantering of the guards, and the faint scuffle of her own feet through the dirt. She felt the muscles in her body beginning to tense, aching for flight. Closer. Closer. Her hands were wet and sticky on the handle of the hoe, her heart pounding. *Just a few more paces*, the voice inside her urged. *Then freedom*.

"You there!" a voice boomed abruptly behind in heavily accented Gaelic.

Stiffening, Finola braced herself for the blow she was certain would follow. Warily, she glanced over her shoulder.

Their weapons drawn, two brawny Norsemen stood less than a dozen paces behind her, scowling. Finola wondered if they had understood her intent.

"That's right," one of them called out in the same deep voice, pointing with the blade of his sword. "You. Are you the one called Finola?"

"I am," she answered guardedly, trying to conceal the quaver in her voice as she turned to them. "What do you want of me?"

"We have orders to take you before Thorgest," the Norsemen replied. "Come."

Finola glanced fearfully at Muireen as she dropped the hoe. Unfastening her shawl, she gently laid Devlin on the ground, then walked over to the two warriors who awaited her. Seizing her by the arms, they started to lead her off.

"Why are you taking her?" Muireen demanded angrily, starting forward.

"Muireen... don't!" Finola cried out over her shoulder. "Take care of my Devlin!"

As the other thralls looked on with sympathy, the two Norseman dragged her across the field and through the main gate, conducting her down a crowded street toward the centre of the settlement. Some of the heathen women pointed and snickered as they passed by. A pack of golden–haired youths began to throw stones and lumps of dirt at her, mocking her in a tongue she could not understand. In an effort to protect her eyes, she tucked her chin into her chest and hunched one shoulder. Then a rock struck one of the guards and he barked menacingly at the young hellions, waving them aside. When they laughed back at him, the warrior touched the hilt of his sword and the boys melted back into the throng. When at last they reached the firehall, Finola's escort nodded curtly to the sentries who stood at either side of the massive doors, then roughly hauled her inside. As they entered, she winced at the nauseating stench of rancid wine and ale. Absorbed in their loud conversations and drink, the boisterous jarls scarcely seemed to notice Finola as she was led through the maze of tables to stand before Thorgest. The Viking leader was seated in his place of honour at the far end of the firehall. Dwarfed by the guards who flanked her, she looked about with dread at the familiar faces of those who surrounded him.

Otta stood at her husband's side, separating him from Taillte who was seated at his right hand. Beside her, Kenan leered down at Finola. As their eyes met, she willed herself to hold his gaze, the terrifying memory of the night he had violated her returning in repulsive images that sent a chill throughout her. For an instant, she considered plucking the dagger from the belt of the guard beside her and rushing forward to slay the man who had brutalized her. But even as she felt the urge Finola knew she would be killed before she had the chance to reach him.

Gesturing the jarls to be silent, Thorgest glanced at Kenan. "Can this be the one?" he asked in Gaelic, raising an eyebrow. "Surely this cannot be the Queen of Leinster!"

"Ah, but it is, my lord," Kenan quickly assured him. "Although I grant you she has changed much since the occasion of my last meeting with her."

Otta stooped over Thorgest's shoulder. "This is the woman who defied me at Uppsala, my husband," she told him scornfully. "I made the mistake of allowing a mere servant to take her place upon the sacred oak."

"Then the gods must have guided your decision," Thorgest answered, glancing up at her. "Dead, she would have proved of little use to us." Resting his elbows on the table before him, he leaned forward and eyed Finola. "I am told you are wife to the Ui Faelain who calls himself King of Leinster. Is this so?"

Finola lifted her head up proudly. "Bran Ui Faelain is king of Leinster, and I am his wife."

"Spoken like a true queen," Taillte mocked as she rose from her place, moving around the table. "But where are your royal robes, my lady? When last I saw you you were attired in the finery of a young bride." Her lips twisted wryly as she halted. "Do you recall? I danced for you that night – the night you became Queen of Leinster. How our fortunes have changed since then, as have those of your husband. Such a pity. His life might have been so much different – had he chosen more wisely."

"The choice was not Bran's," Finola answered defiantly. "But tell me, is it vanity or feeble–mindedness that prompts you to think that Bran could have ever been persuaded to take a whore as his wife?"

Taillte's smile faded. Abruptly, she lashed out and savagely struck the younger woman across the face. Her cheek stinging from the blow, Finola lunged forward, but the guards seized her arms. "How brave you are," she snarled at Taillte. "Have these warriors release me that I may test the courage of a traitor."

Her face flushed and her body trembling with fury, Taillte raised her hand to strike again.

"Enough of this!" Thorgest bellowed. Rising from the table, he strode to the two women and frowned at Taillte. "I did not bring this woman here for your amusement."

"I will not endure her insults," Taillte protested. "Give me a sharp knife that I may send her back to her beloved husband – one piece at a time."

Thorgest scowled down at her. "You forget where you are and to whom you speak. Go back to your man and your wine."

Taillte shot Finola a menacing glance, then marched indignantly back to her place. As she took her seat, Thorgest turned back to Finola, his gaze slowly roaming the length of her body. When he looked up again, there was a glint of admiration in his sea blue eyes.

"You are a woman indeed worthy of a king," he said, nodding appreciatively. "And you have endured much to conceal yourself from us."

"I did not wish to be used as a weapon against my husband," Finola replied flatly.

"What makes you think you will not now be so used?" he asked, grinning.

Finola saw the self–assurance on his face and knew that here was a man who was accustomed to taking whatever he desired. "Do what you will," she answered indifferently. "I know my husband will not jeopardize our people for my sake. For myself, I care not what you do to me for I have come to expect only the worst."

"You have suffered much since your arrival," Thorgest said, his voice almost gentle. "But you brought that upon yourself. Now that we know who you are, you will be moved to better quarters and treated in a manner more befitting your station."

"I prefer the company of those who toil in the fields," she told him haughtily. "There is more honour and civility in any one of them than there is in the whole of your accursed race."

Thorgest sniffed incredulously. "What is it that compels you Gaels to so willingly embrace martyrdom? I have watched your brown robes kneel before our swords and offer no resistance while we slaughtered them and burned their holy places down around them. Where is the honour in that?" He shrugged uncomprehendingly. "I do not understand your people."

"How could you?" Finola snapped back. "You worship craven images and offer blood sacrifices to the lumps of stone that you call gods. Know this. It is through the power of the one true God that the Ard–Ri and my husband will eventually defeat you."

"Blasphemer!" Otta shouted, brandishing her staff. "The penalty for sacrilege is death! Thor cries out for the spilling of her blood!"

"She will be yours soon enough," Thorgest called back over his shoulder. His eyes moved to the gold Celtic cross that hung at Finola's neck. Reaching out, he delicately examined it between his fingers, then abruptly tore it from her neck. Clenching the chain in his fist, he waved it in her face.

"Your god has not helped you – nor will he come to the aid of your husband," he growled. "The gods have nothing to do with victory. When we defeat your husband it will be by the strength of our arms. And defeated he will be. Tomorrow morning I meet with the king of Meath to arrange an alliance that will be the key to Leinster's downfall." He slowly opened his hand and examined the small cross. "I will have Malachy deliver this to your husband so that he understands what is truly at stake."

"Bran will never submit to you," Finola said fiercely. "Nor will the people of Erin."

"Many of them already have," Thorgest remarked confidently. "Munster has long been our ally and soon Meath will follow." He pointed at Kenan. "And when your husband's own brother rules in his place, Leinster too will join us. Ragnar!" he called out over his shoulder. "Take her back to her companions and see to it that our ships are made ready to sail. We leave at sunrise."

CHAPTER THIRTY

The following morning, less than forty leagues east of Thorgest's stronghold, the early light of dawn danced along the surface of Lough Owel, a ghostly mist clinging to the tranquil waters. The Viking garrison that was to be the site of Thorgest's meeting with Malachy had been established months earlier on the eastern shoreline of the lake. The circular ramparts were of uniform height and thickness, and were strengthened internally with beams and externally by palisades of timber. The wall was pierced by a single gateway which was roofed, forming a tunnel to the huge double doors and the inner area was divided into quarters; four groups of four longhouses each exactly alike in size and structure and grouped into a perfect square. Along the secluded beach, the water lapped at the hulls of three longships and a number of smaller fishing vessels which had been partially dragged up onto the shore, their nets stretched out over long poles which had been planted in the sand.

The base, and others like it throughout Meath, had not been intended as foundations for future settlements, but rather military camps designed to establish presence in the province. Although each rarely billeted more than a hundred warriors, Thorgest had been convinced that their strategic positioning would guarantee Malachy's neutrality and eventually compel him to negotiate an alliance, thus inhibiting Leinster and Ulster's ability to consolidate their forces.

As a gentle breeze wafted to him from the lough, Bran stood on the parapet of the outer rampart, looking down into the courtyard where the warriors he had led to Lough Owel busied themselves with stripping the chainmail corselets and helmets from the dead foreigners who littered the ground. They had struck in stealth the previous night, just before dawn, silently eliminating the sentries before moving onto the barracks where the heathen slept. Most had died as they were awakened, staring wide-eyed at the shadowy figures who stood above them while hands reached out of the darkness to clamp over their mouths, muffling their cries as their throats were mercilessly slit.

Ten days earlier, Bran and Rowan had led a small detachment of mounted warriors to the royal crannog of Tigerhnach, the lord of Lough Gabhar. The Meath chieftain, a towering warrior whose unkempt mane and beard matched the hue of his fierce dark eyes, had taken them at once to his modest hall where he had ordered that food and drink be set down before them. The simple meal had consisted of fresh fish and barley cakes, and he apologized repeatedly for his inability to provide more, explaining how his clan had been singled out by the Viking as an example to the others. Burnt crops, slaughtered cattle and murder had been the lot of his people. As Tigerhnach spoke Bran came to understand that his loyalty to the Ard-Ri was surpassed only by his hatred of the heathen and his devotion to his own people.

Etach and a small contingent had reached the crannog the next morning, and in the days that followed their numbers grew as the warriors from Naas continued to arrive in small groups. The message that Bran had sent Etach from Lough Neagh had instructed him to move the remainder of the army north from Naas in secret, and the old soldier had complied by dispatching small bodies of men at intervals along

a variety of different routes. By the end of the fifth day, more
than five hundred eager warriors had assembled at Lough
Gabhar. Even so, Bran and Tigerhnach had mutually decided
that it would be prudent to forestall their assault until the
night before Thorgest's arrival, thus precluding the possibility of alerting him to their presence and intent. The following evening, they had taken the Viking base by surprise, the
logic of their strategy ultimately proving to be deadly in its
effectiveness.

Now, as Bran turned to gaze out across the peaceful
waters of Lough Owel, he drew his heavy bearskin mantle
around his shoulders, chilled not so much by the wind as by
the bitter foreboding that gripped his soul. *What lies beyond
the outcome of this day*, he wondered, peering to the distant
horizon. *If victory is ours, I will send word to Niall and together
we will march on Lough Ree. But what awaits me there? And
what will I do if Finola and the others are not among the captives?
I think it would be easier to bear the pain of knowing that they
were dead than to continue wondering whether or not I will ever
see them again. Yet, in my soul I feel that we will one day be
together. It is that hope, that dream which has tormented me and
laid out the path which I have been obliged to follow. I cannot
believe that the journey which has brought me here has served no
purpose.*

"We are near done, my lord." The voice startled Bran
and he turned to face Tigerhnach who was stepping from the
ladder onto the parapet. Etach followed behind. "My men
have clad themselves in the clothes and armour they took
from the dead," the chieftain told him, wiping his sweated
brow with his forearm. "And you were right about the corpses.

The stench of death already hangs heavy upon this place and the bodies will ripen quickly in the midday sun. It is wise that we have dragged them back into the woods."

Bran's eyes shifted to the dense forest behind the garrison. There was no sign of movement. "Have our warriors taken up their positions?" he asked Etach.

"They have, my lord," the old soldier grunted. "And they are well concealed within the trees. When Thorgest and his escort arrive Rowan Ui Muiredaig will lead his men against one flank and you the other. Whether the heathen approach from land or the lough, we will be ready."

Bran looked at the Meath chieftain. "What say you, Tigerhnach? You know this area better than either of us, for it is your own domain. How will the foreigners come?"

The chieftain's brow creased as he frowned and peered out toward the mouth of the tributary which flowed west from the lake. "There is a network of rivers and small lakes that connect Lough Ree to here." he explained. "The water will give them the speed of a quick escape should they need it."

"You are wise, Tigerhnach," Etach agreed. "Although Thorgest is prepared to negotiate an alliance with Malachy, I doubt that he is ready to trust him."

"Then we must take care to keep his mind at ease," Bran said. "Everything must appear as he expects it. And see that no warrior moves to strike before I give the command. Are your men ready?"

The chieftain nodded. "Warriors clad in chainmail are being posted along the ramparts and those who speak the heathen's tongue will be assembled outside the main gate to greet them as soon as the longships are sighted. Should the sentries

be hailed, it is they who will respond. The others are pitching
the pavilions along the south wall so that Malachy's standards are in plain view." He grinned slyly as he tugged at his
own soiled tunic. "I myself will be attired in garments more
befitting the king of Meath."

"Tell your men to omit no detail in their preparations,"
Bran told them, looking from one to the other. "Thorgest is
no fool and our victory here today will depend on the success
of our deception. So long as we do not arouse his suspicions,
we have a chance. If we fail, he will not give us another."

Four hours later, as the sun timidly climbed the clouds
toward its zenith, a score of longships emerged from the mouth
of the river that meandered west from Lough Owel, fanning
out as they glided onto the glassy surface of the lake. Their
sails furled, twenty pairs of oars propelled each vessel forward,
dipping rhythmically into the water to the monotonous beat
of the drums which gauged their speed.

Thorgest stood on the bow of the lead ship, watching
the dance of the other vessels as they raced one another for
the honour of being the first to reach the garrison on the far
shore. The trip along the winding rivers from Lough Ree had
been uneventful, even boring, and Thorgest reveled in the
competition. Glancing back toward the stern, he smiled confidently as he surveyed the glistening torsos of his own rowers, their grunts marking the pace of their strokes. He knew
that no other crew could match them and that his would be
the ship to win. Turning back to peer at the garrison, he felt
the spray on his face and listened to the gentle sigh of the
water washing along the hull as his ship knifed forward.

I have been too long away from the sea, he thought to himself ruefully. *I yearn to feel the wind in my face, the caress of the waves beneath me and the taste of salt on my tongue. Here, men who are landlocked and have no knowledge of these things struggle among themselves for power without understanding its source. The power of the sea has made the Norse a great people, conquerors, because we have learned to harness her energy and bend it to our own will. That ability alone is what has enabled us to crush our enemies and claim their lands for our own as we have this island they call Erin. Soon, Niall's kingdom will be mine. Even so, I have no heart for ruling a subjugated people, administering taxes and tributes. Petty kings like Feidlimid revel in their own pomp and station, growing fat in their excesses until they forget what it means to be a man. To face the sea and your enemies without fear, believing only in the strength of your arm – that is life. Soon, I will once more stand on the deck of my draken, racing the gods of the sea and seeking a new empire to conquer. Only then will I be – "*

Thorgest's reverie was suddenly interrupted by the strident cawing of ravens, and he realized that scores of the harbingers of death were circling above the woods behind the garrison, which was now less than a quarter league away. Lowering his eyes, he squinted at the Vikings who were congregated on the beach. Behind them, Malachy's banner fluttered above a number of brightly coloured pavilions.

"Eadric!" Thorgest called out as he glanced over his shoulder at the foremost rower. "Look to that flock of carrion birds. What do you make of them?"

"They are an omen... my lord," the man grunted as he drew the oar back, then leaned forward to the next stroke.

"Oden's ravens... sent forth to... sing your praises."

"They honour only the dead," Thorgest replied, frowning. "Give the signal to drop oars."

"But lord, we are nearly..."

"Give the signal!" Thorgest bellowed, his hand going to his sword. "Now!"

The man fumbled with the inlaid horn that hung about his neck, then raised it to his lips. As the haunting tone reverberated across the water, oars simultaneously slapped into the water, bringing the ships to an abrupt halt.

Thorgest cupped his hands around his mouth and hailed the Vikings on the beach. "I am Thorgest, come here to meet with the Gael king. Is he among you?"

One of those on shore, a beardless warrior, stepped to the water's edge and pointed to the pavilions. "His camp is there as you can see, lord," he shouted back. "And we have been expecting you. Why do you not land that we may welcome you properly?"

"Why is it the ravens flock so?" Thorgest called out, pointing overhead. "Our warriors fear they are a bad omen." He watched uneasily as the man said something over his shoulder to his companions. Hoots of laughter erupted from the beach.

"They are a good omen for you all, lord," the Viking answered. "They feed upon the remnants of fish from this morning's catch. Even now it is being prepared for you and your men." Thorgest saw the warrior glance at his comrades. "But perhaps you prefer fowl."

Guffaws rolled across the water to him and the Norse leader's knuckles whitened as his fingers tightened on the gunwale. "We are coming in!" he roared, then nodded at Eadric. Once again the lonely croon of the horn resounded across the lough and the ships surged forward. Less than a dozen full strokes brought the vessels into the shallows and at Thorgest's command the crews shipped oars, their forward momentum carrying them up onto the beach.

Once landed, Thorgest's warriors scrambled ashore, leaving a small party of warriors behind to secure the vessels while the remainder followed him, striding across the sand toward the Vikings who waited. Glancing up at the sentries on the ramparts, Thorgest noted that there was no smoke coming from the inner courtyard and he wondered why the hearthfires had not been lit. *Is not the evening meal being prepared?* he wondered, shifting his gaze to the beardless warrior who stood less than twenty paces from him, smiling.

Surveying the cluster of Vikings ahead, Thorgest suddenly realized that the beards of the man's companions were neither plaited nor pointed as was the Viking custom. But all were heavily armed and several bore shields. Less than ten paces from him, Thorgest wondered why the beardless warriors' kirtle seemed to fit so poorly. Then he saw the dark stain of blood along the neckline. In that instant, Thorgest knew he had walked into a trap.

"It is the Gael!" he screamed, drawing his sword and rushing forward to split the skull of the beardless warrior who had lured them into the ambush. As his men rushed to engage the others, a shower of arrows and spears whistled down on them from the ramparts above. Holding their shields above their heads and stumbling over the comrades who fell before them, the Vikings charged to meet the Gaelic warriors who were now pouring out of the main gate.

Thorgest saw two other groups of Irishmen swarming
out of the woods on either side of the garrison and glancing
over his shoulder, realized the Vikings' retreat to their
longships had been irreversibly severed. Slaying the next
warrior who stepped forward to challenge him, he sprinted
through the momentary gap, leaving his men and his vessels
behind as he fled along the open stretch of beach.

Bran fought alongside his mounted warriors as they
hacked at the left flank of the vastly outnumbered foreigners.
Trapped by the Irish that now encircled them, the crush of
Viking stood back to back against their assailants, unable to
break through the wall of slashing steel that separated them
from their longships. Helplessly encumbered deep within the
press of their own men, most could do little more than hurl
curses and brandish their weapons, jostling one another as
they hastened to take up the positions of those who had fallen
before them.

Over the heads of the warriors who struggled beneath
him, Bran spotted the solitary figure in the distance, running
along the shoreline. Recognizing Thorgest, he reined his horse
about to skirt the fray, water spraying around him as the animal's hooves exploded through the surf. When he was clear
of the battle, Bran guided his mount ashore, then dug his
heels into the mare's ribs. He leaned forward and clutched
his sword tightly as she stretched out her legs, racing across
the sand toward the fleeing Norseman.

"Thorgest!" Bran yelled when he was almost upon him.
The Norse leader pivoted, a scream bursting from his lips as

he thrust his sword high. The frightened mare ploughed her hooves into the sand, whinnying as she reared up on her hind quarters. Clutching his mount's flowing mane in his free hand, Bran managed to keep his saddle, then quickly dismounted as the mare pawed nervously at the ground.

Thorgest stood less than a dozen paces away, braced and waiting, his gleaming blade clutched with both hands. Tearing off the bearskin mantle and throwing it to the ground, Bran raised his weapon, the ruby eyes of the wolf's head on the hilt blazing like fiery embers as they caught the sunlight.

"You," Thorgest growled in Gaelic, his features contorted with hatred. "Wolfblade." Lowering his weapon, he sneered. "Now I understand why you called out to me. Cutting me down from behind would have been the act of a coward and unworthy of you. I am pleased. It is good that warriors such as we stand face to face against each other in battle. It is the honourable way to fight and die."

"Don't speak to me of honour, you murdering pig," Bran shouted. "The soil of Erin has been drenched with the blood of the innocent women and children you have slaughtered. But when you are confronted with those who are not so helpless, you desert your comrades and flee."

"It is plain the battle is lost," he answered, shrugging. "Only a fool dies needlessly. My men have served me well and I will live to see each of them avenged. As for the women and children you speak of, not all of them have been put to the sword – not yet."

Reaching beneath his leather jerkin, Thorgest withdrew a small object and threw it onto the sand at Bran's feet. Slowly, Bran squatted to retrieve it, his eyes focused on

Thorgest as he felt the ground. Standing, he glanced at the delicate Celtic cross in his hand.

"Finola," he murmured under his breath in disbelief, lowering his sword.

"Examine it closely," Thorgest advised. "It belongs to your wife, does it not? You will be pleased to know that she speaks very highly of you. And I have only just discovered that your infant son and your sister are also our guests at Lough Ree."

"If you have harmed them..."

Thorgest thrust out his hand. "Let us strike a bargain Irishman," he snarled. He stepped tentatively toward Bran. "Lay down your sword and your family lives. Yield to me now and I promise that you will die quickly. Your life for theirs. Refuse, and I will kill you anyway, and I swear by Oden's sacred oak that they will follow you upon my return to Lough Ree."

Keeping his eyes locked on Thorgest, Bran glanced at the small gold cross then dropped it onto his mantle. "Come, heathen," he said, his voice low and threatening as he grasped the hilt of his sword with both hands and beckoned with it. "Come."

Lifting his own sword high above his right shoulder, Thorgest began to stalk Bran, gradually circling to his left. Bran turned with him. Watching. Waiting.

Suddenly Thorgest rushed forward with a bone–chilling war cry.

Their blades pealed off one another as the two men met, each sustaining minor wounds as he probed for openings in the other's defenses. But Thorgest was much stronger than Bran had anticipated, and as the battle waged he found himself increasingly hard pressed to fend off the unrelenting succession of well–aimed strokes. Exploiting his advantage, Thorgest began to drive Bran back to the water's edge.

Then, as Bran parried a blow aimed at his head, the two men seized each other's wrists, trying to maintain their balance as they grappled. Abruptly, Thorgest curled his leg behind Bran's knees and together they crashed onto the sand. Pinned beneath him, Bran felt the water lapping at his face. His free hand was still locked on the Norseman's wrists, his arm trembling with the effort as he struggled to hold the gleaming weapon above him at bay. His sword hand grew quickly numb as Thorgest smashed it against the ground repeatedly.

Then the hilt slipped from his fingers.

Releasing his grip on Bran's wrist, the Norseman hammered his fist into Bran's temple. Dazed for an instant, he felt Thorgest scramble to his feet, straddling him as he pulled his swordarm free.

There was a blur of movement above him and Bran instinctively rolled to one side. He gasped as the thrust that was intended to impale him whistled by his back. Reaching out, he caught Thorgest's ankle and wrenched it forward. Pulled off balance, the Norseman toppled into the water. Before he could recover Bran was upon him, his hands on Thorgest's throat, forcing his head beneath the surface.

"Die, you motherless bastard!" Bran shrieked. His fingers tightened on the soft flesh. "Die!"

Thorgest's arms and legs flailed wildly, churning the water around them. But Bran held on and squeezed, his elbows locked as he forced the Viking down. Finally, he felt the body jerk spasmodically beneath him and the struggling ceased. Relaxing his grip, Bran stepped back.

Thorgest's corpse floated to the surface, eyes and mouth agape in the terror of violent death.

Bran crawled ashore, exhausted, and collapsed on the sand. He heard shouts and raised his head to see a group of warriors racing across the beach toward him.

"Are you wounded, my lord?" Rowan asked anxiously, dropping to one knee as Bran shook his head. He glanced at the body drifting in the lough. "Thorgest?"

Bran nodded weakly. "What of the foreigners?"

"Defeated," Rowan answered. "All but a handful who escaped in their vessels. The others refused to surrender."

Struggling to his feet, Bran staggered across the beach and dropped to his knees beside his mantle. He picked up the Celtic cross and held it up to Rowan. "Finola," he said hoarsely. "She and the others are at Lough Ree."

Rowan frowned. "How can you be certain?"

"Thorgest told me," Bran explained as the chieftain helped him up. "If the Vikings should learn that it was I who led the attack on Thorgest..." His voice trailed off. "We must act quickly," he went on, "for surprise is no longer our ally. Send messengers to Malachy and to Niall. Have them say that Thorgest is dead and the time has come to march on Lough Ree."

"But what of the heathen's fleet?" Rowan asked doubtfully. "They will surely escape in their ships at our approach."

"Then we must prevent them from doing so," Bran replied. "You and Etach will ride on ahead with me. The bulk of our warriors are on foot and will not reach Lough Ree in time."

A puzzled expression flooded Rowan's face. "What can *we* do?" he asked incredulously.

"We can do what the army of the Ard–Ri has not been able to," Bran replied without hesitation. "We can destroy the Viking fleet."

CHAPTER THIRTY–ONE

Later that afternoon, the settlement at Lough Ree echoed with the wailing laments of women whose husbands and sons had not been among the survivors aboard the only ship to return from Lough Owel. While rumours of massacre and impending attacks circulated throughout the compound, Eadric stood before the grim–faced jarls and sea chieftains in the firehall, breathlessly recounting the details of the ambush from which he and a mere handful of his companions had managed to escape. As he spoke, Ragnar stared down at him from Thorgest's place of honour, fidgeting with the black tangles of his matted beard as he listened and carefully weighed his options. As Thorgest's second in command it would fall to him to choose the best course of action, a decision that he knew would be both difficult and dangerous. He found himself wishing that the responsibility had fallen to someone else.

Whatever I elect to do my Danes will follow, he reasoned. *But the Norse – their first allegiance is to Thorgest and they will insist upon sailing to Lough Owel in force. And if he is found dead, they will demand vengeance. But against whom? I cannot believe that after all these years of remaining neutral for fear of retaliation, Malachy has finally risen against us. We know not who attacked our comrades, their strength or where they plan to strike at us next. Yet, if I refuse to lead the Norse against the Meath king, they will challenge my authority, insisting that one of their own be placed in my stead. That would be an insult my own countrymen would not be able to overlook, drawing Dane and Norseman alike into a blood bath that would only serve to weaken us. Still, I hesitate to commit us all to battling an enemy whose face we have not yet seen.*

"Did you actually see Lord Thorgest fall?" Ragnar abruptly interrupted Eadric.

"No, lord," came the cautious reply. "But he was surrounded with the others. The Gael were everywhere."

"Then many of them may have survived," Kenan offered, his feet on the table before him as he rocked back on the hind legs of his chair. "As prisoners. My countrymen are not without mercy; it is one of their less desirable qualities. In such circumstances it is our custom to offer the enemy the opportunity to lay down his arms."

"Surrender is unknown to men of Viking blood," Ragnar declared proudly. "And we have already heard of Gaelic honour from those who survived the massacre at Lough Neagh."

Suddenly, the huge oak doors flew open and crashed against the walls as Otta burst into the firehall, a covey of maidservants at her heels. She strode across the room to confront Eadric.

"Why is Lord Thorgest not with you?" she demanded. "Where is my husband?"

Eadric hung his head and stared blankly at the floor. "I cannot say, lady," he stammered. "He did not return with us."

"And you left him?" Otta lashed out and struck him across the face. The slap cracked like a whip in the confines of the firehall. "Coward!"

"There was nothing I could do," Eadric muttered, glancing about the room at the sea chieftains as he rubbed his cheek. "Nothing any of us could do." He stepped past her to take a seat among his comrades.

"And you," Otta went on, her blue eyes flashing as she turned to glower at Ragnar. "Why do you not act? You are his appointed second, the one in whom he has put his trust above all others. How can you sit there and do nothing?"

Ragnar shifted uncomfortably. "I have not yet decided how best – "

"Decided?" Otta exclaimed in amazement. "What manner of loyalty requires a decision before you may speed to his aid? Would not Thorgest himself do as much for you?" she insisted, including the whole firehall in her question. "For any one of you? Did you not all swear an oath of allegiance to him? Go now to your sovereign lord and let our ships be as a wave of terror that swallows the Gael. Go – or forswear the honour on which you all pride yourself."

As indignant grumbles and murmurs of assent filled the hall, Ragnar rose to his feet and gestured to quell the noise. "It is I who will choose when and where to strike the Irish," he announced, his dark eyes sweeping the room. A hush fell over the assembly as he lowered his arms.

Pinned at her shoulders by the two tortoise brooches, Otta's robes flared about her as she whirled. "You dare to defy me?" she called. "I am high priestess to Thor and I will call upon his eight legged horse, Sleipnir, to pluck you up in your sleep and carry you down into the underworld." In spite of himself, Ragnar shuddered at the image. Pushing it aside, he squared his shoulders, knowing that he could not let his warriors see the fear. "Lord Thorgest left me in command," he told her evenly. "And I must think what is best for all before I act."

"Now I see the truth," she shot back, pointing her staff

at him. "You seek to usurp my husband's place of honour. When he returns I shall tell him of your treachery and – "

"I seek nothing!" Ragnar exploded. "I did not ask the burden of leadership be thrust upon me! But now I have no choice but to bear it for there can be little doubt that Thorgest will *not* be coming back!"

Otta opened her mouth to speak, then caught herself. She began to weep. Her maidservants flocked to her side.

"Take your lady back to her quarters and attend her," Ragnar ordered. Watching them lead her from the firehall, he knew that Otta's outburst had been more contrived than spontaneous, an elaborate ploy to elicit the sympathy and support of her husband's chieftains. He eased himself back into Thorgest's chair.

Ragnar sensed the eyes of the Norse jarls upon him and knew he had made a mistake. His confrontation with Thor's high priestess would be regarded as callous, even cruel, and he sensed a fresh tension in the firehall as her countrymen stared disapprovingly at him and the Danish sea chieftains seated opposite them. Frantically, he groped for the words that would shift their focus.

"Eadric," he called out to the Norseman who sat among his comrades. "I am puzzled how you can be so certain it was Malachy's men who attacked your party. What standards did the warriors bear?"

"Only his, lord. Many were clad and armed as we ourselves were. Helmets, chainmail and battle–axes. We took them for the garrison, and it was only when the bulk of their warriors and horsemen charged out from – "

"Horsemen?" Ragnar repeated, his eyes widening.

"There is only one that I know who would lead mounted warriors into battle. Did you see their leader? Wore he a bearskin mantle?"

"I cannot say, my lord," Eadric replied. "There was much confusion as we drew away from the shore and we were preoccupied with getting beyond the range of their arrows and spears."

Ragnar slammed his fist onto the arm of the chair. "Wolfblade!" he grunted. "The one who slew Saxulf, my brother. I know it is he." He squinted down at Kenan. "This is the work of that whore–son who is your brother."

"No," Kenan denied emphatically. "Bran remains in Ulster with Niall. I have heard your own men speak of how it was he who was responsible for the attack on Lough Neagh."

"We know that your high king has marched back to his fortress at Ailech," Ragnar said smugly. "But is your brother with him?"

Kenan shrugged. "You have no reason to believe otherwise. Surely one of your garrisons in Meath would have alerted you if he had led the army south toward Leinster."

"Perhaps," Ragnar agreed, nodding slowly. "But a small number of men would easily elude detection."

"Then he would not have been capable of launching the attack on Lough Owel," Kenan protested, nodding toward Eadric. "Your man has already told us that they were vastly outnumbered. If Bran brought only a small contingent south, how could he possibly mount such an attack?"

"He couldn't," Ragnar replied slowly. "Unless he had been foolish enough to move the remainder of his warriors north from Naas." He grinned maliciously. "And that would mean that he has left Leinster unguarded, at least temporarily."

A smile spread across Kenan's face, then he leaped to his feet. "Then that is where we must strike!" he urged excitedly.

Ragnar knew that greed had sparked the Leinsterman's enthusiasm, and he slouched back in his chair. "My first duty is to Lord Thorgest," he said evenly. "And to the safety of my people.

"You must decide wisely," Kenan reminded him. "It is likely that Lord Thorgest is dead and that means that it is you who must lead us now. To ignore this opportunity would be to demonstrate weakness and fear. Not only to your enemy, but to those you would have as followers. Besides," he added, his smile fading, "you are also honour bound to uphold Thorgest's promise to help me claim my rightful place on the throne. There will be no better time than now to fulfill that promise. Once it is accomplished, I believe you will find me a valuable ally."

"I did not ask for your impudent counsel," Ragnar retorted angrily. "Do you think me also incapable of wise decisions?"

"Of course not, lord," Kenan replied as he stepped around the table to stroll along the edge of the open hearth. "I merely point out that if it is Bran you want, it would be only logical to attack Naas which he will now certainly move to defend. Besides, if indeed it was Bran who struck at Lough Owel and Thorgest is his captive, Naas is where you will find them both. If not, the advantage remains yours for the bulk of Leinster's army still remains in Ulster."

Ragnar scrutinized him for several moments as he considered the possibility. He shook his head. "It is too dangerous. Our draken cannot navigate the shallow rivers between here and Lough Owel and I do not intend to tempt Niall by moving overland."

"Then you must sail your fleet down the Shannon and strike Leinster from the sea," Kenan told him. "Is it not that very tactic which has brought you success in the past?"

"Don't be a fool," Ragnar snorted. "In order to accomplish that we would have to leave our base here completely unprotected."

"Aye," Kenan agreed pensively. "But who will strike at it? A half day will carry you to Leinster and the same on the voyage back. Providing that you can crush Bran in two days, the fleet will be back at Lough Ree long before Niall can reach us."

Ragnar surveyed the hard, weathered faces that looked back at him. "What say you all?" he bellowed. "Do we seek out this Wolfblade who has either captured or killed Lord Thorgest? What say you to vengeance?"

There was a momentary silence, then the firehall exploded into a tumult of frenzied cries.

"Blood for blood!"

"Death to the Leinsterman!"

Ragnar stooped to Kenan. "It would appear you shall have your crown." As Kenan grinned back at him, Ragnar stood and waved down the shouted oaths for revenge. "It will be dark soon," his voice boomed. "We will wait until morning, then every sea chieftain look to his longship. Tomorrow we sail for Leinster!"

While silver–laced clouds draped themselves about the timid moon, its hesitant light snaking across the gently rippling waters at Lough Ree, the cool breeze that wafted over the lake sighed in the stillness of midnight and played amongst the swaying rushes that fringed the strand. Along the eastern shoreline, the heads of malformed creatures rose between the wharfs, the silhouetted prows of the longships nodding in the reluctant light as the vessels tugged at their moorings. The cargo ships were nearest to the shoreline and bundles of goods cluttered the narrow piers. At the southern–most end of the dock, a half dozen sentries sat huddled among bundles of cargo, periodically refilling their drinking horns from the opened cask that rested in the centre of the small congregation. Their mumbled conversation, punctuated by periodic bursts of throaty laughter, amplified as it was carried across the water's surface.

Stripped to the waist, their bodies streaked with charcoal, Bran and Rowan crouched in the darkness and watched the sentinels from the cover of the thickets which cluttered the southern bank. Positioned within a spear toss of the Vikings, each moved with calculated deliberation, unfastening their sword belts and slinging them over their shoulders, the scabbards hanging across their backs.

Abruptly, from somewhere off to their right, came a faint crackling of leaves. Both men pivoted sharply and reached back to grasp their weapons. Etach appeared a few moments later and passed the bow and quiver he carried to Rowan.

"We will not be seen from the towers," he whispered

hoarsely, jerking his head toward the two structures that rose above the palisade walls beyond the harbour. Bran put a finger to his lips, then turned back to his vigil.

His eyes moved to the palisade walls beyond the harbour. *She is there*, he told himself. *Waiting for me. They are all there.*

For almost an hour the three men watched and waited in silence. Then, the voices of the foreigners grew suddenly louder and unsteadier, their light banter evolving into some kind of argument. It was quickly resolved when two of the guards rose unsteadily, collected their weapons and lamps, and shuffled off on their rounds along the length of the dock. The four left behind, the probable winners of the dispute, stretched out on the pier. A short time later, their fading palaver gave way to loud wine—induced snores.

"Etach," Bran whispered, touching the man's shoulder. "Take care of those that sleep. Rowan and I will attend to the other two."

As the older soldier turned and slipped into the darkness, Bran nodded to Rowan. Easing into the icy water, the cold numbing them, they moved silently through the rushes and into the open. Taking care that their strokes did not break the surface of the water, they slowly swam toward the nearest wharf. At the sound of a rasping cough from one of the sleeping men on shore they dove under the water, eventually resurfacing beneath the wharf that had been their objective.

Moving from one prow to the next, Bran led Rowan along the vessels toward the shoreline. As they reached the innermost ship, Bran signalled Rowan to wait, then moved along the hull to the stern. He peered down the length of the dock. The two guards were at the far end, their backs to him as they continued their patrol. Bran made his way to Rowan, then reached up and caught the guy—line which moored the small cargo ship to the wharf. Shinnying along its length to the pier, Bran hauled himself up, then flattened out on the wooden planks. As Rowan followed him, Bran peered ahead to the shadowy figure which had emerged from the brush and was creeping to the dozing sentries, the moonlight glinting on the blade in his hand. He watched as Etach stooped first over one man, then another.

Then one of the victims groaned, a strange gurgling sound that roared in Bran's ears. As Etach's knife flashed again, Bran looked along his shoulder to the sentinels at the end of the dock. They had heard it too and had begun to walk back. Glancing at Etach, Bran saw him drop down among the corpses, his weapon held ready.

"Sigurd? Adeldag?" one of the guards called out, holding his lamp before him as they strode toward their comrades.

Bran nudged Rowan and drew his dagger. Rowan nodded, his own weapon already in his hand. Crouching behind the cargo on the narrow pier, they waited until the two Vikings had almost passed their position, then they sprang at them from behind.

Hooking his free arm around the throat of one of them, Bran plunged his dagger up into the base of the man's skull and twisted. The heathen jerked violently twice, then went limp and crumpled to the ground as Bran released him. Glancing sideways, he saw Rowan easing the other guard down, blood streaming from the Viking's slashed throat.

"What should we do with the bodies?" Rowan asked,

sheathing his dagger and looking about furtively.

"Nothing," Bran answered quickly as Etach reached them. "There is no time." He glanced at the old soldier. "And the others?"

"They will not awaken." He squinted down the length of the harbour. "We will not be able to set all these ships afire, my lord. There are too many. Surely we will be discovered before our task is complete."

Ignoring the remark, Bran dropped to one knee and pried the still flickering lamp from his victim's fingers. He quickly removed the lid, dipped a finger inside and tasted it.

"Oil," he muttered to himself. Striding back to the pier, he quickly pried the lid off several of the casks with his dagger, tasting the contents of each until he found the one he sought. Then he tipped the cask on its side and poured the viscous liquid into the water.

"Quickly," he urged, glancing up at his bewildered companions as he set about opening another. "Find all the casks of oil you can, and empty them into the harbour and along the wharfs."

"What?" Etach mumbled. "What good – "

"Hurry!" Bran pleaded. "We have not much time."

For the next half hour the three men worked feverishly, emptying scores of casks into the harbour until the surface of the water glistened like gold in the pale moonlight. While Etach and Rowan completed the task at the far end of the dock, Bran silently rolled several casks to the palisade walls and overturned them. When he was finished he retrieved the guards' lamp and beckoned his comrades.

Leading them back along the shoreline to the thickets

where they had been positioned earlier, Bran handed the lamp to Etach, then dropped to his knees and began tearing his linen tunic into strips. "Soak these in the oil," he instructed, passing the pieces to Etach. "Then give them to Rowan to fasten to the tips of the arrows."

When a half dozen had been prepared, Bran fitted one of the arrows to the bow, then touched its tip to the lamp's flame. As it ignited, he drew back the shaft, took aim, and released it. Like a small fireball against the night sky, it arced high into the air, then fell among the flotilla of ships, striking the deck of one with a distinct thud. The tiny pinpoint of light flickered for an instant, then disappeared.

Bran cursed under his breath as he fumbled to light another, then launched it. This time, the flaming shaft disappeared between the two ships. For a moment nothing happened. Then, there was an almost inaudible sputtering sound. Suddenly a wall of flame shot up along the entire length of one wharf, spreading to the others like a wave of liquid fire.

"Mother of God!" Etach murmured, crossing himself as Bran prepared another shaft. "It is as if the whole of bloody hell has boiled up out of the Lough!"

Shouts were already coming from the settlement as Bran drew back and took aim at the base of the palisades. His fingers had already begun to release the shaft when he checked himself.

Merciful Christ, he thought in horror as he relaxed his grip. *I may be killing my own wife and child if I set the heathen stronghold ablaze. And if I do not, how many lives will be lost when Niall and Malachy arrive, trying to penetrate defenses that I could have…*

"What is it, my lord," Rowan asked anxiously. "Why do you hesitate?"

Bran glanced at him. "Nothing," he answered softly, then drew back his shaft as he took aim again. *God be with them*, he prayed silently, then fired. As the blazing arrow struck its mark, flames leaped up along the timbers of the palisade walls.

"Jesus," Rowan whispered in awe. "The heathen will think they have been set upon by the devil himself."

"Perhaps they have," Bran muttered as he gathered up his weapons. "But it is us, not he, they will be searching for. Rowan, you stay on this side of the lough and keep watch for Malachy's warriors. Etach and I will move the horses to the west side. In a few more hours it will be daylight and the Viking will be sending out scouting parties." Bran forced himself to smile weakly. "God grant our own find us before they do."

Despite the efforts of the Vikings the fire spread quickly, many of the buildings inside the wall which faced the harbour burning out of control as the breeze off the lake quickly spread glowing cinders and thick choking smoke throughout the settlement. Panicked and confused, scattered groups of men and women worked frantically, using spades, bowls and even their hands to scoop up dirt and toss it onto the flames, but to no avail. In a desperate effort to combat the fire, Ragnar had hastily organized his warriors at the waterfront, the lengthy chains of men stretching from the water's edge to the blazing palisades. But hauling the water from the lough quickly proved to be of little use, the heat from the inferno that had been the fleet forcing them to draw the water from further upshore. The distance had been too great and the process too slow to be effective, so that within an hour of the alarm being raised, Ragnar had ordered the evacuation of Lough Ree.

His mantle pulled up over his nose and mouth, Kenan swept the terrified women and children out of his path as he fought his way through terrified crowds that jammed the narrow street leading to his quarters. Under his breath he cursed Ragnar's decision to lead the entire settlement northwest to the base at Sligo Bay. *These fools march in the wrong direction*, he thought. *It is Leinster they should be marching on. It is closer and from there we could be reinforced by Feidlimid. I feel all I have worked for slipping through my fingers. And yet I have no option but to go with them and hope that they are able to consolidate. I have no other choice.*

As he came up to the small wooden sheiling which had been his accommodations, he frowned at the sight of the half–loaded jaunting cart which had been positioned next to the open doorway. Domhnall and several of his bodyguards were struggling to load yet another chest into it.

"What is all this?" he demanded irritably of the burly, dark–haired warrior who stood apart from the others, supervising the task.

"Your lady's baggage, my lord," Domhnall replied. "She ordered us to see to it."

"Unload it," Kenan snapped, stepping past him. As he stormed through the door, Taillte and Aengus started, glancing fearfully over their shoulders while they remained stooped over the large wooden chest they had been loading.

"What are you doing?" Kenan fumed, frowning down

at the assortment of clothes and articles piled in the centre of the room.

"What does it look like?" Taillte answered sarcastically, turning back to her packing. "You may not have noticed but the whole of this ungodly place is about to burn down around us."

"You can't take all this," Kenan protested. "Here now, Aengus," he said to the ferret–faced warrior who was struggling to lift a rather large chest onto his back. "Put that down and go help the others unload the cart. What little room there is will be needed for food and supplies. The journey to Sligo will be long and hard."

Taillte drew herself up to her full height. "Load it into the cart as I asked you, Aengus," she said, then swung to face Kenan. "I am not going to Sligo."

He met her defiant gaze, then glared at Aengus. "Leave that and get out!" he roared. The startled warrior looked from one to the other for a moment, then rushed from the room, slamming the door behind him.

"What do you mean you are not going to Sligo?" Kenan demanded, peering at Taillte. "You go where *I* go, and I am going to Sligo."

"Then you go alone," Taillte told him firmly. "I have no intention of living like an animal among these barbarians. They lack everything. Besides, I have grown accustomed to a much more comfortable existence. I am going back to Cashel."

Kenan swallowed his anger. "You are returning to Feidlimid?"

"Why shouldn't I?" Taillte pouted. "At least there I

have friends, position, prestige. Here, I am regarded as little more than another concubine." Suddenly her manner changed. Looking at him sympathetically she stepped forward to caress his cheek. "Oh, come with me love. We do not belong among these savages. Let us both return to Cashel. We had a good life there, you and I, and it can be that way again."

Kenan reached out and caught her shoulders. "Don't you understand?" he pleaded. "I cannot gain the crown of Leinster without the aid of the foreigners. I must stay with them."

Drawing back, Taillte shook her head. "It's over, Kenan. The fates have already changed their course. The heathen will be defeated and you will never be king. I have been patient, but I am tired of your empty dreams and promises. And I know now that you will never change. Do as you wish. But I am returning to Cashel."

She started to turn from him but Kenan spun her around. "You will do as you are told," he snarled.

Taillte slapped him, then wrenched her wrist free. "Don't you ever touch me again," she hissed. "You are no better than these savages. It would appear we will both be in good company. Now, get out."

Brushing past him, she strode toward the door. Kenan followed behind, feeling for his dagger. As she reached for the latch, Kenan plunged his weapon deep into her back. Taillte gasped, falling forward against the door, then moaned as he wrenched the blade free. Twisting to face him, her lips quivered and her deep green eyes pleaded for an explanation.

Kenan gently caressed her face, then kissed her. "Feidlimid's court will have to manage without you," he mocked, pressing his cheek on her's. "And you're wrong, love. I will not be going to Sligo alone." He thrust the dagger between her ribs and Taillte flung her head back against the door, sharply sucking in her breath. Her eyes rolled back and she slumped forward into his arms. Pulling his dagger free again, Kenan stepped aside and watched her crumple to the floor. He gazed down at her for a moment, then squatted and wiped his blade clean on her lena.

Rising, he sheathed the weapon and stepped outside. Aengus and Domhnall were standing alongside the cart as he opened the door and he watched their gaze drop to the motionless figure that lay on the floor behind him.

"Now you can unload that cart," he told them, amused at the horrified expression on their faces. "My lady will not be needing her baggage."

While the two men hurried to do his bidding, Kenan strode toward the sheds that quartered the thralls.

CHAPTER THIRTY–TWO

Smoke crept through the narrow gaps between the wood planking of the walls, a thin haze filling the confines of the dimly lit shed. From outside came the pandemonium and discord of a terror–stricken population, the shrill cries of women and frightened children rising above the strained clamouring of the men. Finola threw her weight against the door one last time. As she slammed into it, a sharp pain travelled the length of her arm. But the heavy door, barred from the outside, refused to budge. Massaging her bruised shoulder, she turned and looked down at Muireen who sat huddled in the corner, cradling Devlin in her arms.

"It's no good, Muireen," she said, brushing a wisp of white bronze hair off her forehead as she leaned resignedly against the wall. "I can't move it."

Muireen nodded slowly, then adjusted the ragged blanket carefully laid over the sleeping infant's face. "Can you see anything?"

Finola inspected the wall, then bent down and peered through a space between the planks. The flames were closer than they had been before and she decided not to relay their progress to Muireen. "The settlement is still on fire. And I see people, a great many of them, fleeing out the main gate." She glanced over her shoulder. "It would appear the heathen are abandoning Lough Ree."

"You don't think they will leave us here, do you?"

There was fear in Muireen's eyes and Finola moved across the room, sitting back on her heels as she knelt beside her. She reached out and gently touched the other woman's shoulder. "Of course not," she lied, knowing that the smoke within the shed would soon make it difficult to breathe. Devlin, she realized, would be the first to die. "I am certain the thralls will be collected once the Viking have attended to their own people."

"Aye," Muireen sighed wearily. "And we'll be taken to some other Godforsaken place where they can work us both until we drop. Compared to that hell, the prospect of dying seems almost inviting."

"Don't you say that," Finola admonished her. "Don't even think it. We have to keep hoping and believing that this nightmare will end, otherwise all we have endured will have been for nothing."

Muireen shrugged. "And what future do any of us have now? Little Devlin here will be raised a slave, and you and I will probably die labouring in the heathen's fields. Be honest with yourself, Finola, if not with me. None of us are ever going to see our home again."

"No!" Finola said adamantly, tightening her grip on Muireen's shoulder. "I will not give up – and neither will you. God has not kept us alive this long only to have us perish as slaves. With His grace, we will somehow find the means to escape and return to Naas, to Bran and to our lives. Then all will be as it was before."

"You deceive yourself," Muireen retorted. "Don't you understand, Finola? Nothing will ever be the same. Conor is dead and for all we know Bran as well. Even if we do escape, the home we return to will not be the one we knew. How can you..."

Her words trailed off as Finola touched a finger to her

lips. From outside came the faint rasp of wood against wood as the door was unbarred. Then, as Finola rose to her feet, it burst open.

Otta stood at the entry, the purple mantle and flowing skyrta of the high priestess flapping noisily in the chill breeze while behind her the flames that raged along the palisade walls licked obscenely at the night sky. Strands of her long golden hair, unbraided and disheveled, whipped about her contorted features.

"You have brought a curse upon us," the high priestess moaned as she stepped into the shed. Finola's eyes moved to the dagger held at the woman's side, and she took a cautious step sideways in front of Muireen. "Thor vents his wrath upon his own people because I denied him the proper sacrifice that was his due at the time of Uppsala," Otta went on. "The fault is mine, for taking the maidservant in your place. It was you who should have hung from the sacred oak." Raising the dagger, Otta moved forward. "Now I will put right what was meant to be."

Finola gradually backed away, drawing the crazed woman away from Muireen. "It is not a pagan idol who destroys you," Finola answered. "It is the vengeance of Almighty God."

"Blasphemer!" Otta shrieked, lunging forward. As the narrow blade slashed downward, Finola caught her wrist in both hands. "Die, you Irish sow!" the high priestess screamed, reaching with her free hand to rake the nails across Finola's face.

Turning her head aside, Finola threw herself against the Norse woman, knocking her off balance. Both toppled to the ground. Wrestling Finola onto her back, Otta pinned her to the dirt floor. Her arms quivered with the effort as she struggled to break Finola's grasp and drive the dagger into her breast.

Summoning her strength, Finola thrust her body upward, rolling onto the priestess as she threw her to one side. Otta suddenly gasped, then went limp. Rising to her knees, Finola stared down at the dagger which protruded from Otta's chest. A last breath fled the dead woman's lungs in a rasping sigh.

"Come!" Finola urged Muireen as she scrambled to her feet. "Hurry!"

Finola ushered her through the open doorway then followed. Once outside, they stared in amazement at the horrific scene before them. The palisades and most of the buildings were ablaze now, crackling and popping as they burned. Between the patches of white smoke that drifted by she could see the long procession of men, women and children that continued to pour through the main gate, illuminated in the sickly orange light of the flames. Glancing about, she realized that the guards had also fled and that the fire would soon consume the thrall's quarters.

"You go on ahead, Muireen," Finola said quickly. "Keep to the woods."

"What about you?" Muireen asked tensely. "I'll not go without you, Finola."

Finola's eyes moved along the row of thrall sheds, then she looked back at Muireen. "I cannot just leave the others here to die," she explained. "Now take Devlin and go. I'll catch up to you."

Muireen hesitated, then nodded. "I'll wait for you at

the edge of the woods." She hugged Finola's neck and smiled, then turned and ran off into the darkness.

Moving to the thrall shed nearest her, Finola lifted the heavy wood beam which barred the door. As she flung it open, two young boys stumbled out, coughing and rubbing their eyes. An old man followed, herding the two boys into the shadows. As they disappeared, Finola sprinted to the door of the next shed and struggled to open it.

"Very commendable," a low voice commented behind her. Finola spun about and stared into Kenan's grinning face.

"Your concern for your fellow prisoners is very touching," he continued, striding toward her. "But I do not think their masters would approve." He reached out and caught her wrist. "Come. We have a long journey ahead of us."

Finola struggled in his grasp. "I am not going anywhere with you!" She aimed to kick at his groin, but he quickly stepped aside. As she tried to regain her balance, he swung his fist in a wide arc, the blow catching her alongside her head.

Then all was darkness.

Oblivious to the hawthorns that rended her shift and tore at her flesh, Muireen ran blindly through the dense thickets, her shoulders hunched over as she tightly clasped Devlin to her breast. Glancing frequently over her shoulder, she took her bearings from the sinister red glow that still hovered in the night sky over Lough Ree. The vivid image of Kenan lifting Finola, unconscious and limp, into his arms was still fresh in her mind, haunting her as she continued to press on. She had wanted to lay Devlin down in the soft moss and rush to Finola's aid, but her instinct to save herself and the child she carried had seized control of her legs, propelling her into the darkness. Relentlessly, her shame pursued her.

After a time, fatigue began to override the guilt and Muireen paused to rest, glancing about furtively as she squatted in the shadow of a cluster of willows. Satisfied that they had not been followed, she lifted the edge of the rough woolen swaddling blanket away from Devlin's face. In the pallid moonlight, the baby smiled up at her and cooed happily, then reached out and caught a small handful of her auburn hair. Muireen clucked her tongue softly as she gently pried the tiny fingers loose.

"You do not fear the darkness, do you little one?" she whispered, caressing the infant's cheek. "Nor are you afraid of the heathen. That is good. Then you will have courage enough for both of us." The baby smiled up at her. "So much like your mother. How often I have leaned on her strength these past months, and now... but don't you worry about her Devlin. When we reach Naas you father will know what – "

The hand clamped down over Muireen's mouth without warning, drawing her back against the chest of her unseen assailant. Her skin crawled as she felt his warm breath upon her neck.

"It's me, Muireen," a husky voice whispered. "It's Rowan, Rowan Ui Muiredaig."

The hand was taken away and Muireen turned about to peer into Rowan's face. Paralyzed with disbelief, she stared at him for several moments, then leaned her head against his shoulder. "Thank God," she sobbed as he wrapped his arms around her. "I thought you were the heathen."

"Where is Finola?" Rowan asked quickly. Muireen looked up at him. "She stayed behind and..." Her voice trailed off as she began to weep.

Rowan nodded and laid a cautionary finger to his lips. "We must move quickly and quietly, my lady. The Viking are still about. Bran and Etach are on the far side of the lough. Come," he whispered tersely, helping her up. "I will take you to them."

For over an hour they moved in silence through the darkness, catching only brief glimpses of the lough through the tangled maze of underbrush that surrounded them as they paralleled the shoreline. The rising sun had already begun to chase off the last vestiges of night when they reached a small clearing. There was no evidence of a camp and with the exception of the three horses which had been tethered to the twisted branches of a fallen log, the area was otherwise deserted. The shroud of morning mist which still brooded over the ground underscored the eerie atmosphere of the shadowy glade, and Muireen shivered involuntarily as she padded across the damp moss alongside Rowan.

Abruptly, he gestured her to halt. From the wall of thickets on the far side of the clearing came a faint rustling sound. Glancing up fearfully at Rowan, Muireen started to speak, then checked herself. The young Ui Muiredaig chieftain stood motionless, his attention fixed on the source of the disturbance as he slowly reached over his shoulder and grasped the hilt of his weapon.

Sword in hand, Etach emerged from the dense brush. Behind him followed a tall warrior, the copper tangle of his long hair and beard obscuring his face. He wore a sleeveless tunic that hung in tatters from one shoulder, and the well—defined muscles in his arms and chest rippled as he returned his sword to the scabbard slung across his back. As his blue eyes met Muireen's, he hesitated and peered at her uncertainly.

"Muireen?" he asked with disbelief and hope.

At the sound of his voice, a thousand forgotten memories flooded back to Muireen. Only then did she recognize her brother.

"Bran! Bran!" she cried out, rushing into his waiting arms.

"Thank Christ," he muttered, his voice breaking with emotion as he embraced her. He bent down and tenderly kissed the infant in her arms. "Devlin – my son."

"I did not think I would see you again in this life," Muireen sobbed as tears streamed freely down her cheeks. "But Finola never lost hope – not for a moment. She said you would come."

Bran held her at arm's length, his face full of anxiety. "Is she still alive then?" he begged anxiously. "For God's sake Muireen, tell me!"

Muireen lowered her eyes and nodded, her throat constricted.

"Where is she?" he demanded. "What's happened to her?"

"I don't know!" Muireen blurted out in anguish. "Kenan has her." Between sobs she choked out the details of her escape and how she had watched from the edge of the woods while Kenan took Finola away. "He flees to Sligo, Bran, with the foreigners." She looked up at him penitently. "God forgive me, there was nothing I could do."

Bran nodded slowly. "The fault is not yours." Setting his jaw, he turned toward the horses, but Etach caught his arm.

"Where are you going?" he asked gruffly.

"Leave me!" Bran snarled as he wrenched his arm free.

"Listen to me," Etach entreated him. "What you do is madness. If we go after her now we will all die. The foreigners are many, and we are but a few. Against them we have no chance."

"He is right, Bran," Rowan added, stepping to Etach's side. "We must wait here for Malachy and his warriors. Then we can pursue the Viking in force."

"By then it may be too late," Bran protested urgently. They will be at least a day's march ahead of us if we wait for Malachy. The heathen will reach their ships at Sligo Bay long before we can overtake them."

Etach scratched his beard thoughtfully. "Aye," he muttered. "The warriors of Meath will have little hope of catching them. But Niall might – if we can intercept him. Even now he marches on Lough Ree and cannot know that the enemy has fled."

"Then we still have a chance," Bran said. "We must find Niall and lead him west. If we move quickly enough, we may be able to cut off the heathen's retreat to their ships." He turned to the Ui Muiredaig chieftain. "Stay here with Muireen. When Malachy and his warriors arrive you must lead them to Sligo with all speed."

"But surely Muireen can tell our allies in what direction the Viking have fled," Rowan suggested. "Let me ride with you, my lord."

"You serve me better by protecting my sister and child," Bran told him. "Etach and I will ride north to seek out Niall."

"But how will you find him?" Muireen asked.

"The armies of Ulster and Leinster march behind the Ard–Ri," Etach offered. "Such a body of men will not be hard to find."

"Aye," Bran agreed between clenched teeth. "Together with Malachy we will drive the heathen from our shores." Muireen saw the hatred in her brother's eyes and knew that he would not be stopped. "And then I will deal with Kenan – as I should have long ago."

CHAPTER THIRTY-THREE

For five days the Norse and their Danish allies fled northwest from Lough Ree, their drive for the Sligo coast impeded by the rain that pelted them incessantly, soaking their garments and transforming the road that stretched out before them into a seemingly endless sea of mud. Cursing the chill wind that knifed through their drenched clothing, the exhausted men and women slogged through the sucking mire, the muscles in their shoulders aching with the weight of the weapons and household goods they packed upon their backs. Mothers desperately tried to soothe the children who clutched at the soiled folds of their skirts, whining with cold and fatigue. Heavily loaded carts and wagons creaked along noisily at the rear of the wrangling column, their thick wooden wheels frequently bogging down in the treacherous ooze. Those that could not be moved were summarily unloaded and abandoned.

As they wound their way through the Brickslieve Mountains, some of the disgruntled warriors openly speculated that Thor had deserted his people, adding to the anxiety of those who already believed that the destruction of their settlement at Lough Ree had only been a prelude to the full scale attack that was yet to come. Although Ragnar himself shared their misgivings and had sent numerous scouting parties back along their trail, each time the warriors had returned with nothing to report. Nonetheless, convinced that the Gael would soon be in close pursuit, he had periodically ordered several head of cattle slaughtered and skinned, the hides stretched across makeshift stockades and positioned so that the bloody parts faced back toward the enemy he was certain would follow. Ragnar knew that the horses would balk at such a barrier, and he hoped that the Gael would be delayed long enough to allow him and his warriors to reach the security of their ships.

Then, on the morning of the sixth day, the rain ceased and as the warming sun gradually lifted the mantle of mist away from the saturated landscape, Ragnar caught sight of the distant coast. Beyond the level plain that stretched out before him, three estuaries gouged into the seaboard, the centre one of which served as a natural harbour for the Viking base at Sligo. The settlement itself was positioned near the mouth of the Garvogue, the broad, slow moving river which meandered five leagues inland, linking the peaceful waters of Lough Gill to the ocean. Gazing north to the wooded hills which fringed the southern shores of the lake, Ragnar caught the scent of sea air on the wind and sighed with relief.

"The Gael are no threat to us now," he announced confidently to the jarls who rode with him at the head of the column. "We will reach Sligo before nightfall."

"The people are exhausted, lord," one of them pointed out. "With our destination so close at hand, why not let them camp here for now. One day, more or less, can make little difference."

Ragnar saw the dark smears of fatigue beneath the warrior's red–rimmed eyes. "Only a fool would halt now," he objected, pointing to the highlands that separated the plain from Lough Gill. "We have but to skirt those ridges. The settlement lies only a few leagues beyond. No," he added decisively, "we push on. Tonight we will rest in the warmth of our comrades' firehall." Twisting in his saddle, he peered back along the length of the train. "Where is the Leinsterman?"

"At the rear with Feidlimid's warriors," a robust Norse sea chieftain offered. "He has bound and leashed the she–thrall who slew Otta, and drags her behind him like an untrained mongrel."

Ragnar knew that many of the jarls believed he had tempted the wrath of the gods by not killing the woman who had slain Thor's high priestess. But he had ignored their superstitious whispers, refusing to put his faith in anything he could not see, or entrust his fate to any other hands but his own. The queen of Leinster would die soon enough – but not before he had used her to bait the man who had slain his brother. Saxulf's blood would be avenged.

"We will give Wolfblade the opportunity to save his queen," he told the jarls. "By proposing a simple exchange, the release of his woman for the surrender of the Leinster chieftains – and his consent to take her place as our hostage. Then, both will die and we will conquer Leinster clan by clan."

"And if he does not agree?" a burly Dane queried. "So far this king has proven he will sacrifice much to safeguard his people."

Ragnar grinned back at him. "Then we will send his own brother back to Cashel with a message instructing Feidlimid to march on Leinster. When Wolfblade moves to defend himself, our fleet will sail from Sligo to strike at his unprotected coast. Caught between us and the Munstermen, the outcome will be the same. Then, we look to Niall."

"Feidlimid will never comply with such a demand," the Danish sea chieftain scoffed. "His response to Lord Thorgest's petition for warriors was less than enthusiastic, sending us only a handful of beggars and thieves. What makes you think he will cooperate with us now?"

"The King of Munster will soon find that I lack Thorgest's diplomacy and patience," Ragnar replied. "Feidlimid must decide whether he stands on the battlefield as our ally or our enemy. There are no other choices."

Her hands bound behind her back, Finola staggered along behind Kenan, the rawhide collar chafing her neck as he tugged on the leather thong by which he led her. Glaring at his back, her loathing for him intensified with the passing of each painful step. Night after night throughout the long journey Kenan had come to Finola, brutally violating her before the Norse and Danish warriors who gathered about them, laughing derisively and shouting crude obscenities as she struggled beneath him. Stifling her screams, Finola had channeled the agony and shame into a hatred from which she drew the will and strength to survive.

Now, as she trudged along in silence, a single thought hammered at her consciousness, overshadowing all other considerations.

Revenge. God grant me revenge.

Her eyes stayed on the dagger that hung at Kenan's belt.

Less than sixty leagues southeast of Sligo, Rowan Ui Muiredaig led the clansmen of Meath into the Brickslieve Mountains in pursuit of the fleeing heathen. Five days earlier, Malachy and Tigerhnach had brought their warriors to Lough Ree, and after pausing only long enough to send

Muireen and Devlin back to Naas with a small escort, had set off again to follow the well–marked trail the Vikings had left in their wake. Even so, Rowan knew that the heathen had gained a full day's lead, and though he was anxious to close the gap, Malachy remained stubbornly adamant in his refusal to order the pace increased.

"But the Viking will be in Sligo before the day is out!" Rowan protested hotly to the white–haired king who rode at his side. "We must overtake them now, before they have a chance to reach their ships."

The aging king of Meath, his ashen complexion lined and creased by a lifetime of decisions, scrutinized Rowan. "What would you have me do?" he shot back, his grey eyes searching the young chieftain's face. "If the foreigners should discover we follow them, they could well turn on us, and alone, we cannot defeat them."

"But we do not stand alone," Rowan insisted. "The army of the Ard–Ri marches south to Sligo."

"Aye," Malachy grumbled through his snowy beard. "But where are they? I cannot afford to risk the lives of my warriors by relying on the support of an ally who may arrive too late. If however, Niall reaches the coast in time, let him be the first to engage the heathen. Then, we will act. Until Niall moves," he added as he shifted in his saddle, "we do nothing to provoke the Viking."

Lying on his belly atop the grassy highlands which rose from the southern shores of Lough Gill, Bran peered down at the Viking column as it slowly crept along the valley floor beneath him. *If Finola is still alive she will be among them*, he thought, the memory of her lavender eyes haunting him. He anxiously scanned the dark mass, searching for some sign of her, then realized that they were still too far off to distinguish individual features within the multitude. Still, he sensed she was there, somewhere in the midst of the enemy he would slaughter to find his way back to her – then to the brother he had solemnly vowed to destroy. The obscene vision of Kenan violating the woman he loved came back to Bran, tormenting him before he drove it back into the obscurity of his subconscious.

"Shall I give the order to attack, my lord?" he asked, glancing sideways at Niall who lay prone on the grass beside him.

"Not yet," the Ard–Ri replied, craning his neck as he gazed down into the valley. "It is as you said – the whole bloody settlement from Lough Ree. And they would have slipped by us had you not intercepted us at Enniskillen." He frowned, then looked at Bran. "There are many more of them then I anticipated. Do you see nothing of Malachy?"

"Not yet," Bran replied, surveying the foothills to the southeast that bordered the hazy peaks of the Brickslieve Mountains "But they will come."

Niall grimaced. "We cannot wait any longer. In another hour the foreigners will reach their ships. If we are to stop them we must do it now."

"Then so be it," Bran replied flatly.

Moving back down the gently sloping hill, the two men made their way to the shade of the trees where Etach and Turloch waited with their horses. Captains and chieftains of the clans moved about restlessly, while behind them the warriors of Leinster and Ulster blanketed the lower slopes. Interspersed among the banners that fluttered over their heads were the standards of the Connaught clans who had joined the Ard–Ri on his march south from Ailech. Though many of the Connaught warriors were barefoot and clad in threadbare tunics, their fighting spirit and loyalty to Niall Caille was without equal.

We will face the heathen together, Bran thought as he looked down at them. *All of us. This was my father's dream – the warriors of Erin united under the standard of the Ard–Ri.*

But even though the ranks of the high king's army had swollen considerably, Bran knew they would be hard pressed to defeat the Viking without support from Malachy.

"The numbers of the heathen are far greater than our own," he heard Niall telling the officers and chieftains who had gathered about him. "But surprise is our ally and by the grace of Holy St. Padraic, victory will be ours this day. When the signal is given, strike in the name of Erin and freedom."

As the Ard–Ri strode to his war horse, Bran accepted the reins of his own mount from Etach. "Will you not ride into battle beside me, old friend?" he asked, puzzled that the grizzled soldier was still on foot.

"With your permission, lord, I prefer to fight with my feet planted on solid ground," Etach replied. "I intend to look into the eyes of those motherless bastards before I cut them down."

"As you wish." Bran caught a handful of his mare's mane and swung himself up onto her back in one fluid motion. He smiled down at the aging champion of the clanna Ui Faelain. "God go with you, Etach mac Cennedig."

Etach bowed his head. "And with you, my lord."

Riding side by side, Bran and Niall urged their horses back up to the crown of the grassy hill, then halted and waited as the army gradually moved up into position behind them, silent but for the creak of leather, the shuffling of feet, the muted whinnying of horses. In the valley below, the sprawling horde that was their objective continued to flow across the level plain.

"This day is yours," Niall said as he turned to Bran, the wind sweeping his silver—threaded hair across his face. "It is you who have brought us this chance to drive the foreigners from our land. Let your sword be the one to signal the attack."

Reaching back over his shoulder, Bran withdrew his weapon from the scabbard slung across his back. He cradled the gleaming steel in his hand, transfixed by its deadly beauty. "It was my father's sword," he said slowly, meeting Niall's steady gaze. "His spirit rides with us."

Bran held the blade high above his head, sunlight dancing along its polished surface. He glanced quickly over his shoulder at the tense faces of the mounted warriors who watched him, then stared down at the enemy who had brought so much pain to the people of Erin, to his own family. As he filled his lungs, the images of the massacre at Bray and Conor dead on the beach came back to him, and through the red mist that suddenly clouded his vision he saw Finola, her arms outstretched, waiting for him.

His battle cry exploded, echoing along the rolling hills as his sword slashed through the air and he kicked his horse forward.

"For God and Erin!"

Panic seized the Viking column as the Irish wave of destruction swept down the slopes and onto the open plain. Women shrieked hysterically, clutching children away from the horror and death that was charging down on them. Shouting themselves hoarse in the midst of the confusion, jarls desperately tried to organize their men into shield walls. But the Norse and Danish warriors who had been ambling alongside their families were scattered along the length of the train and few were in position when the Leinster cavalry hit.

Bran's mounted warriors swung their battle–axes with devastating effect, hacking swathes through the disordered Vikings. As they emerged from the opposite side of the disintegrating column and wheeled their mounts about to charge back, the front ranks of the Irish foot soldiers who had followed in their wake slammed into the disordered mass of foreigners.

War cries and the clash of metal on metal resounded across the valley as the battle gradually dissolved into a clutter of scattered melees.

Bran fought as a man possessed, skillfully guiding his horse from one opponent to the next, swinging his sword until his forearm was drenched in blood and the muscles in his shoulder ached with the effort. But still he pressed on, the mounted warriors who guarded him penetrating the innermost reaches of the fray as he searched for her. "Finola!" he shouted in vain, his cries swallowed in the din of battle that engulfed the plain. "Finola!"

Etach was deep in the press of battle, cursing as he roared out advice and criticism to the Leinstermen who fought at his side, many of whom he had personally trained in the skill at arms.

"Keep your shield moving, Murchadh! Mother of God! A wooden shield won't stop steel!"

A blond Norseman suddenly stepped in front of him, his battle-axe singing through the air, the blow aimed at Etach's head. The one-eyed veteran deflected the blade with his shield and swung his sword over the rim, grinning as it sliced into the man's exposed neck. Amid a spray of blood, the heathen crumpled to the ground, clutching at his throat. Etach thrust down into his chest, finishing him, then stepped over the twitching corpse.

"Deflect the blows!" he yelled to his comrades and pushed on.

Breaking through a concentration of Ulstermen, Ragnar and his Danes suddenly came upon the high king of the Irish, Niall Caille, accompanied by only a handful of personal guards as he tried to rally his warriors around him. Ragnar immediately recognized the gold circlet of kingship on his brow and shouted for his men to follow, bolting directly for the Ard-Ri. While his warriors engaged the bodyguards, Ragnar seized the reins of the king's mount and wrenched them violently to one side, the frightened horse throwing Niall backward as it reared. But before Ragnar could capitalize on his momentary advantage, Niall had sprung to his feet and slain one of the dark-skinned jarls, killing him with one powerful stroke. Another Dane threw himself forward and Niall lightly stepped aside, chopping at the Viking's unprotected back as he stumbled past. Screaming, the man dropped to his knees, then toppled forward.

Bellowing like a maddened beast, Ragnar hurled himself at Niall, launching a flurry of blows to bring down the Irish king. But Niall quickly proved to be the better swordsman, parrying Ragnar's thrusts even as they were initiated and countering with strokes that the Dane was finding increasingly difficult to defend against. He suddenly realized that his men had fallen back, deserting him, and for the first time in his life Ragnar felt the icy grip of fear.

"Garder! Rurik!" he yelled over his shoulder, glancing back for his bodyguards. "In the name of Thor, help me!" In that moment, Niall lunged forward, his sword finding the gap in the chainmail under the Viking's arm. A blinding pain shot into Ragnar's chest as the keen–edged steel pierced through to his shoulder blade, robbing the breath from his lungs as he staggered backward and fell.

Ragnar thought he heard the shriek of the Valkryies in the distance, and he willed his eyes to open. Staring up at the clouds, he wondered why the battlefield had suddenly become so quiet. Then Niall's sword flashed again as it cut through the sky above him.

Kenan cursed aloud as he dragged Finola after him, Domhnall and Aengus jogging beside, fleeing in the tracks of Munstermen who had already deserted the battlefield and were retreating south, back toward Cashel.

"The Ard–Ri's army is pushing the foreigners back into

the sea!" Finola taunted him. "Your Viking allies are being defeated! Niall Abu!" she cried out. "Victory to Niall!"

Halting abruptly, Kenan spun about and smashed his doubled fist into Finola's cheekbone, knocking her off balance. But she quickly regained her footing, the daughter of Ragallach Ui Muiredaig and wife to the king of Leinster glaring back at him with defiance.

"You can hurt me no more than you already have," she said soberly. "But you, Kenan Ui Faelain, it is the jaws of hell that await you."

Across the battlefield Bran glimpsed the white bronze of Finola's hair. In that same instant, he caught sight of the figure beside her and knew it was Kenan. Oblivious to the alarmed shouts of his bodyguard who were suddenly engulfed by Norsemen, Bran shot ahead, guiding his mount through the knots of grappling warriors to the open ground beyond, then dug in his heels.

Finola saw the horror flash in Kenan's dark eyes and turning, sighted the horseman who was galloping across the plain, bearing down on them.

"Bran!" she cried out, lunging forward as she recognized the copper hair and bearskin mantle. But Kenan caught her shoulders.

"Aengus! Domhnall!" he barked to his retainers. "Cut him down!"

"No!" Finola screamed, struggling in his grasp as his two warriors sprinted past her and launched their casting spears. The deadly shafts raced through the air toward their target. Helpless, Finola watched as Bran cut sideways to evade one of the spears. The other plunged deep into his horse's chest and the animal whinnied in pain as its front legs buckled, pitching him forward.

Finola gasped as he hit the ground, but Bran scrambled to his feet again. "Finola! Finola!" he called out as he ran toward her, desperation in his cry.

"Finish him!" Kenan snarled. But Aengus and Domhnall were already backing away from the frenzied warrior who was charging at them, bloodied sword in hand.

"Finish him yourself!" Aengus snapped, his voice laced with panic as he caught his companion's sleeve. "Come Domhnall! This is not our fight!"

"Cowards!" Kenan roared after the two warriors as they turned and fled.

Finola saw her chance and flung herself forward with all her strength, tearing the rawhide thong from Kenan's grasp. Her hands still bound behind her, she ran, tears of joy filling her eyes as she raced to meet her husband.

Bran was less than twenty paces from Finola, rushing toward her, when he saw Kenan hurl the casting spear.

"No!" he bellowed in anguish, but it streaked to its mark.

Finola's head snapped back as the spear struck, pain and shock flooding her face. She stopped short, then staggered a few paces and collapsed, the wooden shaft protruding obscenely from her back.

Reaching her, Bran threw down his sword and dropped to one knee. Finola moaned. Cautiously, he extracted the javelin from between her shoulder blades and cast it aside. Drawing his dagger, he cut the rawhide strips which bound her wrists, then gently eased his wife onto her back and lifted her head.

"I knew... you... would come," Finola whispered hoarsely. "I knew..." Then her head listed to one side, and the life in her violet eyes was extinguished.

Bran stared in disbelief at the woman he had loved. Numbed, he was unable to think or move as an overwhelming tide of emptiness coursed through him.

"Come brother!" Kenan's voice reached him from somewhere beyond the void. "I have long awaited you!"

Bran looked up. Finola's murderer stood less than a dozen paces beyond, braced and ready.

"Come!" Kenan challenged, taunting him. "Let me tell you of the pleasure I took from that rotting whore you grieve over."

Hatred and sorrow exploded in Bran. A cry for blood erupted from his lips as he snatched up his sword and flung himself at Kenan, swinging the weapon with blind savagery. A master swordsman, Kenan fended off the wild hacking with ease, then slashed downward with such speed that Bran scarcely had time to block the lethal stroke aimed at his head. The colliding blades pealed out brazenly and the sheer force of Kenan's blow numbed Bran's arm, knocking him to the ground. He rolled quickly to one side as Kenan's sword whistled through the air again, slicing into the soft turf where Bran's body had been a fraction of a second earlier.

Scrambling to his feet, Bran grasped the hilt of his weapon with both hands, his chest heaving as he watched

Kenan's eyes. All thoughts of revenge were gone now, replaced by something much more primitive and calculating. The hunter and his quarry. He began circling Kenan slowly, his teeth bared. Raising his sword high, he suddenly lunged at Kenan and brought the blade down with an exaggerated grunt. The blow fell intentionally short of its mark and Kenan quickly moved in to exploit the opening, sweeping his sword in a wide arc aimed at Bran's extended neck. But Bran ducked under its path and with all his strength swung at his brother's exposed torso. The blade sliced into Kenan's side, his blood spraying them both. He staggered backwards, blood oozing from his mouth, and dropped his weapon; but somehow he maintained his balance and hurled himself forward, fingers catching Bran's mantle.

Wrenching his sword free of his dying brother, Bran did not see Kenan's hand go to the dagger at his belt, draw it clumsily, then thrust upwards.

The blade found the soft flesh between his ribs, and Bran gasped at the searing pain. Peering through the strange mist that had suddenly descended between them, he saw the mocking expression on his brother's face, the bloodied lips moving to speak. But Kenan made no sound. His eyes went blank and he crumpled at Bran's feet.

The ground suddenly tilted under Bran. He staggered back several paces. Gripping the hilt of the dagger which protruded from his side, he caught a deep breath and braced himself, then jerked the weapon free. The blinding agony that instantly followed drove him to his knees and he tightened his grip on his sword, leaning on it for support. Pressing his free hand against the gaping wound in his side, he tried to staunch the flow of blood, but it continued to ooze out between his fingers. He knew arteries had been cut. The wound was mortal.

He tried to rise once, but his legs refused to obey him, and he wondered if this was how death would claim his body, slowly, by degrees. There was no fear in the realization that he was dying, only disappointment that he would be leaving with so much yet to do, so much to tell Devlin.

Then he sensed someone beside him, strong hands touching him and a familiar voice calling from somewhere beyond the ocean that roared in his ears. He tried to rise again, but felt himself restrained. Looking up through the haze that clouded his eyes he recognized Etach bending over him.

"I have sent a runner back for the physician," the old warrior said quietly. "But you must lie down, my lord."

"I will not get up again if I do," Bran rasped. "What of the battle?"

Etach squatted beside him. "Some of the heathen have fled to the settlement and barricaded themselves inside. But we have laid siege to them and cut off access to their ships. Malachy's warriors have been sighted to the south and when they arrive, we will launch the attack."

Bran nodded approvingly, then glanced back at Finola. Reaching out, he caught Etach's arm. "Help me up."

"But your wound..."

"Please, old friend," Bran entreated. "Take me to her."

With one arm around the champion's shoulders and the other using his sword as a crutch, Bran shuffled alongside Etach to Finola's corpse. Kneeling down, he leaned forward and gently kissed his wife's brow.

"We will never be parted again," he said softly, stroking her long flowing hair. He looked up at Etach. "When I am gone, let us rest here, together. We have already journeyed too far. Promise me, Etach, on your word."

"Aye my lord," the warrior replied, his one good eye glistening. "On my word."

Bran caressed the hilt of the sword in his lap, his fingers following the delicate contours of the wolf's head. "Give this to my son," he said, his voice quaking. "To Devlin. It... is his now. Teach him as you..."

Bran wasn't sure if Etach had answered him or not, then realized that it was of little consequence. He would speak to him again tomorrow for there were still so many things he needed to say. But for now it was nightfall and he would rest here awhile with Finola at his side. In the morning they would arise and journey on again, together.

Bran strode through the mist toward the heather–clad hills that surrounded Naas and called out to the familiar figure that walked on ahead of him in the distance. The white–bronze of her hair capturing the radiance of the early morning light, Finola turned and smiled, then ran back to meet him.

EPILOGUE

Despite the Irish victory at Sligo, the Vikings returned the following year in force, their massive fleet the largest ever sent against the tenacious island. Renewing their alliance with Feidlimid, they established two heavily fortified bases within his territory – one at Limerick along the eastern banks of the Shannon, the other on the southern coast at Cork. From their strongholds in Munster the foreigners initiated a series of carefully organized raids, the objectives of which extended far beyond the acquisition of plunder, systematically destroying the military strength of individual clans.

That summer, as he led his Ulstermen to defend Armagh from one such incursion, Niall Caille was pulled from his mount by a pack of screaming Norsemen and drowned in the River Cullan. At the news of his death, Ulster erupted into civil war, the clans battling among themselves as their chieftains vied for the title of Ard–Ri. Without a central authority to govern and unify them, the provinces likewise gradually returned to the old ways, violating each other's borders in an endless series of reciprocal invasions and counterattacks.

Unhindered by any consolidated effort to stop them, the Viking raped Erin at their leisure. In the terror that followed, it was Leinster that suffered the most, her territory ravished as the foreigners established several petty kingdoms along the coastline at Waterford, Wexford and Dubhlinn. And like her neighbours, Leinster had become divided internally between the clans who remained loyal to the Ri–Ruirech and those who challenged his claim to the throne.

Fifteen years after Bran and Niall defeated the foreigners at Sligo, on a dismal afternoon when dark rain–laden clouds blotted out the summer sky, two warriors rode side by side as they guided their horses across the plain which had been the site of the great battle. Etach, his hair now the white–silver of a winter's frost, silently cursed the persistent ache in his joints as his one good eye continued to scan the surrounding hills for any hint of ambush. With the bodyguards left behind to wait in comfort at camp, the detour was considerably more dangerous than it needed to be, and he had not hesitated to say as much. But this time his advice had not been taken and Etach knew the time was coming when he would no longer be needed.

Glancing at his companion, the old soldier could not help but smile to himself. *You have your father's red hair,* he thought as he studied the young warrior's features. *And your mother's fair skin. But there is more of him in you, I think. He and your grandfather were much the same, and if you become but a sliver of them, then we will have both done well.*

When at last they reached the southern edge of the plain, Etach reined in his mount and stared, the memory flooding back to him. "There is the place," he said softly, pointing. "But we should not stay long, my lord. Your parents will be concerned if we are not returned to camp before sunset."

"Rowan and Muireen are not my parents," Devlin reminded him quietly. Upon the youth's brow rested the gold circlet of kingship. "As much as I love and respect them both, they are not my parents. In three days the chieftains of Leinster, Meath and Ulster assemble in Ailech to discuss the possibility of forming an alliance against the Viking. I have not forgotten the stories you told me from the time I was a boy. One standard, one Erin. That was my father's dream – a dream for which he and my mother died. I cannot pass by this place without paying them tribute."

Etach nodded, then watched him dismount and stride to the two massive oaks whose branches intertwined as they rose to embrace the boundless sky. Devlin paused for a moment, the bearskin mantle draped about his shoulders fluttering in the gentle breeze. Then he drew his sword. The ruby eyes in the hilt glowed like embers as he thrust it high into the air.

"For God and Erin!" he cried, his voice echoing across the valley.

Somewhere off in the distance, a lone wolf howled woefully, then was silent.

THE END

GLOSSARY

IRISH TERMS

"Abu!" (a-boo): "Victory!" ie. "Ui Faelain Abu" means Victory to the Ui Faelain"

airechta (err-ach-ta): The warrior who had been declared "champion" of the clan

amhuis (aw-ish): Personal bodyguards retained by a king

Ard-Ri (ard-ree): High King of all Erin

banshee (bahn-shee): A wailing apparition, usually an old woman, that heralds death

Baltinne (bell-tin-a): The Celtic fertility feast observed in spring

bard (bard): A highly accomplished poet and/or musician whose social status was second only to the king

bocanach (bow-ken-awch): The Irish demon of battle that decides who will be slain

boruma (bo-ra-va): Tribute rendered to an overlord or king as a token of fealty

bothachs (bo-tawch): Peasants

brat (braht): A peasant's woolen cloak

brehon (brey-han): Law giver and arbitrator of disputes

brughaid (brew-y): Host and caretaker of a hospitality house

bruideans (breens): Public houses of hospitality which were located at road junctions and maintained by the king for sake of travellers. Food, drink and lodging were always available and provided without charge.

caimsi (kav-shee): Knee–length smock worn by servants

cepog (kap-ogue): A funeral dirge

cland (kland): The sword of a champion

clanna (klan-na): The extended family unit comprised of several houses descended from a common ancestor

coibche (kwiv-cha): A woman's bride price

crannog (kran-ogue): Island fortress built on a lake

cris (kris): Girdle or sash

crozier (kro-zhyer): A bishop's staff

Crom Cruach (krum kroo-ach): A pagan deity worshipped by the ancient Celts

cuirm (kwerm):   Dark beer or stout

curragh (kur-ach): A small boat consisting of a light wooden frame covered with hardened animal hides

daidem (di-a-dem): The ornamented metal headband or circlet which denoted authority

druids (droo-ids): Mystical priests of the pagan Celts

Dubh-gaill (Duv-gawl): "Dark foreigners" referring to the Danes, so named because of their iron body armour

duma (du-va): Burial mound

dun (doon): Hill fortress surrounded with rings of earth and stone

eraic (air-ak): The blood-price for a slain warrior

fingall (fine-gall): The act of murdering a blood relation

Finn-gaill (fin-gawl): "White foreigners" referring to the Norse, so named because of their blond hair

Gael (gale): Name applied to the Irish race collectively

grianan (green-awn): The "sunroom" in a house

keener (kee-nur): A professional mourner retained for funerals

lena (lay-na): Ankle length robe of linen or silk worn by Irish noblewomen

nenadmin (nay-naw-men): a potent cider fermented from wild apples

ogham (owm): The secret system of Runic lettering used by the Druids

ollam (ul-av): A master bard who had completed twelve years of study

oratory (or-a-tor-ee): A small beehive-shaped prayer cell used by Irish monks

Ri-Ruirech (ree-rir-ach): Provincial king. Ruler of one of Erin's five sub-kingdoms

rood (rude): A cross or crucifix

rook (rook): A black, hoarse-voiced bird similar to a crow

samite (sa-myt): A rich, sheer fabric similar to silk

seanachies (shan-ach-ees): Storytellers who orally passed on the history of their clan

Senchus-Mor (shan-chas-more): The law statues of ancient Erin

scriptorium (skrip-tor-ee-um): The writing-room in a monastery

tanaiste (tawn-ish-ta): The elected successor to the chieftain of a clan

truibas (triv-as): Trousers

tuath (too-ath): A tribe consisting of numerous affiliated clans

VIKING TERMS

berserkers (bur-zerk-ers): Viking warriors who painted their bodies and charged into battle howling like animals in a drug-induced "blood-frenzy"

draken (dra-kin): Dragonship. A much larger version of the Viking longship

Freyja (fray-ya): The Norse goddess of love

heriot (hair-ee-ot): Gifts given to a warrior by the jarl to whom he swears fealty

hlaut (h-owt): The blood of a sacrifice

jarl (yarl): Norse or Danish overlord who commanded ten or more sea chieftains

jerkin (jur-kin): A vest worn by the men, usually leather or buff hide

kirtle: A tight-fitting upper garment, like a hip-length jacket

longphort (long-fort): A Viking military camp

Mjolnir (ma-jowl-nur): Thor's war hammer which was said to give off lightning bolts as it sped to its target

Norns (newrns): Demonic imps in Viking mythology that delighted in tormenting humanity

Oden (Od-in): The Viking god of war who bears a spear and is accompanied by carrion-eating ravens, wolves and eagles

shielings (shee-links): Small houses constructed of wood planking

Sleipnir (sleep-nur): Oden's eight-legged mare that came to men in their dreams and carried them to the underworld

Skuld (skoold): One of the mythological Norns who took particular delight in bringing disaster to the plans and ambitions of mortal men

skyrta (sker-ta): The pleated shift worn by Viking women. It was pinned at both shoulders with tortoise broaches

Thor (Thor): The Norse storm god that was regarded as the chief opponent to Christianity

thrall (thrawl): Slave

"Tur-aie!" (thor-ay-ee): "Thor help us!"

Uppsalla (Oop-sa-la): A nine day feast associated with the worship of Thor. Human and animal sacrifices were hung by their necks from the sacred oak, then speared to death as they struggled.

Valhalla (Val-ha-la): The "Hall of the Slain" was Oden's spectacular gathering place in the sky for those who had honourably fallen in battle

Valkryies (Vawl-krees): The "Chosers of the Slain" were Oden's handmaids who hovered above the battlefield and chose those who were to die

Yggdrassil (Ig-dra-zil): The sacred tree of life upon which Oden was hung to gain the wisdom of the runes

SELECTED BIBLIOGRAPHY

1. A HISTORY OF GAELIC IRELAND FROM THE EARLIEST TIMES TO 1608, by P.W. Joyce (Dublin: The Educational Company of Ireland, Ltd., 1924)

2. A SOCIAL HISTORY OF ANCIENT IRELAND, by P.W. Joyce (Longmans, Green and Co., 1903)

3. AN ATLAS OF IRISH HISTORY, by Ruth Dudley Edwards (London: Methuen and Co., 1973)

4. CELTIC IRELAND, by Eoin MacNeill (Dublin: Academy Press, 1981)

5. IRELAND BEFORE THE NORMANS, by Donncha O'Corrain (New York: Irish Book Center, 1972)

6. IRISH HISTORY AND CULTURE - ASPECTS OF A PEOPLES HERITAGE, edited by Harold Orel (Wolfhound Press, 1979)

7. IRISH KING AND HIGH KINGS, by F.J. Byrne (Batsford, 1973)

8. ON THE MANNERS AND CUSTOMS OF THE ANCIENT IRISH, by Eugene O'Curry (London: Williams and Norgate, 1873)

9. THE COURSE OF IRISH HISTORY, edited by T.W. Moody and F.X. Martin (The Mercier Press, 1967)

10. THE STORY OF THE IRISH RACE, by Seamas MacManus (The Devin - Adair Company, 1980)

11. THE VIKING SAGA, by Peter Brent (New York, G.P. Putnam's Sons, 1975)

12. THE WAR OF THE GAEDHIL AND THE GAILL (London: Rolls Series, 1867)

AUTHOR'S NOTE

The Vikings were not the first, nor would they be the last, to invade and terrorize Ireland. Although the motives of its would-be conquerors throughout history were as many and varied as the men who waded ashore, they all possessed one common objective – to plunder the wealth of Ireland and subjugate her people. But as each successive wave of invaders quickly learned, the prize was not to be so easily coveted. Those who did not fall to Irish steel were to flee home with horrifying accounts of the "barbarians" who drove them off. Others remained behind as prisoners or allies, some of them eventually assimilating into the native culture until they became as Irish as the Gaelic people themselves.

It has been said that the Irish have always been at their best whenever confronted with an external threat. At such times they have acted with a cohesion and singularly of purpose that made them virtually invincible. Ironically, it was these same qualities that reinforced the philosophy of absolute loyalty to the clan above all other considerations. As a consequence, individual disputes inevitably escalated into feuds, and occasionally led to bloodier wars between rival provincial kings.

This tradition of the "blood-feud" has been evidenced in recent years in the sectarian violence that has incessantly plagued Northern Ireland. Although the "tribes" and causes have changed, fanatic loyalty to "ones own" continues to fuel the animosity between today's various political and religious factions. And, of course, the cost of prejudice remains the same. A horrendous price has been exacted from those innocent victims caught in the unrelenting crossfire of hatred.

Over the centuries, this legacy of violence has also taken a heavy toll on Ireland itself. Terrorism has further crippled an already depressed economy by driving away foreign investors whose capital and expertise would enable Ireland to participate competitively in the world marketplace. Further, years of violence have steadily worn away at Ireland's most valuable resource – her youth. In a land ravaged by terrorism and unemployment, young people are emigrating in increasing numbers to Europe and North America in search of peace and opportunities. Without them, Ireland will not survive.

Ireland's future rests in the courage and commitment of her youth. They must be re-educated to put aside traditional prejudices and regard their culture and history with a pride free of sectarian influence. Hatred is not an instinctive trait – it is learned. Clearly, what the young people of Ireland are taught today will have a tremendous impact on the Ireland of tomorrow.

Now, for the first time since "The Troubles" began, there is a glimmer of hope. But if the fragile peace initiatives are to have any chance at all of success we must stand united in our resolve to see a definitive end put to the violence. Ireland needs our help and we of Irish decent, no matter where we live, have an obligation to do whatever we can to aid in the peace process.

It is for that reason I have decided to actively support THE IRELAND FUND. For each copy of THE TANAISTE sold, a portion of the retail price will be donated to that organization.

At the back of this book is information on the Ireland Fund of Canada and the remarkable programs with which they are associated. The Ireland Fund also maintains branches in the United States, Great Britain, Australia, New Zealand, France and Germany. If you wish to know more about what you can do to help, please contact an office near you or call any of the telephone numbers indicated.

PEACE FOR ALL

Donald T. Phelan

WHAT EXACTLY IS THE IRELAND FUND OF CANADA?

Founded in 1978 by a group of Canadians of Irish origin, Ireland Fund of Canada is a non-political, non-sectarian, registered charity which funds innovative community-level projects promoting peace, culture, and charity throughout Ireland.

We've been able to distribute over $1.5 million dollars to selected projects since we began our work.

Why is The Ireland Fund unique? We're unique because our projects reach right down into every Irish community – helping them with vital small scale 'people projects' – in their homes, on their streets, and in their own communities.

How does the Fund know it's making a difference? Because they tell us so. The people who receive our funding tell us we can often mean the difference between success or failure in their good work.

And we make the best choices possible by allowing all of our projects to be assessed by an expert Advisory Committee composed of people from all walks of life throughout Ireland. That 'on the ground' familiarity helps us choose projects which will bring the most immediate, peaceful, and lasting change to Ireland.

What does the Fund do here in Canada? We've worked hard to bring Ireland to Canadians through our special events across Canada whether it's a cultural event like an author's reading, a new film debut, a musical recital or through our well-known breakfasts, lunches, and dinners which bring Canadians together to share their common Irish interests in a fun setting.

In addition, our growing leadership and expertise, has made us a thoughtful voice for Canadians on Irish issues – from being asked by the media to offer our perspective on events in Ireland or simply answering the queries of people like you.

MAKING NEW FRIENDS
OF OLD ENEMIES

For 25 years, Cooperation North has been building understanding and friendship between Northern Ireland and the Republic of Ireland, and between divided communities.

Cooperation North challenges the complex set of barriers that promote suspicion and misunderstanding with the simplest of solutions: bringing people together.

Through its programs on youth exchange, business links, cultural contact, and special public events, Cooperation North involves thousands of people, from school children to business managers in common projects.

That's the greatest achievement – getting people to know one another.

THE FOURTH "R"
OF GOOD EDUCATION

Reconciliation. That's what Northern Ireland's integrated schools are teaching Protestant and Catholic children – sitting side by side, in truly equal classrooms, for the first time ever.

The Integrated Education movement has brought together parents, teachers, and school trustees from across the community divide to create a learning environment free of past prejudices, where different traditions are viewed with respect and tolerance.

Integrated Education is catching on. From just 27 students in 1981, there is now talk of having 30% of all students in Integrated Schools by the end of the century – that's 100,000 pupils.

The Ireland Fund of Canada has been there from the start and continued support is crucial to getting new schools started.

HOW TO TAP IRISH POTENTIAL

Ireland is a place of great entrepreneurial potential. But still hundreds of thousands of people suffer the scourge of unemployment.

One of the main barriers facing new entrepreneurs is getting the initial capital to start their enterprise.

First Step is an organization helping people with sound business proposals to get past the first hurdle by providing them with small business loans and expert advice from proven business leaders.

First Step's track record is an impressive 90% success rate with new ventures. That's why the Ireland Fund of Canada is a proud supporter of this program.

MAKING A DIFFERENCE IN BELFAST

Communities in Belfast have traditionally lived in competition or isolation from each other. That's meant city resources, better used if shared, have been squandered.

Belfast Common Purpose is trying to bring the communities together by bringing the leaders together. Prominent citizens from diverse backgrounds – bankers, doctors, community coordinators, school principals, and many others – are brought to workshops on the local economy, institutions, health, housing, and decision making. The Ireland Fund provides bursaries for the voluntary sector participants in the program.

What they take away is a new found knowledge and enthusiasm on how to make Belfast and it's citizens work better together.

To the Ireland Fund of Canada, a healthier, safer Belfast is an important symbol of our work in promoting peace and charity in Ireland.

KEEPING CONNECTED TO IRISH CULTURE

Sir Tyrone Guthrie, the first artistic director of the Canadian Statford Festival, left a very special legacy for Canadians and Irish alike.

 His ancestral home, Annaghmakerrig, has become a centre where young artists and students from around the world pursue their creative passions in an inspiring setting.

The Tyrone Guthrie Centre is jointly run by cultural organizations from the north and south of Ireland. Its one of Europe's leading artists' workplaces where artists from different Irish and world traditions can bridge their cultural gaps by working together.

Talented Canadian artists, with the help of The Ireland Fund of Canada, now have a chance to study and create in Annaghmakerrig – a unique legacy of the man who made such a difference in Canada's cultural life.

NAMED FUNDS

Some Ireland Fund supporters prefer to direct their generosity to a specific project (perhaps one with a personal link) rather than the general project funds.

The Ireland Fund of Canada supports Named Funds that can be set up for special, personal contributions. Some recent examples of Named Funds:

University College Cork Medical Development Fund: Supported by Canadian graduates from UCC.

Coiste Turasoireacht Inis Mór Arainn: Supporting the construction of a senior citizen's residence on the Aran Island off the coast of Galway.

Eaton Lecture Series at Queen's University, Belfast: An endowment for this annual series on Canadian/Irish issues.

Because of the extra administration costs involved in directing this kind of personal gift, the Ireland Fund limits Named Funds to donations of $2,000 or greater.

**For more information on ways to
help right now,
please write or call:**

THE IRELAND FUND OF CANADA
51 Front Street East
Toronto, Ontario
M5E 1B3
Tel: (416) 367-8311
Fax: (416) 367-5931

Toronto • Montreal • Ottawa
Hamilton • Calgary • Edmonton

*A registered charitable corporation
for income tax purposes:*
No. 0513788-09-13

PEACE • CULTURE • CHARITY

PAIX • CULTURE • CHARITÉ

In the year 840 a.d. the people of Ulster were already well acquainted with the savagery of the Viking.

Tightening their grip on Ulster, the fierce Norsemen allied themselves with the traitorous King of Munster. Together they hungrily eyed the three remaining provinces to the south – Connaught, Meath... and Leinster.

THE TANAISTE
AN IRISH EPIC

Donald T. Phelan

When the King of Leinster falls in battle, the burden of leadership is thrust upon his son and heir, Bran Ui Faelain. Determined to spare his people further bloodshed, Bran ignores the menace that is stalking Leinster. Ultimately, he cannot escape the destiny that plunges his kingdom into war.

In the year 840 a.d. the people of Ulster were already well acquainted with the savagery of the Viking.

Tightening their grip on Ulster, the fierce Norsemen allied themselves with the traitorous King of Munster. Together they hungrily eyed the three remaining provinces to the south – Connaught, Meath... and Leinster.

THE TANAISTE

AN IRISH EPIC

Donald T. Phelan

When the King of Leinster falls in battle, the burden of leadership is thrust upon his son and heir, Bran Ui Faelain. Determined to spare his people further bloodshed, Bran ignores the menace that is stalking Leinster. Ultimately, he cannot escape the destiny that plunges his kingdom into war.
